Proud of You

Mary Wood

PAN BOOKS

First published 2014 by Pan Books
an imprint of Pan Macmillan, a division of Macmillan Publishers Limited
Pan Macmillan, 20 New Wharf Road, London N1 9RR
Basingstoke and Oxford
Associated companies throughout the world
www.panmacmillan.com

ISBN 978-1-4472-6736-2

3 5 7 9 8 6 4

A CIP catalogue record for this book is available from
the British Library.

Typeset by Palimpsest Book Production Ltd, Falkirk, Stirlingshire
Printed and bound by CPI Group (UK) Ltd, Croydon, CR0 4YY

Visit www.panmacmillan.com to read more about all our books
and to buy them. You will also find features, author interviews and
news of any author events, and you can sign up for e-newsletters
so that you're always first to hear about our new releases.

For my much-loved and much-missed sister, Rosemary,
who loved the stories I sent in for her when she was
in hospital. To remember is to feel your presence.
Rest in peace, forever locked in your youth,
forever locked in my heart.

Acknowledgements

Thank you to the amazing team at Pan Macmillan who take care of me and guide me, particularly my editor, Louise Buckley. If it wasn't for Louise I would still be self-publishing, which, though I loved and achieved great success doing so, only fulfilled half of my dream. Louise gave me the chance to complete my dream. Her support when I have wavered in my confidence has been steadfast and when I wasn't sure of the way, she has guided me. But above all, her belief in me helps me to know that I can do whatever she asks of me. So thank you, Louise, and thank you too for the structural editing of my work that brings clarity and depth to it, and makes it sing off the page. Thanks also to Emma Bravo, my publicist, and Andy from the sales team – together you have worked tirelessly to promote me and my books and have been there for me every step of the way on my book tours, picking me up when I faltered and taking care of me. Thanks to Ali Blackburn and Laura Carr, and the team of proof-readers who find the errors, correct the punctuation and question anything that isn't clear. Your sensitive handling of my work brings clarity where I have muddied the waters.

A huge thank you should also go to my agent, Judith

Murdoch. You are extraordinary in your field, you are in my corner and always there if I need you. Your guidance and advice keeps me focused when I would otherwise slip into my old ways. Together you and Louise will get me fully into the ways of the traditional publishing world.

And last but by no means least, my thanks as always to my darling husband Roy, my daughters Christine, Julie and Rachel, and my son James, as well as their partners. And also to my grandchildren and my sisters and brothers from the Olley and the Wood family – all have encouraged me, helped me and clothed me in love. Without you I could not have begun to realize my dream. Thank you all.

1

Alice

DUNKIRK, MAY 1940

A MISSION IMPOSSIBLE

They'd pulled it off. No one had noticed she wasn't a man. But now, with the shrill whistle of Luftwaffe aircraft diving towards them in wave after unrelenting wave, she questioned her sanity in persuading Bren to let her come with him to Dunkirk.

'Come on, hold my hand . . .'

The desperate soldiers, neck-high in freezing water, didn't care that the voice urging them to make one last effort to climb into the boat belonged to a woman. Exhausted, terrified and near to death, they found the strength from somewhere to clamber over the side.

The glow of a thousand fires lit the face of the next in line. She looked into his eyes and saw them glaze over. They were young eyes and fearful in the knowledge that he wasn't going to make it. 'Just take my hand. Come on, you can do it . . . Please – no, no, don't give up. You're safe now . . . Help me, someone help me!' No one heard her as the crashing explosions all around them drowned out her voice. His grasp loosened. The blood-filled water washed over his face.

Tears ran down her cheeks. They mingled with the stinging sea spray. She'd failed him . . . *Oh God!*

''Ere, give me a hand, mate. 'Elp me . . .'

The plea jolted her back from her desperation. She had to keep going. Taking the outstretched hand with both of hers and putting her foot against the side of the boat, she hauled with every ounce of strength she had, until the soldier could grasp the side and slither into the boat.

Leaving him, she turned back to the water. Another hand reached for her, and behind him yet another. The line of men had an end. It trailed back to the beach, where thousands of battle-worn soldiers waited – sitting targets for the machine-gun fire ripping through them, making their bodies dance even after they had fallen.

The futility of it all sapped her strength until she felt herself folding with despair, but a voice stopped her desolation. 'I'll take over, lass. Move over, get below for a bit. I'll get them in. I'm Corporal Moisley, Yorkshire Regiment. Some of me muckers are in the line. How many can you take on board?'

'Fifteen.' *Such an inadequate number.* 'Thanks. I'm Alice . . . Alice D'Olivier.'

His face held a look of astonishment, before changing to one of disgust. She was used to that. Her name often provoked such a reaction.

But then, just as if she hadn't spoken, he turned from her and carried on where he'd left off, discussing the business in hand. 'Well, I reckon as this one'll do it, then. Come on, Barrowclough, hitch yourself up. Good lad. You made it.' To the others, in a voice that might have been turning them away from a football-stadium turnstile instead of a chance to

2

survive, he shouted, 'Sorry, lads. But there's more boats coming. A reet Armada of them. You'll catch the next one. Keep encouraging those behind you – good lads! Tell them I'll be back with the skipper on his next trip, as this young lass here is a toff and out of her depth.'

The way he said 'toff' stung Alice and confirmed her suspicions that the disgust she'd seen in his look meant he must have heard of her father. Would she ever live down the shame?

She didn't want to berate him for the insult – she'd allowed so many jibes over the years, unable to challenge them. So what did one more matter? Instead she went to thank him, but the words were subsumed into a blast that blocked her ears, leaving high-pitched sounds zinging around her trembling body. The violent motion of the boat flung her onto her back. Others landed near her; one fell onto her feet. As the motion steadied they lifted themselves up. In the distance behind them flames engulfed a huge ship. A gaping hole showed where its guts had been ripped out, by what could only have been a mine. Wood and steel screeched as the water devoured it. Men screamed the agony of a burning hell. At that moment the thought came to her that the world was coming to an end. *Oh, God, help them, help them . . . help us all . . .*

A hand shoved her. 'Get yourself to the skipper. Tell him we're ready for the off. Go on, there's nowt as we can do for them.'

Pushing through the men slumped on the deck, Alice made it to Bren's side. 'We're full. We need to go.'

'Oh, my darling, you shouldn't have come. I shouldn't have given in.'

The endearment grated on her. She didn't want it. Nor did she want to see his hurt as she rejected his outstretched arm wanting to pull her to him. The edge of her irritation showed in her voice as she shouted, 'This isn't the time, Bren! Just get us out of here. Please.'

'There never will be a time, will there?'

She didn't answer this.

Bren reacted by taking on a professional stance. Handing her a torch and compass, he said, 'Right, I know my way along the coast to where the naval officer said we should head for, but once we get to buoy six, you'll have to take over the navigation from there. He said we were to turn nor'west on a direct course for Dover.'

'How far is it, Skip?' Moisley's voice came from behind her.

'It's thirty-nine nautical miles, according to my information.'

'Reet. Have you any refreshments on board, or fags maybe?'

'We have both. Though whether there's enough or not is another matter. Alice will show you where they are, Corporal . . . ?'

'Moisley. We met up on deck. He helped me to get the last of the men in the boat. Follow me, Corporal. The galley is down here.' Holding the rail and swinging her body downwards, Alice found the steps with her feet. 'I can make tea,' she told him, 'but we only have four mugs, so the men will have to pass them round. We have sandwiches, and . . . and smoked salmon, a salad, cold potatoes . . .'

'Toff's grub, eh?'

'I take it you know who my father was?'

'Aye, and more of your family. But it's a long story, and I ain't for telling it now.'

'I can't imagine how you can possibly know any other members of my family! I accept that you have heard of my father – everyone has – but I am not my father, Corporal. He . . . he died the year I was born. I have no memory of him.'

And the memories I tried to make up were tainted and destroyed when I found out what he had done. Will I ever come to terms with it all? Shaking this thought away, she was determined not to lose her dignity in front of this man, who already held her in disdain. Instead she set about gathering what they would need for the tea. 'There's some tobacco in that drawer. We took a minute to buy plenty before we left, guessing it would be the first thing the men would want.'

He ignored her attempt at a smile. His insolence made her angry, and she found anger a better companion than the thoughts of her father or the fear of their situation.

Trying to make tea with the boat rocking precariously from side to side took all her attention. Water ran around her feet. Looking down, she saw about an inch swirling around, but it wasn't enough to worry about. The lamp she'd lit after pulling the blinds down creaked as it swayed, but thankfully the noise of the battle raging behind them was lessening, though it didn't wipe itself from her mind.

Moisley left her, his hands filled with packets of tobacco and papers. Picking up the matches, she caught up with him and shoved them into his pocket.

'You may not be your da, but you're still of him – and that's enough for me to hate the guts of you,' he said.

A sob racked her throat. The tears followed. Tears of stupid, bloody hurt pride. Wiping them away, she was determined not to give in. If she did, she'd be lost.

The day had started out with the excitement of being with Bren. He'd asked her to accompany him on a trip on his boat to Henley. 'We'll take a picnic, and I have a surprise for you,' he'd said. His voice had held an expectation that told her he meant to propose. She had thought if it was that, she could handle it – even hoped that she would have a spark in her that would enable her to accept. But with the scuppering of their plans, none of it had mattered.

The order had come whilst they were filling the cupboards in the galley with food. The owner of the local boat-building yard had called out to Bren, 'Not a good day for messing about on a boat, sir. I've bad news, I'm afraid.'

Explaining further, he'd told them he'd been charged with letting the owners know that the Navy was commandeering all shallow-draught boats. The Allied forces in France were retreating and were trapped on the beaches of Dunkirk. 'Everything and anything that can float is needed to get them off,' he'd said, and then told them, 'There are upwards of three hundred thousand of them, sir. A disaster.'

Fear had dried her throat. If the forces had failed to keep back the Germans in France, then the invasion of their shores must be imminent!

Bren saying he would go and help with the evacuation had overridden her fear and given her a way to try and wipe out the stigma of her father's name. She would go too; she'd show that not all D'Oliviers were cowards.

None of Bren's arguments had dissuaded her. Running to the boatyard owner's office, she'd telephoned home, leaving a message with her mother's maid to say that she would be staying at Bren's overnight. There had been no need to say more, as her mother wouldn't care one way or the other. Bren had phoned his own mother. Telling her the truth, he'd begged her to keep up the charade of the overnight stay.

When they reached Ramsgate a naval engineer had met them and told them they were to leave the boat and allow Navy personnel to take it from there. Bren had stood firm, telling them, 'I'm Brendon Wellingham – Officer Wellingham.

Completed my training at the Royal Naval College, Dartmouth last week. On leave for three weeks awaiting deployment. This is my yacht, and I am taking her over myself. I have an experienced mate with me.'

The engineer had looked over at her. She'd prayed that her huge sou'wester and the height of a man hid the fact that she was a woman.

Saluting and clipping his heels in respect for Bren's rank, the naval engineer told them they would be given their orders when they reached Dover. But before they were allowed to set sail, their boat had to be checked over by him and his team and passed as seaworthy.

As he'd left them, Bren had turned to her and asked, 'Alice, do you think you can march?'

'I should be able to,' she'd told him. 'You drilled me enough when we played military games as children.'

The lightness of this statement hadn't moved him from his anger at her. He just said, 'Well, do so as we walk over to the mess-hut, otherwise the men will cotton on that you're not a man. I'll be in all sorts of trouble if they do!'

This had been the longest sentence Bren had uttered to her since they had left his mooring on the Thames. But she knew that he dealt with his feelings by remaining silent, so she had accepted it.

His anger with her hadn't just been because of her stubbornness in asserting her right to come with him on this mission, but encompassed his need to change their lifelong friendship into something deeper. She wanted that to happen too, and had been determined to try, but it wasn't easy for her to accept love, or to give it, not even to Bren. And yet Bren was her life. For most of it he'd been the only normal presence she'd known, and his weekly visits when they were children had been the one good thing she'd had to look forward to.

Those visits were something Mother couldn't stop happening, though she often threatened to. Threats, Alice knew, along with all the other cruelty she'd suffered at her mother's hand, were Mother's way of punishing her for being who she was – her father's daughter!

But in all this Alice had an ally. Lady Elizabeth, Bren's mother and the only friend Mother had left – and didn't want to lose – had insisted on Alice and Bren spending time together.

Although reverting to her pre-marriage title of Lady Louise Fuller, Mother had never been fully accepted back into the society from which she'd been ostracized when her husband's wrongdoing to his king and country had been made public. The only real contact with society that she'd had, and the only chance of getting the occasional invitation, had lain with Lady Elizabeth.

Alice often wondered if Lady Elizabeth had realized what was going on. If she had, surely she would have intervened and stopped the cruelty? She had to believe that Lady Elizabeth hadn't known, and remained grateful to her for accepting that a child should have at least one friend, and for making sure her son was allowed to visit each and every Saturday afternoon.

Bren and his mother had been her sole contact with the outside world in those days. Never leaving her house and garden, she had been brought up by her nanny and schooled by her governess, and rarely even had a chat with the servants scurrying around her large home, which stood on the border of Bexley's Danson Park in south-east London.

When that wonderful day had come for her to leave home and go to boarding school, parting from Bren had broken Alice's heart and marred her joy. But she had found her school in Belgium to be both a release from the horrors of her home life and a bringer of new experiences – not least the language used, which alternated between French and German, with very little English being spoken. It had taken her a surprisingly short time to adapt to that aspect, but a little longer to adjust to life in what had been to her a strange environment.

At first afraid of everybody and everything – and in particular the noise made by hundreds of children – she had grown in confidence over time. She'd become a leader, and had been popular with the other girls. Holidays had been spent in France with her father's kin, her Uncle Philippe and his family, and her ancient grandmother – a woman who had taught Alice that she had a backbone and that she had to strengthen it in order to deal with life's knock-backs. It had worked: she'd found a way of dealing with everything. At least she'd thought she had, until at eighteen she'd returned and met up with Bren again. Oh, they'd picked up the threads of their bond easily enough, and had found them woven just as tightly as if they'd never been apart, but there had soon been challenges to the foundations of that friendship as other feelings started to develop. But she wouldn't think about them now. They spoiled what had always been so simple, and made it all complicated.

Bren had grown from the shy, gangly ginger-haired boy she'd known into a tall, handsome man. They'd always been the same height as children, but he now stood a couple of inches taller than her, at six feet. His hair had darkened to a rust shade and suited the short-back-and-sides that the Navy had given him, making his strong features, square chin and freckled complexion all the more defined.

He'd chosen to take up a career as a doctor and was in his fourth year when war was declared last September, and he'd been called up. He'd omitted to tell the naval officer at Dover that his training in sea warfare had been limited to a few weeks for fear of them refusing him permission to go.

He was to continue his training in the medical field with the Navy working in the naval hospital in England at first and then later wherever he was needed.

Alice had gone on to work in the War Office as a secretary and driver to General Stuart Westlin, a key figure in the talks leading up to that fateful day last September when Britain had declared war on Germany. But although Westlin had played a significant role in the planning of the Allied forces' co-operation in this initial defence of France, she wasn't sure of his role at present. It seemed less defined, as greater responsibility had been given to a team of coordinators of which he was a part. The generals made decisions together, and all decisions had to be passed by the PM; only an elite few had a specialized area. The secrecy was such that leading up to the outbreak of war all personnel at the War Office were conscripted into the Army and had to swear an oath of allegiance. Most, like herself, held the rank of officer.

As if tuning into her thoughts, Bren took the mug of tea she offered him now and asked, 'What is Westlin's view of this retreat, Alice? Did you know the scale of the rescue operation that would be needed?'

'No, there was no talk of an evacuation. I knew, like everyone, that the Germans were pushing us back and we were struggling to stop them, but this is a disaster!'

'That's an understatement. God, those poor chaps! I'll have to go back for more, once we get these unloaded. But, Alice, no matter what you say, you're not going back with me. Moisley has offered, and I think that best.'

'I agree. I haven't the strength to give it another go. It wouldn't be fair. Has Moisley said anything to you?'

'About what?'

'Oh, you know . . . about me and about my father.'

'No, why should he? How can he possibly know anything? Let it go, Alice. For God's sake, let it go.'

Turning from him, she wished it was that easy, but what her father had done had driven her whole life from the age of ten, when she had first been told. The trembling started at this thought, and she fought against the memories that were surfacing, but that never helped. As she sat down on a bench next to the helm, they possessed her once more, filling her with loathing and disgust as she relived how her mother had disclosed the truth.

'You are your father personified. That disgusting, disgraceful man lives in you and makes you as evil as he was!'

She'd stood, bewildered and stinging from the constant assault of slaps that her mother metered out as she said this, taking her punishment for whatever imagined misdemeanour she was thought to have committed and telling herself, *Mother isn't well in her head. I have to remember that.* And she had also to remember that her own birth had been the cause of Mother becoming unbalanced.

She'd learned this from their doctor. In an effort to help her to understand, he'd told her, 'The difficult pregnancy and birth, and all she endured during it, has left your mother mentally sick. She cannot help her outbursts, Alice.' It was as if this made it all right that her mother knocked her about until she was almost senseless.

This talk had come after the doctor had been fetched, following a violent attack that had left Alice unconscious. She'd learned afterwards that he'd told the household and garden staff that they should look for the signs of Mother becoming agitated and keep Alice out of her sight until the bout passed – and that was it, that was all the protection she had been offered. There was to be no other help for her. And worse was to come.

Being hit and abused became a normal everyday occurrence in her life. Nanny had done it too. Huh! There was never a more inappropriate title for the woman whose graveside she'd stood beside only weeks after the most shocking revelation of her life.

Although Alice had stood with dignity and made herself look as if she was sorry, inside she'd been cheering. She'd even imagined dancing on the woman's grave, scattering the flowers with their kind endearments written on little cards. And the thought of doing so had lifted her, for never again would that evil woman be able to vent her cruel streak on her, or do those vile things to her body.

Nanny starting to abuse her and Mother spitting out the truth of her hatred for Father, during a particularly violent and vitriolic attack, had both happened on the same day. 'Your father was a traitor! A filthy rotten traitor to his country. And he was shot! Shot by his own regiment for giving information to the Germans – information that led to the death of thousands in the Great War. The dirty womanizing coward!'

For a ten-year-old this had been hard to take in, but she had understood what was meant by the word 'traitor', and the information had shaken her world. In her room she'd taken the framed photograph of her father from the dressing table and thrown it against the wall. It had smashed into a thousand pieces.

As she'd curled her stinging, bruised body into a ball on her bed, it felt as if she'd lost everything. The only good thing she thought she'd had in her life – the picture of her smiling father standing proudly in his officer's uniform – had now gone. As had the world she'd made up about him and herself, and the things they would have done together; the protection he would have given her; the hugs she'd imagined and was almost able to feel . . . All gone. Thinking him a victim of the Great War, she'd put her father on a pedestal and he'd not deserved it. The shame of it had crucified her, and she'd never felt more alone.

The noise she'd made had woken Nanny from her afternoon nap. The sound of her heavy footsteps coming across the landing lived inside Alice and still filled her with terror. Going to the window, she'd been frantic to catch someone's attention, but had known that it was fruitless. Her bedroom overlooked the back garden, and the only person who'd ever shown her any kindness – Bill, their gardener – had been away on a week's break. Sometimes he'd been able to save her. Sometimes, when she'd opened her window and screamed, he'd come into the kitchen and send one of the maids to tell Nanny that he'd have her guts for garters if she touched Miss Alice again. This had stopped the evil woman on occasions, but she'd always had her revenge.

The thought of how Nanny took her revenge that day, and many times afterwards, had Alice wrapping her arms around her waist. Bile rose to her throat. Jumping up, she climbed the few steps to the boat's deck, only just making it to the rail before vomit billowed from her. Weary eyes behind curls of smoke looked over at her, but none of the men commented or moved towards her. Moisley spat into the wind, before looking away from her. She wanted to go up to him and shake him and scream at him, 'Yes, I am his daughter, but can't you see I'm not him? Hasn't what I did today told you that?' And to tell him that she'd paid – she'd paid dearly and was still paying. God, she was still paying.

The child she'd been took over and blocked this thought with her own screams. They were silent to the outside world, but scorched the inside of her as she slumped down on the deck and released them in sobs that did nothing to let free the voices of the past – Nanny's voice as she'd helped her out of her clothes, a strange voice not like Nanny's usual one. This voice didn't tell of the expected beating: 'There, there, Nanny will make it better.' And then, 'Nice. Good girl. Nanny loves you', each word spoken to a caress, a stroke of little Alice's naked body. Frozen with the shock of it, she'd been unable to move. 'Pretty little Alice. Look at your lovely golden curls, angelic, innocent, fresh . . .'

With these words entering her memory, there also came a picture of the distorted light of the lamp. The pain assailed her afresh as she remembered that it seemed to have happened in time to the elongated streams of light, as Nanny moved in and out of the beams that shone across the room.

'Put your hand in there, that's right.' Taking her hand, Nanny had forced it inside her blouse, holding it on her fleshy breast, then moving it over the hard nipple. 'You should have been Nanny's good girl before, then Nanny wouldn't have punished you. There, you like that, don't you?'

'Stop it! No . . . No, it hurts. Please stop . . .' Lifting her head now, Alice wondered if she'd said the words out loud, but the soldiers were no longer looking at her, not even Moisley.

Unclenching the muscles of her vagina, she sighed away the horror. They were nearing the point where Bren would need her help. As she rose, the warm dampness of her body told of her sweating. Opening her sou'wester, she climbed back down the steps.

'Are you all right, Alice? Has this been too much for you?'

Making an extreme effort, she made a joke with her reply, 'Well, it isn't like my usual working day, I'll give you that.'

His smile relaxed the moment. 'And your usual day's work is all the excitement you are going to get for a long time, old thing, if I have anything to do with it.'

'Huh, and who says?' It wasn't the best time to tell him, but the lead-in was perfect and he would have to concentrate rather than argue with her. 'Bren, I'm taking a new job. I'm to move to being an interpreter.'

'What? Good God, you kept that quiet! What will it entail?'

'I had to, in a way. Anyway I will still be working at the War Office, but moving to one of the basement offices. Everything I deal with will be top secret. I am hoping my skills will be needed in the field, too . . .'

'No. Not active service. Not that – oh, Alice, I couldn't bear that.'

'It might happen that I am sent to where the action is. Interpreters will be needed as the Allied forces work closer together. That is, if this lot doesn't bring a swift end with an invasion. Don't . . . I – I'm sorry.'

His arm reached for her and pulled her close – too close. She wasn't ready. She'd moved herself away from him.

'Alice, it has been four years since I first told you how I feel about you. I cannot go on any longer. I understand, I do, but this is me, Alice. Your Bren. I would never hurt you, you know that. Today I planned . . .'

'Please, Bren, not now.'

The tense moment was broken by Moisley shouting down at them. 'Need a hand with navigation? I'm trained in that field.'

'Thanks, I was going to do it, but as you're making the

next trip it would be a good idea for you to show that you can cope.'

Moisley's look didn't mar her relief. Back on deck, she watched the clouds drifting, some of them thick and increasing the gloom that had descended on her, others fluffy and dancing away as quickly as they came, throwing shadows that matched those covering her heavy heart as it visited the turmoil it was in over Bren. *Please God, keep him safe. And help me. Help me to be able to unlock the feelings I have for him, and to give myself to him as I am meant to do. And please help me to let go of the past.*

2
Lil

DISILLUSIONED

Lil Moisley stood by the window and watched as her husband turned into the street. Her heart leapt. He was safe. The note saying he was on his way had arrived five days ago, and every day she had looked out for him.

In the distance behind him stood Croughton Mill, grey and bleak against the blue sky. Its chimney belched smoke that soared high today, but often choked the atmosphere as it travelled on the wind towards them. Not that folk ever complained. If it stopped, it would mean the livelihood of the town would be at an end.

The imposing building had misery etched into its walls by its history of child-labour and below-the-bread-line wages for the folk who had peopled the workhouses and were used as forced labour. Lil had been born in one of the workhouses nearby and had come to learn the wrongdoings of the mill's previous owners. She had seen how the mill had flourished and then almost closed as demand had wavered, but the war had once more breathed new life into it and work was plentiful again.

The need for all things military – uniforms, parachutes, tents, everything and anything that required the basic cloths they spun there – meant the mill's looms never stopped working. But although the townsfolk all depended on the work the mill gave, its legacy held many a heartbreak, and part of it lay at the root of her husband's discontent and, she knew, was the source of his surliness.

She looked behind her at Mildred, her ma-in-law, sitting proudly in an armchair next to the fire, and went to tell her that her son was on his way, but stopped herself. For a moment she watched this woman, the bearer of the sin from which Alfie was born. For the umpteenth time she wondered how Mildred had stood resolute that Philippe D'Olivier, the owner of the mill at the time, had raped her and that Alfie had been the product of that rape, when all the gossip maintained that she went willingly with him.

Alfie had allowed bitterness to possess him when, as a child, he'd seen the riches the D'Olivier family had as they'd driven past him in the first cars ever invented, whilst he and his ma hadn't two pennies to rub together. He'd suffered the indignity of having a lackey shove him into the ditch many a time, when all he'd wanted to do was to gaze at his da as he rode his horse down the lane. One lackey even took a whip to him once, as he'd jumped out in front of his da to confront him; he was only a lad of twelve at the time. But, he'd told Lil, the incident had settled in his mind once and for all that he was Philippe D'Olivier's son, as the man had gasped at the sight of him – not just because Alfie had startled him, but because he'd seen the likeness between them: Alfie had been the elder man's double. Even down to the large brown mole on his left cheek.

Then as rumours circulated about his uncle – his da's brother Ralph – being shot as a traitor, Alfie had suffered further, as folk had taunted him. He'd followed the story as best he could, finding out more after the Great War by visiting the office of the *Bradford Tribune* and asking questions. He'd been disgusted by the facts. Not long after that the mill had been sold and, with nothing coming to him or his ma, his anger took root. He vented a lot of it on his ma.

In some ways the war had brought a relief from all of that for Alfie, and for Lil. Loving him as she did, she'd hated the thought of him suffering over all that he'd found out. And both of them had thought the war would be over in a few days. It had seemed like a chance for him to escape for a while. Nothing had happened here on British soil, and word had it that the French-fortified Maginot Line was a solid defence that Hitler wouldn't be able to get through. When the news changed, she'd feared for Alfie. Sleepless night after sleepless night she'd prayed for him, and now here he was, safe and sound.

Checking her appearance for the umpteenth time in the mirror that was set into the coat stand that stood by the door, Lil felt pleased with her appearance. Her chestnut-coloured hair cut in a bobbed style fell in soft waves to just below her ears. Her skin glowed, helped by the rosiness her excited anticipation had given to her cheeks. Her large hazel eyes twinkled – always folk remarked on her eyes. Some called them kind-looking, others said they held happiness and still others called them smiling eyes.

She loved the frock she was wearing and knew Alfie liked it too. Yellow with tiny roses dotted all over it, it had a fitted bodice and a soft flared calf-length skirt. Its belted waistline gave shape to her slight figure. Feeling pleased with the effect she opened the front door, turning as she did and asking, 'You coming, Mildred?'

'Naw, I'll leave you to greet him, lass. I'll see him when he gets here.'

Poor Mildred. Lil knew she was just savouring the last moments without the look of recrimination that Alfie held in his eyes whenever he looked at her.

Running towards him, Lil began to giggle, such was the joy inside her. Dropping his kit bag, he held out his arms to her. 'Eeh, me little lass.' Tears brimmed in his eyes, but she didn't give any heed to them. To do so would embarrass him.

'Alfie, Alfie, my Alfie. Oh God, I can't believe you're home.'

'Aye, but for how long no one knows. It was like visiting Hell. And we ain't done yet.'

'I know, Alfie, but we have now to savour.'

'Aye, we do. And I can't wait to bed you, lass . . .'

'Alfie Moisley!'

'Ha, don't say as you've not missed it. How you love it – you're bound to have.'

She laughed, but inside she didn't like him talking like this. It seemed to cheapen what they shared. Aye, and what they shared had a tale to tell, for she was with a babby. Five months, but he'd not noticed, not that anyone would as the small roundness the pregnancy had caused to her stomach was hidden by the folds of her frock and her belt hid the thickening of her waist. 'Your ma's waiting. Alfie, be gentle with her. She's suffered with you being away and not knowing how you were.'

His grunt at this put a lead weight in her heart. She loved her ma-in-law and hated to see her pay for summat that wasn't her fault. Gentry had power over folk in those days – they still did, if it came to it. In Mildred's day you did as they said, even if it was to open your legs for them when you didn't want to. You lost your position or suffered terrible consequences if you didn't comply. But Alfie, being a man who thought there was no such thing as rape, wouldn't have it.

'Please, Alfie. She's your ma and has done her best by you.'

'Her best! First she lays with that scum of a bastard toff, then she has me and lives hand-to-mouth, starving me to feed herself and all them so-called "uncles". She's responsible for it all. I've told you. See that? That massive mill and all it stands for? As me da's eldest, I should have come into all of that. Not doff me cap to him and his younger son . . .'

Oh God, he's off already, and he's not stepped inside as yet.

'Can you imagine how that makes me feel? Cheated – cheated of what's rightfully mine, that's how. And all because of Ma. If she'd have had me in wedlock, like other women round here had their young 'uns, then at least I could have held me head up high, even if me da had been a drunken no-good! But I'm a bastard, an unrecognized bastard. And that's the lowest of the low! *She* did that to me, and you want me to greet her like a good son? It ain't going to happen, lass. I'll take care of her, but that's all. Anyroad, on the subject of me family, I have news. I've met a lass who's me cousin: the daughter of that bloody coward who was me da's brother. She's another bloody toff, and stuck right up her own arse, just like me da and the rest of them were.'

'Your cousin? Eeh, Alfie.'

'Aye, but let's get in first, then I'll tell you of it.'

During Alfie's telling Lil began to wonder if this D'Olivier lass was as bad as he wanted to paint her. Aye, it sounded as though she was a bit pompous, but Alfie was probably to blame for that; he'd have been surly with her and put her back up, no doubt. Besides, the lass had been born a silver-spoon-fed bitch, so would naturally have a side to her. But her risking her life for all those men . . . That said something about her, didn't it? She couldn't be all bad. It was funny how she had similarities to Alfie: fair curly hair, blue eyes, olive-coloured skin, tall, good-looking, and with a tongue on her that wasn't afraid to say what she thought. Come to think of it, he'd noticed a lot, considering that he hated her!

She knew better than to say all of this, though, so when he finished his tale she just said, 'Well, what did you expect of one of them lot? Forget her now, and say hello to your ma. I told you, she's been waiting for you, Alfie.'

'Aye, I can see. And I see as you're still sitting on your fat arse, Ma.'

Lil's heart went out to Mildred. 'Don't, Alfie . . .'

'Our Lil said you were back. Well, glad to see you, son.'

'Huh, I'll bet. Bane of your life, ain't I, Ma, eh? Well, your sins shall haunt you, as they say.'

Trying to distract them, Lil said, 'Well, there's news waiting for you, Alfie. You're going to be a dad.'

'By, Lil, lass, that's good news! You kept that quiet. Never said a word in your letter.'

'I weren't sure, but I am now. And only four months to go. Aw, Alfie, how long will you be home? Will you be here for the birth?'

'Naw, lass. It ain't on the cards. We don't know what'll happen next, but we know as Churchill's not one for giving in. Did you hear his speech on the wireless? Me and the lads loved the last bit, we were saying it to each other for hours. It went summat like "We shall fight on the beaches and on the landing grounds, in the fields and in the streets, and we shall never surrender."'

'Eeh, Alfie, you sounded just like him. You're a proper mimic.'

'Aye, well, it were a moving moment, listening to it with the men who had made it back from France. We felt defeated. We were of a mind that our country would be conquered by Hitler, because of us. But Churchill made us see it all in a different light. We all cheered till our throats burned. And all of us agreed: we'll do as our king asks of us and follow Churchill's direction, to the last man.'

This had brightened his mood a bit, and it was good to see a smile on his face.

'But what do yer reckon will happen next? Surely they won't send the lads anywhere, after what you've been through – not yet awhile, anyroad?'

'I reckon they will. When they said we could go home for a bit, they said it wouldn't be for long. The fight has to continue, but we're on our own at the mo. All the rest of Europe is conquered, so we've a long way to go. It's down to the RAF, as I see it. They have to keep them Germans back from invading us. But us Army blokes will have our bit to do. We were told there'd be extra training in desert warfare, so I think we'll be going to Africa.'

'No! Oh, Alfie, I can't bear it . . .'

'Come on, lass. Let's not talk of it now. Come and say a proper hello to your man.'

Taking her hand, he guided her towards the stairs. A glance at Mildred told her that this turn of events didn't bother her. She just nodded and turned her gaze back to the fireplace.

Embarrassed, but excited at the prospect of having her man

back with her and making love to her, Lil put Mildred out of her mind and went with Alfie.

In his haste he seemed to have forgotten to take care. More than once he hurt her when he tried to enter her whilst she still had her knickers on. They were tight with the extra weight she had around her middle, and it meant the elasticated legs cut into her. Not having the success he craved, he tore them off her and shoved himself at her but missed, bruising the delicate area around the entrance to her vagina and making her cry out.

'Come on – give me a hand. I have to have you. I'll come in a minute, and then you'll have nowt.'

'Slow down, Alfie, love, you're going at me as if you're an animal. It's been a long time. We need to love each other a bit first.'

'I ain't got no time for that malarkey. What's up with you? Get it in you! I want it, and I want it now!'

Disappointed, she guided him in and lay back, hoping for that special sensation as he thrust in and out of her, but the moment had been spoilt and there was nothing for her, other than a feeling of being used as he gasped his pleasure and slumped down on her. His sweat wet her face and the taste of his tobacco and a faint wisp of alcohol wafted over her from his heavy breathing. Her stomach heaved. Pushing him off, she grabbed the pot from under the bed and emptied the contents of her stomach into it.

'Christ! Carrying a babby's done nowt for you, lass. That weren't a bit like it used to be. Oh aye, I came, and that were good, but that's all. But I could have done that with me hand. I've never been so disappointed in me life.'

'I need a drink of water. Sorry, love, maybe later, eh?'

'I ain't bothering with later, if that's all you have to offer, you stupid cow. A man comes home from war, having tasted the fires of Hell, and all he gets is a struggle, a few groans and a chance to pump his load. It ain't good enough, I'm telling you. Aye, and I'll tell you summat else while I'm on: I stopped for a pint earlier, and that Joan Parfitt gave me the eye. Lads have allus reckoned she were worth a poke, so you'd better buck up your ideas.'

A sob escaped her. This was the side of her Alfie that she didn't like. It didn't always show itself, but if things didn't go his way, then it would appear in a flash. She'd not tell him it was his own fault for hurrying too much and not giving her a chance to show her love for him. Instead she'd leave him to cool off a bit – go and make him a nice cuppa and bring that up to him, and then he'd have a sleep. It'd be better next time, she was sure of it.

'You been crying, our Lil? Has that sod hurt you?'

She'd emptied and cleaned the pot and was passing by Mildred to put it on the bottom step, ready for taking back upstairs, when Mildred said this. Making herself sound cheerful, Lil smiled as she said, 'Naw, it's all right, Mildred. I'm fine. I'm making a cuppa. Do you want one?'

'Aye, I will, ta. Sounds like that were no more than a rape of you. It's to be expected, with him being away so long and what he's been through, so don't hold it against him. It'll be reet.'

'Aye, happen.' Mildred was never one to let things go. Well, she had some things she didn't want to let go of herself, and suddenly the moment seemed right. 'Mildred? You've never told me what happened to you. You know, what led you to have Alfie? Oh, I know as you've said it was rape, but talk . . .'

25

'Aye, I know what is said. And, naw, I've never told anyone what really happened. But I don't mind talking of it to you. I'd like you to know the truth of it. It was partly me own fault. I had a crush on Philippe D'Olivier. I worked at mill, and he was the boss's son. Handsome, he was. He'd had to learn the business from the bottom up, and so was on the factory floor a lot of the time. He had an eye for me, or so I thought. I was naive. Me, from the workhouse, attracting the likes of him? I was mad to think it. He'd talk to me a lot and then one day he asked me to walk out with him. I don't mind telling you, lass, I thought all me Christmases had come at once. Mrs Skeldon was the supervisor of us lasses and was reet put out, as I didn't need her permission to go, with him being who he was. But she warned me. She told me as he were only after one thing. I didn't believe her. Anyroad, when we got out of sight he attacked me straight away. I tried to fight him off, but he hurt me bad. And so it happened. I thought when I went with a man it would be good, as all the girls sniggered about it, and in a way as if to say it were something to look forward to, but it weren't. It was the worst thing that ever happened to me.'

As she fell into a silence Lil thought, *Aye, it can be. I've had experience of the worst of it, but then I've had the good an' all. It just depends on Alfie's mood.* 'I'll get that pot on the go.'

'Well, I should tell it all now. You've took something from him too, because of it.' Her head nodded towards the stairs. 'You see, that weren't it all, and though I think I caught that first time, he used me a lot after that. Most nights after work he'd take me into the woods and have me. It weren't so bad as time went on. I began to enjoy it, and he said I were good, so I had thoughts that something might come of it as, even though he were married, he didn't care for his wife. But when

I told him as I'd missed me monthly, he dropped me like I were a hot poker. Not long after that he went up to London for a while. I was given this cottage, well, in a sort of way. It's mine for the rest of me days, or until I don't want it any longer, and then it reverts back to the estate. After that I were left to fend for meself, so I took in lodgers.'

Dashing into the scullery, Lil drew some water from the pump next to the sink. The noise would drown out anything else Mildred said. She was sorry she'd asked her in the first place, as now there was doubt in her mind that the initial rape of Mildred had spawned Alfie. It could have happened on one of the occasions when she had begun to enjoy giving herself to Philippe D'Olivier, and that changed things. But one thing she didn't want to hear was the confirming of what she'd heard about her ma-in-law taking in men as lodgers. She didn't like to think of Mildred being more than a landlady to them, to earn extra to keep bread on the table. What she'd told her so far was enough. And it confirmed what Alfie had said about who his father was, for she'd had her misgivings about that, given Mildred's reputation. Alfie never had. He believed himself a D'Olivier through and through.

But then she should feel pity for Mildred. Oh aye, she'd become willing. All sins of the flesh are weakening, they say. Mind, that was a revelation: her being given this cottage, for as long as she needed it. Alfie had never said this. She'd always assumed it was rented.

Alfie's mood had lifted by the time she handed him his tea. 'Eeh, I'm sorry, lass. I shouldn't have reacted like that. It was my fault.'

'Aye, it was. You never gave me a chance to give you the enjoyment of it, and there was none for me. And while I'm on it, Alfie Moisley, you just think about going with the likes of Joan Parfitt – or anyone else – and you'll feel the wrath of me. I'll hit you with your ma's heavy iron frying pan, and that's a promise!'

'Eeh, that's me lass! There's a line I shouldn't cross, I knows that. And I won't. I have no desire to. Come here, let's give you a proper one. I'm calmer now and I'll take care of loving you.'

This time, in his taking of her, he gave pleasure as well as enjoying it himself. He patiently used all the old skills that she knew him to have, caressing her body with his hands and his tongue, finding all the spots that drove a wave of thrills through her. Turning her, he entered her and gave himself to her in the position she loved, until she cried out her joy as the sensations splintered the very fibre of her. Then, laying her on her back, he had his own pleasure, until their moans of completeness joined in a sound that all in the neighbourhood must have heard.

Giggling as they uncoupled, Alfie said, 'By, me little lass, that's what I come home for.'

Slapping him playfully, she went into his arms and knew that the memory of the last time had been wiped away. She should have expected it. It didn't matter, as everything was right between them again.

Sipping his tea, Alfie went back to the subject of his cousin. 'You know, it were a shock to discover her. I didn't know she existed. And though I hate her for who she is, I have to hand it to her, she showed courage like I've never seen a woman show before. Oh aye, she gave way to tears after she knew we were safe, but before that she was like a rock – a shining light in all the horror. Talking to the men, encouraging them, and even pulling great big blokes out of the water. I'm proud of her, thou knows. Reet proud of her.'

'Well, it's nice to hear you say summat good about one of them, for a change. I couldn't have done what she did. And it couldn't have been easy for her to live with what her da did, either. By, I'd be so ashamed, I'd hide meself away from the world.'

'Perhaps that's what she's done. I went back, thou knows – me and me posh cousin's boyfriend, he were a good sort – and we rescued another two loads of men.'

'Alfie, you didn't!'

Listening to him, she felt proud of him, though it put a fear in her for what could have happened and she wished he'd just accepted the fact that he was safe and left it to others to save the rest of them. 'Well, I reckon your family did good that day, Alfie. Cos I'm proud of you, too – proud of the both of you. I wish things could be different and you could know one another. I reckon you'd get on well together. You seem to show the same courage, anyroad.'

'Aye, you're reet, we do. Well, you never know. Though I know one thing: I already hate her a little less.'

This settled a peace in Lil: for Alfie to say what he had about someone from that side of his family suggested that some reconciliation had taken place inside him. She hoped so, for bitterness could corrupt the fibre of a man, and she'd seen signs of that in her Alfie. It wasn't too late for him, though. It was never too late.

3

Alice

A LOVE FOUND – A LOVE LOST

'Mother, don't fuss. I will get ready later.'

'But I am so excited! A party! We are throwing a party!'

Watching her mother skipping around the room like a little girl tightened the muscles in Alice's stomach and set up an alarm inside her that she didn't want to feel. Maybe Mother was too joyous? Was this a different kind of warning sign? Was she on the point of having one of her attacks? Often a deep low in her mood began with an over-the-top high.

'Mother, please calm down. There's hours to go until the party, and look at you: you are already dressed in your finery. You look very beautiful and it is going to be wonderful, but I want you to be well for it. This is an important occasion for me.'

Her mother stopped dancing and for a moment looked delicate and sweet. Her dark hair was swept back off her face and rolled at the front, shining in the shaft of sunlight coming through the window. Her gown clung to her wonderful figure and billowed out at the bottom, giving her the shape of a mermaid. It was a vivid red, with a large mock-collar sweeping down from the neck to the waist, leaving a peep of cleavage where it bordered her breasts. The colour showed off her creamy skin. The whole effect made her appear much younger than her forty-eight years. Smoke curled from the end of her long cigarette holder. Alice smiled at the picture she made, but that smile turned to anguish as her mother's face creased in an ugly rage and a familiar screeching tone entered her voice. 'I *am* calm. Stop being so selfish! You know I have not held a party here for years and years, not since before . . . Oh, that's it. It's *HIM* talking. Your bastard of a father! God help Brendon, that's all I can say, because taking *YOU* – you bitch! – to be his wife, he's going to need it!'

'Don't, Mother. Stop it. Stop it, now! I won't stand for it. Calm yourself. You know you can. You can use the techniques Mr Chou-Wong has been teaching you. Sit down and start your breathing exercises. Do it, Mother!'

The moment held tension as they stared at each other. The flash of loathing in her mother's eyes sliced pain through Alice. Would she ever get used to these outbursts? Adulthood had brought understanding, but it didn't stop the agony of being on the receiving end of her mother's hate-filled illness.

An easing of the strain came with her mother's slow acceptance. Her body folded. Her demeanour changed as she gave in and sat down. Trying to help the process of bringing her to a calmer place, Alice spoke gently, 'Breath slowly, that's right. Now, think good thoughts. How lovely it is going to be to have guests in our home. How we have enjoyed planning the occasion, and in the future, when the war is over, we'll plan the wedding together.'

Though all of this had the desired effect on her mother and she relaxed her body back onto the couch, for Alice there was no calm. She battled the turmoil of emotions set up inside her. At times she felt happy about her forthcoming wedding to Bren; at other times, forced by their situation into making the commitment.

The papers instructing Bren to join HMS *Arklantis* on 8th September had brought things to a head. Taking her to dinner, he'd told her of his deployment. He'd explained that the *Arklantis*, a hospital ship used to ferry home and treat the wounded from the battlefields abroad, was an excellent posting for him, but he could be away for very long periods of time. He begged her not to let him leave without knowing there was some hope for them both in the future.

Alice had seen him becoming more and more frustrated with her over the last couple of weeks. With his posting delayed after Dunkirk for extra training, they had seen each other reasonably often and everything had been amicable between them, even though Bren had been unable to accept her loving him, but not wanting anything further.

Suddenly, as he neared the end of his course, it was as if they had their own battleground. Bren had insisted he could make everything right for her, if she would only let him, but she'd feared letting go and allowing yet another person to have control over her. And, for her, his saying that he loved her didn't allay her reservations. Her own mother couldn't love her – not enough not to stop hurting her. Her father hadn't been able to love her enough to want to protect her, his unborn child, from the horrors of the Kaiser, or from the consequences of his actions. And the love that her nanny had eventually shown her had only damaged her.

Pinning her hopes on time making things right for them, she had plumped for peace and agreed to the engagement. In doing so she had found some happiness in Bren's delight and in his unselfish approach to her. He hadn't minded when she'd stopped things from going too far, at times when his kisses held more than she wanted them to. It had been hard on him, she knew that, and she wished things could be different. She wished she could unravel the part of her that held her feelings in what seemed like an unbreakable iron grip.

Everything had moved at a fast pace after that, and now here they were, a few days later, making it all official.

She hadn't minded the party being arranged. It had given Mother and Lady Elizabeth something to concentrate on, and at times it had been quite fun, as Lady Elizabeth had insisted that Alice should be involved, when Mother would have excluded her.

Contrary to her usual nature, she had enjoyed shopping for an outfit for the occasion, and had chosen a satin gown in a soft gold colour. The skirt flowed in a simple line to the floor, moulding itself to her figure rather than clinging to it. But its beauty lay in the tiny pleats of the bodice, which hung in a graceful swirl from the peekaboo neckline and the batwing sleeves. With her arms stretched out, it formed a perfect half-round shape. She adored it and felt elegant and beautiful in it.

Her mother sitting up and squealing, 'You are not to wear that gold gown – I forbid it!' startled her. For a moment it was as if she had been lost in her thoughts.

'Why, Mother? We bought it together, and you loved it on me. What possible reason can you have for me not wearing it?'

'You will make me look gaudy, and I am not having that. I am the hostess, and I should outshine everyone!'

'Oh, Mother, don't be ridiculous. This is my engagement

party. Besides, I could never outshine you. I want to wear the gown. I have no other – nothing else I have is suitable.'

'You can wear one of mine. I have wardrobes of them, some of them never worn. Oh, I was meant to be feted by society, and to attend all the best society do's. But no, that was curtailed by your father's disgraceful and despicable betrayal, for how could I hold my position after what he did?'

'Mother, please. Why don't I get your maid to take you up to rest? You shouldn't have your gown on yet anyway. There are hours to go till the guests arrive . . .'

'No . . . No . . . !'

Fear from her childhood clutched Alice in a spasm that she couldn't move from, as her mother leapt at her, clawing at her face. The pain of the deep gouges brought tears to her eyes. Pushing her away, she stared aghast at the demented woman that her mother had become. Framed against the window, her hair loosened and hanging in strands around her face, she sprayed spittle into the air with every gasp of breath she took. Her head swivelled from side to side as if in search of something. Terrified of what she would do next, Alice could only wonder at what her mother was looking for, until she saw her eyes, wide and manic, resting on a heavy silver candlestick.

'No, Mother! No!'

Resembling a wild animal, her mother lunged forward, the candlestick raised like a bayonet fixed for charging . . .

There was nowhere to go. The wall behind her didn't have a window or a door. Alice's instinct told her to hit out, but she couldn't – not at her own mother. Instead she put her hands out to ward off the stinging blow. The agony of it had her pulling her hands away, then reeling back as the candlestick smashed onto her head.

The impact trembled through her, her body crumpled into a heap on the floor. Unable to focus properly, and with vomit choking her, she allowed the blackness to take her.

'Alice, come on, darling. Fight. Don't give up. I love you. Oh, Alice . . .'

The distorted voice came to her from a long way off, and sounded the way her records did when the gramophone needed winding up. She knew it was Bren's voice, but couldn't reach it. It came again, pleading, telling her of his love. Part of her wanted to laugh, as he sounded so funny in slow motion, but a desperate part of her wanted to catch his voice and stop it from going away from her.

As she tried to reach out to him, she felt a net of close-knit fibre holding her back. Entangled in it, she saw her mother's head, thrashing from side to side. When her face turned towards Alice, her eyes were pleading. *She needs me . . .*

'Mother. Mother?'

'What are you trying to say, darling?'

Another voice answered, 'I think she said "Mother".'

'Your mother's all right. She is in—'

'No!' This was an urgent whisper from the person she didn't recognize.

But Bren didn't take any heed, and with his voice clearer now she heard him say, 'I have to tell her. She would expect it of me. She needs to know her mother is safe. Alice, darling, don't worry about your mother. She is in a sanatorium, where they are looking after her. My mother is visiting and is seeing to her needs. Your mother doesn't know what she has done, but keeps asking for you. She keeps saying she needs you. And, darling, she has said more than once that she loves you . . . Truly, she has said that.'

She loves me? My mother loves me? Never have I felt that love, although I have wanted to. Oh God, I have wanted to . . .

The net that had prevented her from reaching Bren, and that had entangled her mother in her anguish, thinned and then left her. Now she could see Bren clearly, and in his eyes she saw his love for her. A moment of clarity gave her the knowledge that this was a love that was real – what she had been searching for, but had been blind to. It soothed her. She wanted to return it, wanted to tell Bren that she did love him.

'Don't try to talk, darling. You've had a tube in your throat to help you breathe, and it will have made your voice hoarse and your throat sore. I can read your message in your eyes. I know you love me. I know you always have, but couldn't let yourself show it. It makes me happy that you can now.'

Her attempt at a nod caused her pain, but the physical pain was nothing to her heartache at Bren's next words.

'I have to start my journey to join my ship tomorrow, darling. My—'

'No!' The word came out as a hoarse whisper, and tears washed it away from her.

'Oh, Alice, I'm sorry. I didn't expect you to take on, old thing. Don't cry, my darling . . . don't.'

His tears matched hers. Taking her hand, he laid it in his, not holding it, but allowing it to rest there. She had so many questions she wanted to ask. Tomorrow? Was he sure? She had thought he had a week before he had to leave. Then realization hit her: *God, have I been here that long?*

'Be strong, darling. I will stay with you tonight, but I have no choice other than to leave then, as my ship sails tomorrow evening and I have to get down to Portsmouth. I'm thankful, though, that you came round before I had to go. And . . . and – well, that I know you love me.'

There was so much she wanted to say. She tried to speak again, but nothing would come.

The voice she'd heard earlier and now knew belonged to a nurse interjected, 'She's getting too distressed. I will have to fetch the doctor. He will give her something to put her under again.'

No . . . No . . . Let me stay awake as long as my Bren is here.

A man in a white coat appeared. Finding her voice, she pleaded, 'Bren . . . No . . .' This time he heard her, and thank God he stood firm for her. 'Doctor, she'll be all right. She is calmer now. It was the news I gave her. Please let her stay awake a little longer. We have to part tomorrow. We need these few hours together. I . . . we need time to say things to each other.'

An agonizing moment passed while checks were made of her pulse and temperature. She tried to keep calm during it, praying that the doctor would listen to Bren.

'Very well. I will leave the sedative for a while, as she is stable, but let me know if that changes.'

'I promise I will call someone. I am a doctor myself – well, in my fourth year in Civvy Street, but have further qualified with the Navy. I'll be staying all night with her.'

'Oh, I see. Well, then I can't see that there is a problem. I will ask for as much privacy for you as we can manage, given the checks we need to do to monitor Miss D'Olivier.'

Thank God, thank God! As best as she could she smiled at Bren. It surprised her how her heart hurt at the thought of him leaving tomorrow.

'You won't smile when I tell you what my further qualifications are: I have had to learn the skill of amputating limbs!'

She knew they shouldn't laugh at this, as the implications of it were horrible, but at this moment it did seem funny.

Though it hurt to do so, she giggled with him, and the laughing healed her just a little more.

Within a few minutes it stopped abruptly for them both, and an uncomfortable silence fell. A kind of 'what next?' feeling descended. Bren broke it first. 'Darling, I know you've suffered at your mother's hands in the past, and that your father's betrayal has made you close yourself to any kind of love, but we can find happiness together. It doesn't all have to rely on the past. Some things cannot heal, so we have to find a way of living with them without punishing ourselves.'

'I – I know. I will try. And, Bren, if . . . If I were well at this moment, I would be able to give love to you in the way you . . . you want me to, as I – I love you. I know that now.'

He didn't reply. She knew he couldn't. He just laid his other hand on top of hers and she could see all he wanted to say written in the depths of his eyes.

At some point they must have both fallen asleep without realizing it. Waking suddenly, Alice found Bren leaning back with his eyes closed and his mouth slightly open. Watching him held pleasure for her, but a slow wailing in the distance broke the moment. A chill shivered through her and pebbled her arms with goosebumps – *oh God, an air-raid!*

'Bren . . . Bren!' Her cry merged with the wailing noise. Bren woke, but with the siren now blocking out all other sound, his shocked expression didn't give way to words. Instead he catapulted into action. His strong arms gathered her up out of the bed. Someone opened the door and motioned for them to follow.

Ear-splitting explosions rocked the building. Dust sprinkled onto them and clouded in front of them. A disembodied voice urged them to keep moving. Other figures brushed by, running and screaming, in a surge that had Bren losing his balance and letting her go. She landed heavily against a wall, just as another crushing blast took the light into darkness.

Debris clogged her mouth and throat, making it impossible to call out. Something fell across her, trapping her. Feeling around, she tried desperately to find Bren. At last she managed enough spittle to clear her mouth, but more falling rubble drowned out her cry of Bren's name.

An eerie silence descended, into which came a whistling sound. Then terror gripped her in a vice, as cold air swept around her body and another explosion lit up the space around her. And that was all it was: space! Everything to one side of her had gone.

Fires turned the night sky into a kaleidoscope of reds and golds, and wails of agony competed with the drone of retreating aircraft. Only the beam that lay across her, wedged between two jagged walls that jutted out into the nothingness, had prevented her from falling into the vast hole beneath her. A hole of Hell. Inside it, vicious flames licked at everything before devouring it, and from its bowels came the screams and hollers of death. But none of it penetrated her as her body numbed with the shock of realization: Bren, her Bren, had fallen into that hole . . .

4

Lil & Alice

YORKSHIRE & LONDON,
NOVEMBER 1940

CHANGES AFOOT, CHANGES EMBRACED

Lil trudged up the steep slope from her home to the mill. The factory bell tolled. 'All right, we know,' she told it. Weary, and in her eighth month of pregnancy, she wished she didn't need to answer the demand of the bell calling them all to work. A stream of women of all ages walked the same path, their boots clunking on the stone slabs of the pavement, their hair tied up in scarves knotted at the front of their heads. Fags hung from the lips of most of them. Some were chatting, some coughing – all were reluctant.

The chat held the news of the nightly raids on London. 'Poor buggers!' Enid, her next-door neighbour, put in. 'We allus say if there's owt going, them down south gets it. Well, this is summat I don't envy them. Must be like living in Hell.'

'Aye, Gracie's started a collection for them,' a woman walking behind chipped in. 'She wants sixpence off each of us on payday. She has family down there and wants to help. She says the money's going to them Red Cross folk.'

'Well, they can have mine willingly, though I wish there was some way as I could help other than just giving a handout.' As she said this, Lil knew she meant it. If it hadn't been for this babby she was carrying, she'd apply to the Red Cross to become a volunteer. She could do it after the birth, though, as Mildred would take care of the babby. It was planned that she would anyway, so that Lil could carry on working. But then the Red Cross might send her anywhere, and she didn't know if she could cope with being away from her babby. This thought put a dread in her that she couldn't explain, but didn't stay with her long, as the talk changed to gossip over a new lass in their midst and took her attention.

'That lass over there is the one that was evacuated from London. Gillian, she's called. By, she's going to set some hearts fluttering! Our Mick stands staring through the window when she comes up the road – aye, and he has his hands in his pockets fiddling an' all. I clouted his ears last time and he took it without a murmur, as he daren't shout out, in case Gillian looked over and saw him catching it from his ma.'

'Ha, Enid! Poor lad, you should've ignored it. It's part of growing up.'

This came from the woman behind Lil and incensed her. 'No, it's not. Enid did right. The lad should learn respect for women, and for himself.'

'Eeh, 'ark at you . . .'

'Well, ain't all of you sick of the way men treat us at times? I know I am.' The minute Lil said this she regretted it, as the woman jumped on it.

'Well, that's a revelation. We thought your Alfie were the bee's knees and treated you like a queen. Seems as there's more to you, lass.'

'Leave it, Brenda. You know Lil didn't mean that. I'm with

her, anyroad, and no lad of mine's going to think it's normal to stand and gawp at a lass whilst he plays with what he has in his trousers.' This came from another lass walking just in front of them and put a stop to the conversation, as they'd reached the gates. Lil wished she could take her words back; it wasn't the time to put down their menfolk, with most of them away fighting.

She'd not heard from Alfie since he'd left for Africa. Huh, some training he'd had! He was only gone six weeks before he was home for a forty-eight-hour leave, and that was that. He'd told her they'd trained on a beach. He couldn't say where, but said that most of the time they'd been laying mines and erecting wire-mesh fences to keep the civilians off the sand and hinder any invaders who got past the mines. All of this meant he didn't really feel ready for Africa. And, he'd told her, he dreaded the heat in the deserts there, and didn't know how he would cope.

It hadn't been a happy few hours. Alfie had drunk more than he usually did and, though he wouldn't admit it, held a fear in him, which she'd supposed had contributed to his mood. Twice he'd taken her in a rough way, hurting her and not having a care for her needs – rape she'd call it; even though she was his wife and he was entitled, the way he'd gone about it wasn't right. She'd seen bleeding after both times and had feared she'd lose her babby, but the bleeding had stopped. Funny, though: she hadn't felt the babby move since then, and this worried her as she was near the end of her pregnancy. She'd felt off-colour these last few days with it all.

Attending to the loom took away these thoughts, though the noise grated on her nerves, and her back ached with standing. Clutching her side, trying to relieve the dull ache there, Lil wiped the sweat from her face with her other hand, using the corner of her pinny. The room began to sway. A voice next to her steadied her.

'Boss says I've to give you an 'and today. Me name's Gillian. I'm—'

'Aye, I knows who you are, Gillian, and I'll be glad of your help.'

'Are you all right, missus? You don't look well . . . Hey, 'old on! Gawd help us, give us an 'and, someone. Lil's fainted!'

'Naw, I'll be reet, I'm just feeling giddy. I – I . . .'

'Oh, Lil, what's to do? By, lass, it's a good job you fell onto Gillian and not onto the loom. Eeh, love, has it started?'

'I don't know, Enid. I've a pain, here, in me side and round to me back, and I don't feel reet.'

'Well, that's a sign, lass, you should be at home by rights.'

'Enid's reet there. Get yourself home, Lil. Young Gillian'll go with you.'

This from Mrs Oldham, the supervisor, surprised Lil, but then it was known that she had some sympathetic feelings where childbirth was concerned, having been through a few herself.

'Ta, Mrs Oldham. I'll make me time up.'

The supervisor clucked at this and pushed Lil towards the door. The fresh air helped. Taking a deep breath, she felt better and able to cope without Gillian's help. 'I'll be all right, lass. You stay and get your hours done. It's all downhill to me home.'

'If you're sure, missus?'

'Aye, I am.'

How she got home she didn't know, but by the time she did, things had worsened and she could do no more than make it upstairs to her bed.

*

43

It seemed to Lil that a week had passed, but she knew it was just a few hours. Exhausted, and with her throat sore from her screams of agony, she begged Mildred and the midwife to help her. The reaction from the midwife put fear into her. 'Summat's wrong, lass.'

Lil's heart dropped as if tied to a lead weight. She looked at Mildred, but found no comfort in her expression. Turning back to the midwife, she could hardly speak the words she wanted to ask, as she dreaded the answer. 'Wrong? You mean me babby's in danger? Naw, it can't—' Pain ripped through her and flung her back onto the bed, the intensity of it reducing her to pleading, 'Help me . . . Help me . . . Aaargh!'

'Eeh, Mildred, we've a job on. Fetch doctor, and be quick. She's haemorrhaging. Come on, lass, push . . . Push with the pain. Come on now.'

'I can't . . . I can't. Help me, Nurse, help me.'

'The doctor will be here in a mo. He'll have to use forceps if we can't get babby here soon.'

Horror at this had Lil trembling with fear. She'd heard of this contraption and how it was like a big pair of scissors with spoon ends, which they clamped onto the babby's head. 'Naw . . . Naw, I don't want that. Not that.'

'You'll have no choice, lass.'

Another pain scrunched through her. Her scream split the air, and her insides bore down, leaving her cry tailing off into a growl that rasped her throat.

'Good, lass. I can see the head. Another like that and the babby will be here . . . That's it, it's here, you have a – a boy!'

Slumping back, Lil waited. Nothing . . . nothing. *Cry, cry, my babby.* The sound of her own blood drummed in her ears. Anxiety clenched her throat muscles and dried her mouth. She couldn't move; all life had drained from her.

'Right, Nurse, how long has she been bleeding? Mildred, open my case while I wash my hands.'

Not moving her body, just her eyes, Lil saw the doctor plunge his hands into the bucket of hot water that Mildred had brought up earlier. She tried to ask about her babby, but her lips wouldn't form the words. Looking over at the nurse, she saw her shake her head at Mildred. Mildred gasped. The truth seeped into Lil. Fingers knotted around her heart – fingers of grief that she had to release before her life's blood was strangled from her. 'Naw . . . Oh God, naaa . . . aaw!' The holler came from her bowel and ripped her in two, fragmenting who she was and leaving her an empty shell.

'Don't take on, lass. Don't! You have to think on. You need your strength. There'll be others.'

'I don't want others. I want this one. I want me babby!'

'Your son has been dead for some time, Mrs Moisley. I'm sorry.'

The doctor's words seared her. The pain they gave unleashed in her a burning hatred. '*Alfie killed him!* Him wanting his way – any way he could, whenever he had the urge, and without heed of the cost to me or our unborn . . . *His actions killed our son!*' The words found their own way out of her mouth. They chafed her throat and filled her with loathing for the man she'd loved since she was a youngster.

No one spoke. Mildred held her hands together and let her tears plop onto her frock. Nurse Riley looked shocked, and the doctor carried on with whatever he was doing to the part of her that she would let no man touch ever again.

The days turned into weeks. Nothing lifted or moved Lil from the pit of misery she'd descended into – and nothing touched the soul of her: not the stories of war, or the fact that no letters had come from Alfie. She didn't care. It didn't matter to her if he was alive or dead.

She had to get away, she knew that. She had to leave this town, with its endless days of spinning cotton, churning out cloth, and its folk. Oh aye, they were well-meaning, good folk, but they ground her down. Even Enid. Though Gillian, who was young and still taking life as it came, provided some relief for her.

Looking up the street from where she sat on her doorstep, she saw Gillian heading towards her. It was as if she'd conjured her up. The lass had an old head on her sixteen-year-old shoulders and could make her smile. But not today, by the looks of her. 'Eeh, lass, what's up? What's made you cry? Has anyone hurt you?'

'Yes, bleedin' Hitler! He's took me mam . . .'

'Oh God! No! Eeh, I am sorry. What happened, lass? Come on. Come in for a cuppa.'

From what she could make out between sobs, it seemed that Gillian's mam had been caught in a bombing raid. She'd been on her way home from her job in the cinema. 'Eeh, lass, I don't know what to say.'

'Will you come with me, Lil? I want to go to her funeral, and I want to stay in me 'ome. I don't want to come back here. I have an older sister, Ruby. She'll take care of me, only they won't let me travel on me own, as there's no one allowed to go back into London who was evacuated out. Not of my age, there ain't. But with you I won't be questioned. You can tell them we have a funeral to go to.'

The idea shocked Lil. She'd never thought to go to such a place as London! And yet she could do it: what was stopping her? She'd use the money she'd put by in the pot for her child. Her earnings had been good since the first talk of war and, unbeknown to Alfie, she'd put away every bit of the allowance the Army deducted from his pay for her. Some of it had gone on the burial. Even though her lad hadn't a plot in the graveyard, because he weren't baptized, she'd seen to it that he was laid to rest in the best way she could.

Maybe she could stay a while at Gillian's, if this Ruby would have her. Aye, it'd be something different. Looking up, she glanced out through the window at the street outside with its rows of back-to-backs and its memories, and thought, *I will do it . . . and if I get the chance, I'll not come back!*

Life hadn't been easy for Alice since Bren's passing. It no longer had any core to it, no one who cared.

Two months had gone by and Alice had regained her physical strength. There hadn't been any further injury other than bruising, as the beam had trapped her by its proximity to her, rather than crushing her. When the rescuers arrived they had told her she was lucky. *Huh, that was the understatement of the year!* Though she knew that, in the scale of things, she was. The lives lost – including that of her dearest Bren – had totalled 811. But many more, like herself, had had their world turned upside down.

The funeral had been a non-event, with no body. But the memorial service had been wonderful – as far as such an occasion could be. Bren's commanding officer had talked of a brilliant doctor lost to the world, and of the waste of all he'd put into his short life. Alice hadn't seen it as a waste, but as a contribution to so many others' lives. Looking around the cathedral had shown her that. There hadn't been room for even one more person to attend.

Lady Elizabeth had held her hand throughout the hour-long

service, and this had reassured Alice that she wasn't to be held to blame, in the eyes of Bren's mother.

Oblivious to it all, Mother had no concept of what she'd done, or of the consequences her actions had led to: putting Alice and Bren where they were not meant to be. Whatever they were giving Mother in that place had turned her into a happy soul, who sometimes didn't recognize her own daughter. *But then, had she ever?*

Shaking this bitter thought from her, Alice concentrated on her future as she crossed the vast hall of the War Office and stated her business to security. They were two men she knew well from her days of working in this building, but they still did their duty and checked out Alice and her appointment. General Westlin, her ex-boss, had summoned her. She couldn't imagine what this meeting was about.

The building teemed with uniformed staff, most with at least one crown on their shoulder, as she had; but many of them with two or more crowns, making it necessary for her to salute every few minutes to show her respect.

Hoping the general wasn't simply summoning her to offer his condolences, she knocked on his office door.

'Come in, Alice. How are you? Bad do, all of that.'

'I'm fine. Well, obviously still grieving, but keeping busy is helping that, and it's the reason I reported for duty as soon as I could.'

'Yes, good – always the best way. And your mother?'

'Not well, I'm afraid, but in the right place. They have innovative techniques that should help her. I only visit once a week, as they say it is unsettling for her. Sometimes I think they would rather I didn't visit at all. Lady Elizabeth, her friend, visits and my mother is fine with that.'

'That's sad. Poor Lady Louise. Mental illness is a terrible

thing . . . terrible. Yes. I know Lady Elizabeth, Brendon's mother. Another one suffering, as you are, from his loss. Well, now, I have something I want to discuss with you. You won't have heard of it, but I have put your name forward for the newly formed Special Operations Executive – SOE for short. It's a hand-picked elite who will carry out secret operations in occupied countries. Dangerous but very necessary work.'

'What kind of work, sir?'

'You could be asked to do anything: assisting Resistance groups, operating wireless communications, organizing supplies of ammunition, passing intelligence back to us, disrupting the enemy in any way you can, delaying their progress, sabotaging their equipment. You are ideal, with your command of languages – and because you are a woman. Women can move around, blend in and look as if they are doing their normal thing.'

'It sounds just what I am looking for, sir. Something to get my teeth into. And to make me feel that I am really helping the war effort.'

'Churchill himself is involved with this one. It was an idea of the Minister of Economic Warfare, Hugh Dalton, and a cracking one it is, as far as I can see, although some are dissenting and calling it "ungentlemanly warfare". The training's tough. You will be given a new identity and interrogated until you become that person; taught unarmed combat, how to kill with a knife, parachute-jumping, wireless techniques. And not just sending messages, but how to assemble a radio. Codes, map-reading and being put through rigorous fitness routines . . . My only worry is that you might struggle with the physical side of the training, given your recent illness and bereavement, but I think you can do it, my dear. You have your father's determination and strength of character.'

None of this gave her any concern, but only played to her spirit, which had been dormant for so long, and fired her imagination. She had no questions she needed to ask – her acceptance was total, and anything she needed to know would, no doubt, be fully explained. But now seemed the time to tackle something that had often been on her mind. The general always spoke well of her father, but she couldn't imagine why. Being from the same regiment, he must have been disgusted to find that one of his own – and a best friend at that – had committed such a vile act. She'd never asked him about her father, but with this mention of him, and all that had happened recently, she found she wanted to know. And to know from someone who admired him instead of hated him, as her mother did. But first she would accept the assignment.

'I understand. And am willing to give it my best shot, sir. Thank you, sir. I am glad of the chance this gives me to be of real use in the war effort. I'm looking forward to hearing more about it and to getting stuck into the training.'

'Good. Your first meeting is with Captain Bellows. His interview with you will be designed to test if you are of the right calibre. But I don't think you will have a problem with any of it. Now, have you anything you want to ask?'

'No, sir. But may I have permission to speak off the record, sir?'

'Go ahead, Alice.'

'My father – I know about his betrayal, and it confuses me that you always speak highly of him.'

'Oh, I see. Well, I liked the chap, and . . . Look, just how much do you know?'

'Only that he was a traitor and passed information to the Germans that might have helped them, if they invaded. Mother said he was responsible for thousands dying, but I haven't been able to find out anything that supports that.'

'There is no evidence, as far as I am aware. Where did you look? These things are top secret for at least a hundred years.'

'I . . . well, I snooped in Mother's papers. There was an official paper that said he – my father – had been shot. Then she had another letter from yourself, sir, saying how sorry you were, and that the woman involved had escaped to France, but you would do all you could to track her down.'

'Good God, she kept that! I asked her to destroy it. Are there any others? I mean, no, of course there aren't. How could there be? It's just that these things lead to all sorts of questions. It was a private piece of information that I chose to share with Lady Louise. I really am shocked she still has it. You must find it and destroy it. My whole career is at stake! I'm sorry, I didn't mean to snap. But this is vital, Alice. On second thoughts, bring it to me as soon as you can. I will see to it myself that it is destroyed.'

'Of course, sir. I had no idea. I'm sure no one else has seen it. Mother has only one friend, and there is no one who would see her private papers.'

'I . . . Look, Alice, I was in love with your mother. Yes. I'm sorry to shock you with that, but it is the reason I wrote what I did. I would have done anything for her. Oh, I know how it looks – me, a friend of your father's and in love with your mother, sending her a letter that would hurt her further. But I thought it would help her to cope, knowing that he wasn't worth it. He wasn't, you know. I liked him, but he deserved what he got.'

For a moment this hurt. There had always been a place in her that held an expectation that this man knew something different from what she had been told, because he spoke well of her father. She had held onto a hope that somehow the general would exonerate her father a little, but now it seemed he couldn't – and held the view that justice had been done. But she couldn't leave it there. 'So, this woman my father was involved with, did she play a part in his spying activities?'

'Alice, I cannot talk about it. Even the transcript of the court martial is archived and classified.'

'I understand, sir. I just thought . . .'

'Yes, yes, I know. Well, now, back to the matter in hand. You are to report to sixty-four Baker Street, HQ of the operation, on Monday morning at nine-thirty a.m. sharp. Don't be a minute late, Alice. Captain Bellows is expecting you. I shall follow your progress; but I hope to see you anyway – and very shortly – with that letter. Let me see . . . tomorrow? Yes, I will make an appointment for you to see me here at two-thirty p.m. It has to be official, so that I can get you clearance at the desk. I cannot be seen socially with you or have you come to my home, as things can be misconstrued in the times in which we are living. Right, Officer D'Olivier, that will be all. Do as Churchill has asked and *set Europe ablaze*! Oh, by the way, you are on leave from your current position, and it will be terminated if this goes ahead.'

'Sir.' Her salute was crisp, the clip of her heels precise. She understood his sudden formality. Even though she had always enjoyed a relaxed relationship with him, now was the time to think on a different level.

Coming out of the door, she looked across the road at 10 Downing Street and felt a sense of pride. The Prime Minister, Mr Churchill, must know that she was being approached, and he must know her background, but was willing to give her a chance. He would have known her father; he fought in the same war and couldn't have missed knowing what her father did. Churchill's own record was amazing: his daring escape from capture during the Boer War had been followed by the whole world, and had marked him out as someone of great courage. Yes, this war wasn't going so well, but under his guidance she knew things would turn around. Well, she would do her damnedest to help. She would bring some pride back to the D'Olivier name . . .

5

Gertrude

PARIS, NOVEMBER 1940

RESISTANCE WORKER

Gertrude stood a few yards away from Herr Eberhardt's desk. Her nerves jangled as she listened to him. Could she pull this off? He had to be convinced of her cover story, as it was vital to so many of the Resistance operations that she gained this job. Doing so would put her in a position to seduce him, and that could lead to her having access to so many secrets – information that would further the cause.

'You will oversee the care of my children, and you will teach them French, too. Now, tell me, where did you learn to speak German? You speak it with a Berlin accent. I find that strange. And not only that, but you have the look of a Frau. I am curious, very curious.'

'My father was German, Herr Eberhardt. My mother died at my birth and my father insisted that I speak German around the house. He died when I was six, just when he was about to take me back to Germany. He had been sent here as an engineer in the last war and married a French girl. His sister, my aunt, brought me up. She had come to France to join her brother after the war and met and married a Frenchman, and so did not want to go back. She insisted I take her husband's name, Bandemer, but continued to speak German at all times when we were alone, though not in front of her husband, as he did not like it.'

'And your father's surname was?'

'Schäfer.'

'A very common name, and hard to trace who is who, through it. How convenient for you. Are you still living with this aunt? I should like to meet her.'

Gertrude's throat dried. Herr Eberhardt didn't sound convinced. 'No, I moved to Paris two years ago. I originally came to finish my schooling, but my aunt does not want me back. She says I am to make my own way in life from now on.'

'Where does she live?'

Oh God! This is getting complicated. 'I don't know.'

'Oh?'

'I . . . She moved and did not tell me. She did not like taking care of me and only did it as a duty. Her husband didn't like me at all, and complained constantly at having to provide for me after my father's money ran out.'

'I don't like this. My inner sense is warning me that all is not as it seems. Staff here may hear things and if any of them are spies, they could make it their duty to see things they should not. I am wondering if you are such a person. You are too good: you have every qualification I am looking for, you worked in a kindergarten for two years, you speak my language, and you have certificates that show a very good education . . .'

Her heart jumped painfully. Small beads of sweat broke out

55

over her body. Using extreme control, she held her head high. 'No, I am not a spy, merely someone who needs a job. And the one you are offering is just what I am able to do, and want to do. I know no one who would want information – how could I?'

'We shall see. I can check your credentials, of course, but births and deaths and so on, these things have become increasingly difficult to trace. Many records were destroyed in the last war, though I suspect you know that. So, what am I to do about you? I could have the SS interrogate you . . .'

'No! I have done nothing wrong.' The fear that had gripped her at his mention of spies increased its hold on her, and in a begging voice she pleaded, 'Please, I have only applied for a job. I will withdraw my application. I knew this would be a mistake, but there are so few jobs available, and I am about to become homeless and haven't eaten for two days.'

'You don't give the impression of someone who hasn't eaten. You have the fine figure of a Frau.'

A flash of inspiration hit her at his words. This was her chance, not only to create a diversion, but to test her ultimate goal of seducing him. Her handbag clattered to the floor. She dropped it as though by accident and made sure it fell behind her, 'Sorry, I . . . You made me nervous.' Turning, she bent to pick it up, knowing that he would see her seamed stockings and the outline of the clasps that fastened them to her suspender belt. If the rumours about him having an eye for women were right, he should feast his eyes on these and her rounded buttocks, tightly held in her pencil-slim skirt.

Herr Eberhardt was the chief of all military operations in France. Intelligence gathered by Gertrude's stepbrother told that he had been widowed three years ago. On his appointment he'd chosen to take this large Parisian house, which was once several apartments, in Place d'Anjer, and make it into a home where he could work and have his four children with him.

Straightening and turning back towards him, she could see that her ploy had had the desired effect. His eyes narrowed and his voice thickened as he said, 'Nice! Yes, you do have all I need. I think I will engage you for a time at least. I need to check you out.'

The emphasis he put on the last few words, and the look he gave Gertrude, told her that he intended doing so in more ways than one. *A small victory won,* she thought.

Smiling at him, she kept her thanks to a minimum, wanting to spit in his face now that she knew the seeds of her mission were sown.

She'd been recruited into the small Trudaine Resistance group by her stepbrother, with the sole intention of having her apply for this position with Herr Eberhardt. Everything to do with the German occupation and its furtherance of their standing in the war had to come through him – every transaction and all military decisions, as well as outside operations. She had to succeed in her mission to become his mistress. She had to get close to any information going through his office that might prove vital to the work the Resistance was doing.

The thought of being his lover didn't worry her. An experienced prostitute in her teens, she had no compunction about lying with Herr Eberhardt, and knew tricks that would please him. She had told Juste he needed a foolproof story for her cover. The one he'd given her had so many flaws, she feared. *Oh God, this shows we have so much to learn . . . I only hope it's true that the British are sending agents over to help us!*

Somehow she had to improvise and sound more convincing, as there was no doubt in her mind what would happen if Herr

Eberhardt found out the truth. Not only would she face execution, but their Resistance cell would be compromised.

'You're very beautiful, my dear. Come here.'

Walking across the few yards that separated them, she put a swagger in her step. She was rewarded by his obvious look of appreciation, but then he threw her by saying, 'You demonstrate that you are worldly-wise in the ways of seducing men. Where did you learn your technique? Are you married or . . . ? Well, you tell me.'

'No, not married. I – I . . .' Dare she tell him the truth? 'I have had a relationship . . .'

'There is more to you, Frau, or is it Mademoiselle?' His expression hardened. 'What are you not telling me?'

There was no fooling him; she would have to embellish her story – incorporate some truthful bits, to make it altogether more believable. Putting a sob into her voice, she told him, 'The truth is, I ran away from my aunt's house when I was thirteen because her husband wanted to do things to me that I didn't want him to. I came to Paris and prostituted myself, to enable me to eat and continue my education. I graduated with a degree in languages and went on to do a degree in teaching. I secured the job at the kindergarten, and my life became more normal. But then the invasion happened, and the defeat of the British and the Allied forces, and most people who could afford to have their children educated in languages at a young age fled. There was no work. I have been living hand-to-mouth, waitressing, cleaning – anything to keep going. When I saw your advert in the Café d'Anjer I knew this was the job for me. I made up lies, because I thought you would not let me near your children if you knew the truth!'

'Ah, so now we have it! Well, well. You are not planning

to teach my girls to become prostitutes, are you? Or my boys how to access them?'

He smiled as he said this. It changed his face. Already she had decided he was a handsome man, but now his smile gave him a roguish look. Taking off his cap, he ran his fingers through his blond hair. He had a surprising amount – more than she'd thought from the shaved sides of his head. And he looked younger. When he'd stood she had seen that he was a tall man. She liked that. Being tall herself, she hated looking down on men. For a moment she wondered if her own father had been tall – her real one, not the fabricated one or her late-stepfather, but the man who'd spawned her. The man who had loved her mother. The man who, before she was born, had been betrayed . . . No, she would not think of that. She still had too many hurdles to jump through, she couldn't allow herself to think about sad things.

Smiling back, she told him, 'No, Herr Eberhardt. I wish with all my heart I could wipe away that period of my life. I was often told I was made for loving, but my heart only ever wanted to lie with one man, not dozens. I always dreamed I would copy what my father told me about his life with my mother. He told me they were soulmates. He told me, when he said goodbye to me, as he knew he was dying, that I was to think of him always with my mother, and how very happy they would be to be together once more.' *Where are all these lies coming from?*

Yes, it was partly true: she had run away from her real home – a large farm on the Vichy border – and at a young age, but not because her stepfather did anything sexual to her. He had hated her and vented his anger on her. And yes, she had prostituted herself to feed herself, but her stepbrother, Juste, came looking for her after her stepfather was killed in an accident on the farm, and she returned home with him.

Her beautiful mother forgave her and insisted that she continue her interrupted education. When the invasion came and then the defeat of the Allied forces, Juste moved to Paris to join a Resistance group. Their friend, Antoine, went with him, and Gertrude had been able to put them in touch with Esther, a dear friend from her university days. Esther knew Paris well and had helped them find a place to stay whilst they made contact with other Resistance groups.

Two weeks ago Juste had come home to beg Gertrude to seek this position. He had been devastated to have to ask, but it was a massive opportunity to have someone inside the home of this man. No local girls fitted the criteria, and though Esther was willing and originated from Germany and had the language skills needed, her being a Jewess made it impossible to consider her doing so.

Gertrude had put Juste's mind at rest and had agreed. Yes, like him, through their mother, she was part German; but, like him, she would do anything for her beloved France.

As she had left, her mother, unaware of the full extent of the mission, had said, 'Not only do you look like your father – though an Englishman, he had everything a German loves: blond hair, beautiful blue eyes, a tall gracefulness and a handsome look – but you have his courage. He did have courage, remember that.' For a moment she had looked sad, and Gertrude had known she was thinking back through her memories of the past. It was good to know that Mother's true love hadn't been the evil stepfather, but her lover during her time in England, the man who had fathered her. After a moment her mother had said, 'I hate to think of you doing this, as you will be in grave danger, but there does come a time in our lives when our decisions don't just affect ourselves and we have to take the decisions we wouldn't normally take. Go with my blessing, my darling daughter, and know that I am proud of you.'

Herr Eberhardt had been silent for a few minutes, his gaze not leaving her. Holding his mouth with his thumb and fore-finger, he was considering Gertrude, trying to read her and make his mind up about the truth of her story. She prayed he would believe her, because now, with the embellishing of her tale, it did sound feasible. When he spoke his voice held a lightness, a satisfaction. *I'm sure he does believe me*, she thought.

'Very well. I understand why you made up those lies. The truth is not something that would endear you to a prospective employer. However, I have decided to give you a chance.'

'Oh, thank you, Herr Eberhardt, thank you.'

'There will be ways you can thank me.'

'I will do my best to please you in every way I can.'

'Good. But, for now, I have an important meeting pending.' Pushing a button on his desk, he told her, 'Frau Mauers, my secretary, will show you to your quarters. I think you will be happy with them. You have today to collect your things and settle in. You will be shown the nursery and classroom, and I want you to make a list of all the materials you think we need for them. I have four children. My girls, Greta and Adelheid, are four and six years old, and my sons of eight and nine are Bernd and Nikolaus. The boys have their own tutor, so you will liaise with him as to the times when you can have them for their language class. He is German and does not speak French. I expect you to cover other subjects with the girls, though – all things to do with their basic educational needs. I will test them regularly, as I do the boys. You will otherwise be in charge, with the help of a nursery nurse, of all the needs of my children: their recreation, their diet and their general well-being. For this you will have staff that you can call upon to take direction from you and to help out. You will have one day a week off, but I would expect that you will have made adequate arrangements for the children's care for that day, and not leave it to me to do so. That is all for now. Expect a visit from me later this evening . . . Ah, Frau Mauers.' A good-looking woman of around thirty years of age entered the room. 'This is Mademoiselle Violetta Bandemer, the new nanny and governess. Please show her to her quarters and make sure she has a password, so that she can come and go as she pleases.'

For a moment Gertrude hadn't thought he was referring to her. *I must get used to being called Violetta!* For the last two weeks she'd practised and practised, but still, when Juste had called her by the name when she hadn't been expecting it or hadn't been looking at him, she had failed to answer him.

Leaving the office quarters of the building transported her into a new world: one of thick carpets, chandeliers, beautiful antique furniture and artwork that took her breath away. Renoir graced the walls of the main hall, Picasso's clown paintings the long corridor leading to the nursery quarters, and Beatrix Potter prints the children's sitting room.

Her own room lacked any ornamentation, but to her the soft furnishings of blues and greys, the walls of Regency striped white and silver, the royal-blue velvet drapes and matching Queen Anne chair, and the bed, huge and with an ornate headboard, were enough. If she were to add anything, it would be elegant figurines. Maybe of ladies and gentlemen of days gone by: dancing, walking, or sitting on a bench. For the walls she would choose Claude Monet, as so many of his paintings had the rich blue that would tone perfectly with the curtains and carpet.

Twirling round in a happy dance, she forgot for a moment the reason the room was hers. When she remembered, she sat down on the end of the bed. The ripples this caused in the silk bedspread matched the ripples of fear trembling through her. And once more she asked herself, *Could I pull this off?*

Thinking of Herr Eberhardt, she was shocked by how much detail of him she had taken in: his square chin, his overly thick eyebrows and his grey eyes. The picture she conjured up replaced the ripple of fear with one of expectation. What would it be like to make love to him, for she knew that was what would happen – and this very night! How would he summon her? How would he make her feel?

Frau Mauers had told her that the children would be ready to be presented to her after their evening meal at around six-thirty, so she should have settled herself in and be waiting in their sitting room for them then.

Would *he* bring them to her and introduce them himself? Would that be the time when he would let her know where and when he wanted her? The thought clenched the muscles of her stomach in a way that gave her anticipatory pleasure. Trying to fight the feeling and evoke her earlier repulsion didn't help. She wasn't any longer repulsed by what he expected of her, and neither did she give any consideration to the reason she had to do it. The only thoughts she had were those of not being able to wait.

Trying not to think about it right now, she explored further. A door to the right of her bedroom led into a bathroom. Nothing about it was out of the ordinary, and this she found disappointing after the splendour of her bedroom. A further door led to her sitting room, and this did not disappoint: rounded, comfy sofas of a pearl-grey colour and dark-wood carved occasional furniture, against the same blue carpet that extended from the bedroom, and with the same deep-blue curtains at the French windows, made the two rooms blend perfectly.

There were two sets of windows, and both, to her delight, opened onto balconies. She skipped around the room. She had never known such luxury. Hugging herself, she crossed over to the window that looked out towards the front of the building and stepped out onto the balcony.

Below her were the stunning gardens in the centre of Place d'Anjer – a place of such elegance, with tall buildings surrounding the grassed area and trees shading the benches. She had only ever been here once before, and the beauty of it and the people walking around her had captivated her. She wondered if the apartment she could see across the road was still occupied by the client she had visited that day – such a long time ago now, but she could still remember him. A man in his forties, he had taken her to his apartment and dressed her like a postcard depiction of a French maid, before giving her a feather duster. With this she had to dust the room, but when he said 'Now' she would tickle his naked body with the feathers until he told her to stop. She had never laughed so much in all of her days of prostitution. Her laughter had enhanced his pleasure, leading him to pay her double what he had promised. Afterwards she had gone into the cafe on the corner – she could just see it now by leaning forward. There she had enjoyed a chocolate drink that had transported her to Heaven, and had giggled again as the eyes full of disdain all around her tried to make her feel out of place. They hadn't succeeded. She'd always known her own worth.

The playroom and classroom were nothing out of the ordinary, except that they lacked anything to stimulate the children's imagination – there wasn't anything to build with or to mould with, and no artistic materials. She found this surprising, as Herr Eberhardt had an obvious love of paintings. She herself loved to paint, a discipline she would have chosen for her degree if she'd thought she could make a living at it, but it was now something she did for pleasure. Making a list of things she would need for the nursery and classroom, she then took a quick glance at the two bedrooms that the children occupied and at their bathroom, before hurrying out. If she didn't make haste and get back to the grotty apartment Juste had rented for her, to give credit to her story, she would not have time to return with all she wanted to bring before the children arrived. Luckily the tram went by the end of her road, so she wouldn't have to walk. And she could note if there was anyone following her. Not that this bothered her – nothing about where she lived would raise suspicion if her story was checked by anyone.

Back in her new apartment she changed her white blouse for a rose-pink one with a V-neckline. It wasn't of the quality she was used to wearing, but it was practical and she admired herself in the mirror. Her hairstyle suited her strong features, with the long blonde strands held prettily in a net at the back of her head and the front swept over to one side, finishing in a curl just above her shaped eyebrows. Resting her hands on her hips, she turned this way and that and liked the way her figure was enhanced by the pinched darts sewn into the front of her blouse from underneath her bust to her waist. Altogether she presented a demure picture with a hint of promise and seduction. Perfect! And right on time, as she had just a minute to get to the children's sitting room down the hall.

Herr Eberhardt's eyebrows lifted in appreciation when he entered, holding a little girl's hand and with his other three children just behind him.

'Children, come on in and meet Mademoiselle Bandemer. Mademoiselle is to be your new nanny and governess, my girls; and for you, my sons, she will be on hand to see that everything is as it should be for you, as well as teaching you the French language and seeing that your recreation time is well organized. Mademoiselle, this is Greta, and Adelheid, and here we have Bernd and Nikolaus.'

Greta hid her head further into her father's trouser leg, Adelheid gave a small smile and a curtsey, and the boys, wearing those ridiculous leather shorts with braces, both put one arm across their middle and bowed.

'Greta!' Herr Eberhardt's tone held anger and brought the little girl to tears. Ignoring her for a moment, Gertrude greeted the others in German. 'It is nice to meet you. And I hope you like making things – castles and fairies, aeroplanes and tanks – as well as drawing and painting. What about animals, pets. Do you have any? Do you like animals?'

Bernd spoke first. 'Horses, I love horses, and I would like to paint them, Mademoiselle.' This broke the ice, as the other two chipped in with what they would like to do.

'Well, I have a list of things we will need.' She handed it over to a very surprised-looking Herr Eberhardt.

A little tearful voice came from behind his knee. 'I like cats.'

'Well, then, as you are the youngest, that is the first thing we will draw, and the best one can be pinned above your bed, Greta.'

This had the girl's head popping out and a smile creasing her pretty face, taking her straight into Gertrude's heart. But she would have no favourites, for she liked them all. The older ones were a little stiff – or, rather, over-polite, but that would go in time.

'Well now, children, it seems you are going to get on well with Mademoiselle. Good. I will order this list of materials for you tomorrow, and once you have mastered how to draw you can all do a picture for me and I will treasure them. Thank you, Mademoiselle. Now, Adelheid and Greta, it is time for you to go to bed. Bernd and Nikolaus, you have your music lesson.'

After saying an affectionate goodnight to his children, he asked Gertrude to join him after dinner, in his domestic office. 'Your dinner will be served in your suite at seven-thirty. I will expect you at eight-thirty. I wish to discuss all of the children's domestic arrangements and schedules.'

He hadn't left long before the nursery maid came in. Introducing herself as Della, she had a sour look and immediately quelled the children's enthusiasm – *something to sort out another time*, thought Gertrude, for now she had the excitement of the meeting with Herr Eberhardt.

For a moment the anticipation of being close to him made her wonder if perhaps she was being a traitor. God, she hated that word. But then she was on a dangerous mission and was in as much peril, if not more so, as those out in the field were. And it was important that she gain his trust and spend moments with him when he would be off-guard. Besides, she couldn't help the pleasure that gripped her at the thought of intimate moments with him, though she would never forget that he was the enemy and would never – *never* – let her heart rule her head. So what was the harm?

'There are still some things about you that I am not sure of. Your name, Violetta, for one. A pretty name, but not one I can imagine a German man calling his daughter. And nothing is coming back on our searches of your French surname, though the records are scant; and as for your father's surname, I knew that would be difficult to sort out. There are so many families with the name Schäfer.'

Gertrude stood in front of him feeling disappointed, she had to admit, as he had greeted her formally and opened with this sentence, spoken in such a way that it gave no hint of his earlier insinuations.

'Where did you live when you lived with your aunt?'

More interrogation! Somehow, though, she wasn't afraid this time, and that helped her to answer all his questions in a way that wouldn't give him any chance of finding her out as a liar. She used her real background in farming, but placed the supposed farm where she told him she had lived as a girl, in a different area from where her mother's farm really was. And she embellished it by saying that it was rundown and had been up for sale.

She found him knowledgeable about farming, but he didn't catch her out. 'All of your answers are feasible. Yes, I believe you were brought up on a farm, as I myself was, but it is convenient that it is now sold and the owners have disappeared. I shall try to find out all I can. My instincts tell me I must. I will be extra-vigilant, because I fear your strong connection to France, and how convenient your past is and your application for this job. This will be in addition to the normal security that has to be carried out on all personnel that I engage, especially if they are French. Most are German, and I like it that way. They hate the French as much as I do – at least the principles by which the people of France live, and the importance they give to trivial things. Though I love their food, their art and their women.'

She could have said that she hated the Germans, but instead chose to be diplomatic, and although his continued mistrust added to her fear, she made an extreme effort to keep that fear out of her voice and to answer him in a way that she hoped sounded genuine. 'I have the best of both countries. I have an upbringing by my German aunt, who taught me all the good things about her homeland. And my schooling and my own experiences taught me the good about my own country. I consider France my home, and I do not like what is happening at the moment, but I also consider myself to be part of the "master race". My father was proud to be German and wanted me to know about his roots. He often said he would take me back there to live, but became ill before he could do so. And of course the only family he had left – his sister – lived here.'

'What did he tell you about Germany?'

Again that was easy, for her mother had told her so much, but she had to be careful to tell only the things that a child would remember. 'He told me of the cakes – beautiful creamy cakes – and how when you went to a neighbour's they always fed you. And he made me laugh when he told me that he went from one house to another one day, as he had messages to deliver, and at the end of his deliveries he could hardly walk, he was so full!'

He laughed at this. 'Is that all he told you? He didn't tell you any more serious things about our culture?'

'I was only six at the time.'

'Yes, of course.'

Thank goodness her mother had told her such trivia. Yes, Mother had left Germany in 1910, but she hadn't wanted to. She'd been eighteen when she'd left, so she had many memories. Her own mother had died and her father had taken her

69

to England. Many Germans were emigrating there in search of work, but so much happened to her mother in England that it made it impossible for her to stay. Though she had wanted to support her lover in his quest to prove his innocence, being German she was heavily implicated, and he wouldn't hear of it. Instead he helped her to escape with the aid of one of his friends, a Frenchman whom she later married. Gertrude shuddered as her hateful stepfather came into her mind.

'Has someone just walked over your grave?'

'All of this is bringing memories back to me, and it scares me. I am wishing that I had never applied for this position.'

'But you have – and a big part of me is glad about that. These measures of caution are important, as I have already explained. I have to take great care. Now, a few things about the children, and then we should do something about the hints we gave each other earlier. I meant it when I said I would expect more of you.'

'And I meant it when I agreed. I – I . . .' For some reason her mouth had dried. 'I am willing to serve you in any way you need of me. I – I mean . . .'

'I know what you mean.' He stood and crossed the room towards her, and when he reached her he grabbed her and pulled her roughly to him. His lips pressed onto hers, in a way she could not call a kiss, but a demand. It hurt as his teeth knocked on hers and caught her lip. She gasped and pulled away from him. But he grabbed her hair, dislodging the net and forcing her face to stay next to his. His body pressed into hers. She could feel the hardness of him. His eyes glared an anger at her. Through closed lips he snarled, 'You will not fight me. You will let me take you how I please and when I want to, whore!'

This shocked her and shattered her earlier dream. She detected a bitterness in him, but thought she knew the reason why. 'Herr Eberhardt, you don't have to force me. I am willing. It doesn't have to happen like this. I understand.'

Letting go of her hair, he stepped back. 'What? What do you understand? How can you understand?'

For a moment she thought he was going to cry, so she told him gently, 'I think you are grieving still, and find it more acceptable just to take to appease your needs than to want to give of yourself.'

'Shut up, whore!'

This time he turned away and stood with his back straight, clutching his hands behind him. On the desk she noticed that a picture had been placed face-down – a picture of his wife maybe?

'Will you let me help you, Herr Eberhardt? I can. I am skilled in many aspects of healing through massage and close contact, and can help to dispel guilt from sexual activity. It is what made me such a good whore.'

'Please leave. Please just go back to your quarters. I will speak to you tomorrow about the children's routine. I will send for you when I am ready. Just take over from the nursery nurse after you have breakfasted and spend a free day with them, doing as you please.'

'Very well. Goodnight, Herr Eberhardt.'

As she closed the door she heard the sound of a sob coming from him.

6

Lil

A DECISION MADE

'Eeh, Gillian, I never thought as I'd ever see London, but look at it! Oh God, it's all in pieces.'

'Not all of it. This is the East End, where I live. We copped most of it. They say the West End had some, but nothing like this. Oh, Lil, I can't wait to see Ruby. She'll go mad when she sees me. She didn't want Mam to send me away. It was enough that her two boys had to go. That broke her heart.'

'I allus envied you all living down here, but not any more, lass. Come on. Let's get on our way. I feel exhausted. By, that were a long journey. That train rattled me bones. I thought we'd never get here.'

'You're right there, I feel like a shaken-up bag of bits. But, you know, Lil, with every mile I could see the tension lifting from you.'

'It did – it were a relief to get away – but I could see your sadness clouding you as we got nearer an' all. I reckon you need to be with your Ruby as soon as possible. How far is it?'

'Only up that road there, and then turn at the top. Mam's

72

is a bit further. We'll go there later, as I want to stay there. I don't want us under Ruby's feet.'

'I didn't realize your mam and Ruby didn't live together. Is Ruby's man at home?'

'Yeah, he has flat feet, so can't go to war, but he is in the Army. He works in a supply depot, seeing that supplies are shipped or flown out. He's all right, is Joe, but a bit stubborn. He wouldn't hear of his boys staying at home.'

'I reckon he were reet with that decision. Better they are sent to the country than coping with this lot. Eeh, just look at them young 'uns over there! They look like little lost urchins, mucking about in that rubble.'

'That big one, Charlie Wright – the rubble he's standing on used to be his house. Here, Charlie, what happened? Are your mam and sister all right, mate?'

'Hello, Gillian. Yeah. We were all in the shelter. I've come looking to see if I can find some of our stuff. Sorry to hear about your mam. Are you back for good then?'

'I am. I shouldn't have left. This here's me mate from up north, Lil. She helped me to get back here. I haven't taken it in about me mam yet.'

Charlie touched his cap and nodded at Lil – something she'd only seen done to gentry. She smiled back, lost as to what she should say, after listening to what she thought to be a strange conversation: two young 'uns talking about death and destruction as a normal event in their lives. She'd always thought those from the north were resilient, but these folk showed a strength beyond any she'd previously seen.

'See you later, Charlie. Give me regards to your mam.'

'Will do, and we'll be there on Friday.'

Gillian turned a little pale at this. Lil knew this was the first time she'd heard about the funeral, and imagined that the reality of what had happened must be hitting her. 'I'll stay an' all, Gillian, lass. I've a mind, as it is, not to go back. I can't bear me life there after . . . well, you know.'

'Will you, Lil? I'd like that. Our Ruby will be more inclined to let me stay in our mam's house if she knows you are there with me. We can get work. I could get me old job back in the boot 'n' shoe factory, and I could get you set on, if you like.'

'Naw, but ta anyroad, lass. I'm thinking of doing war work, maybe with the Red Cross. They have a lot to do here, by the looks of it.'

'That's dangerous stuff, but there's danger in just living round here at the moment, so you may as well be in the thick of it. It's not summat I could do, though. Here we are. There's our Ruby, the one with the red hair. Me mam used to say it was her hair that prompted me dad to call her Ruby . . . Hey, Ruby!'

Lil couldn't decipher all that was said. She'd got used to understanding Gillian, but Ruby sounded as if she was from another country, as in a flurry of hugs, kisses and tears she heard something about her 'skin-and-blister' and 'Let's have a cup of Rosie Lee'. But it did her heart good to see the love between the two of them.

They were sitting in a small, welcoming kitchen-cum-living room before Ruby started to ask questions. So far she had only said, 'Hello, love, pleased to meet you.'

Between the two of them, Gillian and Lil answered everything about who she was, what it was like up north and how they got here, until Gillian sobbed and asked, 'Is Mam's funeral on Friday, Ruby?'

'It is, love . . . Aw, come 'ere, sis. Mam didn't suffer. The ARP bloke told me she was knocked off her bike by a great lump of concrete that killed her instantly, so that's summat, eh?'

'I know, but never to see her again . . .'

Both girls were crying huge sobs now, and Lil had to get her own hankie out to dab her face dry. There was so much to cry about that it took all she had not to give in completely and cry her own heart out.

Once they had themselves under control, Ruby asked, 'Are you both planning on stopping here with me, then? Only I ain't sure I have space for you both.'

'No, we thought about stopping at Mam's. And, Ruby, I ain't going back up north, and Lil might not, either.'

'Oh, what you planning to do, then? I tell you, Gillian, love, it ain't no picnic here, and if you had any sense you'd go back up north.'

As Gillian talked about their plans, Lil was silent. She was anxious to have Ruby's approval, as now that she'd seen the devastation for herself she wanted to help more than ever. But more than that, having escaped the oppressive mill and the folk who reminded her of everything she didn't want to be reminded of, she didn't think she could go back. Alfie could do nothing about it; he'd probably be away for years. And if he heard about her leaving for London from his ma, well, she didn't care. She'd deal with him when all this was over, but not in the way he might like, because all love for him had gone from her when she'd held her stillborn babby. That love had been corroded anyway, but to her mind he'd killed their son, and that had finished anything they'd ever had between them.

Gillian's mam's house stood in a row. Well, it had once, Lil thought, but now the end one had gone, as had a row of houses that had once stood behind it and was now a pile of burning wood and charred bricks. Here and there a blackened bedstead or the end of a sofa stuck out from the rubble – relics of the folk whose lives had been left in tatters. When Gillian had told her which house was her mam's, it had been with a shocked, hoarse voice. Without taking a breath, she'd then reeled off a list of those neighbours who had lived around them just a short time ago, and whose houses were now gone.

When they opened the door, it was to an uncanny silence. Lil knew that hush. She'd experienced it when she'd returned to clear out her own mother's cottage after her death. It was as if the dead walked the rooms. A shiver made the hairs on her arms stand up.

'Me mam would never do you any harm, Lil. She may have her spirit in these rooms, but then she was torn away without preparing. That wouldn't suit Mam. The minute we get this place sorted, she'll settle. You'll see.'

She'd thought it previously, but this confirmed for Lil that Gillian had a wise head on her shoulders. 'We'll start straight away, eh? There's not much as needs doing. Your ma was a good housewife, by the looks of it. Let's get her peaceful as soon as we can.'

'Ta, Lil. I'm glad I met you. I know that you're only a few years older than me, but you're like having a mam to take the place of me own.'

Pulling Gillian into her arms, Lil held her for a moment. 'Eeh, lass, that were a nice thing to say. But, you know, I may not be here for good. I have a lot of plans and some of them, if they happen, may take me away.'

'I know. And I understand. But we'll always be mates, won't we?'

'Aye, we will, lass.'

It didn't take them long to sweep through the two-up, two-down little house, or to dust the few ornaments on the hearth, polish the table and chairs that stood in the window and clean around the deep-pot sink. Mopping the lino and shaking the rag rugs was the last of the chores. It was uncanny, the peace this brought to the place.

A knock on the door shattered it just as they were about to sit down and have a cuppa. The scruffy lad she could see with his head around the door hadn't waited to be asked in. *Well, that's summat we have in common with this lot, as our door's allus open to all.* What the lad said, though, made her think again that she'd moved to another land. 'Gillian, it's me, Tommy Rat-Arse. Charlie told me you were back. Come on, the bloody kin' and Nellie Dean are round the Hammer and Tack. Honest. They're 'ere ter say they're sorry for us. Come on . . .'

'Tommy Rat-Arse?'

'Ha, his dad named him that when he told his mam he'd seen his dad kissing Dilly Watson. It all happens here – at least it used to. Do you reckon he was telling the truth?'

'About what? I've not a clue as to what he said!'

'He said the King and Queen are round the back and they've come to say they are sorry for us.'

'Well, there's only one way to tell, but it wouldn't surprise me, from what I've heard about our lovely Queen Elizabeth. Come on!'

A great crowd had gathered in the street behind Gillian's mam's house. An ordinary street, or at least it had been before Hitler's Luftwaffe had all but flattened it. Funny to think of the royals even considering coming to such an area, but the sheer number of folk around implied that they had. Pushing their way through, Lil looked upon the gracious face of Queen

Elizabeth and was rewarded with a smile she knew she'd never forget.

Someone shouted something about it being good to know they were staying in London with the rest of them, and the Queen nodded and waved. All around cheered. It was like a day at the fun fair and it lifted Lil's spirits so much that she couldn't wait to visit the Red Cross the next day.

Looking to the left of her, she saw an ambulance with the familiar sign on the side. 'Hold on here a mo, Gillian. I'm just going to ask a question or two of them over there.'

'I'll not leave till the King does. Oh, look, he's talking to our Ruby . . .'

Lil was beside Ruby by the time this came from Gillian. She heard the King ask Ruby how she was, as he understood she'd lost her mother. By, he were a nice bloke. She could see he couldn't understand a word Ruby was saying back to him, but she could have hugged him as she saw Ruby standing proudly and talking about her mam. A flash went off beside her and frightened the wits out of her. Looking round, she saw a reporter. Pushing by him, she ran over to the ambulance. 'Hey, sorry to trouble you. Can I ask summat of you?'

'Of course, young lady. Where're you from? You ain't from round here.'

'Naw, I'm from the north. I just wondered: can I join up with your lot? I've not got a job as I've just arrived, but I want to do war work.'

'All are welcome. Have you any skills?'

'Naw, but I can learn.'

'Here, go to this office when you can.' He handed her a card. 'They'll sort you out, mate.'

'Ta. Ta ever so much. I might see you again in the future.'

When she turned to go back, the King and Queen were in

their car and driving off. Never in all her born days would she feel as she did at that moment. The Queen looked at her once more and lifted her hand. Lil felt moved by her beauty and the knowledge that she'd suffered the bombing of her own home too, and yet, though the Queen could move away from it all and send her young daughters to another country for the duration of the war, she hadn't. The thought of this strengthened Lil's own resolve; as soon as she could she'd go and see if she could join the Red Cross.

The Red Cross office turned out to be a makeshift hospital not far from Gillian's mam's house, but nearer to the docks on the Thames. The building surprised her, as it stood defiant and grand amongst all the rubble around it. She imagined it had been an old shipping warehouse, which had been specially commissioned for this purpose. A sign, underneath the words 'RED CROSS', stated 'Enter'. Pushing open the heavy door, the smell of fresh air was swapped for that of antiseptic and carbolic. An elderly lady manning a desk just inside greeted Lil with, 'Helpers are to go straight through there. Heaven knows you're needed. Wash your hands and leave your outdoor clothes in the cloakroom on the right there.'

Before Lil could protest, the woman disappeared through a side door. Not sure if she should follow, she did as the woman had bade her. A scene she never thought to witness met her eyes. Blood dripped from arms – handless arms – and stumps of legs hung over the side of the many stretchers lined up along the length of one wall. Nurses scurried around and moans of pain droned on, giving background noise to a scene of horror.

'If you've come to help, get the bloody Hansel and Gretel on – the kettle, love . . . over there.' One of the nurses shouted this over her shoulder, without stopping in her task of bandaging a wounded man's arm.

The kettle was already on. Steam angrily lifted the lid of the huge thing and water spat from it. What she was supposed to do with it Lil had no idea, so she just shouted, 'Anyone need hot water?'

'Here, bring me a bowl full . . .'

Filling several bowls from the pile she found next to the sink, she delivered them to each person who'd called out for one. This resulted in a list of other jobs, as the doctor and the nurses attending the injured asked for bandages or more swabs, or for her to take debris away.

Pity vied with her need to keep strong and be of the greatest use she could, wherever she was needed. The clock showed eight o'clock in the morning, and these were the last of the injured to be dug out from the horror of the air-raid of the early hours.

During the night she'd known the same fear that they must have felt when the wail of the siren had filled the air, waking everyone from sleep. She'd only had time to grab a coat before being dragged out into the night air. Aircraft had screamed above her, large explosions had lit the sky and bits of debris had rained down on every part of her, cutting and bruising her skin as she'd made her way into the shelter. But somehow she and Gillian had made it. There, huddled in the dugout under the garden of the house that used to stand next door, they had found Ruby and another two families.

The time had been spent laughing and singing. Someone had filled a flask and taken it down earlier in the night. The warm tea had tasted better than any she'd ever tasted before. A knotted, sick fear had loosened inside her, and though she'd worried for those who hadn't made it to a shelter, she'd settled into the company as if she was at a free-'n'-easy down at the pub.

Morning had brought the sight of more devastation: crying, wandering, lost folk, mumbling incoherently.

For a time, shock had held her rigid as she'd gazed on buildings she hadn't seen when she'd arrived – tall and broken, hidden only a day ago by other tall buildings that now lay dying in a heap. The sound of water flowing made her look up at one that had somehow kept its shell. What remained told her that this was once a majestic, proud structure. Water now ran from the gaping windowless holes in its sides as though it had shed a million tears. Her heart cried with it.

A voice brought her out of these thoughts. 'Help me . . .'

The cry had come from a form on a stretcher on the floor next to her. It was covered, as if believed dead. As no one had called out an order to her for a moment or two, she went to take a look to see if she could answer this plea. When she pulled the covers back gently, the sight that met her shot her body backwards. The form had no forehead or eyes, only black-and-red flesh. The mouth, dry and leaking blood, asked again for help.

Pulling herself together, Lil found a hand – a beautiful hand with long fingers. A male hand with a feminine feel. 'I'm here,' she told him.

'Luke?'

Unable to think how she could have sounded like a man, she thought better of disillusioning him. In her deepest voice she whispered, 'Yes, I'm here.'

A contented sound, as though a bellow had been squeezed, came from the man, and then nothing.

As she crossed one hand over his chest with his other, a tear that she didn't know she'd allowed to form plopped onto the waxy skin of the hand she'd been holding. *Rest in peace, Luke's friend*, she thought.

'Over here! Bring me some of them bandages.'

Taking a second to put the sheet back over the body of the man, she went over to the chap who'd called her, picking up a large roll of bandage from a shelf as she passed it.

'Why aren't you in uniform? We have to minimize the risk of infection, Nurse. You know that. There is never an emergency that cannot wait for us to sterilize ourselves. Get your uniform on at once!' This angry retort, from the doctor who had looked at her for the first time since she'd entered the room, had her floundering for a moment.

'It's there in the bleedin' Mother Hubbard in the corner.'

As the young male orderly who'd said this was pointing to a cupboard, she didn't have to ask for a translation. Something in her wanted to giggle. It was as if she'd been dropped into a land of nursery rhyme. But then, as she walked across the room, she passed the body of Luke's friend and knew this was no children's storybook. This was real. This was Hell on Earth.

No one seemed interested in whether or not she was a nurse, so she donned the uniform and did whatever she was bidden to do.

As the last of the wounded were loaded into an ambulance, someone said, 'Right, time for the brown bread to go. We'll put them all into the next ambulance and get them to the morgue. Start to scrub down, Nurses.'

'This way. I'm Jean. What's your name, love?'

'I'm Lil. I'm not a nurse, Jean. I'm just a lass as wanted to do summat to help. But by 'eck, I didn't expect this.'

'You're a northerner. Well, we don't get many of them down here. Come on, let's make a cup of Rosie Lee before we wash the decks. The menfolk could do with one.'

'I'll do that, if you want to get on with summat else. I can make a good pot.'

'All right. I'll make a start.'

'Eeh, Jean, is it allus like this?'

'Mostly, love. You did well. Consider yourself one of us.'

'Oh, is that it then? By, I thought it took a lot more to become a nurse.'

'Ha, it does. But there's no doubt they'll take you. That man who snapped at you – he's one of the top ones. He's a doctor. I 'eard him ask who you were. No one knew, so he said, "Well, don't let her escape; sign her up. She'll make a good nurse."'

'Really? Eeh, that's grand! What do I do next?'

As Jean told her the procedure, a feeling of belonging clothed Lil. These folk weren't that different from her own. They had a sense of community. They had courage in the face of anything that was thrown at them, and they were accepting of their lot. Once she'd mastered how to rhyme everything, she'd be one of them. 'Eeh, I'm reet chappy.'

'What?'

'Chappy, happy . . .'

Jean creased up, her body bent double, and her laughter echoed around the now empty room. 'Oh, Lil. You two-foot rule. Ha . . . I've never laughed so much. Rhyming don't make you a cockney, love. But you're one of us, just the same. Come on, pour that Rosie Lee. I'm gasping.'

Lil couldn't help laughing with her. Maybe she was better not to lose her own roots. Now, what was a 'two-foot rule'? A fool – of course! *Aye, I've been one of those in me time, but not any more . . . Not any more. Me new life's begun. I can't wait to write to Mildred and tell her. I know as she'll be happy for me. Well, I hope as she will, cos this is me from now on: a nurse's uniform, helping the injured to get well and the dying to die with a bit of dignity.* She picked up her enamel mug and straightened the white pinny that was now spattered with blood. She didn't ever want to take it off.

'Cheers, Jean. Here's to me new life.'

7

Alice

CHESHIRE, FEBRUARY 1941

FINDING HER TRUE SELF

The train chugged along. Resting her eyes on the white-coated countryside of Cheshire as it sped by, Alice's thoughts focused on trying to put in order the events of the last few weeks. Gruelling training in the Highlands had left her feeling exhausted at first, but, after a time, exhilarated and fitter than she'd ever been.

She had acquired knowledge and learned new skills in things she never thought she would be called upon to learn: how to undo handcuffs with a piece of thin wire and a diary pencil, and how to kill a man with a knife. *Please, please, God, don't let such an occasion happen. But should I ever face this situation, give me strength to follow through and do what is best for most people, whatever the circumstances.*

She had said this prayer so many times, but deep inside her she knew the futility of the first plea. The very nature of her job would put her in a position of carrying out such an abhorrent act. At this moment she didn't know if she could.

But, despite her concerns, she was proud of how well she'd done in her training. She'd gained passes in everything she had been taught, and was now on her way to Parachute Training School at RAF Ringway. With nervousness a constant companion, but not causing her to waver, she knew she had chosen the right path for herself.

After this final part of preparation the only remaining thing to do was to pick up the papers for her new identity and the clothes being made for her – clothes designed to help her blend in. And that would be it – she would be off to Paris to begin her assignment.

Her links to France were not strong. Her grandmother had died a long time ago, and she'd never cared for her Uncle Philippe and his wife, or her cousins, who all seemed to consider themselves a cut above everyone else, so she hadn't visited them since her schooldays. Nevertheless, she still felt an affinity with France.

As the train moved along, her mind wondered, as it often did when she thought of her Uncle Philippe. She'd try to picture her father. She knew the brothers had looked similar, with the same blondish hair as herself. They were also tall and handsome, and yet Philippe had calculating eyes, whilst in the picture she had of her father his eyes held a gentleness, and yes, an honesty. Surely he couldn't have been a traitor. A shudder rippled through her. *Don't! Don't think about that. Let the memories die.*

'Altrincham and Bowdon station!' The voice of the guard became louder and then faded away as he walked up and down the corridor of the train. It warned her that she had arrived and provided the distraction she needed. She didn't know exactly what would happen next, but at least she would be in the right place at the designated time. Hauling down her suit-case, she stepped onto the platform.

'This way, Miss.'

The smoke from the train curled upwards, enveloping the man who'd spoken, but after a second he came fully into view. Despite wearing plain clothes, she knew this was a soldier by the clipping of his heels, though he stopped short of saluting. Not knowing his rank and not wanting anyone to know she was army personnel, she proceeded with care.

'I'm sorry, you must have the wrong person. I am visiting my aunt, and she hasn't said she would send anyone to meet me.'

Skirting round him, she felt very alone as her heels echoed on the stone slabs, even though a crowd of people milled around her. Cold bit into her cheeks as she wove in and out of them, keeping her walk steady and unhurried, in an effort not to show the alarm she felt. A shrill whistle to her side made her jump. *Stop it! Act natural – you're on a station, idiot! The guards blow whistles . . . It's what they do!*

She put her case down and took a deep breath. Somehow she had to check she wasn't being followed. Slipping her shoe off, she emptied a pretend stone from it. It wasn't the best idea she'd had, as her stockinged toes stuck to the iced slabs of the platform. Wriggling them, they came free. Beads of sweat trickled down her neck, warm and uncomfortable on her cold skin as she took a quick glance around. But no, the man who had surprised her wasn't anywhere to be seen. Maybe he had just thought she was someone else and there was nothing sinister in his approaching her after all.

The same voice came from behind her, though quieter, as the sound of the train's wheels chugging into motion drowned it a little. 'It's not my usual chat-up line, but can I assist you? Carry your case maybe? Or even give you a lift somewhere?'

Relief flooded through her. The first part of what he'd said was one of the coded sentences she been taught. *But if he is meant to connect with me, why did he not use one of the phrases straight away?*

Still feeling the edge of her nerves, she answered in the way she should, incorporating another coded phrase into her reply. 'I would be grateful, thank you – for the lift, that is, not the chat-up line. I am not open to one of those.'

In an even lower voice he said, 'Steve Henderson. This way.'

She'd almost said, 'Alice D'Olivier', but decided to use her alias. They'd had it drummed into them that they would be tested on their ability to keep their cover many times before they left these shores.

'Madeline Fontes.'

'Well done, old thing, that's twice I tried to trick you. Come on, Madeline, I have a car at the front of the station – we'll talk when we're in it.'

As she followed him, the tension in her settled a little. Her first test, and she hadn't faltered. Perhaps she'd taken in more than she'd realized, as this job wasn't just about having the knowledge, but about putting everything into practice and living the role. She'd just done that, and although she'd felt fear, she hadn't let herself down.

Madeline, I think you and I will do well together, she told her namesake. A smile played around her lips as she thought of the baby girl whose name she'd taken, and to whom she'd often talked like this. It had helped her, as it wasn't easy assuming someone else's identity, especially a baby's. Talking to her made it feel that they were in this together.

The real Madeline had died at six months old, but now has a documented, false life. Born in the south of France in the same week that she herself had been born in London, Madeline had died in Russia, where her father and mother had gone to live with her mother's family.

But now Madeline's life reads as if she didn't die, but her French grandparents went to Russia to try to persuade their son to come home, although he wouldn't leave his wife. They kidnapped the child, only two years old at the time, in a desperate attempt to make their son leave the ever-threatening circumstances in Russia, amidst the fear that no one would be allowed out of that country in the near future. The story goes that it didn't work – their son did not follow – and they brought their grandchild up in France, never hearing from their son again.

Madeline is supposed to have met a Gertrude Alberto at university, and they developed a friendship whilst they studied languages. She is also supposed to have been to Gertrude's home on several occasions. Though none of this happened, Gertrude Alberto and her family are real, as are their circumstances. The plan is now to place Alice with the Albertos once she is in France, under the pretence that her grandmother has died, leaving her without a home. According to the guide notes, Madeline went to see her friend Gertrude, but found that she had gone missing. Gertrude's mother took Madeline in until she found work.

In truth, Gertrude and her brother Juste work with the Resistance group that she is to be assigned to. Juste will meet Alice when she is dropped into France and will take her to their home. Once there, she will be briefed about what position Juste has found her in Paris and will move into a safe house, which he will have secured for her. He will also bring her up to date on the group's activities and its members.

Without prompting, Bren suddenly rose to mind. A picture of his smiling, concerned face, only minutes before the bomb took him from her, filled her thoughts. She could almost feel the love he had for her.

A poem she'd written for him six weeks after his death was going to be her special code when she contacted headquarters by radio. She remembered how, the day she'd composed the words, she'd run to the bottom of her garden at home and squeezed herself into the treehouse that the gardener had made for her when she was a child. When Bren came to play they had loved to hide away in it. There she'd scribbled her thoughts:

> *I'm like a stone covered in moss*
> *For time has stagnated me*
> *The layers have locked in the pain of your loss*
> *And you, and you alone, hold the key.*

Sobs had prevented her from saying the words out loud then, but now she would say them with pride whenever she needed to and know that Bren would be with her, looking after her.

Layers of moss. She'd been almost able to feel them, and they hadn't dropped away until she'd begun her training. Then she'd started to feel less encumbered by her grief and more able to cope.

Henderson's voice broke into her thoughts. 'Here we are, Madeline. Jump in, I'll put your case in the boot and crank the engine.'

'No . . . I mean, thank you, but I prefer to have my case in here with me.'

'Of course.'

At times the roads were tricky. Glistening ice caused the back wheels of the car to slide around, bringing Alice's heart into her mouth. Steve made light of it, his easy conversation relaxing her a little, but still she was careful not to divulge any personal information to him.

'Steve's my real name, by the way. I'm a solicitor, working in London – or, rather, I was. I was called up, went for my officer training at Sandhurst and was then commissioned into the SOE – one of the first, I pioneered some of the training. Oh, not the running up and down the hills, but the technical stuff.'

'Well, thanks for that; couldn't you have made it more difficult?'

His laugh had a nice sound. He was one of life's tall men (she thought him around six foot one) and had a foreign look about him: dark hair slicked back with Brylcreem, olive-coloured skin tone and very dark eyes. Even his moustache had a continental look, if there was such a thing for a moustache. He was a Clark Gable lookalike. She liked that – *Gone with the Wind* was a wonderful film. She'd seen the premiere of it in April last year and it had her falling in love with Rhett Butler.

Becoming serious, Steve said, 'Well, when I realized the danger that agents would be in, I felt the same as the main body in charge of training. That we – and I mean we, in the sense that I too am to work in the field – should be elite in our knowledge and expertise. We will need more than just physical fitness to give us the best possible chance to do our job, and to remain safe. Unfortunately we need parachute training too. I have been too busy to do this before now. It is the only part of the job that frightens me. I am dreading it. What about you? Does jumping from a great height terrify you, too?'

'No, I have always wanted to do it. I didn't get much adventure time as a child, just a few make-believes that Bren and I used to play.'

'Bren?'

His question held a note of disappointment.

'Yes, my lifelong friend who became my fiancé . . . He was killed.'

'Oh, I'm sorry.'

He sounded relieved. This made her look at him again. This time not as a stranger to be wary of, but just as a man. Something about him touched a part of her.

'Have I passed?' His voice held amusement.

Embarrassment flushed her cheeks, 'Oh . . . sorry, I – I didn't mean to stare.'

Again his laughter filled the car. She liked him. And knew she could trust him. But no, she'd been told not to trust anyone. Not even if it was Churchill himself . . . *I wonder if Steve trusts me. And if he really is Steve Henderson even?*

A smoke-hazed layer hung above the crowd. The music excited her, as jazz tones filled the officers' mess – a low building that looked more like a hut, but whose interior belied this, with its highly polished floors and furniture more suitable to a gentlemen's club. In a way that is what it had been before the war, as the army had mostly been a man's domain. Tomorrow they shipped out to their various postings. Tonight they would enjoy themselves. The laughter, high and shrill, held merriment, but in its depth a fear of the unknown filtered through. This was a good bunch of young people, all willing to risk their lives for their country. All afraid, but none willing to give in to that fear. Alice knew she stood in a room full of courageous people.

The last six weeks of training had been all she'd hoped it would be. Falling from the sky gave her a feeling of freedom that she'd never thought she could experience, and now she was truly ready for whatever the future held for her.

'Alice, will you dance with me?'

She didn't have to think about it, but placed her gin and tonic on the table and glided into Steve's arms. They tightened around her. Nothing in her wanted to resist. His head snuggled into her neck, awakening feelings inside that gave her sensations she'd never really let herself explore. This body of hers shocked her and betrayed her, as it let in now what it had always locked out. Regret nudged itself into her at the thought that she'd never felt like this with Bren, and he'd wanted her to. He'd tried so hard to make her feel what Steve evoked without even trying. *Why was that?*

'You all right, Alice?'

His voice held the feelings that had gripped her – emotion and, yes, desire.

'Oh, Steve, hold me.' The plea had a depth that he didn't question. Her body snuggled into his, swayed with his, felt his need and gave back her need for him.

There was no choice. Steve had guided them towards the exit door and they slipped through it. Their bodies shivered in the cool night air. Taking her hand, he ran across the lawn with her towards the light of their accommodation block.

The rules against females being in the men's quarters added to her excitement. No one had seen them leave. All were caught up in trying to enjoy their last night on British soil, and those who weren't going were jollying along those who were – talking about anything and everything, drinking, dancing and trying to keep things normal.

But things were far from normal for her. She'd broken out. She was no longer the tight bundle of coldness she'd been before. Now a fire lit every part of her, making her aware of herself in a way she had never been before. As Steve pulled her to him and kissed her, the transformation completed itself as the last thread that held her to her old self exploded.

'I love you, Alice. I don't know how it happened. You are part of me. I love your funny little ways, even how you sometimes don't seem to be inside your own body, but far away, as that doesn't exclude me, but just says you have things to deal with. I love your humour, your sense of justice – oh, everything! I love the person that you are. I love you, Alice. Oh, Alice . . . Alice . . .'

This whispering of her name set free a feeling inside her, as if he'd turned the key to release her emotions, which had been imprisoned for so long. Her spirit soared with joy. 'Steve, my Steve . . .'

His hands caressed her and his lips kissed her and gently took little bits of her skin into his mouth, as he took each article of her clothing from her. Though unsure of herself and what to do for him, she responded to him.

As if sensing her ignorance, he guided her. Nothing repulsed her, nothing closed her. She opened to his love, to his need and to her own. When his hand touched the heart of her womanhood, she felt she would burst with the ecstasy of the near-agony waving through her. Feeling his fingers probing her, she writhed her body towards him, urging him to take her. She knew there would be pain, but she was ready for it. She needed it.

When he did enter her, she felt a moment of discomfort.

A stretching and a soreness. But his gentleness helped. When at last his thrust took him deep into her, all her pain disappeared. Her very soul fragmented with the love and joy that surged through her. 'Steve, my love; oh, Steve . . . yes . . . yes . . . Oh, Steve.'

She clung to him, wrapping her arms and legs around him, and drank in his moans, his cries of love, as together they gave and took a pleasure that she'd never thought would be part of her life. But suddenly that pleasure changed. Something in her began to build – a sensation stronger than the others. Afraid of it, she held back, not sure how to deal with it; she knew it would consume her if she allowed it. But Steve had no heed for this fear and his voice whispered, 'Let it happen, my darling, let it come. Come with me . . .' As he spoke, she felt his warm breath on her neck and the heightened feeling began to take her over. This new sensation was so powerful that it felt as if it was splintering the very fibre of her. She was left at its mercy as it throbbed through every part of her. She let out animal cries of sheer abandonment as the feeling tore through her soul and gave itself to this man – her Steve, her love, her life.

When it subsided her whole self was broken, and yet newly born. Lying limp beneath him, she felt his last thrusts, expecting . . . waiting . . . But at that moment he pulled out of her, before slumping down on top of her. His deep guttural moans told her that he had reached his peak.

'Oh, Steve, I didn't want you to leave me. I wanted to be joined to you at that moment.'

'I know, I wanted to stay with you, to give you all of me, my darling, but I couldn't. The consequences . . .'

'Of course. Oh, darling, I'm not complaining. I just wanted to have you in me, to take you with me as part of my body.'

'Sweetheart, it will happen one day, but now is not the

right time. Come here, my darling, let me hold you and soothe the disappointment.'

The warm dampness of his body enclosed her and banished the niggling sensation of something missing. 'I love you, Steve. I love you like I have never loved anyone in all my life. I have let you through the barrier that held me from giving all that I am and, now it has gone, I am yours – you are in my soul. And there you will always be. Oh, darling, I cannot bear to part with you.'

'I know. But, Alice, I . . . well, I want you to know that I understand if Bren is still in your heart, and that is fine. I wouldn't want him not to be.'

'Poor darling, he never had from me what I give to you. I don't mean what we just did, but the inner me. Oh, there is a lot to tell.'

'I have guessed that you have been deeply hurt. That things happened to you that shouldn't have happened. But I realized Bren had never known and experienced the real you. You don't have to tell me anything until you're ready to. And, Alice, I hadn't realized you were a virgin. It was such a joy to me to know you were – not that it would have mattered, in the circumstances. I knew you had been engaged to be married, but, well . . . I didn't hurt you, did I?'

'No more than I thought would happen. In fact a lot less than I expected, but it was only momentarily. I'm so happy, Steve. And yet very unhappy. Tomorrow is like a terrifying, deep, dark tunnel that I know I have to enter without you.'

'Tomorrow is tomorrow. Let's always have tonight.'

'Will you do something for me? Each night look up at the stars and remember tonight. I will do the same. Try to look out at around ten p.m. here, and know that I am looking at them and remembering, too.'

'That's lovely, Alice, it will bring us together. I love you, darling. I . . .'

His kiss drowned out what he was going to say. A gentle kiss that took on a passion greater than she'd just known and, as they moved together for a second time, he gave all of himself to her, she could feel that – she relished it, and took him to her in a way that sealed what they both knew: that no matter what the future brought, this deep love would always be there.

They had to shout to be heard above the drone of the aircraft. How soon the time had come to be dropped into France. Alice didn't know whether the wobbly feeling in her stomach was because of her forthcoming jump and not knowing what the outcome would be, or because she was to part from Steve. She looked over at him. His nerves showed in his face. Every parachute jump they'd done had been an agony to him. He hated every minute of it, from the moment the hatch opened and the rush of air hit them, to the crawling towards the opening and then looking down at the toytowns below. But then he had admitted to her that the adrenalin rush took over as he launched himself into thin air. She knew what he meant and wished she could take away his terror of the rest of it.

His gaze on her told her so much. She tried to convey the same, but now – surrounded by others who were taking this nerve-racking step into the unknown – wasn't the time to put into words what they felt. They'd done that last night.

Staying in the circle of his arms, she'd calmed, but not for long. Soon, to the demands of Steve wanting her once more, the desire inside her had been quickly rekindled, as if a pilot light had flickered within her and burst into life, once triggered. This had been the pattern of the most wonderful few hours of her life, until with a deep sadness they accepted that they had to part. She'd had to get back to her own room before morning broke. Once safely outside, they had clung together in a hug that tied the last of the cords that bound them so tightly. Cords that she knew would never break.

'Right. Ma'am, you're next. Good luck!'

The cold air stung her face and rasped the inside of her lungs. A tear seeped out of her eye. Responding to the word 'Go!' she threw herself into the jump. Her heart pounded in her ears. She couldn't do this, she couldn't . . . she didn't want to. But then her training kicked in and she pulled the cord. A peace filled her as she soared towards the ground. *Yes, I can, and I will.*

Her poem went through her head. It didn't just belong to Bren now. It was Steve's, too. The two men in her life, whom she loved in different ways, would be with her every time she said the words. And that would get her through all that was to come.

8

Alice

THE PRESENT MEETS THE PAST

Entangled in her harness, Alice removed her goggles and resisted the panic that was threatening to grip her.

Juste Alberto must be nearby. *He'll come to help me, he will.* Hauling in the parachute as best she could, she waited. Beneath her the ground felt hard. The landing had juddered through her body. Tarmac? She was meant to land in a field!

The darkness closed in on her. Unfamiliar noises set her heart racing. Animals scurried, trees rustled their branches. A squeal told that a lesser mortal of the food chain had been caught. But none of the sounds that she needed to hear – of men approaching, reassuring her she would be safe – came to her. She feared that Juste might have been captured and she'd be left until dawn, when the same fate would await her.

She and all the trainees had listened in shock and horror to the tale their instructor had told of an agent dropped into France and shot by the Germans, who were lying in wait. It wasn't known how they became aware of the drop, but it illustrated to them all that they must be on their guard at all times. Thinking about it now deepened her dread of such a fate awaiting her.

Peeling off her balaclava and shaking out her hair helped Alice to feel cooler. Though the padded jumpsuit she wore made her body sweat, she knew she was better for having it. The darkness cloyed at her; if only she could see, she would be able to discern how her legs were trapped. This had never happened in training. She'd always made a good clean landing, and had been up and disposed of her parachute well within the time limit that the tests they had been through demanded.

The sound of a jeep coming towards her instilled a feeling of despair in her. *Germans! Oh God, help me!*

Two circles of light shone in her direction. *My God, I'm on the road!* Lying flat, she made an extreme effort to roll, but the parachute wrapped itself around her like a blanket. Softer ground told her she'd reached the grass verge. One last effort and she dropped like a stone. Every part of her stiffened, waited – had she fallen over a cliff edge? But she didn't drop far before she sank into water. The splash she made let her know this wasn't a puddle, but a deep ditch, or even the river that she knew to be near to her designated landing spot. The same river that flowed through Paris some thirty miles away – on the other side of the water.

Terror seeped into her as the water chilled her body. Trussed up like a mummy, she could not stop herself from sinking. The water reached her neck. *God, help me! Help me.* But as her ears immersed and the water ebbed towards her mouth, her prayer had a futility to it.

Light lit up the area around her, but then ebbed away, trailing on the bushes and disappearing. The vehicle hadn't stopped. She hadn't been seen! But then what did it matter? Either way she was going to die.

Spitting the filthy-tasting water away from her mouth, she took a huge gasp of air and tried to lift her head, but her mouth went under, despite this effort, although her nose hadn't yet submerged. Still she could feel herself sinking and sliding, helpless to resist as the parachute held her prisoner.

A feeling of extreme helplessness came over her. This was it then. This was how she would die. *No . . . No! I can't die – don't let me! Steve, my Steve, help me . . .* Just saying his name in her head helped her to make one last effort to lift her mouth above water level. As she did so, she screamed, praying someone would hear her.

Birds took to the air in a flurry of squalling panic, filling her with a hope that the men in the jeep might have their suspicions aroused and come looking – being shot was preferable to this slow death. But as the birds quietened a whisper came to her, cross and afraid, but an indicator that there was someone who knew she was there.

'*Chut, ne faites pas de bruit.*'

With the relief came a protest, but not one she could voice, as once more water flowed over her mouth: *Hush, bloody hush! Christ, I'm drowning, and all whoever-that-is can say is, 'Hush, don't make a sound!'*

Bubbles formed around her as she breathed in through her nose and blew out through her mouth. It had become impossible to lift her mouth high enough to cry out. The seconds passed, her body slipped once more. Her head slid under. Holding her breath, her lungs burned. Pressure built up in her throat. *They don't care. Oh God, they aren't going to save me!* She couldn't hold on a second longer. Her head hurt, a blackness crept up on her, threatening to engulf her. She was going to faint . . . *Steve, oh, Steve, my love* . . .

'Everything is all right, Madeline, ve are here.'

A French voice, a woman's, soothing but with a German accent to it, and sounding just like the matron at her school had – she had been a German working in Belgium. *Am I dead*? The matron had died, but why would anyone think it would be the matron that she would want to greet her? No. Bren should be the one. 'Bren . . . Bren?'

'Ah, it is her man she is calling for. Poor Madeline; don't fret, you are safe. Juste has bought you to our home. You are very velcome. Ve vill take care of you. Here, I have some broth for you to drink. It vill varm up the inside of you.'

This time, though speaking in English, Alice knew for certain the woman was German. *Oh God, have I been captured*? But no, she thought, the woman had said Juste had brought her here. Opening her eyes and trying to focus, she found that she couldn't. Cringing against the light, she squeezed them closed again, unsure once more. *Is Juste a traitor – has he turned me in? That light is like an interrogation lamp!*

Trying again, she managed to keep her eyes open this time. A woman bent over her, offering her a spoon of steaming liquid. As much as she wanted it, she raised her hand and hit it away. 'I – I will *never* talk . . .'

Though she'd tried to put defiance into her voice, the words croaked out. Shaking her head in an effort to clear her mind, she let her eyes wander around her. This wasn't an office, or an interrogation room, but a bedroom. A peace entered her. Juste had brought her to his home. Ashamed now, she looked at the woman brushing steaming liquid from her apron. 'I'm sorry. *Désolé. Entschuldigung.*' Saying sorry in all the languages the woman spoke made it feel more real.

'It is fine. I know you must feel afraid. I shouldn't have lit that lamp, it is the one my Gertrude used when she did her studies. This is her room. And, Madeline, you have the look of my Gertru—'

'Oh, my God!'

'Vhat? Vhat is it?'

'Why have you got a picture of my father on that dresser? Where did you get it? Oh, God, you can't be . . . ?'

'You mean my Ralph? My Ralph is your father! No, it cannot be . . . You are the daughter of Lady Louise?'

'I am. And you? Are you, I mean, were you, *his* . . . I mean, is Gertrude . . . ?'

Sitting on the edge of the bed, the woman blocked her view of her father's photo – an exact replica of the one whose frame she had smashed all those years ago. Looking into the eyes of the woman she assumed was Madame Alberto, she saw a goodness in her. And a gentleness that defied her heavy-set face. A handsome face, she would call it. The woman had piercing blue eyes that were a mirror to her soul and held no badness in them. When she'd been standing, Alice had seen that Madame was tall, like herself. Her figure, though larger than it should be, did her proud, as it looked both strong and shapely at the same time. Her head nodded. 'Yes, I vas; and Gertrude is your half-sister . . . Oh, my dear, do not cry.'

She saw Madame Alberto falter under a look that had come from somewhere deep within her, as the truth hit her. Gentle? Kind? What was she thinking? 'My God, you made a traitor out of my father. You got him shot, by making him do your filthy work. Are you still at it? Do Juste and Gertrude know you are a German spy, eh?'

'No! No, *Non, ce n'est pas vrai* . . . that isn't true. Your father vasn't a spy or a traitor, and neither vas I. Ve vere set up. My poor, poor Ralph vas innocent.'

Confused, something in Alice told her this woman really believed what she was saying. 'Then who set my father up?'

'Officer Vestlin . . .'

'General Westlin? But . . .'

'He is a general now? He is still serving in the Army? *Non, ce n'est pas possible! Non!* He is a traitor. He vill do harm.'

Lying back, Alice felt sick. Her stomach heaved. Madame Alberto dashed across the room, returning with an enamel bowl. Dirty bile came from Alice's stomach; it clogged her nose and stung her throat, but she couldn't stop retching.

'This is good. It is because there is still some of the river inside of you and you are getting rid of it. Oh, Madeline, Juste is heartbroken he had to leave you as long as he did. But there vas another jeep coming along behind the one that he saw you roll avay from, and he had to keep out of sight.'

She could not answer this as the vomiting continued, but inside her she thought: *What was he playing at? Several minutes must have passed before the first jeep came into sight. Is Juste a coward?*

As if reading her thoughts, Madame said. 'You vere early. Juste and André hadn't arrived at the meeting point. They saw the plane vhen they vere half a mile from you. They ran, but had to dive into a ditch vhen the jeep came along. They didn't know vhere you vere until you screamed. At that time another German vehicle vas bearing down on them. They had to stay vhere they vere, they did not know you vere in the water; they vere on the other side of the road, still a long vay from you. Juste ran across, risking being seen vhen he heard you. Then as soon as the jeep passed he climbed down the embankment and, in the light of his torch, saw a piece of your parachute flapping in the vater. He and André managed to get you out and vorked on you, getting the vater from you. André is . . . vas training to be a doctor and knew how to get you breathing. They did all they could.'

Still choking, Alice nodded her head to tell the distraught woman that she understood.

Madame placed a hand on her. 'Come on, take a sip of this vater, it vill help.'

It didn't, for the water came back quicker than she could swallow it. Madame left the room saying, 'I'll fetch André. He vill know vhat to do.'

Fighting her way through the fogginess of her brain, Alice had no idea if she'd been asleep or if she'd fainted again, but she knew she felt better. The awful trembling she hadn't been able to control had left her. Strange, she'd had a dream that she'd met her father's mistress . . . Sitting up, the truth of it hit her. And there, in front of her, was the evidence. Her father smiling at her. His handsome face showing love. Madame Alberto must have taken it, for her to have a copy. And the look that Alice had always imagined was for her – she now knew it was not for her, but for Madame Alberto. A pang of disappointment dropped like a heavy weight into her stomach. But then she was being silly. How could her father have had love in his eyes for her, when he didn't even know she existed in her mother's womb? *God, did he have Gertrude before me? Was I not his first child? Did he get to see Gertrude and to love her? Would he have loved her more, because he'd had her with the woman he loved . . . ?* Stupid questions of the kind, on different subjects, that had caused her so much pain as she'd grown up. *Stop it, Alice; you always try to see things that probably never happened that way. Of course your father would have loved you. But then, Mother never did . . . Except . . .* Well, somehow a copy of the photo had come into her mother's possession and she had framed it and stood it on her dressing table. Just as Madame Alberto had done for Gertrude.

A cough made her swivel her head in the direction from which the sound had come. A young woman sat on a chair watching her. A woman not unlike herself in looks.

'Gertrude?'

'Yes.'

'We . . . we are sisters . . .?'

'I know.'

Compelled to rise, even though her legs didn't feel as though they would hold her, Alice stood. Gertrude did the same, and within seconds they were hugging and crying.

'It's incredible!'

'I know, and yet it feels so right. Have you had a happy life, Gertrude?'

'Mostly – some was bad, but that can wait. And you, Madeline? Have you had a happy life?'

'I'm not Mad—'

'I know, but I refuse to know any of the group's real identity – those I didn't know when I was growing up, that is. That way I will not slip up. Of course I know your real surname; it is the same one I was born with, and will return to when all this is over. But don't tell me anything more, not yet.'

Alice swallowed. God, she'd nearly told Gertrude her real first name. But she hadn't. And it hurt that she couldn't. 'A good plan. Juste knows my name, but he is the only one, and I know yours and his, and your cover names. But to answer your question: no, I haven't had a happy life, although I found some happiness recently. You know about our father being a traitor? Well, I have had to live in the public face of that, and it has cast a shadow over me all my life, and an even worse one over my mother.'

'He didn't do it.' They were standing together holding hands. Gertrude's conviction held the truth that she'd detected in Madame Alberto.

'I would love to think he didn't. But we only have his mistress's – your mother's – word . . .'

'No, we have our father's account, too. He kept a journal throughout his life, right from when he was a boy, until the accusations against him took root. He asked Mama to keep the journals for him and to use them to clear his name, if the worst happened. She continued the story, or at least what she had discovered. The journals are fascinating. They tell of your mother and his love for her, and how she couldn't return it. You should read them, Madeline, they would help you.'

How this newly found sister of hers knew she needed that kind of help Alice couldn't understand, or ask about. Nor could she refuse to see the journals, even though everything about them made her feel afraid. Did the truth always do that to you? Or was it that she would see that the truth hadn't been written . . . ? But no, she had to believe her father had written what really happened and not concocted a fabrication of the truth.

'I will read them. And gradually I will tell you about my life and you can tell me about yours – we have a lot to catch up on. But I understand, for now, that the less we know about each other, the better. Then we have little chance of slipping up.'

They hugged again and, in its spontaneity, Alice found a comfort and a love. A love for this long-lost sister of hers, and a love that she knew was returned as she heard it in Gertrude's voice. 'You're tired, lie back down and I will fetch you a drink and then I will tell you what I am doing in my role. I haven't long, as I have only a half-day off. And I cannot come often to this home, as I might be followed and this could jeopardize everything we are doing.'

Watching her leave the room, Alice felt an emptiness inside her. Finding Gertrude had filled a little place in her that she hadn't realized needed filling. *My God, I have a sister!* This revelation sent joy surging through her, but she didn't expect to feel bereft when Gertrude left the room! How would she feel when Gertrude went back to her assignment later?

Besides a sadness, Alice held another worry within her as she said goodbye to Gertrude. Juste had told her about the assignment Gertrude was undertaking and that it held life-threatening danger. And there seemed a little more to her affair with Herr Eberhardt than just seducing him for the purpose of getting information. The way Gertrude spoke, it sounded as if she was falling in love with him! *Oh God, what might that lead to?* But no; she should stop thinking like that. She would trust Gertrude as she did Juste – she had to. However, a little voice in her head persisted. *Love is a strong emotion; if it comes to a choice between not betraying us and hurting Herr Eberhardt, how difficult would that be for Gertrude . . . ? Let's hope no such choice ever comes up!*

Putting these thoughts from her mind, she reflected on some of the things the two of them had talked about earlier. It had surprised her to hear that Gertrude had known of their Uncle Philippe, and knew a lot more about him than Alice herself knew. It had been shocking to discover that their uncle had also had an illegitimate child – a son. How this came about was, Gertrude told her, mentioned in the journals.

It had saddened her to learn that Gertrude had once taken

herself to the gates of their uncle's house, but had been afraid to ring the bell. The awful thing was, it happened at the same time Alice used to visit – sometime during her fifteenth year – and Gertrude thought she saw Alice sitting in the garden reading. Poor Gertrude, she'd been lost at the time, and was prostituting herself at that young age. She'd gone there looking for help to stop her being on the game any longer. *If only she'd rung the bell . . .*

Looking at the journals lying on the bed next to her, Alice thought about all that had happened today. Once more the happiness at having found a sibling overcame her and she felt a little giggle escape. *It is incredible – I can't believe it; it hasn't happened, it couldn't have – I really did die in that river . . .* Twice now she'd cheated death, and so much had happened in between: things that scared her, as well as wonderful things like meeting Steve. Oh Steve . . . Steve . . .

Shaking herself, Alice picked up one of the journals. They were larger than expected – the size of a small desk diary, rather than pocket-sized. She'd imagined they would be smaller, as her father had written in them whilst he was away at the war in France. But, she supposed, being an officer, he probably had the use of a desk in his field tent. How little she knew of the previous war, for it had never interested her as a child. And although it had come to mean a great deal to her as a grown-up, she had preferred not to delve into the history of it. It had only held pain for her. Now here she was, fighting her own war, and in more ways than being a special agent in the British forces.

The pages from the 1910 journal had yellowing, almost tissue-paper leaves. Bound in green leather, which still gave off a special aroma of expensive hide, it matched the other six journals. There wasn't one for 1916. This was the year that both she and Gertrude had been born to a dead father.

Wiping away a stupid tear, she realized there were no journals about her father's life before the period when everything of note happened. She thought this was due to Elsbeth – as Madame Alberto had asked Alice to call her – thinking it important that she read about this period of her father's life first. Probably in the hope that Alice would come to know the truth as Elsbeth herself saw it.

Suddenly she knew there was no need to doubt him. Yes, she wanted to find out all she could about her father's life, but Elsbeth's and Gertrude's conviction that he was innocent now made her believe in his innocence without even reading the journals. She felt the pain of grief for him, and all the disgust she'd felt before just melted away. He *was* innocent. Somehow she now knew he was and, somehow, she would prove it.

In doing so, she knew she would need to prove General Westlin's guilt. This thought evoked a frustration with an action she'd taken not many months earlier. General Westlin had been very agitated when she'd told him about the letter she'd found in her mother's things . . . Damn, why had she done that? And why had she given the letter to him? Now he had the only thing that linked him in any way to the conspiracy that had brought about her father's downfall. But she would find a way of making the world believe the truth about him. She felt sure the journals would help with that. With this, all her worries about what the journals contained left her and she opened the first one:

Ralph D'Olivier
My Wedding Day

15th August 1910: I am writing this when I should be snuggled up with my new wife in our bed; after all, this is our wedding night. That I am not was predicted to me earlier.

I did not believe it would be so, but here I am in my study, which is feeling cold, now that the last of the embers of the fire have died. But let me begin at the beginning.

When the ceremony was over I couldn't believe my luck as I watched Louise glide from party to party like a graceful butterfly, chatting to this person and that. Her beauty outshone them all, as it did the grand ballroom of her father's home, where we held our wedding breakfast. All I could think of was that she was now my wife. And how lucky I was.

Her poise and grace today surprised me, as I had found her to be a delicate being, prone to headaches and near-fainting bouts whenever anything upset her. But this made me love her more and want to protect her.

Irritated by the silly chatter of one of Louise's younger friends, I excused myself and, as I moved away from her, I caught the eye of my new father-in-law, Lord Shornham, my commander-in-chief. He looked concerned, and indicated with his eyes that I should be with my wife. If only he knew how I longed to be, but she skirted around me skilfully every time I approached her. Why this hadn't worried me more deeply, I cannot think.

Philippe, my younger brother, crossed over to me at that moment, having chosen today of all days to be the most annoying fart possible. Not that he was ever any different really. A pompous man, his decision to remain a French citizen has been driven more by his pretensions to the titles held by our ancestors than by any real affiliation to France. Why he couldn't have become a British citizen like me, I do not know! I am proud of being a first-generation Englishman and a serving officer of the British Army. I loved my time at Sandhurst, as previous testimonies in my life's log have shown.

Philippe has been trying all day – once his duties as groomsman were complete – to talk about something that has been worrying him. He hasn't given any thought to the fact that our wedding is neither the time nor the place.

Always father's man, Philippe has been enduring life in the north of England so as to carry on the family business – something I could never do. Give me London and the military any day! But at least it has saved me from having to see how Philippe leads his life, which, judging by the scrapes he's got into, isn't in a gentlemanly way.

Our family came to England in the early nineteenth century when my grandfather's foresight saw the potential for profit in the mills of the north of England, at a time when strife tore through the area. Our father, a boy at the time, had been educated here, and was one of the few French noblemen to retain the defunct but honorary title of 'Duc'. Mother already held the title of Countess de Lessing when Father married her. And so I could have taken up other defunct titles, as many people with ties to the old nobility still did. However, I am content to leave all that to Philippe.

What I cannot leave to him, but dearly wish to, is the sensible running of his life. Before Father died suddenly last year, there hadn't been any need for this brotherly counselling of the young whippersnapper. If only Mother would allow Philippe to do what he wanted to do – sell the mill and go back to France to live an idle life. It could easily be afforded, but she won't hear of it. She has some silly notion that they should continue what Grandfather began and keep the ownership and running of the mills in the family.

The prediction I have spoken of happened when I made my mind up that I couldn't avoid Philippe any longer and, to my intense regret, tackled him. I blasted him with all my frustrations and gave him an earful about spoiling my day by wanting to impart his blasted troubles to me. Only to learn, horror of horrors, that the rat had made some stupid wench pregnant! According to him, the girl had pursued him until he gave in, and now he thought he should look after her and her child.

Taking him to an anteroom, I exploded. I told him what he already knew: that he would bring the family name into disrepute and break Mama's heart. Clutching at straws, I begged him to confirm for sure that the child was his. He replied that it had been obvious that the girl was a virgin when he'd taken her down, and this doused any hope I had of stopping this awful situation.

It appears the girl has been opening her legs for him for some time, and he was sure she did not couple with anyone else. The poor girl believed he loved her. And besides, he supplemented her wages as well as threatening her with the loss of her job if she did stray. None of this was out of any feeling for her, but more to ensure that she kept free of disease.

All of it beggared belief. But, on my taking him to account about his unfaithfulness to his wife and counselling Philippe to take care not to cause her any pain by the scandal of it all, he astonished me by hinting at what is coming true at this very moment. He told me that his wife, Annette-Marie, was cold and only gave to him on her own whim, or when she needed to bribe him. He went on to say that I would find out what that meant.

Incensed further, I almost hit him, but instead I listened to him as he continued, 'I've seen the lust in you when you look over at Lady Louise. Well, Brother dear, you have a shock coming. Fainting and headaches, eh? Mostly when she cannot get her own way, no doubt. She knows nothing of what is expected of her, and showed repulsion when Annette-Marie talked to her about it.'

Shocked, I defended Louise as best I could, telling him the reason for that is because the English don't discuss such things. It is well known they have a shyness and consider it distasteful to talk about such matters.

Then he had quoted that well-known saying about English ladies: 'Oh, they all know how to lie back and think of England. Frigid – that's what they are. It is the lower classes here that know how to please a man.'

I couldn't believe I was having this discussion with him and chastised him for his treatment of Annette-Marie, reminding him that she isn't English and telling him he should have more respect for her and to stop thinking with his cock, which it is well known that he does. I further told him that his philandering ways would leave Annette-Marie very bitter and make her believe she is the talk of society. Then, when I told him that will not happen in my own marriage, as I will respect my wife at all times and will help her accept that side of things and come to enjoy it, it alarmed me to see him shaking his head in mockery of me!

Changing the subject, I told him to sort things out. Be more ruthless in his threats to the pregnant girl. Tell her that she and her family will be evicted if word of these misdemeanours gets out. She is to keep the father of her child a secret.

But it appeared he'd done all of this and she is demanding that Philippe buys her a cottage. She says she will make her own money by taking in lodgers. She has no family and is from the workhouse, and hates it. I had no other recourse open to me than to sanction such an action, though I insisted on a proviso that any further claim on us will result in the cottage immediately reverting to the estate.

Pleased at this suggestion, but not done with me, Philippe went on to persuade me to talk to Mama again about selling and moving back to France. It appears that Annette-Marie says she cannot stand it in the north a minute longer.

Even though I knew it would be difficult to persuade Mama, I wanted Philippe out of my hair. And so, to this end, I vowed to persuade her to hire a management team to oversee the business here.

After thanking me for this, Philippe reverted to his warnings about Louise. 'My dear brother, I sincerely hope you find Lady Louise different from what I have told of. But I don't hold out a lot of hope for you. If you have problems, there are some discreet brothels that I know the name of . . .'

A twinge of doubt about my marriage entered me at this point. It took the place of any anger I had felt towards my brother. Nerves joined the niggling worry I'd had all afternoon about Louise's obvious avoidance of me; and what I had been looking forward to all day – our coming together at last – began to feel like a mountain that I had to climb. Unfortunately what Philippe warned of has come true. I am rejected. Louise pleaded a headache, and that is why I am sitting here alone in my study, not having had any luck in wooing my sweet wife. Maybe I will have to visit that brothel Philippe spoke of . . . But no. I will give Louise time. She is afraid, that is all. I will make it right for us.

Alice let the journal drop from her hand onto her lap. She was sad that her father had experienced rejection and that it had affected him so strongly he'd felt compelled to tell of it, and of his brother's misdemeanours, in his journal rather than write about the pleasures of the day, and who had attended and so on.

She wished things hadn't gone the way Philippe had predicted. Now her father, who came across as an honourable man, was already thinking of visiting a brothel – a path that would lead to his downfall. *Oh, Mother, you have done so much damage in your life. Yes, you could not help what you did to me, but to Father . . .*

9

Gertrude

PARIS, MARCH 1941

A FEAR OF TRUST

Kicking off her shoes, Gertrude crumpled in a heap on her bed. It had been an emotional day. But she would not give in to tears. She had a mission, and so far she hadn't achieved anything towards that. Not even getting into the bed of Herr Eberhardt. Though she longed to.

Oh, she'd told Juste, and now Madeline, that she had done so, as it was important to their cause that she did, and she didn't want them feeling let down. After all, she had been in the post four months now, and they would expect her to be in the position they needed her to be in.

In her discussion with Madeline she knew that her sister had picked up on the deep feelings she held for Herr Eberhardt – feelings she couldn't deny. She loved him. And something told her he returned her love, and that is why he hadn't taken from her what he said he would. Taking from a whore when you still loved a deceased spouse was not nearly as difficult, it would seem, as giving to another woman the love he had once given to his wife.

Not that he was going without. She'd followed him one night to the officers' brothel – the German pigs had fashioned it from a Jewish synagogue, as if they hadn't insulted the Jewish race enough. The horrific stories that her friend Esther had told her shuddered through her. All of Esther's family were in a labour camp, but Esther didn't know where. She'd had no news from them, though word had been passed to her, telling her what had happened to them and others. She had begged her mother and father to bring the family to Paris when news began to seep through of how the Jews were being treated in Germany, but to no avail.

Esther had come to France to study and had never gone back. Now there were rumblings about the Jews' status here. Nothing specific, but enough to put fear into people. Most, even her old friends, walked on the other side of the road from Esther, but she understood and had told her friends that she wanted them to do this. They could all still meet in private. She'd told Gertrude to do the same and, although it broke her heart to do so, Gertrude knew she'd have to. She couldn't risk being caught talking to a Jew, for it would have put her mission in jeopardy.

A knock at her door had her sitting up. Her heart pounded. Was it Herr Eberhardt?

One of the maids stood trembling with fear there. 'What is it? What has happened?'

'*Hier ist eine Anmerkung von ihrem Freund.*' The girl scurried away.

Looking at the crumpled paper the girl had given her, she felt fear clutch at the nerves of her stomach. *A note from my friend? But who? And why was it brought to me by a maid?*

The knot of fear tightened as she opened it. Was the maid connected to the Resistance? No, Juste would have told her.

Was this a trick to test her? Was the reason Herr Eberhardt hadn't yet been with her that he still didn't trust her?

The paper crackled as she undid it. A rough piece of brown grocery wrapping, its many folds had corrupted so that it was difficult to read the words. When she did manage it, shock stilled her:

> This is to tell you that Esther has disappeared. I need your help. I'm being followed. I am afraid. I don't know if these are our side or Germans, but it has been like this since I spoke to Esther. She had warned me not to talk to her in public, as she had all of us, but how could I not, when I love her? You could find out what has happened to her. Meet me when you can. Let me know through the maid. Antoine.

As had happened when she first entered her room after her visit home, Gertrude's legs folded beneath her and once more she crumpled to the bed. This time the tears flowed. This time she gave into the helpless feeling inside her. Oh, Esther, Esther; would she ever see her again? Big and jolly, Esther had been a friend since their days in university together. She had worked in Paris and wanted to help the Resistance movement, but it was hopeless as she would not disguise that she was a Jewess. Her features gave her away and, no matter how they pleaded with her, she would not bleach her hair and eyebrows to help disguise herself. Whilst Gertrude admired her need to stay true to her faith and race, it made it very difficult to be open with their friendship, and impossible and highly dangerous to allow her to help them. The pity of it all frustrated Gertrude. 'God, what is it with the Germans and the Jews? They're just people, for Christ's sake . . .'

Her thoughts turned to Antoine. Somehow she must find a way to help him, for she could not let down a dear friend from her childhood days. Tomorrow she must get a message to Juste; check if he knew about this maid, and whether he could do anything to help Antoine. But then the maid might be a plant! The whole story might be a sham to catch her out. She had to be careful. Messages for her were always left at the corner cafe. *Why, oh why, would Antoine have not used that method?*

In a flash of clarity she knew what she must do. She must report the maid. She had no choice. If the maid was a plant by Herr Eberhardt, then the consequences of not reporting her would be dire for herself and for the group. She could not risk that. If the maid was a true worker for the Resistance, then they might look on Gertrude as having betrayed them. But no, they would see her reasoning, for the rules of contact had been breached. She had no choice.

Standing in front of a row of nervous-looking maids, Gertrude pointed to the one who had brought the note to her. The screams of protest from the girl would live with her forever.

'No . . . no . . . no . . . I – I was only working for her friend. I did not know her before. She is an agent, a spy!'

This, said in French, made Gertrude realize, with horror, that the girl was genuine. Bile rose in her throat and threatened to choke her. Her heart was weighed down with guilt, as guards were ordered to take the girl away. She clenched her fists and clamped her teeth together in an effort not to protest, and tried to close her ears to the desperate screams of the girl pleading for mercy. They went on and on, fading into the distance.

Dismissing the rest of the maids, Herr Eberhardt stared at Gertrude for a long moment. His face was cold and unreadable. 'So, Mademoiselle Bandemer, what am I to make of this? Why would a French girl pose as a German to get a job in my house, only to bring you a note and denounce you as a spy? This is very strange, don't you think?'

'It is, Herr Eberhardt, and I can understand why you are confused. I am myself. I wonder if she was testing me out, prior to recruiting me? Maybe somehow she knew I was French, even though no one else has suspected.'

'But this Antoine, are you saying you don't know him? Is he real? Is he a dissident? And who is Esther?'

'Antoine is a common name. I do know many men with that name, but none that would be a dissident. And as for Esther, again it is a common Jewish name. I was at university with an Esther, but I haven't had any contact with her for a long time. I had been told that she and her family had disappeared.'

'No matter – the maid already squealed, as you heard, so we will get plenty out of her. You did a good thing in reporting her.'

There was tension in the silence that followed this. Gertrude could not look away from his stare. His grey eyes clouded over. His voice took on a different note from the cruel, accusatory one he'd just used, as he asked almost in a whisper, 'What is it with you? Why do you affect me so? It is as if you are in my mind. You know, don't you? You know about the pain I suffer.'

'Yes, I know. I know what is behind you wanting to be rough with me, and I think you are with any woman that you take.'

'I find that unsettling. Why should you realize my pain and not others?'

'I saw the face-down photograph and guessed it was one of your wife and family, so I had an advantage. In my training to please men, by a very old and wise madam who used to own a brothel here, I was taught how to get inside men's heads and understand the different types who seek out the favours of a prostitute. Some have mother-fixations, some sister-fixations, some a deep self-disgust. Others are grieving for loved ones and feel angry and ashamed. I put you in this last group. I – I can help you . . .'

'How? This is ridiculous!'

'I would take your guilt into account. I would not allow you to penetrate me until you are ready to do so without feeling that crippling emotion. I would let you talk as I massaged your body. I would bathe you, and lie beside you until you slept, letting my naked body caress you, but not demanding anything from you – just letting you fantasize as to whose body it is. And I will allow you to weep because it isn't the body you want it to be. You will know when you are ready to let go and let your wife rest in peace, and then you will be able to love again, and I will be here for you, waiting.'

He did not speak. Turning from her, he picked up the picture from his desk and stared at it.

'Would you like me to leave, Herr Eberhardt? It is in moments like this that you need to be alone. You have a big decision to make – one that could see you going forward or one that could stagnate you.'

His 'Yes' was controlled, but she heard a deep swallow before he spoke.

'I would like to walk out for a while. The children are having their afternoon nap and I usually take this opportunity to get a little time on my own. Do you object to that, Herr Eberhardt?'

'No, carry on as normal. I will speak to you once the girl has been interrogated.'

Back in her room, Gertrude's hand shook as she wrote a note for Juste telling him what had happened, and why she had done what she'd done. She told him that her heart ached for the girl, but her stomach churned with terror at what would happen once the girl was interrogated. Juste was always ready to receive a communication from Paulo, the cafe owner, at this hour. If he saw her going into the cafe wearing her green jacket with the fur collar, he would know that she was leaving a message for him. As soon as she left, Juste would be in the alley at the back door of the cafe, ready to receive the communication.

The cafe hummed with German conversation. Soldiers sat at every table and low whistles and guffaws welcomed her appearance, until one soldier said, '*Sie vorsichtig, sie ist ein Favorit der Ihr Eberhardt*,' and all turned away from her. From the way in which the soldier had warned his comrades to be careful and telling them she was the favourite of Herr Eberhardt, it seemed that gossip was rife about her. She'd have to take extra care, as this meant she would be scrutinized by any German with whom she came into contact. To be thought the mistress of one of the most powerful countrymen in France would earn her a little respect, but would also make her an object of curiosity.

Picking through the magazines in a pile in the corner whilst waiting for her coffee, she found a copy of *Mode du Jour*. The girl on the cover looked similar to herself, with the same-shaped face, long lashes and swept-back blonde hair. And she loved the little black hat the girl wore – a felt imitation of a scarf wrapped around the back and tied on top of her head in an elaborate bow. It was chic and flattering. Thinking that she must get one similar, Gertrude smiled to herself as she read the caption beneath: *'du neuf avec du vieux'* – 'the new with the old'. Was it possible to stop being the woman she was and fully become the agent she had to be? She knew it was, but *she* could mix both of them, couldn't she?

The wind whipped around her as she took her coffee outside. Choosing a seat sheltered from the breeze, she peeled off her second glove – she'd removed only one in the cafe to help her to sort through the magazines. Taking her time, she managed not to drop the note she had tucked inside. It was easy then to open the magazine with her other hand and slip the note between the front cover and the first page, before relaxing back and continuing to flick through the pages while she drank her coffee.

Though the drink was delicious, and was made of superior beans to those used in other establishments, on account of the cafe's German clientele, it did nothing to lift her spirits or to quell the trembling inside her. Her instincts were to run round to the back of the cafe and find comfort in seeing Juste. Her head told her that she mustn't.

'Mademoiselle has found an interesting magazine, no?'

The voice made her jump. Looking up, she saw that it was Antoine. With hardly a movement of her head she scanned the street. She could see no sign of anyone watching her.

In a low tone that spoke of her anger she snapped at Antoine, 'Go away! Are you stupid? How dare you put me in danger?'

'What happened to my friend – did she deliver you a note?'

'Go away, Antoine, please. The cafe is full of German soldiers who know who I am. Please, go away.'

'I will wait around the corner for you. Oh, and I will take that magazine. I see you have finished with it.'

Snatching it up, she stood. The iron chair crashed to the ground. Two German officers appeared from inside the cafe. Antoine walked away unhurriedly across the street.

'Was he troubling you, Mademoiselle?'

'No, not at all. He merely asked for the time. When I looked and realized it was later than I thought, I rose too quickly. I am fine – there is nothing to concern yourself about. I have to hurry. Excuse me.'

'I'll take the magazine back inside for you . . .'

Handing it to the younger of the two, she stammered to thank him in French and German, '*Merci*. I mean, *Ich bin dankbar*' – knowing that she wasn't grateful at all – and went as if to walk away. *Please God, don't let my note fall out!*

'*Mademoiselle, vous n'avez pas payé!*'

Thank God for Paulo. He must have seen the danger she was in from behind his counter and was causing a distraction by asking her to settle her bill!

Smiling at the German, Paulo took the magazine from him and picked up her coffee cup while she fumbled for the change with which to pay him. Paulo never charged her as a rule. Always he would say: '*Non, je ne prends pas d'argent de mes amis.*' But this time she was more than happy to be a paying customer, and not just a friend having coffee!

Nodding at them all, she turned on her heels and put more than the usual swagger into her walk, hoping that the desire this might invoke would take from their minds any doubt they had about her and the incident with Antoine. *What was the matter with him? His actions are causing grave danger to everyone!*

Once back in her room, the hours dragged. Gertrude's mind wouldn't let go of what might be happening to the servant girl and how much information she would tell the Gestapo. Every sound, other than the usual ones of the girls playing, had her cringing with fright. *Please, God, please let the girl find courage within herself not to tell them anything.* This plea interjected with the thought that the girl might not know much at all about the group, and the names of those active within it, and had her praying even more fervently: *Please, please don't let her know about Juste or Madeline!*

Fraught with worry, every sinew in her body felt stretched as if to breaking point. Every nerve objected to movement. Never had she been so glad to see the nursery maid arrive to take over the care of the girls. It hadn't registered at first that the woman had come earlier than usual, so she hadn't questioned it. Now she could only feel grateful, as all she wanted to do was have a long soak in a hot bath, and the extra time she had would allow for that.

The plumbing in this grand building always surprised her. Never had she known a time when she hadn't had to fill a bath with hot water from a huge pan, kept boiling on the top of a stove. Now she relished the sound of the water hitting the cast-iron tub and the waterfall effect, which filled her with peace, as it filled up. Easing herself into the bath, her body already damp from the steam that fogged the room, she anticipated the pleasure of the hot bubbles. They would soothe her aches and perhaps ease some of the tension from her. Lying back, she closed her eyes.

They shot open at the sound of a key turning in a lock. A

distinctive click. Footsteps coming towards the bathroom froze her. Fixing her gaze on the bathroom door, she waited, not daring to breathe.

Cooler air hit her face. Through the steam that blurred her vision she saw the outline of a man. 'Who . . . who are you, and what . . . what do you want . . . ?' But as she asked, she knew. 'Herr Eberhardt?'

'Yes. I haven't much time before the children's dinner, and I always sit with them. But, well, I wanted to try your treatment. Is half an hour long enough?'

Knowing that he must have come through the locked door in her sitting room, through which she had no access, made her realize that her sitting room must lead to his office somehow – though not directly, as that wasn't possible. There must be corridors that connected them. She liked the idea of hidden corridors, and the thought that he had planned this visit and had ordered the nursery maid to relieve her earlier than usual.

'We can make a start. It is good you came now, as putting it off would have made it more difficult for you.' Standing as she said this, she gave him a moment to look at her wet body.

'You're beautiful, Violetta.'

She wrapped a huge white towel around her, loving the embrace it gave her as she stepped out and moved towards him. 'You are too, Herr—'

'*Kristof – mein Name ist Kristof.*'

'Kristof? I like that. Well now, Kristof, it is best just to do as I ask. Is that all right with you?'

He nodded.

'First of all, take off your clothes.' As if she had spoken to a child, he removed his shirt and trousers. She helped him with his vest, then from behind him slipped off his pants, taking a moment to savour the feelings rippling through her at the sight of him. His body belied what his fair hair colouring had given her expectations of. His skin, tight and bronzed, stretched over muscles that told of a man who did more than his daily dozen. It also told of a man of power, but she sensed his vulnerable side and knew that she had hit on exactly the right way to handle him. He needed someone, sometimes, to take the lead. To give him orders and to care for him. She knew she could play that role.

'You are beautiful, Kristof. Step into the bath and, as you haven't much time, tonight I will just bathe you.' Once more, and without protest, he did as she said. 'Relax, Kristof – Kristof, I love your name. I could say it and say it.'

'And it sounds nice when you do. I have never met anyone like you. It is as if you undo me and find my core.'

'That is because I know you. I knew you the moment I met you. I got straight into your soul and took you into mine.'

The action of soaping him with her hands was the most sensual thing she had ever done. It brought every part of her in tune with every part of him. Her desire for him raged inside her, but she knew she must not take him to that – not yet. His need for her, too, showed in the hardness of him and in the way he looked at her. With his breathing coming in deep but short and heavy spasms, she wondered if together they would resist, but knew they must. 'Know that you cannot take me, Kristof. You are not ready, in an emotional sense. When you do take me, it has to be perfect, not tarred with the scars of grief and guilt.'

'I don't know if I can resist . . .'

'You must. I must, too. The satisfaction wouldn't be worth the aftermath for you, my darling.'

The endearment brought tears to his eyes. She allowed him to weep, even though it wrenched her heart to see the silent tears flow from him. She gently rinsed him, filling the sponge and squeezing the water over him. When his crying stopped, she asked him to get out of the tub so that she could rub him dry. As she did so he said, 'Thank you. Thank you, my Violetta.'

For a long time his eyes held hers. In them she could see healing; it wasn't complete, but some of the coldness and the aloofness had gone.

'Please, Violetta, don't turn out to be false. I have feelings for you. If you are deceiving me it will break me.'

Taking his hand, she kissed it all over, turning it and placing her lips on his palm. It smelt of the roses that her soap had left on it. She wanted to take each finger into her mouth, but she knew the time wasn't right to tap into any more of his sensuality. She just needed the distraction of this small act to get herself to a place where she could lie to this man, whom she loved.

Her heart ached to have them transported to another time – a time that held peace. A time when deception wasn't needed. Their time. But it wasn't to be, and so much depended on her, so many lives. She had to live the lie.

'I can understand your doubts, Kristof, and they are natural. You know I am French – yes, half-German, too. But you know I love the country I was born in, and am unhappy at how things are for my people. But I have to live. I have to work. You are the only one offering the work I am trained for, and you have given me a position within your house. That makes me valuable to those working against you. So, as I think happened this afternoon, they will try to recruit me. I think the maid was doing that work, and will do anything – and say anything – to make it look as though it wasn't her fault, because she is afraid for her life.'

At that moment she hated herself for what she was saying, but she knew she had no choice. Her own brother and beautiful new sister, and the other members of the group, were at risk. 'If I had pursued it, I think the man I would have met would have tried to talk me into helping them. But I think their cause is hopeless, and what we French should work towards is living in harmony with our superiors, who, I believe, will make France a better land, given time. And I hope that, as we come to conform, Herr Hitler will relax the regime of occupation and put in place a government that will rule us fairly and help us to prosper.'

'That is it! That is exactly how he sees it. He knows that Germany is the superior race and should rule the world. Our race has qualities beyond those of others. A superiority given to us by God, but one that has been suppressed for too long. We can see the evil of the Jew, an evil that God used his son to fight against. Jews are scum and need disposing of. They corrupt with their greed and vile practices. They suck others dry to make themselves rich. Herr Hitler has a vision, and it is the right vision. He will also rid the world of the evil of those travellers, homosexuals and disabled persons who have not been born in God's perfect form. There is a struggle to go through; nations have to be conquered, but once they are and we can put into action our plans for the world, it will be a better place. A place where the strong live and prosper and all the badness has gone.'

This frightened her. To hear God's name being taken to justify what Germany was doing to the rest of the world, and to the Jews in particular, made her feel sick, but she knew better than to argue. Not yet. One day she hoped to make him see it all in a different light, but that was for the future. All she hoped for now was that he did not believe anything the nursery maid said, and that her job here could continue.

His next words shot her out of this complacency. 'You say she may have led you to someone working against us – a dissident? Yes, you're right. Maybe we should let her do that. We could have you followed and maybe catch a whole group!'

'No, I will not do it. You can have me shot – I won't care. I would rather that than do as you say. I could never help you in your fight against my people.'

'Good God, Violetta! I was just beginning to trust you.'

'You *can* trust me, as I will not help them, either. Look at how I told you about the girl! That should show you I wouldn't help them. I could have just gone to this whatever-his-name was . . .' Beads of sweat ran down her neck.

Kristof had put his trousers back on and she helped him with his shirt. As he buttoned it he looked once more into her eyes. She held her gaze steady. Relief entered her as a smile creased his cheeks. 'You are unreadable, and still some doubt niggles me. But then, what can you do? What can I do? I know I don't want to suspect you, and you haven't given me any reason to.' Again he was quiet. After a moment he said, 'Very well, we will see what we get out of the girl. I will make a judgement then.'

'Thank you. You are strong when you are in your role of power. It is the part of you that holds your emotions and your feelings that is fragile. Come back to me when you feel able. Together we will get you well. Not that it is a weakness in you. No, rather it is your strength, because you have the capacity to give a great love that does not die. I am not trying to help it to die; I am trying to help you to live with the knowledge that you can't taint one love by having another; when that one is no longer accessible to you.'

'You are a very special person, Violetta. I . . . I – well, I have a deep feeling for you.'

Tears stung her eyes. This wasn't right, and yet it felt so right. With a heart torn in two, she told him, 'I love you, Kristof.'

His arms moved around her, taking her into the warmth of his body, the place that was made for her. *Why did that place have to be circled in the world of the enemy?*

To see the tree in the square, which had only ever held beauty, bearing the dreadful burden of the bloodied and bruised body of the young maid swinging by her neck, backwards and forwards from one of its branches, struck horror into Gertrude. She would never get the image out of her mind. Nor would she ever forgive herself.

Antoine, too, had died. Seen as a traitor, he had been shot by members of the Resistance. But was he a traitor? Or was he just like her, a slave to the love that he held inside him. His love for Esther and hers for Kristof – forbidden loves. Oh God, poor Antoine . . . and that poor maid. And, Esther, where is she? The pity of it all brought the tears flowing again.

'None of this is your fault, Gertrude.' Madeline tried once again to console her, but the words she uttered, though well meant, did not penetrate her pain, or wipe away the guilt. 'Listen to me, Gertrude. Antoine betrayed us for his own reasons. He caused the maid's death; he left you no choice. You did the right thing. The repercussions may still not be over. But the early signs are that, in the end, the maid did not break. If she had, we would all have been rounded up by now.'

She knew this to be true, if only she could accept it. 'Who was she, Madeline? Why didn't I know there was one of us in Herr Eberhardt's house?'

'Antoine recruited her. Her name was Hélène de Agusta. She met Juste and, as far as he could tell, she was a good candidate. Her ideals were sound. He did not know that she worked at the house. Again, this demonstrates Antoine's guilt. He must have persuaded her not to disclose that fact. She hadn't been used on any assignments, or introduced to any safe houses or members other than himself and Juste, so she knew little. Antoine said she was the daughter of a soldier who had been killed as he fought with the Allied troops, and Hélène wanted to avenge him and fight for her country as her father had done.'

They were in one of the safe houses – a dark, dingy, dank place, the home of a loyal family whose son was one of their group. The smell of damp walls and poverty took Gertrude back to a time she did not want to visit. A time when such places were all she could afford. Places that often held only a bed, on which her body was used to gratify the sexual urges of many a pervert. No one should endure such conditions, but so many did, and not just prostitutes and lowlifes, but families – good, hard-working families. Would there ever be a better France, a free France? At this moment she could not see it happening.

'Will you be all right, Gertrude? Do you want us to get you out of there?'

This question from Madeline shocked her. *Take her out of Kristof's home – no, that must not happen!* 'No! No, you cannot! I – I . . .'

'Oh, Gertrude, my dear, be careful. Don't let your heart rule your head.'

'I won't. I would never let you down. I am near now to a time when I should be able to get you information that will help you plan your missions. Isn't what I just did proof enough that I will always make the right decisions? It ripped me to pieces to do it, Madeline. To betray two of our own, for the greater good of our cause – especially Antoine, a friend. It has almost broken me, but not my conviction. What Antoine did was wrong. He did what you are urging me not to do; he put us all, and our mission, in jeopardy for the sake of his love for Esther. I understand that, but I would not do the same. Always know that, Madeline. No matter what happens, I would not do that.'

'I know.'

Feeling herself wrapped in Madeline's arms helped. But it did not erase all the pain; only time could do that for her, as she knew it would for Juste. Her eyes held his, over the shoulder of her sister. Her dear brother, once a carefree pest, who always shone in his father's eyes, and whom she'd seen blossom into a man, now looked a shadow of his former self. His face was ashen, his eyes big and dark in their sunken sockets. With sculptured cheekbones that now protruded, his face held the same pain at the loss of Antoine, and even more so at being the one to order his execution.

'Juste?'

He came forward. Madeline released her. Juste took Gertrude into his arms and together they wept.

10

Lil

THE CONSEQUENCES OF
A 'DEAR JOHN' LETTER

Dear Alfie,

Yes, it was me in the picture, and yes, I have moved to London. I'm training to be a nurse and then may go to the front line to tend the wounded. I am very happy . . . something I don't think I could have been if I was with you any more. You changed, Alfie, you stopped caring about me. And, well, I reckon as what you did to me when you were home last – the rough way you took me – caused our babby to come early and to lose his life . . . There, I've said it now. And though I am weeping and find these words hard to say, they need saying. You should know what your rape of me caused. I cannot stay married to a man like you.

I know we can't divorce – that isn't possible for folk like us – but I have to separate from you. So, whatever you get up to, do so with a clear conscience, as none of it

135

*will matter to me. I hope you can find it in you to write
to your ma and treat her with some kindness. She has
never done a wrong to you. I wish you well, Alfie, and
hope you keep safe.*
  Lil

Writing the letter to Alfie had upset Lil more than she
thought possible and still, four months later, when she had a
moment, she thought about it and a part of her wished she
hadn't done it. But then that was probably due to the fact
that she should have had a reply by now, and her nerves were
on edge as to why she hadn't.

It had taken all her courage to write it, as she knew she
would be vilified for doing so. Folk looked on such letters as
shocking. 'Dear John' letters, they called them. It was thought
that no matter how a woman felt, or even if she found someone
else, it was cruel to tell her man whilst he was away fighting.
Despite that, Lil felt justified in going ahead and sending it.

It had been a letter from him out of the blue that had
prompted her. She'd been incensed that he'd never bothered
to write to her about the death of their child, and yet he had
felt it okay that he should write when he'd seen a picture of
her in the newspaper.

Mildred had written to Alfie to tell him about their baby's
death at the time it had happened. Lil had told Mildred to
inform Alfie that she wouldn't be writing to him herself just
yet, and he needn't apply for compassionate leave. She needed
some time to come to terms with everything that had
happened. To her, Alfie was to blame, and she couldn't face
seeing him at that time.

From then on it had been only Mildred who had written
to Alfie, and she never received anything in return. But then

a letter had arrived from him and Mildred had posted it on. It seemed that Alfie had seen a picture of Lil standing behind Ruby, talking to the King. Unbeknown to her, it had been on the front page of the *News of the World*, one of the papers sent out in Red Cross parcels.

The letter conveyed his anger and said things like 'What do you think you're up to?' And 'Get yourself home, where you're meant to be, and I'll sort you out when I get back!'

It was then that Lil had known that she had to write and tell Alfie the truth. But not yet receiving a reply had got her agitated, although she knew that if anything serious had happened to prevent him writing, a telegram would have come to inform them, and Mildred wouldn't have kept that from her.

Mildred had informed her that her name was mud back in Yorkshire. Northern folk didn't like the soldiers receiving 'Dear John' letters, but to Lil it seemed the kindest thing she could do – be truthful and let Alfie deal with it. He was man enough. At least he thought himself to be. He was probably having what he wanted from the black girls in Africa. Well, she felt sorry for them, because he'd forgotten how to love, and make a girl feel good and have that special feeling. He'd become selfish and only wanted his own relief. Repulsion shuddered through her as she thought of this.

She hadn't told him her address. If he did get home on leave, she didn't want him finding her, and she knew Mildred wouldn't give it to him.

London was her home now, with Gillian and Ruby, though she didn't get to see them that often. She now worked in Kent, in this grand old house. It was called Crescent Abbey and had been commissioned by the government to house wounded officers. Sometimes she looked at the magnificence of it – it looked more like a palace than a house, and stood in acres of beautiful gardens – and wondered about the family who had lived here.

The Red Cross had put her forward to train as a nurse and had sent her here. For a trainee, she was given a lot of responsibility and had to live in the Abbey during her working shifts. Her room, like every room in the house, was grand: high ceilings, with carvings so beautiful that she often lay on her bed just gazing at them. Some of the carvings had tips picked out in a gold so shiny that she was convinced it was real. Nothing was plain – even the balustrades of beautiful wood were all intricately carved. Flock wallpaper still adorned the recreation areas, and the furniture was like none she'd ever seen before. Only the wards had been stripped back and whitewashed. She loved the place and felt like a queen gliding around it.

Leaving it was always a wrench, though exciting, too. Every two weeks she travelled to a nursing college in London, where she'd stay over with Gillian. She had one of these days coming up, and a leave day. She'd take Gillian to the pictures – she'd like that. The poor lass was still a bit lost after the death of her mother. Perhaps Ruby would come with them, and they could get a bottle of beer from the pub on the way home and make a night of it. Thank God the air-raids had finished now and some normality was seeping back into London.

Mildred wrote to her at Gillian's address and, every time Lil went there, a letter had arrived for her. She always looked forward to reading it, though she worried about Mildred. She was alone in that cottage and didn't go out much.

This had her thinking that she would write to Mildred's old next-door-neighbour, Enid. She'd ask her to look out for Mildred, and explain why she'd sent the letter to Alfie and why she couldn't give her address. She should have done this a long time ago, and then Enid could have stood up for her.

'Lawd above! 'Ere you are.' Arthur, the male ward orderly, made her jump by saying this as he came up behind her. 'Tea break's over – it's time for the patients to have a cup of tea. And they don't need to be served it from a weeping woman. Keep your moment to yourself, love. They have more to cry about than you do.'

She hadn't realized she was crying. Rising from the step outside the kitchen where she'd taken her break, she hadn't noticed how stiff her bottom had become, either! Patting it, she said, 'Sorry, Arthur. I'm coming. Have you done all the bed-baths?'

'Not all of them. Fred felt sick and had to go outside, so I did what I could on my own. It was the smell of that young man with gangrene that did Fred in. He had just started to clean him when it turned his stomach.'

'Aye, it does that to me at times. Leave Officer Rigmay to me, I'll see to him. Bless him, he's from the north like me, and he feels at home hearing me voice. Eeh, lad's got a lot to put up with. I reckon that leg will have to come off, or we'll lose him.'

As she entered the ward and looked around, the plight of these bed-patients tugged at her heart. None of them would recover sufficiently to live the lives they had dreamed of. *It just doesn't seem fair what they are going through*, thought Lil, *and all because of bloody Hitler's whim to rule the world*. Her heart ached for them and their families, but she had found a way to cope and give of her cheery best to them. They needed her to – they needed someone's strength to latch onto.

Even though a trainee, she was the most senior on the ward today and only had the two male orderlies, Arthur and Fred, to help her. Sometimes it frightened her, having to make decisions that she didn't feel should be on her shoulders, as there wasn't always time to fetch the doctor or go to matron's office for advice.

The smell hit her before she reached Officer Rigmay's bed. His moans of agony cut at her heart. 'Eeh, lad, you're in a bad way with that leg, but don't worry. I'll telephone an emergency through. They'll sort it. I'll be back in a mo.'

With the call made and the promise of an ambulance on its way, Lil felt cheered, but on going back to the officer she wondered if it would come in time. To her mind, the doctors should have taken the leg off straight away. The wound was old and infected by the time the lad was brought off the hospital ship. They'd had too many to cope with on board and had prioritized treating the dying first. But it should have been obvious that gangrene could set in, when all they'd done was clean it, set it and send him here. She wondered at the mentality of those in the big hospitals sometimes.

'Rigmay? Officer Rigmay?' His face had paled even more. 'Hold on, sir. They're coming for you. I've asked the local doctor to come over as well. He can give you summat to help the pain.'

'I'm not going to make it, Nurse.'

'None of that talk! You're a northerner – oh aye, a posh one, but we don't give up, now, do we, lad?'

'What's your name?'

'Lil.'

'Lil, that's a nice name. My nanny was called Lil. She was like you: *Never say die.*'

'Well then, do as your nanny told you, eh?' Wiping the sweat from his brow frightened her, as she felt the cold yet clammy signs of a high fever.

'My name's Adrian. I have a sister your age . . .'

'Oh, and how old is that?'

'Twenty-four, I'd say.'

'And you'd be reet. Now, stop talking and rest.'

'I have a long time to rest. Oooh . . . !'

'Arthur! Run to the doctor and tell him I've sent for an ambulance, but Officer Rigmay needs some strong painkillers, which I am not allowed to administer. Tell him to hurry.'

'There's no time.'

'Please don't say that, Adrian. Please fight. A lot of getting better is willpower.'

'Tell Mother and my sister I love them.'

'Don't give up. Adrian, please don't give up.'

It didn't seem to matter what she said, as she knew that Adrian couldn't take any more. He'd chosen not to fight and couldn't face the pain. His eyes closed, his breathing became shallow. Nothing she did could stop him slipping into a coma. But although fear for him gripped her, she took comfort in what she had been told: in some cases when this happened the body's own survival instincts took over. She hoped with all her might that this would happen for Adrian, as she set about fixing an oxygen mask on him. *This bloody war! How I'll get through it, I don't know, but somehow I'll have to.*

Gillian met her at Shadwell Street station. Her face was lit with a smile Lil had not seen for a long time.

'Eeh, lass, it's good to see you. Let me give you a hug.'

'You're crying, Lil, what's wrong?'

'Everything and nowt, as they say. We lost a lad last night. Oh, I know, we lose a lot of them, and deal with stuff that would turn some folk grey, but there was something about this one. He seemed to go against what others do. He didn't even try to fight. He gave up. As if he had no life to live, after what he'd been through.'

'It must be bad dealing with all that every day, Lil. I feel for yer. I couldn't do it. Think of 'im as at peace now, and he couldn't 'ave 'ad anyone better to tend to 'im in 'is dying 'our. Now cheer up, love. Lawd, it's good ter 'ave you 'ome. 'Ow have you been?'

Drying her eyes, Lil felt a warmth enter her. This young lass had become like family to her. She was the only family she had other than Mildred. She didn't think of Alfie as family any more, or of those in the workhouse she'd grown up in, as that place had taken her ma from her. Those thoughts brought only misery to her and, such as it was, meeting up with Gillian was a joyous occasion that she didn't want to spoil. So for a few hours she'd put what went on in Crescent Abbey behind her and enjoy her time off. 'You're reet, lass, I did me best, and now I have to put it behind me and carry on. Come on, let's get going, I'm dying for one of your Ruby's Rosie Lee's.'

'Ruby's not been so well, Lil. I'm worried about her. She coughs like mad, and them fags don't 'elp her.'

'Oh?' Lil felt fearful. Ruby had seemed a bit under the weather the last couple of times she'd visited. 'She's not picked up yet, then?'

'No. 'Er man keeps saying she'll be all right. That it's a cold landed on 'er chest, but it's not the weather for colds and I can't remember 'er ever 'aving one . . . Oi, watch where you're going, mate!'

The man who had nearly knocked Gillian over turned to face Lil. She couldn't believe her eyes. 'Jimmy, Jimmy Gibbins? What're you doing here . . . ? What . . . ?'

'Grab her, Brian, I'll get the young 'un.'

'Eeh, what d'yer think yer doing – leave her alone . . .
Argh!' The swipe knocked Lil backwards, and her body
smacked against the wall of the alleyway the two men had
dragged them into.

She couldn't understand what was happening. Jimmy and
Brian were neighbours from up north. A rough couple of
crooks who'd do anything for the price of a couple of pints.
They'd missed the call-up by dodging from here to there and
lying low; both were wanted by the police and the military.

Jimmy's ugly tone raised her fear to terror. 'Write a "Dear
John" letter to a man serving his country, would you? You're
a reet whore, doing summat like that – and to one of ours.
Well, we've come to avenge him. He saw the name of the
street you were in, written under that picture of you in the
paper. And it were easy for us to find out everything after
that. Reet little Nurse Nightingale, aren't you? Aye, we've
watched you; and that Arthur as works with you has a loose
tongue in his head when he hears some coins rattling. Alfie
wants you to get what's due to you. He said that you called
him taking his due "rape". Well, he wants you to know what
real rape is, and it ain't what a man is allowed to give to his
missus.'

Gillian's scream took Lil's attention from the horror of
what Jimmy had said. 'Leave her alone, she's nothing to do
with it – let her go.'

'Naw. She might not be owt to do with this business, but
I allus fancied her when she lived up our end. And what I
fancy, I get. Now, shut your mouth, lass.' Pulling Gillian round
to face him, Brian punched her, sending her flying. Her body
hit the wall before slumping to the ground.

Fresh courage entered Lil. Twisting herself round, she freed
herself from Jimmy's grasp and kicked out with all her might.

143

Her foot squelched into Jimmy's privates. He sank to his knees, crying out like a babby until vomit shot from him, choking him. Tears ran down his face.

Righting herself, she turned on Brian. 'By, lad, you're well known as a coward – hit a young girl, would you? Eeh, come on then, try it on me and see what happens.' The fear inside her made her words tremble as Brian moved towards her. Picking up her case, she went to swing it at him, but Jimmy grabbed her ankle and upended her. She landed in his vile-smelling vomit, only to look up and see Brian's foot coming towards her.

The room she awoke in closed in on her. A putrid smell of years of rotting rubbish and dank soil stung her nostrils. Damp had formed a furry growth on the walls. There were no windows and the weak bulb above her didn't give off much light – a cellar? Choking on the foul-tasting rag they'd stuffed into her mouth, a despair settled in her.

A noise. A grunting, coupled with crying and pleading, came to her from an adjoining room – oh God, Gillian!

Trying to move her arms and legs stretched a pain through her ribs. Realization filtered through her fuzzy brain that the men had tied her feet and wrists together behind her. Anxiety made her sweat, even though the room was cold. Tears wetted her face. The screams went on and on. *Oh, God, help Gillian . . . Please help her!*

Gillian was a virgin. Rape hurt, Lil knew that, but to be a virgin suffering it – oh God, she couldn't think of it. *Gillian, oh Gillian . . .*

'Hurry up, it's my turn. I were the one who wanted this one.' It was Brian's voice, thick with his need.

Then Jimmy answered him. 'You're not having a turn,

you're doing the other one. This is to get you ready. You know how you have a problem – blokes your size allus do. Anyroad shut up, you're putting me off.'

A moan came from Gillian that held desolation. Lil knew that Gillian could take no more and had no fight left, only acceptance. This must have triggered Jimmy, bringing an end at last to his assault on Gillian as his holler filled the space around Lil. When it died down there was a moment's silence. Lil strained to hear if Gillian said anything, but all she heard was the vile half-laugh of Jimmy. 'Ha, me legs have gone – that were summat else. Not had a virgin afore. Light me a fag, Brian.'

Lil's body crumpled into itself. Wretchedness seeped from every pore and guilt burned her. Her letter to Alfie had brought this down upon Gillian.

The door crashed open. A brighter light shone through, giving her a view of Brian standing there with an animal-like expression and the stance of a thug.

Grabbing her, he turned her over onto her front. A whimper of pain came from her throat. Lying on her stomach, tied as she was, took away any chance of her fighting him. She felt a tugging on her legs, which increased the pain for a moment, and then released it as her legs flopped away from her body and her toes hit the ground.

Even though her arms were still tied, she moved in a twisting and turning fashion, trying to kick out at him. But it did nothing to stop him. He just laughed as Jimmy came through the door and goaded him, 'Go on, Brian. Show her. Let her know she did wrong.'

The feel of Brian's hand slithering up her thigh made her want to scream, but she couldn't. The grunt that came from her grated in her throat. The tears, already running down her face, now flowed into her mouth and added a salty taste to the stale rag.

His hand reached inside her knickers.

'Get on with it, Brian. I want to see her squirm. Here, let me take that rag out of her mouth. Let's hear her beg for mercy. Not that she'll find any.'

Even though she knew it was fruitless, she tried to reason with them as she pulled herself away from Brian's probing fingers. 'Why? Why're you doing this – what have I ever done to you? You weren't no mates of Alfie; you were the ones who rigged him as a kid, cos of his da. And you've given his ma hell whenever you've had fun at her expense, so what's going on, eh? How could you do what you just did to a young lass?'

'Alfie's paying us, that's why. We don't give two hoots about him – the Nazis can kill him, for all we care – but he'll have a nice packet sent to his ma, once he knows you've been punished. But while we're at it, you're worse than us: you've sunk lower than any of us could. You abandoned one of our soldiers, and you're going to pay.'

'Aye, and I had good reason to. But for all that, at least Alfie's not a coward. You're both stinking, rotten cowards. Why ain't you out there fighting, eh? How long d'yer reckon you can get away with it? They'll throw you in prison, and I'll be glad of it. Everyone hates you both, they—'

'Shut your filthy mouth!' The kick caught her shoulder and sent a stinging pain down her back.

'Reet, Brian, if you can't handle her, I'll have to help.'

Undoing her arms, he stretched them out. The weight of his knees crushed them, causing Lil agony, but this was nothing compared to the sick humiliation of seeing him take himself from his trousers and realizing that he was going to abuse her too. As he lowered himself towards her mouth she moved her head to the side. 'Ha, you're going to have it, no matter what.' His sick laughter as he said this echoed around her. When Jimmy paused she became aware of Brian wedged between her legs. His weight came down on her, forcing the breath from her. His hand fumbled, trying to guide himself into her. His fingers scratched the delicate skin of her vagina as he prised open the entrance. His struggling bruised her inner thighs. Trying to get into her, he shoved with all his might. Then she knew what Jimmy had meant when he'd said 'blokes your size'. It felt as if she was being forced to take something the size of a rolling pin into her.

Tensing made it worse, and caused scars from the birth of her son to be ripped open, searing her with soreness. Brian's cries of sheer ecstasy increased her despair. *How long would it take? Please let it end.*

Her back rasped on the concrete floor; the rawness of her insides stung. Jimmy's words made her want her own death. 'Brian, give me a hand. You can still pound her while I have mine in her mouth.'

Try it – go on try it, and I'll bite it off. She dare not say the words, but cringed as he said, 'Hold her face, Brian, stop being so selfish. Get your fingers in her mouth and hold it open . . .' His words faded into a look of shock. His body fell forward. Panic seized Lil. She couldn't breathe with the weight of them both on top of her. *God, help me . . . help me . . .*

The help came from Brian. Crushed himself, he raised his body and Jimmy slid off him. Lil looked up. Above her stood a demented Gillian, bruised, cut and with eyes protruding from their sockets. In her hand she held a bloodied knife.

Brian pulled himself from her and rose to his knees, his

mouth slack, his eyes staring at the body of Jimmy and then back at Gillian.

Lil couldn't move or speak. Her fear for Gillian, and the enormity of what had happened, had taken everything from her. Froth lathered Gillian's chin and gathered around her lips. A sound that Lil couldn't compare to anything she'd ever heard before came from Gillian as she lunged forward. Brian ducked to one side. The knife went into his neck.

Blood spurted over Lil. Warm and sticky, it hit her face and covered her breasts. Still she couldn't move, as she watched Brian's body sway and then, as if in slow motion, fall to one side, trapping her legs.

Gillian sank to her knees. A terrible hollow moan came from her. With all her strength Lil moved Brian off her legs and crawled towards Gillian. Taking her trembling body into her arms, she wept with her. Huge sobs verging on hysteria came from both of them. It joined their anguish in a desperate feeling that Lil didn't see them ever rising from.

11

Lil

A Separation That Hurts

The yellowing walls that showed layers of paint peeling off their brick surface had been stained by the smoking of a million fags, thought Lil, as she breathed in the stale smoke of the detective's third fag. A small room, it contained only a table and four chairs. A wood stove gave off fumes, but little heat. Trying again, she begged, 'Please let me see Gillian – please.'

'I've told yer, Miss. You two cannot be together. One of you is the witness, the other killed them blokes. She is saying it is her, you are saying it is you. Now who are we to believe, eh? As one of you is fibbin'. You didn't both kill them, nor did you kill one each.'

His pudgy eyes held a hint of kindness, but his attitude was one of impatience. Nothing about him spoke of him being a detective. She'd imagined detectives to look smart and to wear a uniform like the bobbies on the street. But his shirt strained over his belly, leaving each button looking as if it would pop open at any minute. He constantly ran his finger between his neck and shirt as if to relieve the pressure. The action caused grime to lie around the top of his collar. The sight brought Lil the thought that she'd like to get it on her washboard and give it a good scrub. *Funny the thoughts that popped into yer head.*

'Well?'

His voice made her jump. Why did she keep going into a dreamlike state? Lifting her chin she said, 'It was me. Gillian is hysterical . . . She—'

''Ow come she had the knife, and you hadn't got any clothes on? Look, Miss, I reckon you're trying to protect her. And if what she is saying is true, there ain't no need for yer to do so. As I see it, them bastards raped the pair of you. 'Er first, then you. When she could, she came to 'elp you. If I'm wrong, where did you get the knife and 'ow did she get it off you?'

'I – I . . .'

'She knows where she got it. She says it was in the jacket pocket of the bloke that done her first.'

Lil slumped forward. She couldn't defend Gillian any longer. Her ragged mind wouldn't give her any answers to make it sound plausible that it was she who had done the killing. Lifting her head she asked, 'What will happen to her?'

'She's already gone. She's on 'er way to the mental hospital – she don't know what day it is. Turned her 'ead, it has. But she knows what 'appened, and so do you. Now, let's have a proper and truthful statement, eh?'

'You can't do that. You can't charge her, when she don't know what's going on!'

'We know that, and that's why we 'aven't charged her. Not yet. She needs 'elp, and they can give it to 'er and at the same time keep 'er secure, pending our investigations. 'Er sister's been sent for. She will look after 'er. Now my advice to you is to tell the truth, word by word as it 'appened, and let me get it all down. Give me something to work on. I reckon this case could be chucked out, 'ow it's lookin'. Self-defence, I'd call it.'

Lil sighed. She had no choice but to comply. The tiredness ached her bones. It had been a long night.

She and Gillian had made it out of the building and begged a passer-by to fetch the police. At first he'd looked as if he wouldn't help them. His eyes had searched up and down the street, probably thinking their attackers were still lurking. She hadn't been able to tell him they were dead, but had just stood there shivering and crying, trying to support Gillian.

Before attempting to leave the cellar they'd put their coats and boots on over their battered bodies, but still, she knew the bloke she was asking to help could see what they'd been through. Her face had been covered in splashes of blood. He'd have seen that in the light of his torch – something he shouldn't have had, as it was past blackout time.

After a moment he'd said, 'Look, I don't want any involvement, but there is a phone in the hall of the flats where I live. It ain't far. I'll ring the Old Bill and tell them about you, but that's it! I ain't getting dragged into this.'

Together she and Gillian had huddled in the police van. Both in pain, both weeping and unable to speak to each other.

In the police station they had stood at the desk whilst an officer said, 'These two were apprehended at the scene of a murder – two blokes, knifed in a cellar. Their names are unknown, as these two 'aven't spoken either to me or to each other yet.'

'It looks like they need a doctor. See to it, Robinson.' This came from the desk sergeant and gave Lil some hope that all would be all right. The doctor would see to Gillian, ease her pain and give her something to calm her. But the doctor hadn't come for an hour or more, and in the meantime they had separated her from Gillian and she'd found herself in a dirty cell with a bucket in the corner. The smell had brought the vomit from her, leaving her empty and dry; but no drink, no wash or comfort of any kind had been offered. Not that she had worried for herself, but for Gillian. All night she had begged to see Gillian and they had ignored her. The doctor had made things worse, examining her in a way that spoke of his disbelief in rape. 'You weren't a virgin, I see. So you knew what it was all about then?' Those words had turned her blood cold. It was as if he was calling her a prostitute. She could only imagine what an examination of that kind had done to Gillian. Already sore and torn, especially as she'd been a virgin, any further intrusion in this rough and uncaring way would have been agony for her. But at least it was ordered that they were to be washed and given soothing ointments. A woman had done this – a kind of nurse, Lil supposed, but not the same kind as herself. This one had a judgemental attitude that made you feel guilty, even though you were innocent. It felt good, though, to have her body clean at least, though she doubted she'd ever feel clean inside again.

And now Ruby, poor Ruby, would have to face the shock of all that had happened to her sister and how it had left her. On top of this, Ruby was fighting her own battle with what Lil was sure was cancer. Life was unfair sometimes, and more so for the likes of her and Ruby and Gillian.

'Can I get another wash and a pot of tea, before I tell you what happened?' Her plea expressed the disgust she felt for herself: she could still feel Brian inside her and see him slumping, his life's blood pumping all over her.

152

'Not a wash – you've 'ad one, and we need your statement while you're thinkin' of givin' it. So just start talking. The quicker this is done, the quicker you can get some tea.'

'But I need a drink, I can hardly talk.'

'I'll say what yer need or don't need – look, all right. I'll give in over the cup of tea, but that's all. And don't think of me as 'eartless. I want to see you're all right, but I also want the truth, so we can get yer out of here. I don't 'appen to believe yer should be prosecuted, but it ain't up to me, and you telling lies ain't 'elping me to convince those that make the decisions. No matter how well-intentioned your lies are, they ain't 'elping!'

'Aye, I understand. And I'm sorry.'

Although it was painful, she managed to tell him everything that went on – though not about the reason Alfie set them up, or of his involvement; she just said that Jimmy and Brian had a score to settle with her husband. Something stopped her from telling the truth. Pride – a pride that didn't want them knowing she had accused her own husband of raping her, and that he had arranged for those men to show her what real rape was. Nor did she tell him about the orderly, Arthur, revealing where she was at a given time. He weren't bad, Arthur, just a bit misguided in his decisions and a penny-grabber, no matter what it took. To her mind, the police had no need to know either of those things.

Three hours later, making her way to the house she still referred to as Gillian's mam's, but which she looked upon as her home, Lil wouldn't have cared if she died. What was the use of her life? Everything around her lay in ruins. Her life was turned upside down once more and, through her actions, young Gillian, who'd never done anything bad and who'd befriended her when she most needed a friend, had been subjected to indescribable horror. *Oh, Gillian, lass. What have I brought down on you?*

Weary to the extreme, she almost wanted to ignore Ruby's house as she passed it, but knew she must call in. She dreaded knocking on the door. In the half-light of the early morning all the houses still standing were blacked out against the threat of more air-raids, which Lil felt confident wouldn't come again. With no lights showing, the houses looked dismal. But she knew that wasn't the case in the daylight. Each housewife, proud of her little home, would soon be outside, hair tied in a headscarf, a pinny on and a kneeling mat at the ready, scrubbing her steps and wiping her windowsills, and looking with scorn on those who didn't do the same! The thought made her smile – something she never thought she'd do again. But it was the spirit of these London folk that allowed her to smile. No matter what hit them, they came up smiling and spouting their rhyming slang. Used to their way of speaking now, she sometimes even slipped into it herself.

Lil knocked timidly on Ruby's front door. When it opened, Ruby leaned on the doorframe looking down at her. A tear trickled down Lil's cheek as she gazed back at her. 'I'm sorry, lass. I'm heart-sorry.'

'Come on in. Tell me what 'appened. 'Ow did me little skin-and-blister get into the state she's in, eh? Look, I'm not blaming you. Gillian has told me it wasn't your fault. I just need to know what 'appened.'

Sipping the hot tea that Ruby poured from a pot standing on the side of her stove, Lil didn't flinch at the stewed taste of it, but told Ruby all that had gone on. As she talked she could feel how raw the wounds still were, the disgust she'd felt at the sordidness and brutality of it all and, mostly, at the blood and gore from the deaths of Jimmy and Brian.

For some reason, as she spoke she kept thinking of Jimmy and Brian's mams. The two women were staunch members of the community in the little town of Rawston. Neither deserved the way their lads had turned out. *How will they be feeling when they find out what their sons have done, and what happened to them?* And when they got to hear that Lil was involved, what would they think of her? Would they take it out on Mildred? She must write to Mildred and explain. And find some way of telling her, without involving her son.

'Oh God, Lil! Oh, my poor Gillian; she's still a young girl and yet she's been through so much. ''Ow will we mend her from this – 'ow?' Ruby's body slumped from the defiant stance she had taken at the door. Holding her in her arms, Lil felt the pity of it all; aye, and the guilt. It was no wonder Ruby felt broken, with Gillian in the throes of a breakdown, violated mentally and physically, and she herself battling against illness and having to face all of this.

'I – I don't know how to say how sorry I am, Ruby.'

'Don't. I know this all came about because of folk attached to you, but I can't see that any of it is your fault. If you told them coppers all what you've told me, then surely they won't prosecute. I mean, Gillian saved your life and her own, by the sound of things.'

'She did. I reckon as they would have killed us after. I mean, they couldn't have left us to tell the tale – they were wanted criminals as it was. Anyroad, thanks for saying what you have, love, it's good to hear you are thinking that way. Though this isn't at all what you need, with your health problems and everything. How's things going for you, lass? Is the treatment having an effect?'

'I don't think so. But they say it will. I've put in a request to 'ave me boys back from evacuation. I can't wait to see them and hug them, but I 'ave me reservations. In some ways I don't want them to see me dying.'

'You're not dying, Ruby.'

'Look, love. I ain't said anything, but they've told me it's cancer – it's in me lungs and they reckon it may have spread. And at times like this families should be together, shouldn't they, Lil? I should have me boys with me. What if something happens to me – I'd never see . . .' Ruby's tears engulfed her. And although in her heart Lil had known the nature of Ruby's illness, having it confirmed took away the last drop of hope she had in her, although she couldn't show that.

'Oh, Ruby, lass. Ruby, don't. I don't know what to say. But I do know you're doing the right thing. And it will help Gillian an' all to know the lads are with you. She misses them and hates to see you pining for them. Let's hope the authorities agree. I think they will, as one or two young 'uns are beginning to come back, as it is.'

'I know, but some parents have had to go and snatch them back. They live in fear of getting into trouble, but I don't think those that put the scheme into operation care any more, now that the raids have stopped. It wasn't right what they did, Lil, taking our kids like that. They should have taken families together.'

'I know. Have you heard much from them?'

'Ronnie writes – he begs me to fetch him. He says the folk who have him don't want him. They make him eat on his own, and call him a scruff. It breaks me 'eart, Lil. But I don't think they are all like that. Ronnie said there's a couple of lads with a farmer up the road from him and they are as 'appy as pigs in muck. And Gillian were all right, weren't she? I know she missed home, but she doesn't say anything bad about the people who took her in.'

'She was fine. She brought a new lease of life to the place. The Baracloughs were reet sad to have her leave. Anyroad, lass, you'll soon have your lads with you, I'm sure. Now, Ruby, love, I can see as you're exhausted. I'll fill you a tub and you can have a bath. And I'll get you some breakfast – I'll fry off some tatties for you, then make sure tonight's supper's on the go an' all.'

'Tatties? What's them when they're 'ome?'

'Ha, it's time you southerners learnt a bit of our northern way of speaking. Tatties are potatoes, and when they are fried they're delicious. You're in for a treat, lass. Now, have you still got that bit of scrag-end Gillian told me you were going to cook for our tea last night? I could do a stew and leave it on the side of the stove all day; it'll be done nice for when your man comes back.'

'Lawd only knows if he will. He don't come 'ome much at all. Says he has to stay at the depot as there's so much to do, but I reckon he's got 'imself a floozy, the bastard!'

'Naw, not Joe. If he says he has to work, then I reckon as that's the truth. You're not thinking straight. Come on, let's get you that bath, and I'll peel them tatties while you soak.'

'I can manage, Lil. I've got all day. You've been through Hell and don't look as though you've had a wink of sleep.'

'I haven't, but that's not important.'

'Lil, you didn't deserve all of this. You're a good person through and through. What you must be feeling inside, after what that bloke did to you, I can't think. But here you are, more concerned for me. You're a champion.'

As she lifted the heavy pot off the hob and poured the boiling water from it into the tin bath that she'd dragged in from the yard, Lil didn't feel like a champion – she felt more like an animal, as that was how she'd been used. But at the end of the day her lot was nothing compared to Ruby's and Gillian's, so she was just going to get on with it. *Life has to go on* – that was the saying everyone had on their lips. But that didn't stop her questioning: how? How could life go on after what had just happened?

She poured some more water into the bath and helped Ruby to undress. Seeing the bones jutting out through the tissue-thin skin of her body took away any pity Lil felt for herself and set up a prayer in her heart: *Please, God, help us. Make Ruby well, bring home her boys, and most of all heal Gillian. Heal her mind and her body, for the lass doesn't deserve what's happened to her.*

Walking the few hundred yards or so to Gillian's mam's house, with a hot pot of stew wrapped in a towel under her arm to finish off cooking later, even though she didn't know whether she could eat it, Lil thought about the last few years. It seemed she'd been transported to Hell; not that she'd been in Heaven, as it were. Life before the war had been humdrum and centred around Alfie's whims. But she'd known some happiness then, despite everything. Alfie could be funny and used to make her laugh. She'd loved going to the pub with him on a Saturday night and joining in the free-'n'-easy, singing her heart out. Aye, and she'd enjoyed what followed when they'd got into bed an' all. When did it all change? How did she, a married northern lass, end up here in the derelict East End of London, separated from Alfie, nursing the sick and having stuff happen to her that she'd never dreamed would? She didn't know; what she did know was that she didn't want to keep thinking about everything that had happened – she wanted to forget. She would get more involved with the war effort than she currently was, and then she wouldn't have time to think about it all.

The Queen Alexandra regiment came to her mind. She'd thought about it a few times, ever since an officer had told her about the lasses belonging to this army of nurses. They had saved his life on a hospital train that operated near the front line, picking up the wounded, caring for them and then seeing they were shipped home. He'd told her that the Queen Alexandra regiment had a long history. Funny that she'd never known about them till she entered nursing. He'd said they really went back to the Crimean War, when Florence Nightingale started to train nurses in military nursing. Now Lil did know about this wonderful lady, and probably wouldn't be doing what she was now if it wasn't for Florence and her work. He'd gone on to tell her that the late Queen Alexandra had taken on the forming of a proper regiment of nurses and had been its president. Lil had been fascinated by it all and could have listened to him for hours, and in her heart a longing had awoken to do the same as those nurses.

She could join the Auxiliary Territorial Service. As a nurse, she would be attached to the Queen Alexandra regiment. She couldn't join them directly, as they only seemed to take on girls from middle- and upper-class families. *Eeh, it sounds just the job for me, though. Aye, and when all of this is behind me, and Gillian and Ruby are sorted, because I could never leave them until they are settled, I'll see about joining. I can see meself out there, on the front line, keeping the wounded alive.*

She'd be doing similar work to what she was doing now – only she'd be away from all that she had experienced here.

It felt good to have something to look forward to, and it lifted her spirits as she picked her way over piles of bricks that were once part of a house that a family had lived in. Where were *they* now? She hoped they were safe . . . She wished everyone could be safe and live a normal life once again, but she couldn't see a time when that would happen.

12

Alice

CONTACT MADE, MEMOIRS REVISITED

Radio Londres crackled. Juste turned the dial.

'Hurry, the messages will begin soon. There must be one for us before long.' Alice's anxiety showed in her voice. She needed instructions – an assignment for the group to carry out.

Over the weeks since her landing she had settled in and had taught the group all she could about the techniques of the undercover war they were fighting. They had proved to be quick learners and had many useful skills among them, even an explosives expert – a man who had worked in a mine in Alsace, but had left when the Germans had taken it over. He told of many miners working for the Resistance movement all over France.

Not that the learning had all been one way, for she had picked up a few new tricks, too. But they all knew that until they had carried out a directive from London, and done so successfully, their worth could not be measured.

They listened to the personal messages broadcast every day.

All agents had codes that made no sense to anyone other than the one person meant to receive them – a fact that maddened the Germans as they sought to decode them. They'd had great success in the beginning, as well-known poems had been chosen as code-breakers and identification, but now British agents had to make a code up, or have one made up for them. No one, other than HQ, knew the poem. Alice had never shared hers with anyone.

More crackles. Looking around the room at the men, all listening intensely, she thought of their bravery. Juste, young and single, could be at home working on the family farm with his mother, Elsbeth, and leading a comfortable life hardly touched by the war, but instead had chosen to fight. To all intents and purposes he was at university in England, which meant that his visits home had to be done after dark and in secret.

Juste had false papers in the name of Dedrian Handrian, but preferred to be called by his real name when they were in private. She didn't know the real name of the others in her group, or even whether the names they used were their own – François and Breshna, a Polish lad, and Gerard – just as they didn't know her real name. She knew François was a lawyer in his 'other life', and Gerard was a shopkeeper whose shop had been destroyed. He now traded from a kiosk on a street around the corner, selling cigarettes and newspapers. Breshna had been in his last year of study as an engineer in France when the invasion happened, and had stayed to fight here rather than risk being captured on the way home to his occupied country of Poland. His knowledge was the most practical and, she thought, would prove most useful to them, though all of them brought their own intellect and courage to the group and all of them were invaluable.

These were the main members of the group, but smaller pockets of trusted helpers existed: bakers, business owners, farmers and doctors, like Andreas – all of whom could be called upon at any time and might play useful ongoing roles in communication, storage for equipment and expertise, as well as providing safe hiding places for them, when needed. Each member was highly skilled at moving between safe houses. They had become like cats, able to scale walls of great height and creep along roofs without making a sound.

Their faces held the same gaunt, haunted look as they sipped the coffee that Madame Chappelle had provided. This was her house. She too showed great courage in allowing them to meet here. Madame had influence in the area. Many people came and went from her house, due to the business that she and her husband ran from home. She was a seamstress and her husband a tailor, and they numbered many high-ranking Germans amongst their clientele. They were strange bedfellows for the group to share lodgings with, but in a way this worked for them, as did the Chappelles' standing with the Germans, because they were trusted, and the last place to look for dissidents would be a place that the Germans themselves frequented.

All Resistance work was carried out in the cellar: not a good place to get a signal and so, though it was a risk, they had brought the radio up into the kitchen for the broadcast. Here they were greeted by the smell of freshly ground coffee – a real luxury, although Madame never disclosed her supply source. The addition of bread proving in the oven gave the sparse but clean room a homely French feel.

At last a voice on the radio broke Alice's anxiety: '*Avant de commencer, quelques messages personnels.*'

She breathed a sigh of relief; the personal messages were about to begin. *Please let there be one for us . . .* But first she had to get rid of the others. 'You must all leave me now. Go on, I will call you if the radio plays up. Hurry, you must not hear any words from my poem.'

Alone, she listened intently.

'*Le chien est noir.*' The dog is black. *Not words from my poem.*

'*Remplir le cœur du feu.*' Fill the heart of fire. *No. Come on, please* . . .

Two more and then: '*Lapide-moi, pour une clé couverte de douleur.*' Stone me, for one pain-covered key . . .

'That's it! Yes, at last!' Calling the others back in, she waited for their cheers to die down.

'Now, bear with me, as I have to decipher the code.'

Every letter in her poem had to be numbered. In this case the 'one' in the message meant that she was to start with the first letter of the alphabet. The messages would always indicate which letter she had to start her numbering with. Thinking it through, she remembered that although she had to start with 'a', each repeat of the letter had to have a number of its own, which the code-makers had told her would prevent all the letters having sequential numbers. Using this system, she took some time to convert the words from her poem into letters, which would then need sorting into the real message that HQ was sending her.

A full half-hour had passed when François, always the one in a hurry, showed his frustration. 'How long is this going to take?'

'I'm sorry – it's complicated. There! I have all of the letters. I just need to solve the anagram.'

Screwing her working paper up, she threw it into the fire. Not even with trusted people must she be careless with any of the words in her poem. It took the group's local knowledge and joint effort finally to work out the words of the message: 'Versanté factory – drop is one a.m. on second, or day after'.

A low whistle from François showed his thoughts on the difficulty of the task. Juste shook his head. 'This is almost impossible. The Versanté factory makes parts for all manner of warfare equipment. Most of its operation is underground and it is heavily guarded. How are we to destroy it?'

'And what about the workers? My cousin is one of them. This has to be planned for night-time when the factory is closed, or I will not take part.'

'Of course it will be night-time, François. This cousin of yours, would he help by giving us inside information?'

'Yes, he hates working there. It goes against his principles, but he has no choice. He is part of the forced-labour programme the Germans have in place. I am exempt from forced labour, as my court work is valuable, to maintain some stability.'

'Good. But he must be prepared for some reprisal, for they will know someone helped us. Are we willing to risk that?'

'We have to be. And I know my cousin will think the same, although it is terrifying to think what they might do. Their atrocities know no bounds – it is as if the Germans are not human.'

'Don't think like that, François. Our fight is as much for the German people as it is for France and England and Poland – well, all countries really. There are many Germans who do not want this. Think only of the regime, the Nazis, as the inhuman ones.'

'Of course, I apologize. I forgot your mother is German, Juste.'

'I live in dread of others finding out. Where she lives they accept her, but . . .'

Alice hadn't thought of this before. Elsbeth could be in danger. What if a son of one of the villagers near her was killed in action or . . . *Oh God, what if they find out her history!* True or not, it wouldn't look good for her.

Bringing the subject back to the matter in hand she said, 'You are right, Juste, and we must remember that. But back to the message: the drop of the equipment and so on that we need will take place where I landed. As it is in the country, it is well-known by the night-flyers and has a good landing strip. The message contained a coded number allocated to that location. The exact date will be determined by the weather, but we have two alternatives in July to get a clear night.' A shudder trembled through her body as she remembered the horror of her near-death at that place; it iced her blood.

'Are you afraid, Madeline?'

'Yes, Juste. And I know it's natural to be scared, but I'm also concerned. We really need a new place for the drop. You all have to think of somewhere, because there's a danger of the consignment falling into the river.'

'No, we cannot. Everything is set up there. We have a runway fashioned. Though it is hidden by undergrowth it only takes us half an hour to clear it, when we need it. And there are bunkers that we have dug out, and the false tree trunks sent to us before your arrival are all in place. All are good storage and hiding places for the equipment they send us, and will be safe until we can move it.'

She'd seen those tree trunks, and many other gadgets of disguise and subterfuge, being designed and made at both the Thatched Barn in north London and The Frythe, a secluded house near Welwyn Garden City. Hollowed-out and hinged, the trunks looked realistic enough and could lie undetected in any wood.

'Right, then we'll go with it. It's probably too late to change it anyway. Now, are there any more questions?'

'What if none of the days are suitable, weather-wise?'

'I will have my field-phone with me and will receive an abort message, Breshna, so don't worry . . .'

'But surely you will leave that part of the mission to us? We cannot risk you being present. It is too dangerous.'

'I need you all to forget that I am a woman. I have demonstrated my skills to you. You know I am capable, and you must trust me in the way you trust each other. Besides, the pilot will contact me to verify that he is in position and there is no ambush, and therefore I must be present.'

'And if there is an abort?'

'In that case we will receive another message. One of us has to listen in to Radio Londres every day and, if it's not me, then whoever it is must jot down all the messages word-for-word.'

'You're right, Madeline.' Alice was glad to hear François say this, for he wasn't given to listening patiently to women and had been more than a thorn in her side at times. But he had a way – a lawyer's way, she supposed – of calming situations and making the others understand what was needed. She listened, as they all did, as he continued, 'Now we must decide who will do what, in the strategy we have to put together. This will be a real achievement for our group. Destroying this factory will greatly hinder the Germans, both in building new equipment and in repairing damaged ones. So, firstly, maps . . . ?'

The mission was taking a great deal of planning, which Alice found both fascinating and exciting. Her first real involvement in sabotage! But as the proceedings drew to a close, tiredness seeped into every part of her and settled in her bones. It became difficult even to think of riding her bicycle home to her small apartment. On top of everything else, she was due to begin her new job tomorrow, as assistant to the stationmaster of the Gare de l'Est.

Juste had secured the position for her. Alice's ability to speak German had made her a good choice for the job and meant she could assist the many German passengers. Besides this, her duties would be to coordinate timetables each day, as many train services were disrupted at the last moment by the need for German transportation of men, prisoners and supplies. These were never planned in advance, and so some shifting of the schedule was necessary every day. The job held many opportunities for her to gain useful information, not only for her own group, but for others too, about exactly what was moving and where the Resistance could sabotage it. It rankled that no train carrying Jews or dissidents was to be interfered with. But then they had no contingency plans to house, feed and look after such people, if they freed them.

'Well, I think we have covered everything. Let's call the meeting closed. Curfew will be imposed soon.'

Thankful to hear Juste say this, Alice asked if she could be the first to go home. Wheeling her bicycle out onto the street, it seemed to her there was an uncanny silence. Nothing moved. Not even a wisp of wind disturbed the scraps of rubbish on the pavement, nor were there the usual hungry dogs scavenging in the bins and the gutter. The Café Romane had its blinds down.

Every part of her tuned into the danger in the air. *Had they misjudged the time? Had curfew already begun?*

'Halt!'

The pit of her stomach changed places with her heart. *Oh God!*

'*Zeigen Sie mir Ihre Papiere.*'

167

The huge soldier stepped out of the shadows. Searching for the papers he'd asked her for, she undid the concealed inner lining of her bag. The cold steel of her knife reassured her. As she handed over her ID card she rehearsed her cover story in her mind, in a bid to ensure that she did not say the wrong thing. His torch blinded her. 'Blonde – not usual for a French girl! What were you doing in that house – is it where you live?'

'No. I was visiting a friend, Madame Chappelle, who is making me a new outfit.'

'Ah, the seamstress, I have heard of her. My wife is looking for one of those outfits. Come, you can introduce me.'

Please let them have seen what is happening and have got away!

A flicker of the curtain told her the others in the group hadn't yet left, and that the next one to depart was checking to see if it was clear for him to do so. Now she only had one choice. Taking her papers from the soldier, she tucked them into her bag.

The knife felt heavy as she clasped her fingers around it. Putting a caressing tone into her voice as she looked up at him, she said, 'It is disappointing to hear you have a wife. It seems all the handsome ones amongst you are married.'

'Being married doesn't stop us giving you whores what you want.' He moved closer. Her knife sunk into his breast. His body weight took her down with him, and her bicycle crashed down on top of them. The noise resounded along the empty street.

Alert to all possibilities, she pushed her way free. When she pulled the knife out, it squelched as it tore muscle and caught on a rib. A watery sigh, which was not drawn back in, told her the soldier was dead. Rolling away from him, she stood up. Still nothing stirred in the street, but she knew this could not prevail for long. The Germans patrolled in twos. Maybe they had each taken one end of the street, intending to meet in the middle. Looking in the direction that the other soldier would come from, she saw a small light glow and then fade. How often had they been warned that smoking could give your position away. Grabbing her bike, she rode it in the opposite direction, pedalling for all she was worth.

François flagged her down. He appeared from a narrow alley leading down the side of a row of shops. Looking around, she could see nothing behind her.

'This way!' His whisper carried as if it was a shout. 'Come on, Madeline.'

He took her handlebars as soon as she was in the alley and straddled the bike in front of her.

'Hold on! We will freewheel to the bottom of the lane, where I can hide your bike in a friend's yard. Then we will climb the steps leading to his roof and escape across the rooftops.'

She didn't argue. Once on the roof, she used all the skills she had learned to move like a feline. In silence they man-oeuvred around the chimneys and travelled the length of the street behind the one where the incident had taken place. A jeep roared along below, making its way towards the scene. They lay flat out on the apex of the roof until it passed.

It took them a long time to reach her place. After coming down from the roof they clambered through yards, climbed over high fences and sprinted across alleyways. At last they reached the street where she lived – usually just a five-minute bike ride from Madame Chappelle's.

Crouching behind a wall, they watched the commotion that had erupted. The street had come alive with motorbikes and jeeps. Germans shouted to one another. People hung out of their windows, wanting to see what all the fuss was about, but quickly closed them when they saw what was happening. Soldiers banged on doors.

'Oh God! Where can we go?'

'Come.'

Like a graceful lynx, François set off running along a path, then jumped the wall that formed a barrier across the end. Keeping up with him proved difficult, as Alice's lungs already felt as though they would burst. When she landed she saw they were beside the river. Taking off his jacket and shoes, François waded in, holding his belongings above him. She had no choice but to do the same, lifting her bag high above her head.

The water froze her to the bone, but she would not give up. Ahead, the form of a wooden shed stretched out over the water. It took on a beautiful outline against the moonlit background of the shadowy trees straddling it and making lace-patterns in the water.

'Stay still a moment!' François ducked under the water. The doors of the shed opened and a boat emerged. Hauling Alice inside wasn't easy, for her strength had gone and the cold had paralysed her muscles.

'Here, wrap my jacket round you – it's mostly dry.'

Some warmth entered her, and her teeth stopped chattering. Again François whispered to her, 'I have a farmhouse downriver. It was my grandfather's. It is in need of repair, but we can get shelter there and food. I can light a fire to get us warm.'

What was it with her and boats? They seemed to figure in her worst moments lately, instead of her happiest, as they had done in her teens with Bren. *Oh, Bren – carefree days.* As this thought hit her, she found she could not answer François, as vomit threatened to choke her. She leaned over the edge and emptied her stomach. *I killed a man . . . God, I killed a man!*

'Your first?'

She nodded. They were sitting on an old and sagging sofa, drinking cocoa that François had made. The cocoa tasted of smoked water and stale chocolate, but she clung to her mug and sipped, as if it was the best drink she'd ever had, blowing the steam away from her eyes. The fire crackled and spat in protest at being loaded with damp logs, and she felt some peace settle inside her. With her naked body snuggled into an old dressing gown, she thought, *So, this is war then? One moment full of fear, trying to save lives from an unforgiving sea whilst being shot at; the next being blown up and losing loved ones, and knowing the terror of drowning, unable to move. But, worse, being forced to carry out atrocities, as I did tonight. But between these horrors I have experienced moments like those I have shared with Steve, and like this one, snug and cosy in front of the warming flames.*

'Best to just forget it. And if you do think about it, tell yourself you saved lives – and the group from being caught – by doing it. Don't ever think of the man in a personal way, or about his life.'

'I know. We trained for this, but the reality is different. I will get used to it.'

'The main thing is that you know when to act quickly and don't baulk at doing so, and because of your actions the rest of our group got away. Madame Chappelle's attic leads into all the houses in the row. After being alerted by what you were doing, we all crawled along the rafters. Each person got out through a different skylight and disappeared over the rooftops. I was the last one, and saw you riding for all you were worth towards me. But I am sure the others are all safe.'

She hoped so, but couldn't speak to answer him. Tiredness closed in on her. François rose and pushed her head down, then lifted her feet onto the sofa. 'Stay as long as you need. My advice would be to have a rest, then root around in my grandmother's things. Burn your own as they are blood-stained. My grandmother was about your size and, from what I remember of her clothes, they could be adapted to wear as if they are the fashion of today. As you are taller than Grandmama, what was long on her will be the length that women wear now, on you. And her jackets were of a good cut, so will pass, I am sure.'

'Thank you. Can I get a train nearby? I need to get to the Gare de l'Est station. I begin work there tomorrow.'

'Yes, I remember. When you leave, walk for about ten minutes in a westerly direction and that will bring you to the village. They have a station there, and regular trains pass through that go to most stations. Juste told me about your job. Good luck with it, and keep a low profile. Mind your own business, no matter what you see. What you find out from there is going to be very helpful. We will know exactly when to grease the track, and which track to grease. Goodnight, Madeline.'

After he'd gone she closed her eyes. Trying to block out the horror of earlier on, she thought about her mother and father. She had her father's diary with her, tucked into a side pocket of her shoulder bag, which she had managed to keep dry. Taking it out, she snuggled back down to read:

Sunday 6th September 1910: it has been three weeks now, and still Louise is refusing to have me in her bed. I have given her an ultimatum. I have told her that I can have the marriage annulled, and have her tested to prove she has not allowed the consummation of our marriage.

This distressed her greatly and, as a consequence, I felt like a cad of the worst order. But although she begged me not to annul our marriage, I told her that her behaviour was ridiculous, and no man should have to suffer what I am suffering.

She pleaded with me, telling me she was afraid about what would happen in the bedroom, but would allow me to come to her tonight. This nearly undid my resolve, and I told her as tenderly as I could that there really was no need to be afraid, saying, 'I love you and will be very gentle. Everything will be all right, I promise, darling.'

At that moment the tree above us rustled, filling the quiet between us with a peaceful sound. The hustle and bustle just a street away continued as normal, with businessmen and shoppers thronging along the busy London street. Yet none of it intruded on us. I could already feel a stirring of anticipation inside me.

I had been looking at the magnificent garden with its views over Danson Park. My hammock swayed gently, lulling me as I lazed idly. Louise sat in the garden chair next to me. A contentment came over me. Closing my eyes, I tried to imagine the delights of the evening ahead, until a movement disturbed me. Louise had risen and, when I asked her where she was going, she said a sickness and a headache plagued her. She said she needed to lie down and would see me at dinner.

Disappointment coursed through me at this. Louise seemed to be resorting to the same old trick, which Philippe had warned me about. This was her way of planting the idea within me that maybe I should leave her alone. I watched her go, wondering how someone so beautiful could reject what would make her into an even more self-assured and beautiful woman?

The gentle sway of her layered skirt played on my senses. Turning away, I tried to get myself under control, but it didn't work. I made up my mind to go to her now. Headache or not, she *must* see to her husband's needs!

Alice ceased reading and turned a few pages. She knew she wasn't giving herself a chance to learn properly about her father – his thoughts, his feelings and what led him to Elsbeth – but her own knowledge of her mother told her that Louise would have manipulated him, had him begging for morsels, and would have given very little of herself to him. This was confirmed by a passage a few pages further on:

23rd October 1910: Today was a pleasant day in the garden, unusually warm for the time of year. The dead leaves had been swept from the lawn and a game of croquet had got under way. The women giggled and skipped around like children, distracting the men from their conversation. Ferdinand remarked to me that he thought me the luckiest of fellows, as Louise is a stunning woman.

I could not stop myself from agreeing that she is, but – with gross disloyalty – went on to tell him that she is as cold as ice. I confessed that I no longer knew what to do. That I had been very patient with her, but nothing worked.

His shock showed in his question, 'You mean it hasn't happened yet? Good Lord!'

Shame reddened my cheeks as I admitted that it had, but it was nothing like it should be, and I was left feeling like a rake every time. Not that there had been many occasions.

The feeling was compounded when he told how he saw Louise as the opposite of what I described. He saw only her charm and her flirtatious ways. In fact he envied me. He even suggested that I was at fault and that, were he so inclined, he felt sure he could seduce her perfectly well!

His guffaw had me cringing and made me question whether I lacked the ability to arouse my wife. To prove I didn't I was almost tempted to encourage him to try, as I didn't see anyone managing to get through the self-centredness that Louise possesses. If they did, I would say they deserved a medal. But no, he might succeed, and I couldn't bear thinking of another man having her.

Why I was surprised at his suggestion then, I do not know, but he implied that I should take my need elsewhere, even telling me that he knew of a place, if I was interested. When I replied that Philippe had told me he was visiting such a place that very evening, Ferdinand surprised me further by saying he often saw Philippe there, and asked how Philippe had got out of that spot of bother up in the north.

Unbeknown to us both, Philippe had by now come up behind us and asked, in his stupid way, 'What spot of bother up in the north?'

Ferdinand laughed at this, which drew the boast from Philippe that the girl had given birth to a son and that he'd neither recognize the boy nor pay her a penny. I hadn't realized the girl's pregnancy was so far advanced when Philippe told me about her!

It appears the girl is already taking in lodgers – all of them male and so, in Philippe's opinion, all seeing to her, no doubt. He even had the audacity to say it had been a blasted shame, as she had been good to lie with, but for him life has improved. He now has a mistress in France.

But I have to confess to feeling a certain admiration for Philippe, when he answered Ferdinand's enquiry as to whether it was tiring living in France and having his business here, saying, 'The only tiring thing is keeping all my women happy. I was just going to say that I also have another up north, an Irish girl who lets me have what I want and makes no demands. And then there is the brothel you were just discussing.'

To this I sharply counselled him to be quiet, for the sake of the family name! To which he declared that he was perpetuating it, as he happened to know that Father did his share of putting himself about, too. Then he speculated that we had many a sister and brother, from here to France. My toes curled in embarrassment as Philippe and Ferdinand laughed, only to have the conversation worsened by Philippe saying, 'Besides, haven't I just heard that you are leaning towards finding extra pleasures elsewhere yourself, dear brother?'

I must confess that I have given much thought of late to the needs of the male species and how those needs can gnaw away at you, making you do things against your honour. Inside I feel I have done that to Louise – lost my honour in pursuit of satisfaction with her. Oh, damn it! The brothel it is . . .

Something in Alice didn't blame her father. Her thoughts went back to Steve; her own longings burned a desire into her and she understood her father's actions. Maybe Father had learned from Elsbeth that many women had these desires, and wanted to please their men and receive the pleasure they gave. She imagined that Elsbeth was one of these women, and this was the reason Father had fallen in love with her.

Wrapping her arms around herself, she wondered what had become of the boy that her Uncle Philippe had fathered. Was he still alive? Did he and his mother still live in the north of England?

For some reason Corporal Moisley came into her mind. She supposed it was because he was the only northerner she'd ever met. And, thinking about it, he was about the right age. Funny how he knew of her father. But then Father was notorious, so she shouldn't wonder at it really. Then again, why should that make Moisley hate her with such venom? *It was strange . . .*

13

Gertrude

PARIS, JUNE 1941

A LOVE RETURNED

It has to happen soon, but how do I instigate it? Gertrude asked this of herself a dozen times a day.

There had been several encounters similar to their first. They'd chatted and she'd bathed Kristof. And on the last occasion she had even massaged him, but still they hadn't made love. Each session had ended with him in a flood of tears. She'd held him until these moments had passed, and in doing so had seen his arousal pass, too.

At least she knew he wasn't seeking pleasure elsewhere any longer, and this pleased her. He was hers – she knew that and, as she savoured the thrill this knowledge gave her, she also knew that in other circumstances she'd be prepared to wait as long as it took. But now it had an urgency to it, as Juste and Madeline had given her the task of finding out anything she could about the Versanté factory – and gaining access to plans of its layout, if she could. For this she would need the keys to get from her apartment to Kristof's office, and those for his office and his safe.

Madeline had given her what she would need to make an impression of Kristof's keys, from which replicas could be made. But he rarely brought any keys with him, except the one for the door in her living room, which he used to access her apartment.

In preparation for the time when she would visit his office to seek information, she had already begun to look for signs of an alarm system: where it led to, and to which doors it was connected. She'd been surprised to find there wasn't an inner alarm, but of course there was one huge obstacle – there was always a guard on duty outside Kristof's office.

Frustration soured her mood. Helping him to recover from his demons was one thing, but it was all taking such a long time. She needed to move things along, and she needed to do so by having him come to her on an unplanned visit, when he was more likely to have his keys with him.

Making up her mind that there was no time like the present, she picked up her internal phone and dialled his office. Her hands shook as her finger twisted the dial round and it sprang back to its original position – the number she rang should only be used in the event of an emergency. She feared the anger she would incur for using the phone flippantly. Her heart thudded as he answered, 'Yes? Are my children all right? What is wrong?' Despite the worry in his voice, its softness soothed her.

She kept hers low and husky, 'They are fine. I am not.'

'Oh?'

'I rang because I need you. I need you to be ready for me. Have you reached that stage yet?'

The silence went on and on. Into it came the sound of his quickening breath. When Kristof spoke, his hesitancy gave her hope. 'Violetta, I – I do not know . . .'

'Can you get away? Can we try? I am aching for you. I love you, Kristof.'

'I know. And I have feelings for you that sometimes surpass those I had . . . for my wife.' Again he fell silent.

'It is all right to feel like that. We can have two loves in our lives. I won't ever eclipse your wife's memory, and in time she won't eclipse my being with you. You will cope with us both in different ways. I promise that if you cannot, it will not matter. I will bathe you as usual, but I want you inside me. I want to give myself to you, and for you to take from me all that you should take from the woman you love.'

He was silent again. Her sham was despicable, and although she meant every word about her love for him, it didn't sit well with her that she was luring Kristof to her not just to love him, but to dupe him.

'I will come. Run me a bath. We will bath together, and then we will see.'

She took a sharp breath at the involuntary clenching of the muscles in her groin. Her whole body tingled with the anticipation of having him at last. A warm dampness trickled from her. *God, I want him so badly!*

As she undressed him she kissed every part of him. The feel of his uniform, rough to the touch, gave her a sensuous sensation when she ran her fingers down his arm while he was still wearing it. His aftershave gave out a subtle aroma that reminded her of the woodlands she had played in as a child. And as she removed his shirt the smell of his body added to this and further heightened her senses. She wanted to suggest they make love now and forgo the bath, but could sense a tenseness in him and knew she had to deal with that first.

'I am sorry, my dear, I hold back because I know that once we make love, it will be a beginning and yet an end. None of those other women meant anything to me. I may even have taken them were my wife still alive. They were just extra needs that I had. But I know that coming together with you will mean so much that it will hurt. It will scar the memory I hold of my wife. I don't mean it will taint it, but it will take some of it away and replace it with a feeling of disloyalty.'

'It doesn't have to. All our sessions have been about making a place in you for your wife, without holding anything back from me. That place she has can be sacred. I need you, my darling, I need you so much.'

Something in what she said, or the proximity of her, triggered his passion. He pulled her to him, his lips bruising hers. His tongue prised them open to explore her mouth. Dare she let go? Dare she give her all? What if he rejected her or stopped her, wanting her to bathe him as they had planned? But the decision wasn't hers to take. Her resolve collapsed, leaving her no choice as he guided her towards the bed.

He unclothed her, his hands probing, his mouth kissing, licking, sucking little parts of her skin and bringing her desire to an orgasmic peak that needed release. It came the moment he entered her. A crescendo of sensations gripped her, pulsating through her in powerful waves that left her gasping and crying tears of joy. It was a freeing of her soul, a splintering of who she had been. From this moment on she would be changed forever. Part of her would belong to Kristof. Without him she would be nothing.

She knew he'd felt the power of their union, for his gasps told her he couldn't cope. 'Be still, my darling. Rest in me a

181

while. We are too sensitive to each other. Hold me . . .' This was where she belonged, filled with him, snuggled by him and loved by him.

His movements, when they happened again, gave her feelings she had never experienced before. This wasn't a sexual act; this was the strong bonding of a man and woman who were one soul. A joining of lives. Taking all he had to give, she wrapped her legs around him and rocked with him. The moans that came from deep in her throat had started in the pit of her, where a fire burned that she knew would never be extinguished. His cries told her he was feeling the same. His kisses covered her face, his gentle nibbling of her breasts seared her with an exquisite pain. Words of love tumbled from him as they rode a crest of sensations, taking them to a peak so intense it hurt, before showering them with a release that had them gasping for breath and clinging onto one another as if they would never let go.

They lay, still joined, not speaking – looking at one another. They had no need for words. She watched a bead of sweat trickle down his cheek. When it reached his lips she bent towards him and licked it away. His smile lit his lovely grey eyes. She smiled back.

The soft dampness of him as he pulled from her left a trail on her leg. It reminded her that they hadn't taken care, but then it didn't matter. If she was to have his child, it would be a gift she would treasure.

Her mind left this thought and gave her another – one that dampened her happiness and brought back to her guilt at the reason she had lured Kristof to her. It hurt to re-engage with her deceit of him. But then she thought of what Kristof and the regime he belonged to were doing to her people – and to the world – and her resolve renewed itself. She had to get access to his keys. But how?

She could see nothing in the way he lay looking at her, and twirling a lock of her hair, that said he was ready to move from her side. This suggested that even if she encouraged him to take his bath, he would want her to stay with him and to wash him, as she usually did.

'How long can you stay with me, Kristof?'

Turning and looking at his watch on the bedside table, he shot upright. 'I need to go very soon – I have a meeting. I will take a quick dip in that water you have ready for me . . . I am sorry, my dearest, I should not be leaving you after what we just shared. But I have to. Thank you, my love. My precious.' He kissed her forehead and then her lips, allowing his kiss to deepen for a moment before he pulled away. 'Tonight. I will come back tonight and we will lie in each other's arms all night long.'

She had never heard anything she wanted more in all her life. Placing her hand on his chest, as if she would help him on his way, she told him, 'I can wait. And I will be ready for you. Go . . . go on, have your bath. We mustn't let anyone suspect anything. The boys will be coming down from the schoolroom for their French lesson soon, and the girls will be back from their walk with the nursery nurse. So hurry.'

He did not object or ask her to go and bathe him. She rolled over at the sound of Kristof moving in the water, and pulled a case from under the other side of her bed. It glided soundlessly, although its latches clicked as if a gun had been fired. Keeping still, she waited. Still the water splashed. Grabbing three of the square tins that Madeline had given her, Gertrude removed the lids and rolled back to the side of the bed where Kristof's keys lay. With her heart pounding fear all around her body, her hands shook as she took the keys one by one and pressed them into the soft moulding clay in each tin. One, two, three. And then a small key, which she pressed into the side of one of the indents. Sweat trickled in little beads from her forehead, leaving a cold trail as it ran down her cheeks. Somehow she managed to replace the lids and put the tins back in the case. Now for the final stage. Grabbing the damp cloth she'd prepared earlier, she pushed the case back into its hiding place, not daring to close the latches for fear of the noise they made.

Frantically rubbing each key clean of residue, she'd just finished the last one when the bathroom door opened. In the split second that followed, and with her nerves making it difficult for her to breathe, she tucked the cloth and the keys under the bedclothes. Putting the keys back where they were would be impossible without Kristof seeing her do so.

His gaze held hers as he approached the bed. Trying not to appear frozen with fear, she knew she had to cause a diversion. His question – 'Are you all right, darling?' – held concern. Answering him released some of the tension within her and allowed her thoughts to process an idea concerning how to get rid of the keys. Her hand closed around them.

'Yes, more than all right, but disappointed.' Swinging her legs off the bed as she said this, she purposely knocked her trinket box off the bedside table where his things were, then stood up and, under the guise of picking up his undergarments, dropped the keys close to her necklaces and bangles, which were sprawled out in a glittering pile. 'Oh, now look what I've done!'

'Never mind that. Why are you disappointed? I thought we had—'

'No. Not disappointed in you, darling. It's just that I wanted to come in and dry you, but you were so quick.' She moved towards him, but he stopped her.

'No, just hand me my pants – I will see to myself. I cannot let you near me. I am already feeling the need to take you again, and that cannot happen.' He grinned, a boyish grin that released more of the tension in her, causing her to give a little giggle and ask, 'Why not?'

'Because, I am supposed to be working, and I will miss my meeting with Herr Dansk. But I will secretly dream about doing so, whilst he drones on about what he must have and what I must agree to.'

'Ha, you'd better remain seated behind your desk then, as you know what that will do to you!'

He laughed out loud at this and she relaxed further.

While he dressed, she gathered up her things and his keys, and put them back where they had been. He showed no sign of noticing anything.

Still naked, she ignored what he'd said about staying away from him and helped him on with his jacket. The magnificence of his body curled her insides into a delicious knot. Though she hated what his uniform stood for, she loved him in it and the feel of it. Kissing him, she told him, 'I love you. I don't know where that will lead us, as we cannot be public with our love. I will be vilified and maybe even killed for fraternizing, but we will have my rooms as our haven, our love nest.'

'Oh, you French! That is ridiculous – we are not your enemy, or won't be the minute you realize that we're not. You will see, things will improve once this war is won. Anyway this will not be our only place to meet. I will invite you to my suite. I have some trusted servants. They will see us dine in the manner that we should, and I will have things prepared for you the way I want them to be for my woman. I will buy you gifts and shower you with all that I have. I love you with a completeness. And I know my wife has her place in me and is at peace. You did that for me. You, my love.'

She drank in Kristof's gentle and loving kiss, allowing her deceit to find a place to rest easy in the part of her conscience that held her devotion to France and its people. This meant she was able to send him away with a promise of good things when he came to her later, instead of feeling the guilt of her actions.

Relaxing into the bath water, Gertrude didn't let her thoughts linger on the part of her that Kristof had unlocked and made his own. Like him, she dared not think about what had just happened, as still she tingled with a need for him. There was so much they had to explore together. This first union had been a miracle in unlocking a broken heart and allowing the fusion of two people in love.

No, the thoughts must stop there! She had to plan how and when to get the tins with the moulds of the keys to Juste, so that he could take them to a locksmith. They had one, a genius with all metalwork, in their group. For a small group they were lucky to have the skills amongst them that they did. Forced labour had kept many experts in different fields in the area, instead of having to go into the German Army, as was the fate of so many.

She had to be quick, for Herr Dansk headed the SS assigned to the factory. He probably wished to talk about the security there. If he wanted to increase it, he would need Kristof to authorize a request to go to Himmler for more men. She knew, from the intelligence gathered by agents before she moved into this house, that all communication and requests had to go through Herr Eberhardt. And so the quicker she had access to his office and found any information on the factory, the better. The thought of having to secretly enter Kristof's office set up a palpitation of fear in her heart, which upstaged any lingering feelings of their lovemaking that she'd been harbouring.

An idea occurred to her. She would take the boys on a walk to teach them some French through experience: have them name things they passed, and then take them into the cafe and ask them each to order their own drinks. Somehow she would find a way of giving the tins to Paulo whilst they were occupied. He would help her, as he would know by what she would wear that she had something to pass to him.

The coded message had said 'Keys ready' and had given her instructions about where she should rendezvous with Madeline to pick them up. Thank goodness the urgency of her request had been adhered to, Gertrude thought, as she read it. It had been imperative that she collect them today, not only because this was her only day off this week, but because after the meeting Kristof had held with Herr Dansk yesterday, they had to act quickly. If decisions about security were being made, there might still be vital information in Kristof's office – information that would help the group in its mission to destroy the factory.

Holding the message to her breast for a moment before ripping it into small pieces and disposing of it in the nearest rubbish bin, Gertrude had felt a moment of elation and had thought, *At last I will meet Madeline again and have a chance to carry out my first real assignment!*

Now she had the keys in her hand.

'Are you sure about this?' Madeline had asked, as she'd passed Gertrude the keys from her position directly behind her outside the cafe. The pavement narrowed where their two tables stood.

As she had turned the corner into Rue Abel, just a short walk from where she had alighted from the bus, Gertrude had seen Madeline standing outside a shop a little way away. The tables they were to sit at had been occupied. Through Madeline's gesture not to approach she had known there was going to be no social contact between them. This had disappointed her, but she should have realized it would be so.

Taking her cue from Madeline, Gertrude had stood looking at the items in a shop window, marvelling there still was jewellery of such beauty and high price for sale.

They hadn't had to wait long. Unlike Paulo's, where they dared not meet, this wasn't a cafe where people lingered, but more somewhere they stopped for a quick refreshment before continuing their shopping.

Gertrude had crossed over to it first and sat with her back to the chair facing the next table. Madeline had followed and claimed the one behind her. The other tables were around the corner. In answer to Madeline's question she wanted to say, 'No, I am not sure. I want out. I want to go back to Mama's and be safe again.' But instead, while pretending to look through the magazine she had brought with her, she said, 'Yes, I will be all right. I wandered near Herr Eberhardt's office the other day and no one questioned me. The guard at the door chatted with me. I told him I was exploring, as I hadn't seen much of the house other than the children's and my own quarters. He was quite friendly and a little suggestive. Most of them are lonely for a woman's company. I will use that fact tonight in my quest to have him turn a blind eye to me entering the office.'

'Tonight? You're going to attempt it tonight? And what is your plan to get the guard to let you into the office?'

'I will lure him into a side office to have sex, then tell him before it gets that far that I will scream rape unless he gives me a few minutes inside Herr Eberhardt's office. And yes, it must be tonight. Herr Eberhardt had a meeting yesterday with Herr Dansk, the officer who heads security at the factory, and it is likely there is still information in his office relating to that meeting. I will start in his PA's in-tray. I noticed on the day of my interview that she had a lot of work outstanding. I just might get lucky and find she hasn't yet dealt with the papers from yesterday's meeting, and then I'll be able to get in and out of there very quickly.'

'But it all sounds so dangerous. How can you be sure the guard won't squeal, once you are in the office?'

'I can't . . . Oh, it's hopeless.'

'I think this is something I will have to handle. The guard will need to be disposed of. Can you sneak me into your room, so that I can gain access to Herr Eberhardt's office from there?'

'No, that is impossible, for everyone has to have clearance. I cannot just arrive with a guest, and I have no way of getting you in without you being seen.'

'Couldn't I climb into your room from that tree? The branches hang very close to your balcony.'

'I don't know. Let me think about it for a moment.'

Sipping her coffee, Gertrude screwed up her face at the bitter taste. *Obviously not a cafe frequented by the Germans, and that's probably why Madeline chose it.* Around them the street buzzed with shoppers. Mostly elegant women who gave an air of the war having had little impact on their lives, whereas she and Madeline had to meet in this clandestine way to work out ways to help the liberation of France. Somehow it didn't seem fair.

Brushing the thought away, she focused on Madeline's

proposal. It did sound like a good idea, but could they pull it off? What if Kristof came looking for her . . . ? That's it! As if a light had been switched on, a foolproof way that Madeline could get into his office without encountering Kristof came to her. She could make sure he visited her tonight, and keep him busy in her bedroom. That would leave the lounge and the route into the corridor leading to Kristof's office clear. She could leave the window to the balcony open . . . But no, there would be too much danger for Madeline, she couldn't suggest it.

'Gertrude?'

'Oh, sorry. Look, I have a plan, but you must get one of the others to do it. I don't want you to – it is too dangerous.'

'Don't worry about me, Gertrude, I am highly trained. I have skills the others have never seen. Just tell me what it is, and let me decide if I can do it.'

'Well, what if . . .' Telling of her plan and having Madeline shape it, it seemed feasible. Yes, they could do it. But if only Madeline would agree to one of the others carrying it out.

14

Alice

A DANGEROUS MISSION

The branch swayed up and down. Alice hung on, praying it wouldn't break. Beneath her was the balcony, which was a drop of about ten feet. Gertrude had placed the flowerpot in the centre of it, so that Alice would know she had the right one. This only left her a small space to jump onto on each side. The light held by the SS guard walking the pavement flicked upwards, missing her, but lighting up Gertrude's window. *Please, God, don't let him shine it on me!*

His steps, precise and short, resounded around her. Counting his paces, she knew it would only be a few seconds before he turned the corner to check that side of the house. As he had done before, he saluted his comrades standing guard on the door. Then he was gone, and she knew it had to be now.

Dropping her feet and holding onto the branch with her fingers, she took a leap of faith and let go of it. The branch snapped back into place; birds squawked and flew into the air. A guard below blew a whistle. *Now – I have to get inside now!*

191

She tried the handle, but it didn't give way to her. *It's locked! Christ, Gertrude, why have you locked it*? Lying flat on the floor, she prayed.

Below her she heard a voice saying something had disturbed the birds in the tree. Brightness bathed everything around her and then went away. An argument broke out. From what she could make out, one SS guard wanted the house searched, whilst another said it was probably a cat. A third said that he'd seen Herr Eberhardt going towards the nanny's room and they should leave things well alone. As if by a miracle, at that moment a cat squealed and the SS men burst out laughing.

'Look, it was the randy tomcat chasing his love.'

'Well, he has caught her now, lucky thing. Look at him, he's having his fill!' A beam from his torch shone onto the green, where it lit up the two cats. The moaning sound of the female took up the space around her.

One of the guards said, 'I could fuck anything that moved – it's been that long.'

The taste of cigarette smoke filtered up to her with the next voice, 'Me too. We will have to go to the brothel.'

'But that's only for officers . . .'

'Not the one I've heard of. And I have heard the women are good, too.'

'We will go, but for now stop talking about it. Gustrad's trousers look as if he has his baton in them.'

Their laughter calmed her nerves. *Thank you, God. Now, if you could just get me in here . . .*

Trained to pick locks, she took what she needed from her overall pocket. She'd donned these over her clothes in anticipation of there being a bloody mess when she dealt with the guard. If that happened, she could discard the overalls and make her escape in clothes that didn't tell of her involvement, if she was apprehended. The overall's many pockets enabled her to carry everything she needed, or might need.

As she went to tackle the lock, a sound on the other side of the window had her shrinking back into the wall. A lock turned. A voice – distant, but one she could just make out – asked, 'What are you doing, darling?'

'Just fixing you a drink.'

'I don't want a drink. I want you. Come here, I am already in bed. I cannot wait any longer.'

After a few moments Alice tried the window and slipped inside. She became tangled for a moment in the net curtain as it returned after billowing out, but freed herself and made for the door in the corner.

From the other room she could hear moans of pleasure. It awakened a memory and played with the muscles in her groin. Tensing that area shortened her breath. She had to get out of earshot of what Gertrude and Herr Eberhardt were doing, and let the fear take her once more, so that adrenalin pumped around her body and not desire.

The key to open the door into the corridor fitted perfectly. She didn't know why she had worried that it wouldn't. Emile was an excellent locksmith.

Once through the door, she crept along the corridor. She unlocked another door ahead of her with the same key. Now she was in a wider passageway. It was dimly lit, so that she had to count the doors that led off it. At the third one she used a key with a piece of wire wrapped around its ornate top; this was for identification purposes, in case she wasn't able to distinguish it in the half-light.

Sweat ran down her forehead and into her eyes. Blinking

it away, she turned the key very slowly. This door would lead her to the hall outside Herr Eberhardt's office.

The click of the lock made her jump. The staircase, which Gertrude had told her led to Herr Eberhardt's quarters, blocked her view of the office door, which she knew was situated at the bottom of the stairs on the other side. Holding her breath, she waited. Nothing happened. Stepping into the hall, she crossed over the parquet flooring. Her overshoes squeaked on the polished surface. Standing suspended, she listened again, but still she hadn't been heard. Taking care to tread on her toes in a movement that lifted her feet, she felt her nerves jangle as she nearly lost her balance.

Tears threatened when she saw the SS guard sitting outside what she knew was Herr Eberhardt's office. His back was to her, his head bowed as if he might be bent over a book, reading. She could see that he was just a young man. The thought of what she had to do sickened her. But there was no other way. Stunning him might not work, for he might come round too soon and raise the alarm. Straightening her back, she steadied her hands as she held them flat against the wall. The feel of the flocked wallpaper gave her a moment's memory of home. Often with Bren she had played hide-and-seek and, in her attempt to remain hidden behind a curtain, she had pressed her body like this against a wall and her fingers had felt the soft, velvety wallpaper. How she longed for those days now. Even though they held pain, they were a million times better than being in the same position waiting to pounce upon a man and take his life – or maybe even lose her own.

Wiping away her tears, she wished for a moment that she had given in to Juste and allowed him to take this assignment, but she'd been worried about his clumsiness. In her training she had been taught to emulate a cat in her movements in such situations, while Juste was more like a bull, charging at things with too much enthusiasm and insufficient stealth.

Taking a deep breath, she pulled her emotions in check, felt for her knife and closed her fingers around its stubby handle. She had to be swift and precise in her actions. Counting herself down, three-two-one, she leapt at the unsuspecting soldier. The blade scrunched into his neck. Blood ran over the fingers she held over his mouth. Pulling her knife out, she heard him groan. *I missed*. Pulling his head back, she sliced his throat. When she let go of him, he slumped forward. The chair scraped on the floor as his weight shifted. The hall echoed with the noise of it. Once more she froze.

After a moment, when no one came and no alarm was raised, she continued with her plan. She had to be quick: there were time limits for her escape. Gertrude had said that the guards often took it in turns to meet outside the kitchen window, where the guard she had just killed would pass them coffee. Thinking of this set a panic inside her, as she had already been delayed in getting to this point, with the window being locked and her fear freezing her at times.

Taking items she would need from her overall pockets – the keys, her Zeiss Ikon camera and her folding kit of penknives – she moved away from the blood and placed them on the bottom step, in readiness to transfer them to the trousers she wore underneath. The camera she would have to clip onto her belt. A moment of irony hit her as she remembered buying the camera during her finishing year in Belgium in 1931. It had been made in Germany. She prayed there would be enough light to enable her to take clear photos, but she had a notebook, just in case.

Her overall clung to her, resisting her attempts to peel it off. Calming herself, she told herself it was always so with these garments. The trick was to get her arms out, and then jig about to loosen it. When she did this, it fell around her ankles. She stepped out of it, and out of her overshoes. Using the cloth she'd brought with her, she wiped the blood off her hands. Leaving all that she didn't need in a pile, she stood still and listened. Along the corridor she could see the steps leading down to the kitchens. This was her escape route. Gertrude had said there was a window that Alice could climb out of, but she must do so the moment she saw the guard go around the corner to the front of the building, then she would have time to sprint to the end of the street before he returned. But this had to be before four a.m., as that was the time the guards would expect their coffee.

With everything now ready, she freed the keys from the pocket of her trousers and opened the office door. Here she took photos of everything in sight, without bothering to check whether or not it was of importance. Taking the papers from the PA's in-tray to the back window helped, as the strong light from the yard would ensure that she got a good shot. Each item she placed on the floor once she had photographed it, turning them back over so that they were in the right order to put back in the tray.

There were no exposed documents or filing cabinets in Herr Eberhardt's office. Not being able to find the safe anywhere, she realized it must be in the only locked cupboard. None of the keys fitted this and so, using her skills, she unpicked the lock and opened it. Her large key slid easily into the safe's iron door. The plans she found inside were marked 'Versanté factory' and were rolled up. Excitement clenched her: *My God, these would be so useful!* Worried about the time she had left, she hurried back into the PA's office to get the plans into the light and searched frantically for something to weight them down and keep them flat. An inkwell and a paperweight did the trick. If only these photos came out well, they would be heaven-sent.

With this done, and although desperate to get out of the office, Alice took the time to make sure nothing looked as though it had been disturbed – if, after finding the guard, the authorities thought someone had had access to everything, they would probably change all their plans for the factory and she would have done this for nothing.

Locking the door, she smeared blood on the handle so that it looked as though it had been tried. She hoped they would believe that, after trying the door handle and not being able to get in, the intruder had escaped.

Stale cooking smells met her as she opened the kitchen door. A huge iron saucepan simmered on the blackened stove. From it came the stench of kitchen cloths soaking. The clock above her told her it was almost four in the morning. A light flickered on the window that she wanted to escape through. It threw a shadow across the floor and lingered longer than she liked. Standing against the wall, she heard the guard shout. Another voice answered him, asking what was wrong. It seemed the guard thought it strange that there were no lights on in the kitchen, and he wondered why their colleague wasn't yet in there making their coffee.

She held her breath and listened to them decide they should check inside the house. *Oh God, no!* Fear gripped her afresh.

Instructions were given by the first voice she'd heard. The others were to use their keys to access the front of the building and check everywhere, as they made their way to the office. They were to avoid the rooms of the nanny, in case they disturbed Herr Eberhardt. The one speaking said that he would stand guard over the back entrance.

Frantically searching for a solution, her eyes rested on the pot on the stove. This was her only hope. Seeing through the window that the guard stood outside the door with his back to it, she watched him draw on his cigarette. She slid open the window, then dodged away from it. The guard squared up in front of it within seconds, his movements jerky, his gun ready to shoot. Grabbing a small saucepan from a row of pans hung on the wall next to the stove, Alice scooped steaming-hot water into it from the simmering pot, stepped nearer the window and, with outstretched arm, threw the hot liquid into his face. His gun discharged into the air.

His screams of pain echoed around her as she climbed through the window. Hardly able to breathe, she jumped down and ran. It seemed that the end of the road was moving further away from her. Voices, shouting and panicked, came to her. Looking back, she saw that lights now shone from every window of the house, illuminating figures with guns looking in her direction. She prayed they couldn't see her in the dimness.

At last she reached the corner of the street and dodged around it. Across from her she could see the narrow lane where she had hidden her bike. Sprinting across the road to the sound of heavy footsteps coming towards her, she made it. Her legs didn't seem to belong to her as she straddled her bike and pedalled away, wobbling at first, but then gaining control and whizzing down the street.

Braking at the end and looking back again, she saw there was no sign of anyone following her, but in the distance the sound of vehicles turned her blood cold. This was still curfew hour. Patrolling cars drove around every now and again. Had they been alerted to a fugitive? What if they turned into this street?

Remembering her escape with François, she opened the gate next to her and pushed her bike into the garden. Scaling the drainpipe got her belly-down on the rooftop. Edging her way along, clinging to the apex of the roof, her progress was slow. Deciding it wasn't worth the effort, as she was getting nowhere, she lay still and waited. Shivers of cold and fear shook her body as night gave way to early dawn. Throughout the hour or so she'd been lying there she'd seen the comings and goings of soldiers – some of them kicking open gates before searching gardens and sheds, others driving past, illuminating the street with their headlights. But now, with their search of this street over, the noise of them had faded into the distance. At last Alice could retrace her steps to her bike and, if challenged, could say that she was cycling to work.

Sticking her camera under the saddle and feeling for the clip to make it secure, she checked her special pass, which would allow her to travel during the last hour of curfew to get to the station on time for the first trains. Well, not the first, because trains moved all night long. Trains with Jew-filled carriages.

Her heart felt heavy thinking about them. She hated this bloody war. She hated the regime that thought it right to imprison people because of their culture, or because they were homosexual, crippled or mentally sick. This thought had her longing for life as it had been – if only she could communicate with Steve . . .

Digging deeper inside herself, she found the strength to distract her thoughts. Riding the streets of a Paris that hadn't yet woken to the day had its merits. Crossing the Avenue d'Héloïse, she came to the Seine. Its waters gave a peaceful lapping sound. Ducks slept with their heads beneath their wings, whilst a busy water mole slipped in and out of the river from the bank below her. Looking to her left, she could see the top of the Eiffel Tower gracing the skyline – a landmark that symbolized all she was working towards. A liberated France: the gateway to enable the Allied troops to push the invaders back and defeat them. It had to happen – it had to.

One week later Alice still couldn't lift her spirits. It didn't seem as if any progress was being made in the war, and her experience in Herr Eberhardt's headquarters had laid her low.

'Why didn't you let me do it?' Juste tried to look angry with her, but his voice softened, as did his stance when he realized her distress. 'Oh, Alice . . . I mean, Madeline. Look, don't – don't cry.'

'It's the killing. I thought I could do it. You see, when I trained I was a cold person. I won't go into it, but my life had closed me. Then someone opened me up, just before I came here. And now it feels as if all these emotions were released. I feel everything more strongly now. I keep thinking of that young man, and the other one – my first. They had their whole life in front of them . . .'

'Yes, *ma chérie*, they did, but so do millions of others. Think of all the young Jewesses holed up in the camps. Will they survive all of this? What atrocities are happening to them? Think of all your own countrymen, who were happily going about their lives – working, seeing their girlfriends or wives and planning a future – and now thousands of their corpses are rotting on the beaches and on the battlefields. What we do, we do because we want freedom, and we do it for them *and* for us. We want to lead normal lives again.'

'I know. Oh God, I need a break, so much has happened.'

'Maybe you should go to church, talk to a priest. We will

go together, tonight. Get some sleep. Then, as we aren't destroying the factory for a couple of weeks, why don't you request some time away? You could go and stay with Mama.'

Alice said she would try going to church, though she wasn't sure it would make her feel any better. And she would ask for a few days' break, but she knew in her heart of hearts that what she needed was for all this to be over, and to be with Steve. She wanted to be with him more than anything in the whole world. Or even just receive a message from him. But she knew that was impossible, for agents were forbidden to contact one another unless they were working together. She didn't even know exactly where he was – somewhere in Brittany, but that was all.

Alice had begun to feel slightly less weary as she got ready to go to the church service. It had helped to focus on something other than her longings, and the service itself lifted her spirits. Getting back to her flat just before curfew, she and Juste shared a weak cup of coffee. The one packet of coffee beans that she'd been able to buy six weeks ago had only two beans left and she hadn't seen any in the shops for a long time. Supplies of everything were getting short, and people were going hungry. The gaunt and haunted looks on the faces of people in the streets tore at her heart. She had prayed fervently when the priest had offered up a blessing for all those working to save France, and the world, from the evil grip that held it, and something in her had lightened and a new determination had entered her.

'Juste, thank you for that. I do feel better. So much so that I won't ask for that leave. We have to press on – and soon – with destroying the factory.'

'You are right. And I am glad you feel better. We do need

201

to act quickly. Those papers you photographed were mostly useless: information about placements for different ranks, pay enquiries, new rules for men stationed in France, that kind of thing. But two documents will help, and make what you went through worthwhile. One is the set of plans for the factory – they are vital, and Breshna is already studying them with Agard. You haven't met Agard yet; he is another explosives expert. He is old now, but his knowledge in that field is extremely important, and he can advise us on where to place our charges. Then there is a document that sets out Herr Dansk's request: he is asking for his guards to be doubled and for extra security towers to be built. So we have to strike before this happens.'

'I know. Have we layout plans for the factory yet? I mean, the plans I got will be too detailed for us to follow. They sound perfect for what Breshna and your new man need to do, but to find our way around the factory we will need a layman's copy.'

'Only a rough drawing done by François's cousin, but using the two documents Breshna will come up with an accurate, easy-to-read layout. But there is bad news. The men and women working there have been told there will be round-the-clock shifts at the factory, starting at the end of next week!'

'Oh God, no! No wonder Dansk needed more security. Can we be ready before then?'

'I don't think that's possible. The day of the drop is still a week away, the second or third of July.'

'We need to get the radio from Madame Chappelle's and install it where it will be safe. We cannot go back there. As soon as we are somewhere else I will send a message at once, to request that the drop is sooner.'

'We must inform the British now. But you are not to worry

about the radio. I forgot to tell you: when we saw what happened outside, when you killed the officer, I ordered that the radio be taken with us as we made our escape. I was afraid a search might be made of Madame Chappelle's home. We are looking for a new place to install it. What about using your emergency radio?'

This surprised and worried her. 'Juste, I haven't got a radio.'

'No? But all agents are equipped with them, are they not? I thought . . .'

'Well . . .' So, he had assumed. What to do now? Alice wasn't sure if she should reveal that she had one. An agent's secret radio was meant to get them out of bother if they found themselves compromised. That could be by anyone – even those they trusted – and so it wasn't healthy that others knew she had such a device to help her if she needed it. But then this was an emergency.

'All right. But what if the frequency is picked up? We don't know if they scan the area.'

'They have taken to scanning all areas. We have to take the chance. Make it very quick and to the point, so that you can come off-air within seconds. I will go to your kitchenette to make us another wishy-washy coffee, as you English call what we have to drink these days, while you do what you have to. I have a view of the street from there and can warn you if I see any patrolling vehicles.'

The assembling of the radio didn't take her long. It was another art Alice had excelled at in training. Once ready, she tuned in. 'London. Ajax needs help – the dandelions are dying. Over.'

Switching it off and taking the radio apart, she stowed it away in a hollow doorstop. An ingenious creation, it had folded flat to let her bring it with her, but assembled into a dog shape. Inside she could fit all the components of her radio.

She dared not wait for confirmation that her coded message had been received – a message designed to convey urgency, and just one of many she had been given to use in different circumstances. This one would let HQ know that the planned mission needed to take place sooner. Now all she could do was hope. In the morning she would tune into Radio Londres and pray that she received a message back. The urgent nature of her message would ensure that any answer would come as soon as HQ could arrange it, even if it was just to tell her it had been received and they were dealing with it.

'All done?' Juste asked from the other side of the door. On her calling out that it was, he entered, 'Good. No sign of anything in the street. Here, drink your coffee.'

'Ugh! Coffee? More like pigswill. You've used that liquid stuff – I hate it.'

'Cheek! I am renowned for my chicory-essence brew.'

They laughed at this and it lightened the tension inside her. 'Have you heard from Gertrude? I'm worried about her, Juste. I think she is in deeper than she should be with Herr Eberhardt. I didn't tell you, but I have been worrying all week about the implications. When I got onto her balcony, the window she was meant to leave open was locked.'

'Gertrude is fine. You must not worry. And, please, never express these worries to the others. One or two of them are mumbling about her, and I am more afraid about that than about Gertrude's loyalty.'

'Oh, I didn't mean Gertrude had done it deliberately. But if Eberhardt suspects and checks things, like the security of her rooms when he is there . . . I don't know. But I would never suspect Gertrude. Oh God, why? Why would the others question her loyalty?'

'For the same reason you are worried. They can see that she has fallen in love – it is obvious – and that is a concern, especially if choices have to be made. Anyway, she contacted me and was mortified about the window being locked. But she feels she is totally above suspicion by Eberhardt, which is good. He hasn't even questioned her about the death of his guard, and she has heard nothing that indicates they think anything in his office was disturbed. They think the intruder broke in through the kitchen, and they have now had all the windows barred. It seems she did not have to lure Herr Eberhardt to her, for he came to her, and before she was ready for him, which is why he doesn't suspect her, as he might have done if she had enticed him away from his office. Gertrude probably told you that the reason she needed him with her was that he often went back to his office to work after dinner?'

'Yes, that is why she came up with the plan of me doing the job, so that she could keep him out of the way. Poor Gertrude. I feel so bad for her. I am glad in a way that she is in love, as it means she is not prostituting herself for the cause. But it is a dangerous situation. And now, if you say the others are questioning her loyalty because of her feelings, I am even more worried.'

'Yes, we must stem it, by letting them know the good work she is doing.'

'I still cannot get over Gertrude being my sister. But I know what I feel for her is a sisterly love, and it hurts to think of her in danger. You know, my mother must have known that your mother was pregnant. She had her sources: General Westlin, for one. She never told me; she never even hinted . . . Sometimes I hate my mother.'

'Don't. Hate is a destructive emotion. Love her for her failings. Often these are done with the best of intentions. But who is this General Westlin?'

'Oh, someone who was in love with my mother when it all happened, and who is now a big nob at the Foreign Office. Has your mother never spoken of him?'

'Westlin – *mai oui*. The one who really did the deed that your father was accused of?'

'Yes, that is him. Tell me, Juste, did your mother know my mother was pregnant?'

'No. I have asked her, and she said she had no idea. In fact it hurt her to find out. I found her crying, after you and she had spoken. She told me she was very happy to know you, as you are another part of Ralph, but that she felt betrayed in some way. "Her Ralph", as she calls him, had always said there were no further relations between him and his wife, and that after the war he would divorce and marry my mother.'

'Oh, I don't know what to say. I mean, he must have slept with my mother – is there nothing in the memoirs? Oh God, I couldn't be Westlin's child, could I! No, that is impossible. One of my cousins, my father's brother's child, is the spitting image of me, and I look so like my paternal grandmother did at my age. And Gertrude: look how alike we are.'

'I haven't read all of the memoirs, but my mother has, so your father must have left out how you came to be conceived, but then he would . . .'

'Yes.' Somehow this tainted the new way in which she had begun to think of her father. She already knew he was capable of deceit, otherwise he would not have taken a mistress; but to deceive that mistress in turn made her wonder what else he had been capable of.

15

Alice

HER FATHER'S PASSION, A DOOMED MISSION

Unable to sleep once Juste had left, Alice pulled her father's memoirs from under the bed and settled down to read more about him. Though she hadn't delved far into his life, her sympathy had begun to lie more with him than with her mother. But now, though nothing she read redeemed her mother, doubts about her father's integrity began to take root. Yes, she could understand a man telling a lie to a mistress he didn't care about, but from what she'd heard, her father was supposed to be deeply in love with Elsbeth. Her mother's manipulative ways came to mind. If Louise had known about Ralph having a mistress, she would have been capable of luring him to her bed, even though she hated what occurred there when she did. *And so I would have come into being through a loveless union.*

It began to look to Alice as if the beginnings of her mother's illness were in place long before she gave birth to her. This thought comforted her, but she needed to read further to find out more:

Elsbeth and Ralph

10th July 1911: I awoke this morning with a new feeling taking root in me. Is it possible for a man to love two women?

I am obsessed with my mistress. At last I know the glorious pleasure I can expect from a loving, giving woman – my Elsbeth. Yes, she is a prostitute, but she is not meant to be. It is not of her doing, as I will explain later.

I must confess it embarrassed me today to be introduced by a cheery call from one of the other girls inhabiting the brothel: 'Look who's here, Elsbeth. It's lover boy.'

This had me blushing like a schoolboy discovered playing in his trousers, though it was a fitting description, as I have visited Elsbeth seven times in as many days. She fascinates me, and makes me feel as I never thought I would ever feel – like a man, a lover, someone of worth. I had thought myself useless in that department, unable to woo a woman; and this was done to me by Louise, whom I loved beyond measure, but how quickly that had died with her rejection. Louise has nothing but the beauty of her face and body, and she is empty. Empty of love, and empty of feeling for anyone but herself.

Elsbeth is a German immigrant of culture. Her paintings are superb and she has a beauty of a different kind from Louise. Large-boned and tall, like me, she gives the appearance of having been sculpted out of the finest porcelain. Her eyes are deep blue and searching, her hair is blonde, thick and lustrous and reaches to her shoulders in waves that start on her forehead. Her lashes are dark and long. Her body is slim and yet like that of a goddess, strong and honed; not pink and soft like Louise's. And then there is the Elsbeth inside all this: passionate, loving, talented, and yet, vulnerable.

Her father brought her over from Germany just eight months ago, afraid of the unrest there, and suffering because of the financial climate. They at first worked in a shoe factory. Elsbeth cried when she told me of the conditions they endured: long hours on their feet, no breaks for food, not even toilet breaks were allowed. The factory was cold and damp and the pay pitiful. Then one day her father brought a man to her and told Elsbeth she must go with him; that he had better prospects for her, and so she landed up in a brothel. Her father hasn't been seen since.

Always pleased to see me, Elsbeth dismissed the other girl and swanned into my arms the moment the door had closed on us. Her words of love and her pleasure at seeing me played like a song in my ears. Stammering, I tried to tell her that I hadn't come to pleasure myself with her, though I would pay her. I had come just to be with her, as being apart from her was becoming unbearable.

She told me that she knew. She understood because she felt the same way. And then she uttered those immortal words, 'I love you.'

That was a magical moment, but was soon marred by my discoveries. When I asked her if we could walk out for a while together, she became afraid, saying that she had never been outside since arriving at the brothel and didn't think it was allowed.

To me this is inhumane. At that moment I vowed to get her out, saying that I would speak to the owner of the brothel. But a deep fear inside her caused Elsbeth to shy away from me. She begged me to help her to get out, without anyone knowing when she went out or where she went. Otherwise, if she was found and brought back, she would be whipped.

It seemed our only chance was to plan her escape and hide her away. But where? I could not consider anywhere near my home or close to my barracks, as she might be seen by those who use this place. Explaining this to her uncovered a shocking revelation. At the mention of the possibility of Philippe seeing her, when he is home from France, if she was hidden near my home, she told me that Philippe is hated by the girls at the brothel, that he is cruel and enjoys beating them, sometimes hurting them badly. She said he had asked for her recently, but she had refused, telling her pimp that they would lose me – a valued and regular customer – for the sake of letting an occasional customer have his own way.

I was appalled. And as I write this I can feel the bile rising in me with my anger. I vowed to Elsbeth that I would cut Philippe out of my life. And see to it that his allowance is stopped!

She counselled me as to the foolishness of this idea, as we do not need an enemy – especially Philippe, who is a particular friend of her pimp, a fact that I am disgusted to hear of.

An idea occurred to me then. I have a trusted friend, a fellow officer called Westlin. He will help us; he has a lot of connections and he owns properties in the streets around where he lives. Good properties. I am sure he will rent one to me for Elsbeth to live in. And he has never been to the brothel, so will not know of this one and its rules. He is a man of honour and of the Church – he is very religious. Not that I am not, but I have lapsed some of late. I am ashamed about this, and yet elated at the same time, as my sin is my greatest love and the source of my happiness.

Somehow nothing I am doing feels wrong. I don't even consider myself to be being unfaithful to my wife, as I have ceased trying to have a relationship with her. She seems a lot happier for it. It is funny, but we get along well in all other ways now, just as we did at the beginning when we first met. It is a pity really. But I am accepting of it.

It does seem as if a solution to our problems may be found. And Elsbeth and I found ourselves making love, despite my promise to myself that I would visit and not take anything from her. But she is my nectar, and I cannot deny myself her.

Alice felt she was gaining a deeper understanding of her father with every detail she read. In his writings she could feel his love for Elsbeth, and how it troubled him that Mother was so frigid. But in the end this was a journal – an intimate friend of her father's. In it he had put some of his deepest thoughts. She didn't want to read all the details: what he and Elsbeth did together, how her father found a place for Elsbeth and so on . . . Besides, what she had read so far had told her that Westlin knew everything, and that her father had put store by him. From that it was safe to assume that Westlin, under the guise of being a good religious man, had continued his friend-ship with them, providing alibis even. *Oh, Father, how trusting we are of our friends, but then who can we trust, if not them?*

Reading on in this fashion, a snippet here and there, Alice pieced together what had happened. Her father and Elsbeth had planned to be together for eternity, and had even dreamed of getting married one day, if it ever became possible for Ralph to do so and keep a certain correctness towards her mother. Louise seemed to be satisfied with her life, but was innocent of her husband's second life until she found out about his affair. What followed were tears, tantrums and what Alice's father described as a beautiful woman turning into a malicious cat. He tried to appease her, tried to make her see that it was the only way the marriage could work, as he could not live a celibate existence or take what she gave so grudgingly. The former was impossible for him, the latter made him feel dirty and guilty.

Then came the war . . .

Not up to reading any further at the moment, Alice wrapped the ribbon back around the journals and lay back. Confusion made her restless, and though she could empathize with all the emotions her father was feeling about how difficult her mother was, she also felt a moment of sympathy for her mother. But then her thoughts turned to Westlin. Did Father know that Westlin had told Mother? Did Mother know how Westlin felt about her? And what about her not being with child? Didn't Louise's own mother – the maternal grandmother Alice had never known – wonder about her daughter not having children? Still, maybe Mother couldn't have them easily, as her father had talked about them lying together a few times before he met Elsbeth.

Alice had been concerned that she herself could be pregnant. Though very glad it had turned out not to be the case, she had worried for a time, as she and Steve hadn't taken care that second time, or any time after that. But it hadn't happened. Maybe it didn't always happen. Funny, she'd never thought about that; she'd always thought that if you went with a man, you had a baby.

It seemed everything she did and thought brought Steve to mind and awoke longings inside her. Now her night would be further disturbed. There was a lot to do and she needed her sleep, but telling herself this didn't help or stop her thinking about Steve. Without warning, the tears came. She let them flow. Maybe they would release this agonizing knot of pain and fear that she held inside her, though she wondered if anything ever could.

'Here are the personal messages for today.'

Feeling tired, Alice found that her hand shook as she sat the next day, pencil ready, listening to the radio and hoping. She, Juste and François were in a shed at the back of a house they had not used before. Juste had only been told this morning that somewhere new had been found. He had informed Alice how to get there and had brought the radio with him in readiness.

The house belonged to a cousin of one of the group and had been derelict since before the war, when his grandmother had died. The family had never been able to afford to repair its roof, which leaked, and had tried to sell it as it was, but the war had stopped those plans. Very few houses changed hands now. Alice hoped this could be a more permanent hideout, as it stood on the outskirts of Paris and had no neighbours to see or report on their comings and goings, as they believed had happened at Madame Chappelle's.

As before, the others left the shed, so as not to hear her message. Swallowing, she waited. The radio crackled. *Please, please don't lose the signal now.* Then it came. Scribbling it down word for word, she was surprised by how long it was. After switching the radio off she went into the kitchen to decipher the message.

The heat of the kitchen oppressed her. Somehow they had managed to light the old gas cooker and had the oven open for warmth. Steam from a kettle on the hob misted the windows. Juste and François stood near her. François had gathered up the radio and taken it down to the cellar, where they had earlier dug up a slab and made a hole big enough for it to fit into. Neither man spoke. Juste crossed over and opened the door. The crisp morning air still had a cold bite, but she welcomed it. Putting her pencil down, she let her head flop forward.

'*Ma chérie*, what is the matter? Are you ill? Is it the message? Did it come through? But no! You are crying, are you not?'

'No, it is the cold coming through the door making my eyes run. Leave it – don't close it, I like the fresh air. Yes, the message did come through. I can hardly believe how quickly they have sorted everything. It told me that the drop is tonight, as the weather forecast is good. It also said that another agent is to join us and help us.' She wouldn't tell him it was Steve, the love of her life. *Steve will be on the plane, I can't believe it* . . . The message had simply said, 'Henderson will join you, code name Giles'.

'We need to prepare the landing strip as they have said the plane has to come in. It cannot drop the explosives and weapons from the air.' *At least my darling won't have to face his worst fear of parachuting in.*

'Is it a man? Do you know him? Why are we being sent another agent? Does this agent have skills that we don't have?'

'I do know him. He is known as Giles. And yes, he has skills.' *More than I dare think about at this moment* . . . 'He is a lawyer, like François, and not only has experience in everything we agents are taught, but he designed many of these things. He is exceptional at planning and designing. There may be something we have missed, or haven't seen as important. If so, he will know how to get round it. HQ must think I will need him.' *Though if only they knew how much I need him, they would be sending someone else!* The thought cheered her that HQ didn't know. She and Steve had not shown their love for each other until the night before they parted, and no one had discovered them. Liaisons between agents were highly dangerous, and left each agent even more vulnerable.

'Aah, you are smiling again. Good. Is there something about this man that makes you smile?'

'No . . . I – I didn't mean to.' Juste's expression made her laugh. 'Well, stop being nosy. What you don't know, you can't tell . . . Oh, I didn't mean that. It's an old English saying – something mothers say to their children.'

'I know. Stop worrying. You are like that other old saying of your country: a cat on a hot tin hat. What? What is it that makes you laugh like that?'

'It's "roof", not "hat"! Sorry. Happiness – just happiness.'

'Who's happy, and why? And what is it that anyone has to be happy about?'

'Gerard! I haven't seen you in weeks.'

'That is because you don't smoke. I only see smokers.'

This had her giggling even more. Juste and François, and now Gerard, looked at her as if she had gone mad. Perhaps she had. *Mad as a hatter on a tin hat, with a cat on it smoking a cigarette . . .*

Her sides ached before she got herself under control. It was the sight of François coming for her with his hand raised that did it. Taking a deep breath she said, 'I'm sorry, I'm all right. Not hysterical, I promise. Just very happy that my friend is coming, and laughing at the "lost in translation" bits. I'll be serious now.'

Blowing her nose with a sound like a trumpet nearly set her off again, but she swallowed hard and then gave them the details of the message, except for Steve's real name, before setting fire to her scribblings by throwing the paper into the empty grate to burn.

Getting the runway ready didn't take long. The men were all practised at clearing it of debris and setting the torches. All was ready, but then they had to abort the drop, as Gerard, their lookout, sent a runner to tell them a convoy of Germans was headed their way.

The drone of the plane in the distance made Alice tense every part of her. Grabbing her field phone, she tried again to make contact with the pilot: 'Abort. Abort.' But still it came nearer.

François extinguished the last of the torches.

God! Please let the darkness make them turn around!

'We have to go. The Germans cannot be more than five kilometres away. Gerard said they have passed his lookout. Come, Madeline, come.'

'No, Juste. I have to find a way of turning the aircraft round. Help me to gather the torches. We will light a message on the ground. They are nearly above us – they will see it.'

'But, *ma chérie*, that will take too long. And what will we write?'

'We can do it. "SOS" will be enough. Help me, Juste . . . François, help me.' Racing away from them, she grabbed the nearest torches from the ground. Looking back into the darkness she couldn't see the others – they must have retreated to the trees. *Well, I will do it on my own, if I have to.*

Taking the torches into the widest part of the clearing, she jumped as two figures joined her.

'How many do we need?'

'Nine for each letter will do. Hurry!'

'I have nine.' Handing them to her, François said, 'You stay here and begin to place them.'

The noise of the aircraft descending made her body sweat with fear. She put the last one in place and whispered, 'Have you all got a torch?' On their '*Oui*', she lit the first one. 'Right, light yours from mine, and run round lighting the others. Hurry!'

With the last torch lit and spelling out the distress message, they ran, each in a different direction, taking their own planned escape route.

Alice ran towards the river. Once there, she kept to the edge of the rippling water, ready to dive in and stay under, with just a pipe to give her air, if the need arose. But she hoped against hope to make it to the little boat – her emergency transport, hidden in the bushes. If she made it, she dare not start the engine, but she was a strong rower and could slip away under cover of the weeping willows.

When she was almost at the boat she stopped. The sound of the aircraft swerving back into the sky gave her a great feeling of relief, but it vied with a deep sadness. *I was so near to Steve and yet so far. And what of the aborted mission?* A sudden noise took her mind from this thought and struck her with fear. *Flak . . . No! Climb, climb – get out of their range, please!*

Voices coming towards her made her crouch down. Her eyes couldn't penetrate the darkness. Were the Germans on the bank? On the road? Stepping back, she fell. Unable to stop sliding down the bank, she clamped her teeth together to stop herself calling out. She landed with a bump and bit her tongue, tasting blood. Not knowing where she was, she lay still. A darkness more intense than that on the bank of the river enclosed her. This must mean she had cover. The voices became clearer. They were just above her now and belonged to two men. Her hand touched the gun on her belt.

But the men didn't stop walking. They hadn't seen her. A light showed through some brambles above her, then swung away again. From what she could work out, one man had said to the other, 'The bastards have got away!' The other one replied, 'That will mean we will be out here all night. They won't let us give up. They know the dissidents who were trying to help the plane land will be hiding somewhere. But they will have to come out sometime, so let us hope it is sooner rather than later.'

As their voices faded, Alice relaxed a little. Now she knew for sure that the aircraft was safe! The breath she'd held released itself with this knowledge. But at a cry of 'Halt!' fresh fear clutched at her chest.

The voice that answered stopped her heart. '*Es ist Kamerad, nicht Feind.*'

Steve – telling them he was a comrade, not an enemy! He must have parachuted in . . . *Christ, what do I do?* Holding everything tensed and still, she listened, interpreting their German as best she could, as one of the men asked Steve, 'Why are you here?'

'I have come to find you, for we have apprehended the dissidents. We need a shooting party.'

'Keep your hands up. I do not recognize you.'

Oh God! Clutching at the grass, Alice pulled herself up. Brambles ripped her face, but she didn't care.

'Show us your papers.'

Now she could see the three men, lit by strong torches. Steve hesitated. Alice unclipped her gun from her belt. Steve's knife glinted in the torchlight and there was a split-second flash before he lunged forward. Death came in an instant to his victim. Shock held his comrade a moment too long. Her bullet took him into the river.

Shouting came from all directions. Steve answered, his German accented with a Berlin slant. 'False alarm – a rabbit. I'll bring it to the car, we can have it for supper.' Someone laughed. Another German shouted, 'If we get supper tonight. We need to catch the bastard dissidents first.' And a third voice, 'We will. Where can they go? We have the roads blocked – there is no exit.' Then another, 'There is the river. They could try to escape that way. We need strong lighting to scan it. Turn the trucks towards it.'

While this had been going on, Steve held her. His lips found her brow, then her cheek. Alice's body shivered with shock. Hateful, terrifying shock at what had just happened, mixed with wonderful, unbelievable shock at having Steve here, when she thought he'd returned to England.

Without uttering a word, Steve pulled out a roll of cloth from his jacket. Placing her hand on it, she felt the pipe that was used to breathe underwater. Taking her cue from this, she took out of the long pocket of her trousers her own pipe, curved like a walking stick and with a mouthpiece. Holding hands, they waded into the water. Just before she went under, she heard a voice ask, 'What was that? Listen!'

The cold iced the blood in her veins. Opening her eyes made them sting, and was futile as she couldn't see anything. Keeping her breathing steady, she clung to Steve's hand. His strength was enough for both of them. On and on they swam, staying close, using one arm only, with leg movements to propel them forward. She prayed they were going in the direction of the other side of the river, but knew they couldn't make it like this. At some point they would have to lift their heads and swim in earnest, or they would die of hyperthermia.

On the other side of the river lay the outskirts of Paris, about ten miles from François's farmhouse, where once before she'd taken refuge after that dreadful incident at Madame Chappelle's, which had been the scene of her first killing. The farmhouse was now their rendezvous point, it had been prepared by the Resistance workers who had built dugouts for storage and had made use of the imitation logs and tree trunks to store their weapons. So far it had proved a perfect hideout.

As long as they turned towards Paris they would come across it. She prayed that Juste and François would get there safely. They were crossing fields and had several safe houses on the way. They had gone on foot, abandoning the van they had all driven in. *Please let us all survive!* As she thought this she wondered who had betrayed them: *Someone must have . . .*

A squeeze of her hand told her that Steve intended to do something. He let go of her. Panic gripped her. Forcing herself to remain calm, she waited. She felt his hand grasp hers again and pull her to the surface. Taking the pipe from her mouth, she gasped for air. His voice, weak with cold, came to her. 'We are in the middle of the river – look how far away their lights are. Come on, darling, swim. Swim as fast as you can, for we need to get our circulation going.'

'I – I can't . . .'

She didn't know where he found the strength, but he turned her body over and, with his arms under hers, swam, pulling her along. Hearing his breath labouring instilled a strength in her that she didn't know she had. 'I'm all right, I can do it.' With this she turned over and began to swim.

They lay on the embankment, shivering and crying. After a moment Steve coughed – a watery-sounding cough that made Alice stand up and turn him over. Vomit projected from his mouth. When the bout passed she held him. 'We have to move. We will die if we don't. Look, there's a light shining from a window just along the towpath.'

They crawled at first, moving closer to the light. But as they got nearer they stood. The smell of wood-smoke tinged her nostrils. With it came the realization that this was François's farmhouse, as she saw the building come into view. They must have drifted further along the river than they had thought. Wanting to check that she was right, she looked behind her. She could see the same view she had seen when she'd looked back from the boat when François had taken her to it. The river, with the lights of Paris sparkling on its distant surface, appeared like a moving ribbon with jewels sewn on the end; and the huge willow tree, just a few hundred yards along the towpath, bent as if in homage towards the water. *Please, God, let François and Juste have made it here and be safe . . . Please, God.*

16
Lil

THE TRIAL

Worry had worn Lil down over the last few weeks. Unable to eat or sleep properly, she had lost weight, and tiredness dogged her. And now that the day had come, her anxiety increased as she wondered whether it would be Doomsday or a day of rejoicing. But, if nothing else, she would get to see Gillian at last.

Calling in at Ruby's house increased the heavy feeling inside her. Ruby's body now showed signs of being ravished by cancer. The burn marks that the radium treatment had left on her neck looked vivid and painful. Her face had sunk till her skin looked stretched over her cheeks. She looked as if she'd already lost the battle. And, Lil thought, if Ruby hadn't got the sink to lean on, she'd fall over.

Lil stood by the table in the kitchen, wanting to go over to Ruby and hold her, but the lass looked as if a hug would break her in two. 'Well, today is the day, Ruby. Are you up to coming to the trial?'

'Yes, I'm ready. We have to face it. But I 'ope and pray

that they're going to do as that sergeant said should 'appen and throw out the case, or pass a verdict of self-defence.'

'I think the last verdict is more likely, as they have to have a reason for the killings. They can't simply act as if nothing happened, though I'm sure it'll be all reet. How was Gillian when you saw her yesterday?'

'The same. Like someone who isn't 'ere. 'Er eyes just stare out into space and she 'ardly speaks. She goes through the motions of the routine of the place, but more like one of them toys that you wind up and set in motion. I 'ate to see 'er in that mental institution.'

'I know, I can't give a thought to it. And the worst thing is them not allowing me to see her, cos I'm the only witness. Ruby, I know I've told you before, but I – I tried. I did. I told her I would take the blame, but she wouldn't let go of the knife, and she just screamed and screamed when the police came. I said that she'd taken the knife off me, but they weren't having it.'

'Lil, love, you can't keep going on about it. Gillian doesn't 'old you responsible – she never has.'

'Aye, well, she's done well to come to terms with it all.'

'I don't think she has, not really. And neither have you, if you told the truth. How you've kept going, I'll never know, Lil, love.'

'I had to. If you could see them lads I attend to every day, you'd know why. They need me. So there was no choice for me, once me physical wounds had healed. I told them all I'd been taken down with a bug. None of them questioned it – neither did the staff. Though Arthur looked a bit sheepish and has had his tail trimmed. I reckon he knows what went on.'

'Aye, well, let's see how he reacts to being arrested, cos

they should take him in, once you tell them that bit. And you should tell on him, Lil; you've got to, love.'

'I know, lass. And I intend to. He's of the kind that would betray you for a few pounds. And them sort need locking up. It was about me this time, but it could have been a German that wanted info, and for the reet money Arthur would give them what he could.'

'I'm glad you've come to see it that way. The coppers have said all along that they don't understand how, even if the men knew you, they knew where to find you. And you should tell about your bleedin' Alfie's part in it as well.'

'Naw, I . . .'

'You 'ave to, Lil, please. Everything should come out. The story you gave of them louts fancying you, and seeking you out for a lark, doesn't sound possible. Them prosecuting blokes will make a case that you're a liar, and then none of your evidence will sound credible. You should tell that defence lawyer before you are called. Your man putting them blokes up to it all is vital evidence, and gives a reason for everything happening.'

'Eeh, Ruby, you're reet. I know that now, lass. By, I still could weep me heart out over it, but that would do no good. I emptied meself of tears when they took Gillian to that hospital and she couldn't speak. And once that were done, I've never cried a tear since.'

'I've cried every night over it all, and not just over that. Look at me boys, Lil. Bless their cotton socks, they're to be left without a mum. I know me man will take good care of them, as will his mam – she's a good person; and Joe's pulled up his socks lately. I think I had it all wrong when I thought he were having a bit on the side. He's been a good bloke to me, and they've given him a lot of time off – compassionate leave, they call it. But oh, Lil, I just don't know 'ow to face it all.'

A lump came into Lil's throat. She could see that Ruby's inner light had gone out and she wondered if it would ever come back on. And she herself felt the burden of that. She feared for what would happen. Would the law really let Gillian off with a double killing? Mind, it was in self-defence and to save them both, so that should go a long way. And what of Ruby and her boys? At least she'd had them home with her for the last few weeks, that was something. 'Oh, Ruby, love, I don't know how you face it all. Are you thinking there's no hope for you? Won't the treatment make a difference?'

'I've stopped having it. It were making things worse. I can't eat, nor sleep, nor nuffin'.' I reckon as they're bleedin' experimenting on me, that's all. No, Lil, I have to face it and make me preparations.' At this she slumped down on a chair.

'Look, love, if you're not up to it Gillian will understand.'

'I'm coming, Lil. I 'ave to be there for me little skin-and-blister; she'd look for me, and not seeing me would undo her. She'd think me dead or summat. Oh God, Lil, she will get off, won't she? I couldn't bear it if they committed her to that place or, worse, took her to prison.'

She hadn't expected this from Ruby. No matter what, Ruby had remained positive. 'She won't go to prison, I'm sure of it. But you must prepare yourself, love, just in case.'

'I will. I'll cope. I just . . . Well, look, if they say she's free of all this later today, I'll die happy. I want her with me, to help me through this. She can, you know. If she gets off I think it will make her better in her mind. I need her, Lil.'

Hearing Ruby say this made Lil's worries about both Ruby and Gillian increase. What if Gillian wasn't let off? It felt that, whatever happened, there wouldn't be a happy ending and nothing could make things right for them. They still had a lot to face.

It was good to see some clearing up going on outside as, with Ruby leaning heavily on Lil, they walked to the police station, which doubled up as the local court. But Ruby's words had made Lil think maybe they could never clear up the deep harm done to everyone. 'It's like everything's broken, Lil. Our lives, the place we live, our families – everything.'

'Aye, well it is, lass. Nothing will ever be the same again. But at least the bombing has stopped and we can sleep peaceful in our beds, eh?'

'I suppose.'

The building in front of them was grey and forbidding, and one half of it was in ruins. Here and there men worked on shifting rubble and repairing walls. Huge steel supports had been fixed to strengthen the half that still stood proudly. A *Police Station and Law Courts* sign in stonework still resided above the main front doors, and there was a stone ribbon with something in Latin inscribed on it underneath.

Climbing the ten steps to the huge wooden door took the stuffing out of Ruby. Panting for breath, she held onto the ornate railing. 'Take a mo, lass. We're early. And don't be afraid. It'll be sorted. It has to be. Gillian's not a criminal. She's not . . .' Lil wanted to apologize again for bringing all of this down on Ruby and Gillian, but she knew she'd made Ruby weary by taking the blame, when neither of them held her responsible.

The coldness of the desk clerk who signed them in and checked their particulars matched the chill of the reception area with its black-and-white tiled floor, dark-green half-tiled walls and stark wooden benches. Sitting on one of these, they stayed close to one another, but didn't speak. Lil could feel Ruby's sense of foreboding. It matched her own.

A man approached them, his robes flowing behind him. His wig sat on his huge, curly hair as though it was a topping on a blancmange. Lil wanted to giggle at the sight of him, but this desire was squashed as he asked, 'Mrs Moisley?'

'Aye, that's me, sir.'

'I am the defence lawyer assigned to the case of Gillian Smith versus the Crown. Will you come this way, so that I can run through a few things with you?'

The court hushed as Gillian appeared through a side door. Handcuffed to a policewoman, she looked a pitiful sight. Lil's heart felt as though it was being torn from her. *Oh God, it's unbearable. Gillian, my precious.* She didn't take her eyes off the tiny frame. Gillian was so thin that she looked like an old woman, and it was hard to believe she had once been the robust, full-of-life young girl she'd known only a few months before. She willed Gillian to look over at her. When she did so, tears plopped onto Gillian's cheek, from eyes that were red-raw and matted with green gunge. Her nose looked just as sore, and she had cracked and weeping scabs around her mouth. Lil had to suppress a gasp of horror. How could they have allowed this deterioration? Ruby had said that Gillian was well cared for! Looking at Ruby, she saw that nothing about Gillian's appearance shocked her. Had she become immune to others' suffering? Surely not that of her own sister?

There was no time to take this up with Ruby, as banging on a desk at the front of the room grabbed everyone's attention. 'All stand!'

The judge entered and signalled that they should sit, as he did. He had a kindly face, Lil thought, and this gave her hope.

Voices droned on for a while: the jury was sworn in and given instructions, the prosecution was invited to state its case and read the formal charge. This brought Lil up short. She hadn't ever thought of Gillian being charged, but then, she realized, she must have been charged, to be here. What were the police thinking? God, the charges sounded so damning: 'You are charged with the murder of Jimmy Gibbins and Brian Foxley on the fifth of April 1941. How do you plead?'

'Not guilty.'

Gillian's words sounded rasping, as if her throat was very dry.

Lil kept her eyes on her, hoping to convey that all was not lost. There was a moment when the big-haired lawyer stood up and said that Gillian would like to submit a plea of killing in self-defence. The judge said he would consider this when he had heard the case.

The case started with a doctor giving the cause of death. A little man, he had an air of being full of his own importance. He went on and on, as if he wanted to hold the stage for as long as he could. In the end what he said amounted to the men having been killed by stabbing. The word brought the scene vividly to life in Lil's mind. She would never forget it.

After this the lawyer defending Gillian turned to Lil and gave her the signal that she must leave the courtroom for a time. He'd allowed her into the public gallery up to this point, but had made her promise that she would leave when he indicated to her, as his chief witness could not be allowed to listen to all the evidence being presented. As she rose, she looked at the jury. They sat on a wooden stage-like structure, with a high partition allowing only their heads to show. Many of them looked to be what she'd call 'chapel-goers': women who felt it their duty to preach their own moral goodness over others. They wore little pointed hats, with noses to match, and expressions that said they – and they alone – were fit to judge their fellow men. The menfolk had bushy moustaches, which looked as if the hair had been taken from their heads and had left them with bald, shining crowns. These men had crisp white collars on and she felt that they looked down on events with disdain.

Further along the gallery sat Brian and Jimmy's mothers. When she caught her eye, Brian's mam looked as though she would murder Lil, but Jimmy's mam just nodded. Ruby must have seen this, and squeezed Lil's hand.

The corridor where she had to sit held no comforts. The wooden bench squeaked and rocked its protest if she moved to ease her stiff bottom. The minutes seemed like hours. A cold draught chilled her. Then came a cry that froze her: 'Mrs Moisley, please.' She walked back through to the courtroom.

'Take the stand, Mrs Moisley.'

All eyes were on her. Her footsteps sounded as if someone was hammering in the quietness.

The stand had to be reached by climbing four steps, and it elevated her to the same level as the jury. Looking across at them, she couldn't see one friendly or encouraging face.

The prosecutor opened by asking her to recount the events leading up to the murders. Some of the jury, and the two women in the gallery, gasped when she told of her husband having plotted the incident and having paid to have her raped. Asked if she could prove this, she said she couldn't, for it was only what the two dead men had told her. After this the prosecution ripped into her, suggesting that she and Gillian met the men by chance and then lured them to the cellar. 'Both mothers of these men you lured and killed have made statements to the effect that their sons knew nothing about London and couldn't find their way around outside their own county. So how come you say that they set out to find you?'

By the time the prosecutor had finished with her, Lil had been made to feel that nothing she said sounded plausible. Then he shredded her character as he mentioned the 'Dear John' letter, making a great deal of the kind of person she must be to write such a thing and leave her husband in the way she did.

It went on and on, and Lil felt her body folding as she lost any remaining pride. By the time the court adjourned for lunch she felt exhausted, and both Ruby and Gillian looked defeated.

When they left the court, Gillian's defence lawyer came up to her. 'Don't worry about what the prosecution was saying. Nothing he has said will jeopardize our position.' He pointed to a woman sitting on a bench.

'Mildred! Eeh, Mildred, you came . . .'

'No, don't approach her. You mustn't be seen together. Mrs Moisley senior has vital evidence.'

'But why didn't you tell me she was going to be a witness?'

'I didn't know. I had a note passed to me whilst I was in court. I will call her this afternoon, once you have finished giving evidence. Now I will work on this Arthur business. I wish you had told us about him before. I have the police fetching him, and they have agreed to make a deal with him. If he tells the truth – as I believe you are – about his part in all this, they will let him off with a caution. Not that they can really charge him with anything, as technically he can take payment for information. There is no law against it, and he wasn't to know what would come of him telling the men about your comings and goings. But at heart the police believe your story – you just didn't give them much to go on.'

Lil's shame at this made her cower in on herself. Ruby did her best to support her, and Mildred made a move towards her, but the lawyer stopped her. 'You go and get a cup of tea, Mrs Moisley. There is a canteen along there.'

Lil and Ruby entered the lawyer's office, a poky, partitioned-off corner of the vestibule. 'Sit down, both of you, you look at the end of your tether.'

'Can I go and see me sister?' Ruby asked.

'No, I'm sorry. But everything is looking good. Now tell me, what sort of a chap is this Arthur?'

'He ain't a bad bloke; a bit cocky and . . . Oh God, why didn't I say this at the time? I thought at first it didn't matter, and I didn't want Arthur or any of them knowing what had happened. I was so ashamed, partly because of my husband Alfie being the one to send Brian and Jimmy – and then about everything that happened after. Look where it landed Gillian . . . I'm so sorry.'

'Here, take this.' The lawyer handed her a huge hankie. It looked as though his mam had bleached and bleached it, for it was that white. 'And I've ordered tea and sandwiches, a sort of "working lunch" for us. I need to know everything there is to know about this Arthur.'

Lil nodded and blew her nose. She'd hit her lowest point, and yet having lunch made her feel that in some small way she was going up in the world. *Eeh, I've never had lunch afore – breakfast, dinner and tea is me lot. By, the way these posh lot live.* But she didn't allow herself even to smile at the idea, as she just needed to know what was going on. 'And what about Mildred? What . . . ? I mean, how can she help?'

'She has a letter that damns her son, as it tells of his plans. It is a nasty letter and threatens her, too. She didn't want to be disloyal to Alfie at first, but then her conscience got the better of her. Besides, she said she'd rather you were saved than him.'

Poor Mildred, this must be so hard for her. Lil wouldn't ask when Mildred had received the letter, because if it had been before it all happened and Mildred hadn't warned her, it would taint the way she felt about her. She'd rather think it had come since. 'So, if I am shown to be truthful in what I have said, will that help Gillian?'

'It will. At the moment you are seen in a bad light, but your mother-in-law is prepared to speak for you. She will talk about the kind of life you had with your husband, and what he did to you. All of this will help the jury understand how he could come to arrange this, and why you came to leave him. They will know that you have been a good daughter-in-law, always writing to your mother-in-law and even sending her a parcel of things that you must have needed for yourself.'

Ruby hadn't spoken much until now, but what she said went a little way to helping Lil cope. 'Lil, love, it is as me and Gillian have always told you – you're not to blame. Oh yes, you shielded the wrong ones, in not telling about that Arthur bloke and your man, but you had the right intentions. None of us knew how important it was to reveal that information.'

'Ah, here are the sandwiches. Now, while we eat, tell me every little detail about Arthur – anything he has done or said that might help me ask the correct questions.'

When the court reconvened, Lil felt hope in her heart. She liked the lawyer, a down-to-earth type, and had every faith in his belief that all would go well. 'I think the judge will rule in our favour and allow a plea of killing in self-defence, and will then instruct the jury to bring in that verdict. Then it will all be over.'

But would it? Gillian was still mentally unstable, and they were both facing the imminent loss of Ruby; not to mention the war and the possibility of Alfie coming home . . . *How am I to cope with it all?*

17

Alice

CAPTURE

Three weeks had passed since the failed mission. The sun scorched their backs as they walked. News had reached Alice and Steve at the farmhouse that the hunt had intensified and the Gestapo were everywhere. Steve had advised all of the group to go to ground, wherever they felt safest. After spending a few days at the cottage, in what seemed like total bliss to Alice, they had decided to try to reach the Vichy border. There were several safe houses along the route whose occupiers would take care of them: a farm was one, a flour mill another. From the first of these they would radio a message to be airlifted out.

'I feel as though I have failed, Steve. I haven't carried out one mission. Oh, some trains carrying equipment and soldiers have been disrupted because of my information, but I haven't physically achieved anything with my group.'

'Don't talk like that. You haven't failed. Because of you, men and women who were undisciplined and untrained for the courageous work they intend to carry out now have the

234

skills, equipment and arms to help them. They are organized, have radios to contact each other, and hope. Above all, Alice, you have given them hope. This mission was obviously sabotaged. It was through no fault of yours – someone betrayed you.'

'I know. And I also know none of the group would. But, well . . .'

'Is there someone you suspect, darling? Look, let's sit down a moment, we've walked for hours now. We should take a break and have a drink.'

Sipping coffee from a steaming flask, she took a deep breath and told him, 'Westlin.'

'Westlin? You mean General Westlin? Good God! How did you arrive at that conclusion?'

Telling him took some time. After she'd finished he was silent.

'I know you don't believe it, but it's true. I am convinced of my father's innocence.'

'You mean Gertrude and Juste are related to you, and . . . My God, yes, I have heard of D'Olivier. He was your father! I can't believe it.'

'I know. But it is true.'

'Have you got the diaries with you?'

'Not all of them. I hid them in my room. I told Juste where I kept them and asked him to collect them and get them back to Elsbeth. But I have the one I haven't read yet. The one that leads up to the accusation of my father. The last bit of it was written by Elsbeth, as she recorded what happened after my father was taken into custody.'

'Well, I think we should read them. I need convincing of this.'

'I understand that, but think of it this way: if *you* don't believe me, how will anyone else? How will I ever stop Westlin?'

'I don't know. And you have a point there. We'll look at the diary together as soon as we are safe. But have you thought about Gertrude? Could she be the weak link? You told me before that it worried you that she had fallen in love and—'

'No, she wouldn't betray us. I know she wouldn't. But, God, I worry about her, because some of the group are beginning to doubt her, and all of this will look like . . . No, I can't think of that. They trust her; Juste will make them trust her. He will look after her. Come on, according to the map we are still twenty kilometres from the safe farm. Let's get there and go through the diary for clues.'

After trudging through woods, wading in deep ditches and some precarious running across open ground, their journey at last came to an end. 'There's the farm. Come on, race you over the last field!'

Though she laughed, she did not take Steve up on his challenge. Her legs wouldn't let her, for climbing the last hill had sapped her strength.

'You've gone soft since training, you . . . Christ!' A shot split the air. Alice fell in agony, her arm splintered. A burning pain seared her. Falling beside her, Steve held her. 'Oh, God, the place is crawling with Germans. I saw them – they are coming towards us from the farm, but how . . . ?'

'Go, Steve! Leave me. Please, you have to escape. Go. Take the diary . . .'

'No!'

Spitting dirt out of her mouth, she begged him, 'Please, they will be here in a moment. You can make it back to the woods. You have to make it home. You have to find out if it

236

is Westlin who is the traitor – he has to be exposed and stopped.'

'I'll get the diary from your pack and bury it inside our sandwich tin. It mustn't fall into the Germans' hands. Here . . .' Picking up her gun, he wedged it under her good arm. Thank God they hadn't hit her right one; she could operate the weapon, though with impaired accuracy. 'When they are near enough, start to shoot. That will give me time. We could still get out of this.'

'There are too many of them. Go, darling, pleeease go . . .'

'Fire. Now!'

Her reaction to his command had her firing into the soldiers. Two of them fell. The others took to the ground, advancing towards them on their stomachs. They were much harder targets now, but then so were she and Steve. From behind her, where Steve had hidden in order to bury the box out of sight, she felt him tap her. 'Hand me your gun and I'll wedge mine under your arm, then reload yours.'

This done, she opened fire again. A crack shot with two arms, she knew the Germans were getting braver and crawling nearer as they weighed up her poor efforts, with shots going all over the place. Their numbers increased, as others out of range ran towards their comrades. Fear gripped her. This was hopeless. Trying to grind her body deeper into the furrowed ruts of the field, she felt a chill from the damp earth seep through her blouse. Her arm throbbed with pain, and blood ran down to her numbed fingers and dripped onto the ground. Into her anguish came the noise of several engines, causing a distraction from her agony. Her hope sank. Jeeps sped along the country lane leading to the side of them. How long before they were surrounded?

'Darling, please! Go, before it's too late. I will keep them at bay.'

'No. We can make it back to those woods. It will take at least half an hour for the motorcade to reach the other side. We can still get out of this, we can!' Swapping his loaded gun for her empty one, he refilled it as he spoke. 'Get ready to run, on my say-so. I will cover you. Hold your gun in a firing position. Go for twenty yards and then down, and fire while I catch up; then we will repeat the loading and running process until we reach the trees. We'll radio in for help as soon as we can. There may be aircraft in the vicinity that will come to our aid. It's worth a try.'

Whilst he spoke the odd shot rang out, but no one fired directly at them. Were the Germans under instructions to take them alive? They must be. They could have killed them both in the first attack. They'd been easy targets. *Oh God, help us!* Thoughts of the torture methods they'd been warned about came to mind: hot pokers jamming into their bodies; skin peeled off, nails pulled out, bones broken or teeth extracted one by one . . . *I can't do it, I can't.*

'Steve, have you got your cyanide pill handy?'

'No! No, darling, not that. Please don't take it. Please give me a chance to get us out of here. Go! Go . . .'

Getting up wasn't easy. She didn't know how she was going to be able to run. Gunfire rattled around her, the noise blocking her ears. Twenty yards felt like a marathon. Collapsing before she got there, she screamed in agony as she rolled onto her shattered arm. Sweat ran into her eyes. She blinked it away, but felt the sting of its aftermath as she aimed her gun through her blurred vision. Her heart pounded in anguish as she watched Steve dodging hails of bullets.

When he fell down beside her, she saw a river of blood running down his face. 'Oh God, you've been hit!'

Voicing her own fear, he told her, 'They want us alive, Alice. That cannot happen. I'm with you, darling, you're right – if it comes to them capturing us, we'll take our cyanide. We'll hold hands as we do it, but for now try, darling, please try to escape with me.'

She felt a new life come into her as he said this. Rising, she ran faster than she could ever remember doing. All pain left her. This time she dived instead of fell and was in position quicker. Clutching the gun as steadily as she could, she fired. There was no target, for the Germans lay low and her bullets went over their heads. Steve ran towards her. One more effort and they would reach the woods and have the blessed cover of the trees and the thicket. The dense undergrowth would shelter them.

In this third run she had almost touched the bark of the first tree trunk when a second bullet entered her body. Her right shoulder exploded with burning agony. Her gun dropped to the ground. A barrage of pain and fear gripped every muscle in a spasm that she didn't think she would ever recover from. She thumped against an exposed tree trunk as she fell. She couldn't cover Steve. *Oh God!*

'Stay down, Steve. I'm hit, I'm out of action.' Tears filled her voice. Tears that hazed her vision of Steve running, then firing, then running. He didn't make it. Blood spurted from his left leg and then his right leg. They had lost.

Through her sobs and his cries of pain she told him, 'I'm coming.' With an extreme effort she raised herself. Reaching him, she begged him, 'Get my pill for me, and yours – we'll do as we said. I love you, darling, help me, help me.'

As he tried to get in a position to reach her pill, a shadow fell over them. '*Bleiben still!*'

'Take yours, darling, do it!' she told him.

'No. We are in this together, my love. If you have to go through their torture, then I will. Please, God, let us come through it.'

There was no time to say more. Soldiers, some looking not much older than eighteen and shivering with their own fear, bore down on them, and from behind them she could hear the sound of a truck. Within minutes it pulled up alongside them. Orders were given to load them onto it. This caused them both to call out in pain from the rough handling of their bodies. The journey to the farmhouse over the rutted field flung them around. Tears, sweat and snot mingled, as they sobbed from the agony of their wounds. No words were spoken between them, nor could they stay close to each other.

Inside the farmhouse everything looked as it should. Nothing was out of place. It looked as a normal farmhouse should look: cosy, with wellingtons in the corner, muddied and turned down at the tops, standing on newspaper beside the stove. It smelt of home cooking. Onions and garlic bulbs hung from the ceiling next to gleaming pots – the haven of the family who lived here had now turned into hers and Steve's Hell. The only thing that struck terror into Alice was the silence, into which came the laboured breathing of her darling Steve, spreadeagled on the floor, a soldier's foot on his back compounding that Hell.

'You ver making for this house? This is one of your safe houses, yes? These people are collaborators, are they not? And you are British agents . . . Tell me!'

His boot thumped down into the small of Steve's back. Steve's moan sounded weak. Blood from his wounds seeped over the tiled floor. Alice knew the loss was too much for him to sustain life. 'Get a doctor, he is dying; please get a doctor!'

'Shut up!' His punch sent her reeling back against the arm of the sofa on which they had sat her. But it didn't matter as the officer, speaking in German this time, told one of the soldiers to fetch the village doctor. Steve would receive help. But with this relief came the confirmation of her fears: the German officers must have orders to keep them alive; they knew of their movements and had plans to interrogate them. *Please let me be brave enough not to tell them anything. God, please help us.*

A noise to the side of her brought the middle-aged farmer and his wife into focus for the first time. Their eyes were wide-eyed in horror as they sat in the far corner of their kitchen, each bound to a chair and gagged.

'You – you tell me! Vhy ver you headed this vay? Confirm to me that you are British agents. Tell me your names and your code names. Tell me your poems.'

Like Steve, she did not answer. A shot echoed around the room. Blood splattered the walls, and bits of flesh and brain slapped her face. Horror-struck, she stared and an involuntary sob escaped her. The farmer was dead, his head a smashed, bloodied mess.

An agonized grunt came from the farmer's wife, a scream muffled by her gag. Now the straight arm of the shooter pointed in her direction. Alice saw her eyes close and her head loll forward as she fainted.

'One of you must start talking to me, or she dies too!'

Agony dripped through every part of Alice. She could not say anything. She could not save this poor, innocent woman, who'd risked everything to help her and Steve, and whose son worked for another group of the Resistance movement.

A quick look around the living space showed no photographs of him, and no reference anywhere to his existence.

'*Werfen Sie Wasser auf ihr!*'

On this command, one of the soldiers threw water over the farmer's wife. She shuddered and shock opened her eyes, but a gunshot closed them forever. He'd wanted her to be awake when she was shot.

'Now! You vill give me the information I vant or I vill kill him.' His gun pointed at Steve.

Alice's heart stopped. A gasp of 'No' came from Steve. She knew he'd meant it for her, and had not been begging for his life. Gertrude came to mind now. How often she had wondered how Gertrude would cope in this situation. Alice had doubted her integrity, but now she doubted herself. Could she hold out, knowing that to do so would mean Steve's death?

'No, no . . .'

Ignoring Steve's plea, she spoke in French, giving her cover name and story as if they were the truth about who she was.

'You are lying! Vhy vould you have guns? Our intelligence told us you are British agents! And you have just spoken in English a few minutes ago.'

Intelligence? For a split second her mind came to Gertrude again. *No, she wouldn't have told them anything. She is my sister. Juste would be in danger too, and Gertrude would never do that. It must be Westlin. Oh God . . .*

The door opened, interrupting the German officer as a soldier returned with the doctor. A look of shock crossed the doctor's face and his mouth opened. The German interrogator pointed his gun at him. In perfect French the officer said, 'You will take no notice of anything here. You have been brought here to make these two fit for travel. Just get on with it.' As he finished saying this he gestured to one of the young soldiers. 'You . . . and you, get rid of those bodies. Stinking collaborators, they deserved to die.'

Seeing Steve in greater need than Alice, the doctor began work on him, telling the interrogator, 'I cannot do much other than stop the bleeding. He needs an operation – a miracle . . .'

'Keep him alive. Nothing more.'

'But it isn't that easy. Broken bones can interfere with the blood supply. He has to have an operation.'

'Are you capable of that?'

'Not here I'm not. At my surgery, and with the help of my wife, who is a nurse, I could sort them both out.'

'Very well. We will take them there.'

'They will have to be transported with care. Get your men to take two doors off. We will have to strap them, one to each door, to keep them still. I will apply splints to prevent further damage. But even at my surgery I can only do a limited repair, enough to make sure they do not die from their injuries. Though infection is a major worry – gangrene and maybe even pneumonia.'

'Just get on with it. They are going to die anyway. But not here. They have information they must give us first. And by the time we have it, they will be begging us to kill them.'

Alice felt a moment of defiance enter her. She would tell them nothing, no matter what they did. And she knew it would be the same for Steve. Yes, they would die, nothing could save them, but they would die not having betrayed the Resistance members or their fellow countrymen.

18

Gertrude

A WARNING

Pacing up and down, Gertrude felt certain that something had gone wrong. And yet she dared not go out to the cafe to try and find out. *Please let Madeline and Juste be all right, please!*

Three days had passed and she hadn't heard anything from the Resistance group. No word. No sign of the factory having been interfered with, or of any change in Kristof that might have told her the mission had been successful. She would go mad if she didn't find out soon what had happened. A sound alerted her to a key being turned. Standing still, she jumped as he called her name.

'Kristof? I wasn't expecting you.'

'I know, my darling, but I had a sudden need of your company. I am very pleased about something, and I need to share it.'

'Oh?'

'Yes. We have foiled an attack by those bloody dissidents. Here, I have brought champagne.'

The muscles that had been dancing in her stomach these last few days clamped painfully at this news. She'd nearly called out 'No!' but stopped herself and instead told him, 'You know I will not celebrate such an event, if it means you have hurt my countrymen. Even though I do not agree with their tactics, I understand their cause.'

'Of course you do, my dear. I know that. But we haven't killed or caught any of the bastard French. Our prize is much bigger. So you can join me in a toast.'

Bigger? He must mean Madeline! There is no other explanation – oh God!

'What prize? Have you found arms, or captured someone of importance?' She didn't expect an answer to this and was surprised when she got one.

'No. Two British agents.' His eyes held hers. Scrutinized hers in fact.

Turning what she knew had been an instant look of horror into one of bewilderment, she took the glass he offered. 'British agents! Are there such things here?'

For a moment he did not answer. His eyes still bore into hers, searching, watching. 'You did not know?'

'No. I don't know anything about such things. I am very sheltered here. I don't get to read the papers or listen to the news. You know that. You banned me from doing so.'

'I did, and for your own good, but . . . Well, for a moment there I thought my news had affected you.'

'Of course it did! For one thing, I was shocked that such things are happening; and for another, I – I . . . Well, look, I have to be honest. I had a moment of thinking that there might be people still trying to liberate us. I mean . . . well, I can't explain.'

'No, I don't suppose you can. I thought you had come to

245

the conclusion that you didn't need liberating from us? I thought you had taken the sensible route of knowing that we Germans are working towards a superior world, and that France is part of that plan. Are you saying you no longer believe this?'

His voice held a coldness. It chilled her blood, but she didn't care to deny her sister and the effort she had made for France and for world peace. She couldn't be sure it was Madeline they had captured, but 'two British agents' fitted – as Madeline was expecting a male agent to join her. *No . . . no! I can't think of it!* Once more she chose the path of truth. 'If there was a hope of France going back to how it was, I would choose that path. But I am realistic and know that won't happen.' To temper this she told him, 'I also think it can be even better, as I have said before, under German rule, but many things will have to change. The killings, the strict regime and the curfews.'

'We go round in circles, and still I wonder about you. Still something gives me a niggling worry as to whether you are deceiving me.'

'I don't know how to allay those fears. I am what I am. A French citizen. I know you have values and beliefs about your country, and I respect them. Maybe you will one day come to respect mine?'

'Maybe. And, yet, I do in a way. Come here. I didn't visit you to pick a fight. Far from it. This capture we have made should supply us with valuable information that will help us in many ways. I am pleased. And, when I am, I want to share it with you.'

Uncomfortable and not feeling like loving him at this moment, Gertrude wriggled in his arms. 'I am not feeling well . . .'

'It is my news – it has upset you. Forget it. These British

pigs are not worth it. Besides they'll be dead by now, I shouldn't wonder. Please, darling. Sip your champagne; it will make you feel better.'

Pushing him away, she ran to the bathroom. Bending over the lavatory bowl, she vomited. *Madeline, Madeline . . . Oh God, I don't even know my own sister's real name!*

'You really are ailing, my dear. I'm sorry, I didn't realize.' Holding her from behind, Kristof rubbed her back gently. The motion soothed her. In moments of anguish she'd want no one but him to help her, but in this instance he'd been the one to cause her pain.

'What is it, darling? You're crying. What's wrong? Don't cry, I can't bear it.'

Taking the towel he offered her, she wiped her lips. Straightening, she went to the sink and swilled out her mouth. The water caught in her throat, making her cough. The coughing turned to huge sobs that racked her body, weakening her, till her legs bent underneath her.

His strong arms held her. 'Darling, please. What is it? Why should you be so upset? Has my news anything to do with you? Tell me.'

Swallowing hard, she lifted her body until she stood in a strong stance. She did have something to tell him. How he would take it she did not know, but at this moment she was happier about it than she had been since she realized her condition, for now it had given her an excuse for her reaction, 'No. I – I think I am pregnant.'

'What! My God, that is wonderful. How long – when did you know? Have you seen a doctor?'

'No. I think it happened that first time or maybe the second, I don't know, but I have missed a period. Though that is the first time I have been sick.'

'I will get my doctor to attend to you. Oh, darling, this makes me so happy. We will be married.'

'No. I cannot. Not yet, and that is what is upsetting me. It cannot happen until the war is over. Not until my people accept you and yours. My life would be in danger. Already people cross the street from me and spit on the pavement. They call me a collaborator. No. If I *am* pregnant, I dare not even go out of the house. I will have to stay here!'

'How dare they? I will not stand for it. You will go down the street and one of my officers will follow you and protect you. They will shoot anyone who insults you!'

'No! Oh, Kristof. I would rather just stay in and exercise in the garden. Especially when it shows, but maybe later today, if I feel better, I will walk to the end of the street to the cafe, just for some air and to collect a magazine.'

'Very well. Now, my darling, lie with me. Like in the early days, I will not touch you, other than having my body curled around yours. I want to hold my woman and feel the round-ness of her stomach, where I am convinced our child is nestled.'

The holding did not last long. Soon she could feel Kristof's need and it awakened her own. Their naked bodies could not just entwine as they once had, for now they had tasted the pleasure they gave each other, and they both craved it.

He took her gently. A slow, loving act that filled her with joy and took away her pain and fear for a little while. Losing herself in the ecstasy of his skilful stroking and thrusting, just where she needed him to, brought her to a state of complete-ness that overshadowed everything else. This only lasted until she came back to earth with his last, almost painful thrust. As he uncurled from her, Madeline's difficult plight ahead hit her afresh, along with the guilt that she could forget about it, even for a moment, and make love to Kristof as if nothing had changed.

'Please don't cry. Talk to me. Are you unhappy about our baby? I can get the doctor to—'

'No! No, I would never cast our baby away. Besides, we cannot be sure until I miss another period. Then the doctor will be able to tell us. It is just that we cannot behave like a normal couple, and I hate the destruction of life that is all around us in this bloody war. I hate it. Oh, I know you and your men have to obey orders – it is your duty to do so – but every time you do, it is against my people or those trying to help us.'

'My sweet, sensitive darling. It will all be all right, just as you hope. I promise. And I will be happy if the doctor confirms our child exists, not only for the obvious reasons, but because you say you will not go out. Then no one can hurt you, and I can protect you fully. Rest now. I will send someone to the cafe to pick up a magazine for you. You should not go out today.'

'Thank you, Kristof. Will you tell whoever goes to say that the magazine is for me? The cafe owner knows which magazine I like, and often keeps one in the back specially for me. Oh, and can they call in on me first, in case I think of anything else I might need that they can pick up for me?'

'I will, my dear. Now I will run a bath for you and you can relax in it. I will have a wash while the tub fills.'

When he'd gone, Gertrude stepped into the tub and allowed the hot water to relax her. In doing so, she could not stop the flood of tears. Her grief punctured her, making her feel that life as she'd known it had drained from her. *Oh, Madeline . . . Madeline . . .*

An hour passed before a knock came on her door. 'I am

going for your magazine and have been asked to see if there is anything else you need.'

The maid looked afraid. Gertrude didn't blame her; none of the staff had approached her or interacted with her since the time when that other poor maid had attempted to deliver her a message. Trying to sound friendly, she said, 'Yes, thank you. Here, I have written them down. You can get them from the cafe.'

In times of emergency there were several codes she could use. One would tell Juste that her movements were restricted; another that she was being watched – that kind of thing. They'd made them up after the Antoine incident. They had never again wanted to use a direct note in a magazine as their means of communication.

Madeline had helped and, besides her and Juste, Paulo was the only other one who understood the codes, in case there was a time when Juste couldn't be contacted, and then he could make sure someone knew her message.

Apart from these simple codes there was another special code for when she had information to give. She would do this by using a greeting to Paulo, which could be deciphered by using something similar to Madeline's code method – a short piece that she and Juste had composed, and from which words could be taken to form a sentence. Madeline had taught them a way in which the letters of the alphabet could be represented. It had taken them many practice runs to get it right, and many times they had giggled about how wrong the message had been. It was this kind of message that Gertrude had written into her note.

'There, please give the note to the cafe owner, as he will know then that the things are for me. You see, some of the things he gets for me from other traders, and keeps them until

I need them. It saves me from having to go too far afield.'
She knew the maid would understand this. All those who
worked here knew the perils of leaving the vicinity, as they
risked possible reprisals.

In her message she'd told of the capture of the British agents
and had asked Juste to find out if one of them was Madeline.

Pacing the floor while she waited for the maid to return
wasn't helping her anxiety; neither was going to the window
to see if she was coming back, for her guilt added to her fear,
making it impossible to settle. How could she abandon herself
to her bodily needs at such a time?

Trying to appease herself, she thought about the possibility
of a baby growing inside her. And although this did bring
happiness, now she knew that Kristof was happy about it, it
also brought loneliness. There was no one she could share
the news with. Her family would be repulsed. Madeline would
be cross that she had made herself so vulnerable. *But then how
can I even share this news with Madeline, if she has been caught?
Please don't let her be one of those captured.*

There was a tap on the door and it made her jump, even
though she had been expecting it. The maid stood there with
a tray of coffee and cakes. On the tray, lodged between the
coffee pot and the jug of milk, lay a rolled-up magazine.

'Paulo said he has some of the things, but will get you the
others later. I will fetch them for you, if you like.'

'Thank you, yes, I would. Please put the tray on my table.
Thank you, that is very kind of you.'

She didn't take much interest in the magazine, as she didn't
want to appear too eager to look inside it. She left it where
the maid put it on the side of the table and took the coffee
that was poured for her over to the sofa, refusing the offer of
a cake.

Sipping the hot liquid and savouring the delicious aroma, she stared at the magazine, almost afraid of it, knowing it held information for her. Paulo's verbal message had told her that. But it also told her there was more information to come later.

The maid left some five minutes afterwards. Unable to hold off any longer, Gertrude scoured the pages. They were there: small dots alongside several letters on many pages. Writing them down, it shocked her as she read: *Do not leave the house. Madeline captured. The group believe you betrayed them. I will prove them wrong, dear sister. But stay safe. I have to disappear.*

Her gasps for breath panicked her. A heat crept over her and yet inside she felt cold. Every fibre of her trembled. 'It cannot be! How can they suspect me?'

Looking around, it seemed as though they were hunting her already and that they were here. *Oh God! How had this come about?* And what should she do with the magazine! What if Kristof browsed through it and noticed the dots! Previously she'd always been able to walk out and dump it in a bin, or leave it on a bench somewhere.

She pulled firmly on the bell cord. The maid appeared at the door once more. With agitation in her voice she said, 'That stupid man. He has sent the wrong magazine! I am half-way through reading a serial – I must have the other one. Please take it back immediately and tell the cafe owner to send the correct one or I will have the order stopped!'

'Of course. I won't be a minute.'

Leaning on the closed door, Gertrude tried to settle her racing heart. All would be well. Paulo would understand. He knew she could not leave the house. He would destroy the magazine and send her a different one. The fact that he had delivered Juste's message told her that he trusted her and cared about her. Yes, Paulo would play his part. He would apologize, send another magazine for her and always send her the new one in future. She'd said it to herself many times, but this time she thanked God aloud for Paulo. A true friend.

The shreds of the decoded message dropped like confetti into the lavatory, and flushing them away gave her the sensation that she was leaving the past and facing an even more uncertain future. Into those thoughts about her future came her possible pregnancy. Now more than ever she needed it to be real, for the path was already laid for her to be able to remain around the house without arising suspicion in Kristof. But soon her prayers changed and she forgot her own plight as she begged for Madeline's life and for some way to be found for her to escape.

Going to the window to get some air, she found that the street below looked no different, for life carried on as usual. The only difference was the presence of armed guards. And that now she could see so much more of the street than she used to be able to. This was due to her begging of Kristof to fell the tree from which the maid had been hanged, telling him that it gave her nightmares. This didn't mean she ever forgot the girl, or her own part in her death, but at least there wasn't that constant reminder when she looked out of the window. The felling had opened up more of the street to her, giving her a view of much more of the central garden and a vista of beautiful tall buildings. The apartments in these buildings had pretty windowboxes and coloured shutters. People milled around, some of them walking with purpose, some walking dogs or children leisurely and others sitting on benches. A warmth entered her as she gazed down on them. Taking a deep breath, the thought came to her that at least she had this view. She could come out onto this balcony whenever she wanted to.

It would make her feel as if she had some sort of normality in her life, as would the birds tweeting, the sounds of cars occasionally disturbing the peace, and the sight of life around her. This thought had barely lifted her spirits when something caught her eye. A shadow moved from behind a tree. A man, moving in a furtive way and holding something. *Oh God, it's a gun!*

Dashing back inside, she moved away from the open door. Everything around her lost its familiarity and took on rounded, wobbly shapes. Her vision clouded and her body crumpled in a heap, as it all disappeared into a zinging noise in her head and a blackness descended over her.

Coming round brought a confusion she couldn't untangle for a moment. Why was she on the floor? Memory caused her blood to run cold through her veins, as the realization hit her of the danger she was in. Already they were trying to kill her. And, knowing those men, she knew they would never give up, never . . . They would go to any lengths – facing their own certain deaths, because once the shot had been fired at her, the guards would be alerted and there would be no escape for them. They would know that, and yet they were prepared to risk their own lives just to dispose of her. Panic gripped her afresh. *My God, they really believe I have betrayed them . . .*

19

Alice

PARIS & KENT,
JULY 1941

RIPPED APART, AND FINDING A NEW FRIEND

The last few days – Alice didn't know how many – had been spent drifting in and out of sleep. Occasionally she'd heard the harsh tones of the German officer, and then the softer ones of the doctor insisting that he needed longer to make sure of saving the captives' lives. Then another dose of the drug he was giving them would be administered, and she'd drift off again into a nightmare world of strange sounds and shapes she couldn't make out.

Fearing this, although pain had woken her, she lay with her eyes closed, hoping to detect a time when no one was in the room.

When all seemed quiet she opened them and looked over to where Steve lay. On seeing one of his legs plastered and the other one bandaged, she surmised that one had just taken a flesh wound, but the other had a smashed bone. The bandage around his head worried her, but she knew it couldn't be serious, because he'd carried on afterwards and had spoken normally.

The dryness of her mouth made it hard for her to swallow. Only a moan would come from her as she tried to get Steve's attention.

'You're all right, my dear. You're both going to make it.'

The doctor had said this. He must have been in the room after all. She must try to communicate with him. 'We c – can't, we have to . . . p – pill . . . in jacket . . .'

'My wife has washed and mended your clothes as best she can.'

'No . . . no, she mustn't. We have pills . . .'

'Hush, all will be well. It is lucky for us that the officer in charge is under strict orders to keep you alive. It has—'

'Ah, so the bitch is talking at last, eh? Vhy didn't you call me? I told you to inform me at once!' The doctor cringed from the glancing blow that the officer aimed at him as he came through the door. 'You vill not talk to them. I vill put a guard in here at all times. You vill find yourself a prisoner with them, or dead even, if you disobey my orders again. Probably the latter, as you are of no use to us once you have them vell enough to travel.'

Steadying himself, the doctor nodded. 'Please may I at least tell them what I need to?'

'Only ven I am present, as I speak French.'

'Very well.' To Alice the doctor said, 'I will get my wife. She will come and wash you and give you a drink. You are making good progress.' Before he turned his back to her he winked. This shocked her. It wasn't the kind of wink a lady expected from a Frenchman; it was not saucy or suggestive, but came with a nod of his head and held a message that said there was hope. *But that's not possible – how could there be!*

Speaking in French, Steve's weak voice came to her. 'How is she, Doctor?'

'Shut up! You vill not talk to the doctor. You do not need to know how each other are.' A slapping sound came into the silence that followed this, as the officer held his gloves in his right hand and tapped the palm of his left hand with them. After a moment he said, 'I have made my mind up. Ve vill ship out tonight. If they are vell enough to talk, they are vell enough to travel. Have them ready in half an hour! In the meantime do as I say, and do not converse vith them. Hey, you . . .' In German he shouted to someone outside. Alice heard him give instructions to stay in the room with them at all times, and to shoot the doctor if he so much as opened his mouth.

Other instructions that she heard him shout as he left the room told of his intention to move them from there to the station to begin their journey, but to where she did not know. Their only hope seemed to lie with the doctor now. Did he have some sort of plan? If not, somehow she must convey to him that she and Steve had to have their pills. But although she knew he'd understood her about her cyanide pill, she doubted if he had any intention of helping them to end their lives. She couldn't blame him, for he had a duty to save lives – his own included, though that hung in the balance. She feared for him.

Looking over at Steve, she willed him to look at her. He didn't. Maybe he thought it was best not to show that they had any feelings between them. The Germans would use that to their advantage. They would probably make one watch the other being tortured. That would be beyond endurance.

Only the loud ticking of the clock above her disturbed the silence as the doctor's wife went about washing her and helping her to dress. With a screen between her and the soldier, Alice tried to mime that she needed her pill.

She didn't want to die, she wanted to live, to be with Steve in a free land, to marry and have his children. But it was better that they died now than risk being broken by the cruel lengths to which the Germans would go in their quest to extract information from them.

Despairing, she realized her miming was useless. The woman continued her nursing duties without even trying to understand, and mostly without looking at her. She seemed preoccupied, and Alice noticed how often she looked up at the clock with an expression that said she was willing the time to reach a certain hour.

Voices drifted to her from the hall outside. The doctor asked the officer if he could be allowed to give pain relief to his patients before they were taken. The officer refused, telling him he didn't trust him. 'Are they in a suitable condition? Ve need to go before it gets dark. Ve need to get them to a train that I have arranged to call in at the station of Valsema.'

This information confirmed her earlier suspicions: the doctor and his wife were in extreme danger. Knowing that he was going to kill them would be the only reason the officer would reveal their means of transportation and the location of their pickup. A fear for the kindly couple dampened her body in sweat. *How can I warn them? But then, if I do, there is no way they can save themselves. Oh God, I can't bear it!*

'Yes, they are ready, but it is imperative they are handled with care. If the wounds are opened again, they could bleed to death, as they have had no time to make up the blood loss they have already suffered.'

The officer barked an order and soon Alice could hear the sound of men rushing around and of vehicles being moved. Two soldiers came into the room. She screamed in pain as they lifted her. One held her by her wounded arms, the other held her feet. 'Get her into the truck – hurry.'

A cry from Steve told her they were doing the same to him.

'Climb in!' a soldier ordered her once they reached the truck.

The truck's canvas sides flapped in the breeze and a smell of stale, damp leather wafted into her nostrils. Her legs were heavy and weak, making it difficult to get up the steps without being able to hold onto anything.

Once inside the back of the truck, she sank down onto the bench. As she did so, they manhandled Steve into the truck and laid him on the floor. Somehow he managed a smile as he looked up at her. How she did it she didn't know, but she smiled back. Inside she ached for him. She wanted to lessen his pain and get him away from here. A sense of desolation entered her, but she quashed it. This journey might be the last time they had together on Earth. She must not spoil it by creating an air of hopelessness.

Mouthing the words 'I love you', she smiled even wider than before. Steve's face lit up. It seemed that while he thought she could cope, he could too. He began to mouth back to her when a desperate plea cut him off.

'No, no . . . Not my wife, No – noooo!'

Cries followed and the sound of a woman weeping. A gunshot rang out. Alice's body jumped, then shook with the horror of realization. A silence followed. It didn't last long before there was another gunshot.

Tears ran down her face. *Why, oh why, couldn't they have spared the doctor and his wife?*

There were no answers, and no time for her mind to adjust, because a louder explosion increased the high-pitched noise in her ears and made all other sounds filter through as if in slow motion. Gunfire penetrated this blankness. It was rapid and from different types of guns – hand-held pistols, rifles and the rat-a-tat of machine guns. More explosions shook the truck. *What is going on?*

'Oh God, Alice, the Germans are under attack! But who could be attacking them?'

'The Resistance?'

'It must be. Oh, thank G—'

A German soldier entered the truck, his gun pointed at her. Her breath stopped for a moment. She acknowledged that now was the end.

Out of the corner of her eye she saw Steve lift his less-injured leg and kick the soldier. The gun went off. Closing her eyes, Alice waited for death. There was no pain, but they say you don't feel pain as you go towards eternity. *How do they* know? *Why am I asking myself this, and why has everything gone so silent again?* She opened her eyes. The shot hadn't hit her. The sound had deafened her, but she was all right. 'Steve, Steve, I'm all right, I'm . . . No. No – nooo!'

'Come on – quick, can you manage?' It was a French voice, but was alien to her.

'Mademoiselle, please hurry. We have killed all the Germans that were here, they are all dead, but when the train comes in and you are not in sight, more soldiers will come.'

She was still and silent, dumbfounded with shock. Steve lay at her feet, his eyes staring blankly at her and blood coming from his neck. 'Help him, help him . . . Don't let him die – please don't let him die.'

'Doctor, over here, quick! One of them has been hit.'

Doctor? She'd thought he'd been shot?

'Help the girl out, Robert. Let me get to the man.'

She went with the one called Robert, but unwillingly; everything in her wanted to stay with Steve. 'Save him, Doctor, please.'

'We must get going. Robert will stay and help the doctor. Come, come, I am Alfonse, I will take you to safety.'

'No. No, I am not going anywhere without Steve.'

'Please, you must come with us. Many men have put their lives at risk to save you. My own parents have been killed . . .' His voice broke.

On hearing this, Alice knew what she must do, but still she hung back, torn.

'You are putting us all in further danger – you must hurry. We have to get out of here. If the doctor saves him, Robert will do all he can to bring him to you. No one knows this area better than him. Besides, there is a plane coming in an hour. We have to be there. The landing strip is eight kilometres from here, and we have to make it. And then we all need to disperse, as the place will be swarming with Germans and our efforts will have been in vain.'

It was the hardest decision she'd ever had to make, but she knew she must comply. She could not jeopardize the safety of these men, nor could she compromise their group by putting them all at risk of capture. There was no time to plead with them to let her stay.

Looking back, she saw the doctor pumping Steve's chest and she prayed – prayed harder than she had ever done in her life. She prayed to God, to Bren, to her dead father and even to her grandparents. But in her heart she felt it was useless.

At the bottom of the steps lay the German who'd entered the truck. For a moment she wanted to spit at him, but his eyes, staring unseeing at her, were those of a young boy and she couldn't. *This bloody war . . . Fuck Hitler!*

On the journey she asked questions. Alfonse told her that he was the son of the farmer whose farm she and Steve had been heading for. He'd left his Resistance group on a mission to travel home and help her and Steve on the next leg of their journey. When he got near, he'd seen the Germans around his home and could do nothing but watch from a hidden vantage point. From there he could see everything, but could hear nothing other than the shots which, he now knew, had killed his parents. When he saw the doctor arrive, he took off to the doctor's house and spoke to his wife. She told him that the doctor had been instructed to keep the British agents alive. Alfonse left instructions with her to ask her husband to take as many days as he could, while he gathered a party to attack the Germans and save the agents. The British agent working with his group, whom he only knew as Hubert, had arranged for the plane to pick her and Steve up and lift them out. She guessed he must have been amongst those who attacked the Germans with Alfonse and the rest of the group, but he could not make himself known to her.

Alfonse told her that he himself had given the instruction that no German should be left alive. He went on to say that when they arrived at the doctor's house, it was to see the doctor's wife cowering in front of a soldier with a gun. Alfonse had shot him, saving the wife and starting the attack. Miraculously, or maybe because of the surprise element, none of the Resistance workers, to his knowledge, had been hurt. Before leaving her, Alfonse promised that he would go back to Steve and do all he could to get him away to safety.

The plane landed at Biggin Hill airport. Feeling like a dead person inside, Alice could not respond to the ambulance men who lifted her off, or to the nurse who had a kindly smile and sat with her on the journey to hospital. Her whole self was back in France with Steve. She willed him to live and to join her. Pleading was the only thing she could give her mind over to, as she'd closed down her emotions. There were no tears – nothing. An icy coldness had clenched her feelings back to how they were before she met Steve. At this moment she felt that if Steve didn't make it, there would be nothing to fill the void that he would leave within her. It would be a barren life that stretched out before her, on a road that was too long for her to travel. She'd not even think of doing so. If Steve didn't make it, neither would she.

Once an assessment of her condition had been made, and the strapping removed and a new one refitted on her arm and around her shoulder, she was declared fit to be transported to a nursing hospital for officers. 'Not tonight, though, eh?' The elderly doctor looked kindly at her. 'You've had enough for one day, ma'am. We'll get you settled in a quiet ward, feed and water you and give you something to make you have a really good sleep, then arrange to have you shipped out tomorrow. Whoever took care of you did an excellent job. You only need rest and time to recover from all you've been through. Crescent Abbey is just the place. I will make all the arrangements . . .'

Crescent Abbey? How ironic! Her friend, Lady Rosamond Flastow, had lived there before this war and her 'coming out' party had been the last one Alice had attended. She hadn't had one herself – a fact she'd been glad of, for she had hated having to accept all the invitations from her friends. Leaning against a wall, she had generally refused all dances, except with Bren. But even he'd found her foul mood too much and had left her alone most of the time.

It had always affected her – being amongst so many people

who knew. Feeling their eyes on her, catching their knowing nods to one another. Even now she cringed inside as she thought of it. But the thinking strengthened her resolve. When she saw her boss, which she knew she would very soon for a debriefing, she would tell him her suspicions about General Westlin. If he didn't believe her, she wouldn't give up. One day those who had made her feel like an outcast would know of her father's innocence.

Facing the debriefing meant more than simply a first telling of what she had learned about Westlin, for as her thoughts moved on, shame washed over her at how little she would have to report. Not one major mission accomplished . . . If only there had been, all she had suffered would have been worth it.

'Stand at ease, Officer D'Olivier. Or, rather, sit. You look all in. I came as soon as I could.'

'Yes, thank you, sir. You could not have come any quicker, as I only arrived here myself two hours ago.'

The officer welcoming her was a man with thick glasses, slicked-back thinning hair and a poky-looking face. The room was one she wasn't familiar with in this house, and she imagined it must have been Rosamond's father's office. One wall held books from floor to ceiling, and another had prints hung in symmetrical patterns, all of dogs. Some of these she recognized as pets of the family when she had visited. The furniture she knew from the familiarity of it. It was the kind every office in every large house held – solid oak desk and leather chairs. The chair she sat in welcomed her into its padded depth, a blessed relief for her aching body.

The two hours since arriving had exhausted her as they'd settled her in and a nurse, who had seemed in awe of her, had taken all her particulars, from her name to her previous illnesses. As she was obviously from the north of England, Alice wondered how the woman came to be working in a hospital in the south, but then that was the war for you. There had been no exchanges between them, other than those that were essential. It wasn't that the nurse had been unkind, just very matter-of-fact, and afraid. Yes, that was it. She had seemed afraid. All the time she'd taken details, changed dressings and generally seen to settling Alice in there had been a nervousness about her.

The officer brought her attention back to him. 'I'm Colonel Young, I am the immediate senior of your boss, Captain Bellows.' He coughed, an embarrassed sound. 'You know the procedure, Officer. You have to tell me anything that is relevant to our continued support of the group you were with, or contacts you made that will allow another agent to regroup them.'

'Yes, sir. But first, is there any news on Steve?'

'Agent Henderson, you mean? No, no word, I'm afraid. Our agent attached to the group who saved you said he thinks Henderson and the Resistance worker who stayed with him must be holed up somewhere. He hasn't heard a word, but is trying to find out. He knows the area is being scoured by the Germans, though. So, and I'm sorry to say this, if Henderson did survive, there is little hope that he escaped the Germans.'

Her involuntary gasp prompted a look from him that showed he'd realized what Steve meant to her, but he didn't pursue it. 'Right. Let's get on.'

After answering most of his questions, one came that shook her. 'Which member of the group do you think betrayed you? We have intelligence that it was the woman Gertrude, known as Violetta Bandemer.'

'No!'

Once more he gave her the same quizzical look, but carried on. 'Every effort is being made to capture her, but she has gone underground and is not leaving the house she works in. If it is her, then she is very dangerous, as she is close to Herr Eberhardt and has a lot of information that she could give him: names, safe houses and so on. It is imperative that she is caught and disposed of. There are plans to do the latter.'

'No! You must stop them. It is not Gertrude.' He listened in astonished silence as Alice told him what Elsbeth had told her, and about her father's journal.

'Good God – Westlin? No, it cannot be. He is a most decorated and honoured soldier. What you have told me is damning, but I believe it is false. Oh, I understand how your father came to make those assertions, and that his mistress would believe them. It is obvious that your father would want it on record that he was innocent, as he proclaimed. And for that to have any substance he would need someone to lay the blame on. Look, I am sorry, this is something I don't like saying, but in doing so your father has shown the kind of man he was. Westlin stood by him as much as he could. But once he saw what was happening, he had to use his friendship to get evidence that would stop it. He could not allow your father to continue jeopardizing our war efforts, and now it seems that your sister – or half-sister, or whatever – is doing the same. Chip off the old block . . .'

This hurt. Not the fact that the colonel didn't believe her, but the inference that Gertrude was a traitor, as he believed their father to be. And the pain of what they intended to do to Gertrude ripped her apart. 'Please listen to me. Or at least have someone go and talk to my father's mistress. Try, please try. Westlin caused all of this – he did!'

Even to her own ears it all sounded implausible. There was no real proof. Unless the writings of her father and Elsbeth, in that last journal, provided that proof . . . 'There is another diary, sir, and it may contain further evidence. Elsbeth told me that, once I read it, I would believe in our father's innocence. I had it with me when we were captured. We had to bury it: Steve – I mean, agent Henderson – and I. It is in a field. The Resistance worker called Alfonse knows where it is, for he watched everything.' *Oh God! Please let that be so. Please let him have seen us bury the book!*

'Well, that's a long shot, like finding a needle in a haystack. And then what if it is all lies? No, the whole thing is preposterous. I forbid you to speak of it ever again to anyone, Officer. And that is a command!'

Drained of energy and locked in a cocoon of fear for Steve and Gertrude, Alice felt engulfed by a feeling of helplessness. All she could do was nod her head.

'Good. We will continue in an hour. You look as though you need a break. I am sorry. Really sorry, for you do not deserve the legacy of your father's actions. No one that I know thinks so. Even Churchill himself expressed his faith in you by sanctioning your recruitment.'

This prompted the thought that maybe the great man didn't really believe in her father's guilt, but, not daring to go down the road of pursuing this, or visiting her anguish again, she did not say so. 'Thank you, sir. That means a lot to me. May I ask if I will be allowed to go back, sir? I feel as though I achieved nothing at all.'

'Nothing? So, training rough-around-the-edges Resistance workers into a disciplined troop with skills they would need, and gaining valuable information on the Versanté factory and details that led to several trains being disrupted represents nothing in your book, does is? Well, in ours it does. You have done a sterling and courageous job. But whether you will be able to go back will depend on the level of fitness that you attain. Those injuries to your arms may leave a permanent weakness, which may impair your abilities. If it is considered at all, then you will have to go through the whole course again. So for the moment get your mind conditioned to the likelihood of a desk job being your future, or some kind of advisory role.'

She walked unsteadily along the corridor, which was once the magnificent landing of this wonderful house, and stopped when she reached the top of the beautiful staircase. Moving further along, she admired how it curved and then framed each side of the wide stairs. A glance over the banister brought back memories. She could almost see Bren standing, his back against the wall, looking up at her and calling to her, 'Where have you been for the last hour? I have been looking for you.' The last part of this echoed into the present as she became aware that someone had spoken to her.

'What? Sorry . . .'

'I said, Nurse Moisley is looking for you, ma'am.'

Astonished at hearing that name, she stared back at the man who had said the words.

'I'm an orderly, ma'am. I'm called Freddie. Are you all right, ma'am?'

'Yes, sorry. Forgive me, I was daydreaming about the past. Did you say Moisley?'

'Yes. Come on, I'll help you back to your room and tell Nurse Moisley you are there. I'll get you a nice cup of tea and help you to drink it, how would that be?'

She wanted to snap at him and tell him not to patronize her, but she didn't. His mention of that name had shocked her. It couldn't be a relation to Corporal Moisley, not down here surely? Moisley had said he came from Yorkshire, and she'd assumed all of his family did as well. But then the nurse who had attended to her was northern . . .

Confused and a little anxious, she allowed the orderly to help her. Glad of his strong arm around her and leaning heavily on him, they reached her room – a partitioned-off part of what she had known to be a much bigger room belonging to Rosamond. Not that she'd had many invites here, and none of them held happy memories for her, but she had spent some of the time of Rosamond's coming-out weekend in this room, with Rosamond and a crowd of other girls. She remembered it had been a sitting room as well as a bedroom, with a dressing room and bathroom. She supposed all of these rooms had been used now in some way or another, and wondered once more what had become of Rosamond's family. She would write to Lady Elizabeth and ask her.

'Help me to the seat by the window, please, Freddie.'

The window reached from floor to ceiling, enabling her to look out onto the garden. But seeing what the war had done to other people threatened to undo the tight knot inside her. Milling around the once-perfect garden, which still held its original design but lacked the finish and floral presentation she had known, were men and women, all of them injured in some way, all tentatively picking their way around or seated in wheel-chairs or on benches. There was a certain Englishness about the scene, but no likeness to any scene that she had known.

'You cry, ma'am; seeing them poor souls is enough to make anyone cry. It does me, and I tend them every day. I want to scream at the injustice of it all sometimes.'

Turning, she saw the nurse who had attended her earlier. 'Nurse Moisley?'

'Yes, ma'am. Here, I saw Freddie bringing you a cuppa, so I took it off him. I'll help you with it – you look as if you could do with one.'

'Thank you. But no biscuits. Sorry, I'm not up to eating.'

'No, I don't suppose you are. But that will come. Once them bigwigs have finished what they have to do, we have other, gentler folk you can talk to. Oh, I know you can't tell them owt much, but they'll help you to chat. That takes a load off you. Just telling someone some of what you've been through.'

'They said you were looking for me?'

'Aye, I have to check on you regularly in your early days with us. See that you have no temperature, that sort of thing; and check on your mental welfare, and help you to settle, as it were. But let me help you with your tea first. That's more important for now.'

'What's your first name? May I use it, or do I have to call you Nurse?'

'Lil, ma'am. And aye, you can use it – most do. I'd like that. But if Matron is about then we have to be more formal.'

'You're from Yorkshire, aren't you? I recognize your accent. How did you come to be working down in Kent, for they must need nurses up there?'

Lil hesitated before saying, 'Aye, I am, and they do, but . . . Eeh, it's no good. You're going to find out. Me husband is Alfie Moisley. You met him once on a boat. Now, this might be a shock, ma'am, but Alfie is a cousin of yours. Oh, not full-blown, as he were born on the wrong side of the blanket, but your uncle fathered him, just the same.'

Even though she'd suspected this, Alice found it a surprise to hear it. For a moment she wanted to laugh. Was she to find relatives everywhere she went? The idea of them popping up and saying, 'I'm your sister, your brother, your cousin, your father's mistress' prompted a giggle, but the giggle hurt. It grated her throat and bubbled up, not into laughter, but into a sob. More sobs followed. She couldn't stop them. Her whole body wanted to cry and scream all the pain out of it.

'Eeh, ma'am, no. Don't take on like that. Eeh, I'm sorry, I shouldn't have told you.'

The feel of Lil's arms around her made Alice feel safe. There had only been a very few occasions in her life when another woman had held her, and it had never been with gentleness. Crying uncontrollably now, she took the comfort Lil offered. She leaned into her and allowed her to lift her to a standing position and guide her to the bed. Lil helped her onto the bed and sat beside Alice and held her – just that, nothing else, no remonstration or persuasion. Lil let her cry out all the misery, the coincidences that war had thrown at her, and her loss, her deep loss, of Bren, and now of Steve. Steve, the man she existed for. Would she ever see him again?

Once she'd calmed, Alice asked for and listened to Lil's story. Something in her wanted to apologize to this lovely person, to tell her she was sorry that her cousin, Lil's husband, had done such bad things, and to make her understand that Alice's uncle had instigated it all. His actions had created a feeling of anger and rejection in Alfie. He'd closed down to feeling positive emotions, just as her mother's actions had closed down Alice herself. Instead all she said was, 'Lil, we're much the same, you and I. People have done bad things to us. But we are survivors. I have a lot to tell you. Nothing is all that it seems. Especially where my father was concerned. Maybe one day I can make up to Alfie for everything he suffered, and maybe then he can change.'

'It won't make a difference. You see, I'm not the same lass as I was back then, ma'am.'

271

'Call me Alice when we're alone. I'd like that.'

'Thanks, Alice.'

Her smile held a gentle love, the kind Alice needed. 'I'm tired now. And my boss will need to see me soon, but we will talk, Lil. We'll get to know one another and become friends. I'd very much like it if that happened.'

'I'd like that an' all, Alice.'

A warmth settled in Alice as Lil said this, and somehow she didn't feel quite so alone.

20

Lil

A DOUBLE-EDGED SWORD

Torn two ways, Lil looked at the letters. Shock at the contents of both of them held her rigid with indecision. *Why, why . . . ? How can I cope? How can I split myself in two?* In three, in fact, for as well as Gillian and Mildred, she had Alice to consider, too. Alice, so frail, so hurt; a broken young woman, whom Lil knew she now loved very much. But that love within her was strong for all three women who were hurting.

In the first letter Gillian begged her to come and help, as Ruby had reached her dying days. The torment of this cut deep. *Oh, Ruby, lass . . . And poor Gillian, what must all this be doing to her?* Her being acquitted at the trial had been wonderful, but it hadn't been the end of the story for her. No, she had a long way to go.

This anguish vied heavily with the contents of the second letter. She hadn't properly taken in what it told her, and didn't know how she felt. Rocked – that's the only way she could describe it. Rocked off the centre of her world, and yet she

273

had to admit to a little relief entering her. Alfie was dead! Killed in action. Poor Mildred had had the shock of receiving the telegram.

Lil felt very differently from how she would have felt, had she received the news a couple of years ago, but her heart bled for Mildred. With Alfie's death, the hope that one day he would show Mildred some love had died, too. That hadn't happened, and now Mildred would have to live with those memories forever. Poor woman!

But what was she to do? Which way to turn? Everyone needed a part of her – how could she give it to them all?

'Bad news, Lil?'

Alice's voice came to her. Lil had taken her letters into the garden. She was up to date with all her morning duties and had allowed herself a moment of respite.

'I'm not intruding, am I, only you looked very distressed?'

'No, I'm glad you have come over to me. I don't know which way to turn . . .' A sudden realization stopped her. *God, I have to tell Alice that her cousin has died!*

'What is it? Can I be of help?'

Eeh, how she longed for a northern voice saying, 'Come here, lass, you look like you've been hit with a shovel, what's to do?' Or even an East End one, like Ruby saying, 'What's clocked you one then, love?' These officers had a stilted tone to their voices, whatever they said, though Alice did try to show she cared – she'd give her that. It was what Alice had been through that stopped her fully showing her feelings.

'I have troubles that are more than I know how to cope with at the moment, lass.' She could speak like this to Alice, but only when they were alone. 'I've had a couple of shocks, and one of them affects you. Sit down, love. I'm to tell you summat as will hurt you.' Alice sat. Her eyes held an inquisitiveness, nothing more – no worry or fear; it was as if nothing could touch her on top of what already had. She'd been here at Crescent Abbey two months, a time that had seen her body healing, although her inner self was still broken.

'I'm sorry, lass, but Alfie has been killed in action.' Just like that. How come she could say that to this near-stranger – as Alice was in a way – and not feel anything? No sadness or gladness, nothing.

'Oh. I – I don't know what to say. I – I . . .'

'There's nowt you can say. Only, I thought with you having thoughts of meeting him and making everything right, it would be a bit much for you to take.'

'No. I mean – well, I don't want to sound cold or thought-less, but it's hard for me to feel anything at all. I was just worried about you and your own feelings.'

'Oh, I'm all right. I'm long over feeling owt for Alfie, and a bit of me is relieved. But I feel for his ma – you know, Mildred, that I told you of?'

'Yes, I remember. I haven't given it all a lot of thought. Yes, poor woman, and never having felt his love – that's . . .'

'Eeh, lass. I never thought I'd say this to anyone, but it's good to see you cry again. I can't bear it when you're so closed up. It's like you're a non-person.'

'I – I can relate to the feeling of others, when it matches my own. Mildred is me in reverse. My mother never loved me.'

'Your mother is dead? By, lass, you've been through summat . . .'

'No, I tried to make her so. Not literally, but well, in my heart and mind. I wanted to be free of her. But Mildred's pain at her son's rejection has shown me that I'm not immune to the pain of my own rejection by my mother. You see . . .'

275

Listening to Alice's tale about her mother helped Lil come to a deeper understanding of her. 'I've said it more than once, lass, we've all been through the mill, but by, your troubles top them all. And I suspect there's even more as you're not saying. Well, don't force it. Let it out in bits like this. It's easier that way. And, if you like, I can find out how your mother is. That might settle you some.'

'No. Thanks, but no, I'm not ready. I've let a bit of her back in, but I'm not ready for any more, not yet. But you said there was something pulling you many ways – what else has happened?'

After Lil told her, Alice said, 'Oh dear, you will have to go to Gillian, won't you? But what will I do then?'

Lil knew this sounded worse than it was meant to. Poor Alice had a real fear within her, and the connection between them was like a prop to her. It wasn't that she felt herself more important than the others, or her needs more pressing than theirs; she just didn't know how to cope without Lil. The feeling this gave her was a good one. Their class, their education – well, everything about them divided them, but the feeling they had for one another bonded them, and that bond was stronger than the divide.

'Maybe they'll give me some leave and let you come with me. I reckon as you would like Gillian and Ruby, and helping them would help you. Give you something to focus on.'

'I would love that. I wouldn't be able to do much on the physical side, but I could help a bit, couldn't I? Oh, I do hope they will let me.'

'I don't see why not. You're on sick leave, and that gives you more freedom. Not as much as proper leave, but you must have some of that due anyroad?'

'I have, as it happens. I'll talk to the doctor. I needn't tell him I'm coming with you – he might think that too traumatic – but I could say I want to go home for a couple of weeks. I have maids at home who would see to me, if that was the truth, so I think it would work.'

'You're on, lass. But you know Gillian's house ain't what you're used to.'

'Nothing is what I am used to. Or rather it all is, now. I am sure Gillian's house is nowhere near as bad as some of the places I have had to stay in over these last months. Don't worry about me. I'm not coming to give you further worry.'

'Naw, it will give me less worry having you there. Then I will know as you're all right. And I didn't mean to imply that Gillian's house is rough, or dirty; it is lovely, just small and hasn't got the luxuries you are used to in your own home. But having you with me doesn't solve everything. There's still Mildred . . . And I'm to face losing Ruby, and poor Gillian's not up to it all. I told you about the rape – well, she's never recovered. Not to become the lass she were, she hasn't.'

'No, it will take her a long time. You have done really well yourself. Look, what if I pay for Mildred to come and stay nearby? I'd love to meet her, and have always intended to take care of Alfie's mother as best I can. I would like to provide for her and see that she has everything she needs, and this would be a start. Do you think she would come?'

'It would be a solution, and I think she would, but she's not used to fancy guesthouses. There's room at Gillian's – she has three bedrooms, and she's been staying full-time at Ruby's, she tells me, and I can't see her changing that until . . .'

'Oh, Lil, I haven't given you a thought in all of this. Forgive me. Of course it is all affecting you, these are your loved ones. I am so selfish. I'm sorry.'

'Naw, don't be. It doesn't matter. I have to go to Gillian

and Ruby, but to have you and Mildred with me will make everything easier. We can all be a help to each other.'

Saying the words didn't make the task sound any easier. All of these folk would need different things from her. Lil just hoped she was up to giving them what each of them would want.

Gillian was shocked when Lil told her the plan. Lil had rung the shop on the corner of Gillian's street and left a message asking, if one of Gillian's neighbours dropped in, would the shopkeeper give her a message to take to Gillian? He never minded doing this, and she had learned that it was a regular occurrence for the shopkeeper: informing this or that person they needed to contact someone. Gillian had rung Lil at the hospital from a phone box.

After telling Lil that Ruby was deteriorating fast, and having a cry together about this, Gillian had said, 'Anyway, love, me 'ouse ain't had a duster round it for ages, and you want to land a posh bitch on me! You take the biscuit, Lil! But they're welcome – especially Mildred, bless her. It'll be nice to have her with us. I always liked Mildred.'

Lil had said how sorry she was to ask, and had told Gillian she hadn't known which way to turn, but that it seemed like a good solution, to have all those she was worried about in one place. Then she had added, 'And Alice ain't like your normal posh kind, I promise. I wrote you about her, remember?'

'I know,' Gillian had said, 'and it's all right. Typical of you, though. You're a regular Miss Nightingale, Lil. You're gathering all the poor sods in the world. But, like I said, I'm all right with it. I have a lot on me plate, so a bit more ain't going to hurt me.'

The guilt that Lil had felt had settled a little with this. She could tell that Gillian was secretly glad of the distraction.

But when Alice's driver took them to the station to meet Mildred off the train later that day, Lil's worries increased. From being a sprightly woman who could hold her head up against anything, Mildred had turned into a crumpled old soul who looked lost.

Holding her was all Lil could think to do. And she did, as the steam and smoke from the train swirled around them. After a moment Mildred stood back and took stock of Lil. 'By, lass, you've gone up in the world. That suit looks like it cost a bob or two. It suits you.'

'Ta, Ma. I don't really like black, but – well, it's more fitting at the moment. By, it's good to see you, Ma.' It was easy for Lil to call Mildred 'Ma' as she had become like a true mother to her, as well as a friend.

'I know, lass. A lot has fallen on you. It sounds as though you are going to have your own "home for the lost and needy". But I'll help, I promise. It's just what I need – to be among folk and to help them, instead of thinking of me own troubles.'

'You're all right with who Alice is then? I mean, you understood the message I sent? I couldn't say it outright, as them at the Exchange gossip.'

'Yes, I understood. The lass you have with you is the niece of that Philippe D'Olivier, who did wrong by me. But none of that was her fault, so I'll not mention owt.'

This brought relief to Lil. 'I'm glad to hear it, Ma. Now come on – you look all in. Let's get you to me home and get you a nice cuppa or, as they say here, a Rosie Lee.'

'A what?'

'Don't ask – all will become clear. Look, there's Alice now.'

The greeting between Alice and Mildred held a kindness. Each of them reached out to the other with their words, but Mildred wouldn't hear of Alice apologizing, saying to her, 'Naw, lass. None of what happened to me is on your shoulders. There's a lot of it on mine, and a huge lump on that uncle of yours, but that's by the by. It's nice to meet you. And fitting to do so at such a time. Come here and give me a hug.'

For a moment Alice looked surprised and held herself stiffly, but Mildred was having none of it, and it brought a tear to Lil's eyes to see Alice melt a little and go into Mildred's open arms. *I'm for thinking that lass hasn't had many cuddles in her time, but the way Mildred has taken to her, she'll have to get used to them.* With this thought she got into the back of the car and left the two others to sort themselves out, and the driver to collect Mildred's bags.

Alice put Mildred in the front with the driver – a nice gesture, and she said as she did so, 'You sit with Jenson; it will be easier for you to get in, and you'll have more room for your legs than you do in the back.'

The astonished expression on Jenson's face as Mildred commented to him about how posh the car was, and that he looked right and proper as the chauffeur of it, made Lil and Alice giggle. Though it wasn't long before they were laughing out loud at Mildred's funny observations on the East End of London, saying how sorry she was for the folk living down here and finishing with, 'Poor things, it all looks like it's been hit by a bomb.' Then she turned to them and asked, 'What's up with the pair of you? You're like a couple of young 'uns going on a charabanc outing!'

'I don't know what one of those is, but I do know, Mildred, that you are a tonic and it is really nice to meet you.'

'Ta, lass. I can say the same of you. Anyroad, I knew I was going to like you, when our Lil said as she did. She's good taste in folk, though they sometimes let her down. I only wish we'd met in better circumstances, Alice, but we've got to make the best of things.'

When they turned into Gillian's road and Lil told them where they were, their mood became sober. Seeing the little house, with the wreck of its bombed-out neighbour still clinging to it, brought home why they were here. And Lil wished with all her heart that things were different and that, instead of slowly dying, Ruby would greet them at the door with her lovely smile, as she often did when she waited at Gillian's for her, and would say, 'You got here all right then? And I bet yer could do with a nice cup of Rosie Lee, eh, darlin'?'

The feeling this evoked in Lil brought her low and, looking at the others, she could see they'd both dreaded this moment. And both looked as if their own problems had come back to crowd in on them.

'Well, let's get in and get settled. Gillian will probably be round at Ruby's. I'm dreading going round there, but I have to.'

'You just see us in, lass, and show us where we're to sleep and where the larder is, so we can make a pot of tea. We'll make ourselves at home – don't you worry about us. You get off to this Ruby's house. I reckon her and Gillian need you more than we do at the moment.'

Though Alice didn't protest, Lil could see that she looked a little unsure of this. It felt natural to pat her hand and give some reassurance. 'You'll be fine with Mildred. You have a lot to talk about, and I reckon as it will help you to do so. I'll try not to be long.'

There was only a weak smile in return, but Lil couldn't devote herself to Alice's feelings at the moment. Alice had known why they were coming here, she'd asked to come along, so she must take it as it was.

Showing understanding, Alice said, 'Yes, we'll be fine. I don't know if I'm ready to talk yet, but we can do some settling in and getting to know one another.'

'That suits me, lass. I'm afraid to talk an' all. I have it all bottled up at the moment, and I'm not sure I can let the cork free. So let's take it as it comes. When we get in, you can get the stuff up to the rooms we each have, and I'll get the kettle boiling.'

'Jenson will take the bags up. I – I mean, well . . .'

'I know what you mean, lass. You're used to folk doing stuff for you, whereas we're used to doing it ourselves. There's nothing in that – just a birthright. Let that be as it is.'

As Lil got out of the car she said, 'It's not just that, Mildred. Alice is used to mucking in and doing things for herself, and in circumstances that you and I can't imagine, but both her arms were injured when—'

'When I stepped out in front of a car. I wasn't paying attention.'

Lil was mystified at this sudden interruption from Alice. But then she realized, by Alice's pleading look, that she wanted Lil to leave it at that. This made her curious, as she had imagined that Alice was shot whilst serving in a supporting role in France – driving an ambulance or delivering supplies – but her need for secrecy showed that it could have been much more than that, and she obviously didn't want to arouse the curiosity or speculation of Jenson and Mildred.

Mildred was saying, 'Well, not to worry, lass. I'll take care of you while Lil's not around. Now, let's do as Lil says and get inside.' This made Alice visibly relax, but Lil wasn't so sure – she knew Mildred. If Mildred thought there was something not quite right with the explanation, she would find out in her own way and in her own time. Not in a malicious way, there wasn't anything like that in Mildred's character, but she liked to know the truth of what was going on around her.

As they opened the door Mildred said, 'Eeh, it's a nice little house, Lil. Cosy. It feels like a lot of happy times have gone on in this home. Pity that bloody Hitler had to spoil it by causing the death of Gillian's mam . . .'

With that thought in her mind, Lil left them. All around her as she walked there were signs of Hitler's spoiling of the lives of folk round here. But then, thought Lil, in a small way Hitler had relieved her of her greatest burden: Alfie . . . *God! What am I thinking! It must be all the upset turning me mind. I know I didn't want Alfie any more, but that's no reason to be glad he no longer has his life, or to not think of his ma's suffering at his loss!*

Reaching Ruby's house, she let go of all of these thoughts and dug deep within herself to find the courage she needed to step over the threshold – something she had been dreading.

21

Lil & Alice

LONDON & KENT,
EARLY OCTOBER 1941

A Release

'Let's go to the free-'n'-easy night at the Red Bull, Lil.'

This, from Gillian, surprised Lil. She hadn't thought Gillian would want to go anywhere tonight, having just come back from Ruby's funeral. Looking at Mildred and Alice, Lil could see they were also taken aback, and both had a look of bewilderment on them, which was probably down to not being sure what a free-'n'-easy was, as much as anything else.

The funeral had been awful. Lil never wanted to experience the like of it again. It had been impossible to imagine the bright-and-breezy cockney girl that she'd known Ruby to be lying stiff and still and cold in the wooden box.

The spread back at Ruby's ma-in-law's house had been a subdued affair, with several people quietly breaking down. But the resilience of Ruby's lads had been good to see. They'd played and argued in the little back yard and seemed to have accepted it all at face value. And now here they were in Gillian's mam's house. Jenson had driven them back, and Gillian had proclaimed that she wanted to go to the local pub for a sing-song!

'Ruby would have been happy for us to go, I reckon, Lil. I can almost hear her saying, "Come on, me skin-'n'-blister, stop being morbid and see me off in a good old cockney fashion." And that's what I want to do.'

'If that's what lass wants, then I think as we should do it. She knows best how to say goodbye to her sister, and what we had this afternoon weren't what you could call a wake. Though I'm not sure what a "free-'n'-easy" is.'

Alice nodded, 'Yes, Mildred, I agree. I didn't meet Ruby, but from what I've gathered, she would have liked a happy send-off and, though I'm not sure what it is either, if I'm invited I would like to go. It will cheer us all up.'

Lil wondered how Alice was ever going to be really cheery again, but she had to hand it to her, she could put a good face on things. And, looking around them, she saw that same strength and fortitude in them all. And although she least felt like it, she agreed. 'Reet. The Red Bull it is. I've allus been one for a good old sing-song or, as they call it down here, a free-'n'-easy. Everyone get ready, and we can get some fish and chips on the way home, as we'll be in need of a bite by then.'

Smoke hung in the air of the bar, and the music from the honky-tonk piano vied with the tinny voices of the patrons – mostly women, as was usual these days, though a few men were dotted here and there amongst them: those who had jobs that exempted them from joining up, the flat-footers, and the occasional service man waiting for orders to join his regiment.

A woman called out to Gillian, 'Lor, luv a duck, Gillian, didn't expect you, love. But glad you came. Come and sit here. There's room for you and your mates.'

285

As they wove their way through the occupied stools, the woman started a slow hand-clap. Then the whole room took up the applause. When it died down, the one who had called out said in a loud voice, 'That applause was well deserved, and I'm glad that you all joined in. These four are very brave women. Gillian came through her own trials to nurse her sister. Her mate, Lil, is a nurse for officers who have been wounded. Her mother-in-law, Mildred, is a mother of one of our lost boys. And Lil's mate, Alice, is an officer who was wounded in action.'

Lil looked around in astonishment as the clapping started up again. Mildred and Gillian wiped tears from their eyes and smiled a watery thanks, but Alice had a stony, cold expression. This embarrassed Lil a bit, but then Alice was an officer type.

'How did they know about me?' she asked. 'Lil, there's a reason why they say that careless talk costs lives! I am very angry.'

'I don't know, but I can guess. Have you slipped out to Mildred that your wounds were caused by you being shot?'

'I – I don't think I did. Oh dear.'

'Well, she must have deduced it, when she saw your wounds or something, and happen she let it slip when she was gossiping in the street, and then word got round. I'll talk to her. But I shouldn't think any harm has been done. They only know you have seen action – that's all. If you keep up the frostiness, they might start wondering if there's more that we're not saying, so just accept it as it is.'

A soldier came over, saluted Alice and introduced himself. 'Private Fulling, ma'am. I don't know what you did over there, but I salute you for it. And you, missus – you gave your son. And all of you. If you can show bravery, then I can. I will remember you all when I'm out there.'

'Aye, you do that, son,' Mildred told him, 'and we'll be thinking of you, won't we, Alice?'

'We will, Private. And all of those fighting. Good luck.'

He sounded friendly enough, Lil thought, but she also thought Alice had been a bit short with her answer – the lad had been looking to her for encouragement. She could be like a piece of cold lard at times. Not that she wasn't kind, but she could just cut herself off from everything. The soldier went to say more, but Lil stopped him, for she could see Alice wasn't happy with the intrusion. 'Look, lad, we're just out for a night together, love. We don't want to be hailed as heroes, or owt else. We're no different from the rest of you. Go and enjoy your beer. Ta for the recognition of us, but we don't want to chat.'

'Oh, er . . . Sorry, ladies.'

'Poor bloke, he were only trying to be friendly.'

'I know, Ma, but none of us want that attention. And you be careful what you tell folk. I know it ain't easy, as talking's what we do where we come from, but down here there's all sorts listening. Like Alice just said, careless talk costs lives.'

'Well, none of us have owt to hide, have we?'

The music drowned Mildred out, as did the singing that started up: 'Show Me the Way to Go Home'.

When it ended Gillian said, 'I'm going to sing a song for Ruby.'

Lil watched her approach the pianist and say something to him. He nodded, before shouting at the crowd, ''Ere, listen up. Young Gillian wants to sing a tribute to Ruby, so shut up your boat-races and listen. Give some respect.'

Lil held her breath. She couldn't think how Gillian would make it through a song, but willed her to do so, when she heard Gillian announce in a voice that shook with emotion,

'I'm going to sing "My Sister and I".' As the familiar notes began, there came a sound that Lil hadn't heard in a long time: the once happy-go-lucky Gillian singing her heart out:

> *'My sister and I remember still*
> *Tulips growing on our windowsill.'*

These weren't the real words. It seemed Gillian had gone to the trouble of changing the lyrics to fit her life with Ruby. This song must mean a lot to her, and Lil prayed harder for her; she'd lost her mother and now her sister: *Please let her get through the song at least, please* . . . Everyone helped Gillian with the last line of each verse, 'But we don't talk about that'. Until, that is, she sang her own version of the last few lines:

> *'My sister and I recall the day*
> *We said goodbye and she sailed a – away.'*

The tears streamed down her face, the pianist faltered and a silence fell. But then Alice stood up and went towards Gillian and, in one of the most wonderful voices Lil had ever heard, sang a version of the last two lines:

> *'But we have friends that are here to stay*
> *And we must all talk about that.'*

Cheers rang out as Alice reached Gillian and helped her down from the little stage, bringing her back to her seat. 'Well done, Gillian. That was a fitting tribute to Ruby. I only wished I had met her.'

For the umpteenth time that evening Lil found herself astonished, as Alice hugged the weeping Gillian to her.

A woman shouted over to Alice, 'Give us a song, Miss! Go on, give us one of Vera Lynn's.' Everyone joined in then, calling for Alice to sing.

Lil thought it was time to go and went to say so, but Alice stood and said, 'Righto, any preference?'

'Eeh, I never thought I'd see the day, Lil, that one of them D'Oliviers sang in a pub! I'd have sooner imagined being whacked in the face with a shovel!'

What Mildred said summed up Lil's own feelings, but before she could say so, Alice's voice, beautiful and strong, filled every corner and silenced her and everyone else in the room. 'A Nightingale Sang in Berkeley Square' lifted the hairs on her arms. And it came to her that this was an Alice she'd never seen before and, she guessed, not many others had, either.

Everyone cheered Alice. Some said she should be on the stage, others told her she'd made their night. Flushed and beaming, but looking tired, she sat down, refusing their requests of 'More!'

'Eeh, lass, you've a lovely voice.' Mildred wiped a tear from her eye as she said this. Lil stepped in. She needed to stop any sentimentality before it put them all down in the doldrums. Speaking in her best nurse's voice she told them, 'Aye, she has, but it is past her bedtime and, as my patient, I am ordering her home. So come on, all of you. It's been a good night, but time to go.'

Linking arms, they walked home. Stopping off at the chippie, none of them could resist pinching a chip, before the rest were wrapped in a newspaper bundle and put inside a brown paper bag. Their antics at trying to bite into their steaming-hot chips, dripping with vinegar, had them all giggling on the way back. The noise they made drew more than one protest, as folk opened a window and told them to think of others who were trying to sleep. But although they tried there was a lightness about them, not altogether due to the beer they'd drunk, but to having given Ruby a proper send-off, and at having cemented their friendship. And that included Alice.

After one particularly nasty warning to 'shut up or be shut up', they walked in silence until they neared their front door, where Mildred said, 'I feel a peace in me now, lass. Tonight I thought of me Alfie in a different way. I thought of him out of danger and safe, because he is, you know. He's safe from them Germans, and safe from the demons that drove him to do things he shouldn't. They say as how your life flashes in front of your eyes before you die, and that would show him the error of his ways. Aye, and I reckon that if he could have his say, he'd say he were sorry for how he treated me and you. Anyroad, I've forgiven him. Do you reckon you can, Lil?'

'I can, Ma, and have.'

'And I have too,' said Gillian.

Lil was surprised at how quickly she'd forgiven Alfie, but to hear Gillian say that she had also forgiven him, for causing her rape and subsequent trial for murder, gave her hope that forgiveness could lead to healing. It would be good to have Gillian at peace inside herself. As it would Alice, but whether that would ever happen she couldn't say. As Lil watched Alice look up at the stars and mouth the words 'I love you', as she did every night to someone only Alice knew, she thought: *Maybe it will take Alice's special person to come home before she can be healed.*

'Well, lass, here we are again.' The familiar smells of the hospital, carbolic soap and disinfectant hit Lil as she opened the door of Crescent Abbey.

'Yes, here we are, and I am already feeling the weight of the place. Lil, I think I will ask to be discharged. It's time to go back to my own home. I am sure I will heal better there. I have a beautiful park at the back of it. The views are soothing, and I love walking amongst the trees. Besides, I have my staff, who are also my friends, to look after me.'

'Oh . . .' Disappointment settled in Lil on hearing Alice say this. They'd spent the last few days with Mildred and Gillian, before seeing Mildred off on her journey back up to the north and Gillian back to work. Things seemed to have fallen into place for each of them. Now Alice was saying that she wanted to leave, and Lil didn't feel ready for that, not yet. Neither did she think Alice was ready. Yes, she'd made strides – huge strides, both physically and emotionally – but there was still a way to go.

'I feel I have to leave. This place depresses me. Oh, it's nothing to do with you nurses or any of the staff, but seeing the other patients – they're all, well, broken. And it doesn't feel as if they will ever be mended. Besides, I have things I need to do. I want to put an allowance in hand for Mildred, and . . . well, visit my mother and get her affairs straight. I need to be busy, Lil. Really busy.'

'I understand. I do. But I'm going to miss you.'

'No, you won't. You can visit me, and I can visit you and Gillian. And we can go up to the north to see Mildred on one of your leave days.'

'I can't! Not that last I can't. They all hate me up there. They see Alfie's fall from grace, and Jimmy and Brian's deaths, as my fault. They think I did wrong sending that letter to Alfie, and that I got my just deserts in the way he got his revenge. Besides, I thought I'd try to get Mildred down here permanently. She ain't treated right up there, either. They have a holier-than-thou attitude sometimes. Oh, they're the salt of the earth most of the time, but when it comes to a lass having a young 'un on the wrong side of the blanket, they are judgemental in their attitudes.'

'Would she come?'

'Aye, I think so. I sort of hinted at the possibility, and she got me gist and didn't show any reluctance. She liked it here.'

'Well, then, I will help with that. Whatever she wants, I will try to provide it. And I will write to my uncle and let him know about Alfie. He should have helped Alfie and Mildred, but he isn't like me. None of them are. Not even my mother. I must take after my father and my sis— My aunt, I mean.'

For a moment Lil thought Alice had nearly said sister. *How strange. As far as I know, she has no siblings – unless her father had a child out of wedlock, as his brother did. Still, if she doesn't want to share it, I'm not going to probe.* With this thought, Lil allowed Alice to change the subject without challenging her.

'Lil, will you come with me and see my mother? You remember I told you a bit about her? Well, there's a lot more to her than I've told you, and I'm afraid to go on my own.'

'By, that's a rare thing – afraid of your own ma. But I dare say as you have your reasons. Aye, of course I will. You just give me a warning as to when, and I'll fix it up.'

'Thank you, Lil. Thank you for everything – not just consenting to accompanying me when I visit my mother, but everything. These last couple of weeks have had their sad moments, but for me they have been wonderful. I feel accepted amongst you. You feel more like family than I've ever had.'

'Eeh, lass, that's good to hear, as I was feeling the same. I've no real family. I have me ma-in-law, but that's all. Though I've long since looked on Gillian as a little sister, and . . .

well, I did look on Ruby as a sister an' all. But now I can add you to that, and it feels good to do so. Oh, we're not in the same league, so we can't socialize a lot, but that don't matter. It's what we feel in our hearts that counts.'

Alice's arms came around her, and the hug she gave Lil told her that Alice had made huge strides, just in being able to give this little gesture of her feelings for another person. It warmed her heart to think there was every hope that Alice would heal completely.

22

Gertrude

PARIS, MARCH 1942

A LIFE GIVEN – A LIFE LOST

If the threat on her life hadn't been in place, Gertrude knew she could have gone outside as normal. Life had dragged these last few months, and she'd felt completely cut off. No contact with Juste, or any of the group. But then, unless she went to the cafe, how could they keep her informed about what was going on?

Even though her pregnancy was nearing its end and had given her an excuse not to go out, as she turned this way and that in front of the long mirror she knew she could have hidden the fact. The child inside her hardly showed its presence to the world. Wearing that flared jacket with the three-quarter-length sleeves over her frock would have hidden her small bump. But fear had kept her inside. Oh, how she longed to go out for a walk.

In an instant she made her mind up to do so. Surely those who wanted her dead couldn't be watching her every movement, or waiting in the street twenty-four hours a day on the off-chance that she might appear? For one thing, the guards would notice them, wouldn't they?

With a defiant flick of her hair she went to her wardrobe, donned a thick, loose-fitting woollen jumper for warmth and then put on the flared jacket. Checking in the mirror, she was pleased with the result. The dark red colour of the jacket suited her and toned well with the grey jumper. The frock she had on underneath had a background of grey, with a pattern of reds and blacks flecked into it. Slipping her stockinged feet into a soft pair of flat shoes, she moved towards the door. But a pain stopped her. It shot across her back and had her gasping in a deep breath. *God!*

As she waited for a few minutes the intensity of it wavered and she was able to take a few tentative steps. She made it back to the sofa and sank down. Sweat ran down the nape of her neck. Sitting up straight gave her relief – the pain had gone. *I must have twisted myself.*

Reaching the door of her room again and opening it gave her a moment's elation – she really was going to go out. Nothing would stop her; she refused to be a prisoner here any longer. Juste would have sorted everything by now. Somehow he would have proved that she did not betray the agents. It had been months ago – it had happened in the first weeks of her pregnancy, and now she was coming to the end of her eighth month.

The guard sitting at the end of the nursery stood as she approached and gave a half-salute. Gertrude nodded and moved past him. Behind her the noise of the children playing in the yard had her stopping again. Should she take them with her? It wasn't that they had been deprived of fresh air, for the nursery nurse took them out every day and was with them now, but Gertrude did love being with them.

Seeing things through their eyes had given her a different perspective on everyday things she'd taken for granted, and their questions had entertained her. Often the four of them had ended up giggling together; the child in herself had come to the fore and had given her a joy she'd rarely felt in her own young years. Deciding it was best not to take the children with her now, just in case there was still any danger lurking for her, her body released a sigh from deep within her. She dreamed of one day in the future when it would be possible to be a mother to them, and not a governess, but that couldn't happen yet. *If only peace would come, then Kristof and I might stand a chance of being open with our love. But this bloody war rages on. And on.*

As she opened the front door, the cool air braced her for a moment. The avenue outside acted like a wind tunnel at this time of year. The guards stood aside, then showed surprise that it was Gertrude coming through the door. One went to speak to her, but changed his mind. Stepping down the first step brought the pain back into focus, but with a gut-wrenching ferocity that tore through the front of her, before settling in her back. Her hand grasped the rail. A guard caught her and said in German, 'Frau Bandemer, what is it? Are you hurt?'

His dialect had her struggling for a moment, but she managed to decipher what he'd said. 'Please fetch Herr Eberhardt . . . Hurry!' A wetness soaked her underwear.

'But . . .'

'*Fetch* him!'

The guard jumped, clipped his heels and hurried inside.

Pain took over every part of her, taking her dignity away and leaving her standing in a pool of water, screaming like a banshee.

'Frau Bandemer, what ails you? Let me help you.' The assistance that the second guard went to give her was quickly withdrawn, as a command from Kristof sliced through the air: '*Nicht berühren!*'

'Oh, Kr— Herr Eberhardt, it is happening . . .'

'Come, my dear. I will help you to your room.'

She had no idea how she managed to get there. Pain after pain waved through her, gripping her in spasms she could hardly bear.

'There, I'll help you onto the bed. The doctor is coming.'

She'd heard him barking orders as they passed the offices. Heads had appeared from them, some acknowledging his orders, others looking astonished, but in her confusion she hadn't heard him asking for a doctor.

'It's coming, it's coming – remove my panties, Kristof, please remove my panties. I need to push.'

'But it is too soon. Wait! Wait for the doctor, maybe he will be able to stop it . . .'

'Nothing can stop it, pleeeeeease!'

At this he jumped into action and, once released from any restrictions, there was nothing she could do but push. It took just two massive pushes, to the sound of Kristof begging her, 'Stop, wait – wait for the doctor, please!' before their baby slithered onto the bed. Instinct told her to clear the baby's mouth and get it breathing and warm. Ignoring the blood covering the eiderdown, she leaned forward and, grabbing the baby's little legs, pulled her towards her. With shaking hands, she gently prised open the little mouth. With the airway clear, she gave one sharp tap on the wrinkled, blueish-coloured bottom, and a scream to rival the one that she'd given herself filled the room.

'She's alive! Kristof, our little girl is alive . . .'

Kristof sank to his knees, his eyes rolled back and he went into a deep faint. Looking down, she saw his motionless body lying on the floor beside the bed. Smiling, she said to their child, 'There, little one, is your father. His welcome isn't very good, is it?'

Cradling the tiny form to her breast, she felt a great love inside her – a love she had never previously experienced. With it came tears of joy, mixed with pity for the troublesome and dangerous situation this little mite had come into.

As if seeking comfort, her baby's tiny fingers, small and dainty, wrapped around her own. 'It's all right, little Elsbeth, Mama and Papa will make your world safe. Everything will be well, you'll see. Mama will wrap you in love, and so will Papa.' The child made a small sound as if saying, 'I know.' It wasn't very loud, but with it Kristof stirred and looked up at her in astonishment.

'What happened?'

'You fainted, darling. Don't worry, I have heard that it happens. Meet your daughter, little Elsbeth.'

'A girl! Elsbeth? You have named her?'

'Yes, I knew at once that she was to be called that. I – I don't know why. Do you approve?'

'I do. It is a good German name. It was my grandmother's name. It is perfect. And I will add Frayda, as Frayda was my mother.'

'Elsbeth Frayda Eberhardt. Yes, it has a nice sound. I like it.'

'Where have you heard the name Elsbeth? Is it a family name of yours, too?'

'No. I heard it somewhere and liked it – that's all. I am so happy that you like it, and that it has a family connection for you. Now, where is the doctor? Elsbeth's cord needs to be cut and tied, and I need to be relieved of the afterbirth. I think you should leave me for these things. But if the doctor doesn't arrive soon, then make sure I have some sterile scissors . . .'

'Oh, don't! No details – I feel queasy.'

His smile told her he was sorry to be so useless, but she didn't mind. These soft qualities of Kristof's were what made him more human, and took away the thoughts of the cruelty she knew he was capable of, when crossed.

Once he'd left them Gertrude lay back. Her mother and Juste came to her mind. They should be here with her, in particular her mother . . . *Oh, Mama, Mama.* Once more the tears came, and she wondered if she would ever see them again.

The agony of this thought ripped through her. But it also put a determination in her to try and re-establish contact with Juste and the group. Once she was strong again she would go out. She'd wear her fur-collared coat, in the hope that Juste was nearby and would know she had a message for him. In her message she'd ask if she was in the clear yet, and for any news on Madeline, and would tell Juste that he was an uncle.

With Madeline in her mind came further agony. Inside her she felt sure Madeline was dead. It had been months without a word. Yes, there had been a time when she'd felt hope, as she had found out that Madeline had escaped. Kristof's anger when he'd been told of the British agents' escape had made him more talkative than usual about matters of war. He'd raged about making it his mission to recapture the agents. But he hadn't discussed it with her since, and she hadn't dared to show any interest by asking.

The door opening and the doctor's arrival with a nurse

stopped any further speculation or giving in to heartache, as the next half-hour was taken up with sorting out both her own and little Elsbeth's needs. She wept as they did this, and neither of the medical staff tried to stop her. 'This is normal for a new mother, especially with such a quick and unexpected birth.' The nurse didn't say this in a kindly way, more matter-of-fact, though her voice softened a little as she continued, 'It is the shock, as much as anything else. But you need not worry, as your daughter is very healthy. A little small, but that is not a problem, as everything is functioning normally. This down that is covering her will drop away. It is because she did not reach her full term.'

Gertrude thanked the nurse, but at the same time wished that both she and the doctor would finish what they were doing and leave her and Elsbeth alone. She had so much to put her mind to.

At two weeks old Elsbeth was constantly hungry and made Gertrude very sore, sucking at her breast for what seemed like most of the day. But Gertrude didn't mind. This contact with her daughter felt like the closest a human being could be with another, and she gazed in wonder at her child for hours. But still her inner turmoil raged, and impatience to know something about what was going on in the outside world got the better of her. Contact had been impossible for months now – it had been as if she was stranded on an island. Even news of the war came with a German perspective, worrying her more and more.

Donning her fur-collared coat, with her message for Juste pinned into the lining, she hugged Elsbeth to her. Handing her over to the nursery nurse gave Gertrude a strange pain in her heart. She almost snatched her baby back, but as she gave the nurse the bottle of expressed milk, the girls jumped up and came to her, demanding that they got a hug too. This welcome distraction warmed her. If the nurse hadn't been within hearing distance, she would have told them how much she loved them, as she had taken to doing when they were alone. She hadn't actually said this to the boys, for it would have embarrassed them, but there was an unspoken knowledge of the shared love between them. 'I won't be long,' she told the girls. 'Look after little Elsbeth, and be good girls for Nurse.'

Walking along the hall, with her resolve holding strong to carry out her plan of venturing as far as the cafe, she once more admired the paintings as she went. Around her she could hear the usual sounds: voices from behind doors and, in the distance, footsteps as office workers hurried between rooms. Then, as she neared the stairs that led down to the kitchen, a clattering of pans and the remnants of breakfast smells filtered up to her.

A door opened behind her. A chair scraped along the tiled floor. As she looked back, the guard who had been sitting outside Kristof's office, and who had barely glanced at her, now stood to attention, with his arm straight out. Her ears cringed at his cry of '*Heil Hitler!*'

Kristof emerged, looking surprised to see her. 'Oh, are you going out? Well, obviously you are, but I didn't expect to see you.'

'I know. I didn't want to disturb you, but I am longing to walk a little way. I'll only go as far as the cafe. I feel safe now . . .'

'And Elsbeth?'

'She is too young to go out yet, and the air is a little chilly this morning. The nursery nurse is taking care of her.'

'Come inside a moment.'

Hoping Kristof wouldn't stop her from going outside, now that she finally had the courage to do so, she followed him into his office. In the outer one he spoke to his assistant, asking her to ensure that he wasn't disturbed for any reason. The woman didn't comment.

Bright winter sun poured through the south-east-facing windows of his office and a million specks of dust danced in its beams. The smell of his aftershave, and the brilliantine he used to try and tame his hair, played with her senses, awakening them for the first time since the birth.

Everything around her was just as she remembered it from the first time she'd been here. Even the picture of his wife still stood on his desk. She felt a pang of jealousy at this. And, as if he knew, Kristof said, 'I cannot live without the picture, but I live happily with it now.'

A warmth blushed her cheeks. She was embarrassed that he'd noticed her reaction. But his response helped her. 'That is good,' she told him. 'I would never want you to shut her out, and I hope one day she will become part of us, but you need to talk more about her for this to happen.'

He did not answer her. In his silence she recognized there was still a part of him that was so vulnerable, although it was an aspect that she suspected he showed only to her.

'Thank you. I will . . . Come here, let me hold you.'

As he came towards her, he placed the photo face-down. *Will anything ever heal him fully?*

The feel of his strong body pressing her to him further awakened her, but it was too early to give herself to him. Still sore from the birth and still bleeding, she couldn't do it. But to be held by him, in this undemanding way, filled her with longing.

'My darling, I love you.' His voice held the desire she could feel him fighting against. Letting her hand wander, she caressed the hardness of him.

'There is no need to do without. I am here for you, darling.' There was no objection from Kristof, just sighs of love and pleasure as she guided him to his chair and released him from his trousers. His moans told of his enjoyment. His hands caressed her bent head, pressing her mouth further onto him. Suppressing her own desires, she worked on him with all the skills she'd learned in her days of prostitution, until at last she drank him in and he flopped back, completely spent. As she rose, she looked down at him. At this moment he looked beautiful. His flushed cheeks, his adoring look, the little beads of sweat on his forehead glistening in the sunlight and the heavy, lush grey of his eyes would stay with her forever.

Putting himself away, he pulled her down onto his lap. Cradled there like a baby, she enjoyed the gentle rocking motion as he swung the chair from side to side. Their eyes held each other.

Kristof broke the silence. 'My darling, how can a man be so lucky as to have known two great loves?' As he said this, he bent forward and stood the photo up again.

The woman in the photo looked at her with a beautiful smile that wasn't dissimilar to her own. Her blonde hair was cut short to just below her ears, unlike Gertrude's own long hair, but her features almost mirrored her own. This shocked her.

'Yes, you are alike, and I cannot deny that is what attracted me to you at first. But you are different people. She was a wonderful person, and I still hold her in my heart. But you are even more wonderful – you are warm and loving. You know me like I have never been known. You don't try to change me; you open me up to be what I am. At least the loving, feeling part of me. The man who is real. The man who has nothing to do with the part of me that is loyal to my country and to Herr Hitler, and who has to do my duty, whatever that may cost me.'

Yes, she knew that man. And she knew that if he found out the truth about her, even though he loved her, he would have her executed. This thought rippled a memory through her that she did not want – that of the maid hanging from the tree. Something told her that her own fate would be even worse, for she had violated Kristof's trust.

'Don't be afraid, my darling. You have no need to be. I will never allow you to see the other person that I can be. I keep him locked in this room. I like to keep the different sides of myself separate, though you have made me break this rule today. But that is what you are capable of doing to me. Now, I have to compose myself and go to my apartment, which is where I was off to when I came across you. I need to prepare myself for a very important meeting. So go and enjoy your walk, but please don't be out long – you are not yet strong.'

Getting up off his knee, she wiped her mouth, then poured herself a glass of water from his jug.

'Washing me away, eh?' His laugh sounded childish. She laughed with him.

'Never, darling, but I don't want to talk to others with the hint of you on my breath. We are for each other only, and shouldn't share that part of us with all and sundry.'

Kissing her, he said, 'I'm all gone. I can't taste me on you.' With this he slapped her bottom, winked and said, 'I may be back there soon, though. I hunger for you, and though I cannot have you fully yet, that is a very good second-best.'

Though she knew he meant this light-heartedly, she had a

sudden urge to tell Kristof how much it meant to hear this. 'Thank you. I never thought I'd be loved in the way you love me. If this is my last day, know that I am yours – always yours.'

'What! What are you saying? Are you in danger?'

'N – no. No. It is just a saying. A lovers' saying.' But even as she tried to put his mind at rest, something in her thumped the fear around her. Every day she thought of the death-threat hanging over her. Surely it had lifted, hadn't it? 'Anyway, I'm going; you get yourself ready. I'll see you tonight when you come to me and little Elsbeth. I love you, my darling.'

Outside the air cut through her. Pulling her fur collar closer around her neck and putting her head down against the wind, she walked unsteadily, but with determination, and kept her eyes forward, resisting the urge to search every nook and cranny of her journey for a possible killer.

The cafe looked the same as always, though the little red gingham curtains appeared to be freshly laundered, giving a cosy feel against the dark-green paint of the windows and the door. Closed against the draught of the wind, the door stuck a little, but as it gave, it rattled the bells hanging above it – a familiar and very welcome sound.

But the person behind the counter didn't give the same welcome. It wasn't Paulo and, as rarely was the case, there were no customers in the cafe. This gave it an eerie silence, when normally chatter and laughter would be bouncing off the walls.

The wobble in her step increased. She tried not to worry and to appear as if nothing was amiss. 'Are you new here? When I was in here last, Paulo owned this cafe.'

'*Oui*. Paulo died six months ago. What can I get you?'

A feeling spread over her as if someone had run a feather down her spine as the shock at his news turned her blood cold. 'Oh, nothing. I have changed my mind. I am too upset by hearing of Paulo's passing to want to eat or drink now. *Merci. Au revoir.*'

Before she reached the door, strong arms grabbed her. The door slammed shut. The sound of the bolt clunking into place made her heart heavy with fear.

'*Rapidement, obtenez les cordes!*'

A hand came over her mouth, making it impossible for her to emit anything more than a groan from her throat. She kicked her leg backwards in an effort to hurt whoever held her, before the ropes that had been requested could be fetched. The blow she managed to give his shin made him release his hold. She reached out for the door bolt, but a punch deep into her kidneys buckled her.

'Bitch! Traitor! I spit on you!'

Wet slime slid down her cheek. All hope of persuading her assailants she was innocent evaporated as she looked into the hate searing the eyes of the man she'd seen behind the counter. A second man, a stranger, stood over her. Thick rope dangled over his arms, and struggling didn't help. Her body hurt as they trussed her, stretching her limbs till they felt as though they would come out of their sockets. The scream that started in her bowel was left rasping in her throat as something was stuffed into her mouth. Then darkness – perhaps the worst thing of all – enclosed her as they placed a tight blindfold over her eyes. Her mind could not untangle the emotions going through her as terror filled her, leaving her unable to grasp the reality of what was happening.

As they lifted her, she wanted to shout out the agony it caused her, but could not. Squeezing her through the gap that led behind the counter, they took no heed of her limbs scraping against the sharp edges. *Please help me! God, help me.*

From what they were saying she knew they were taking her out of the back door and into the alley behind. Here the smell of stale food-waste, cat wee and dog excrement sickened her already-churned stomach. It was a relief when they shoved her into the back of what she imagined was a van. The slatted floor dug into her, but at least every part of her body was supported, and not left to dangle in a way that would dislocate her joints.

The doors slamming shut with a tinny sound, typical of a van, rocked the vehicle. The smell of fresh bread and hams suddenly blotted out the foul stench of the alley. What this told her filled her with despair. Delivery vans often moved around the area, even during curfew, without being challenged, so it was unlikely that any patrolling German soldiers would call them to a halt. Even random spot-checks were becoming fewer as German complacency set in.

The movement of the vehicle, driven in haste, caused her body to rock backwards and forwards. Loaves of bread dropped onto her. Soft and delicious normally, they now felt like weapons with hard exteriors that scratched and bruised her.

The journey went on and on. With each mile she imagined the horror of what she would face when they reached their destination. Into the turmoil of her thoughts came her mother, smiling down at the child she once was – showing her the photo of her father and telling her what a lovely man he had been. *Oh, Papa, am I to suffer the same fate as you? I know you were innocent, too. Help me, Papa, help me!* Then there was Juste, marching around the garden with a stick held on his shoulder as if it were a gun, playing his war games. *Games – how soon those games had turned to reality!*

A picture of her stepfather came to her, wielding his belt, his smile holding a sick pleasure as he whacked the leather strap into the palm of his hand. As then, a terror trickled through her now. *Oh, how I would prefer to be facing his wrath than the unknown horror awaiting me* . . . But she mustn't think about it. Something would happen to save her. Juste must know of their plans. He must have his contacts who would tell him that she'd been taken. *He must have!*

Madeline entered this frenzy of thoughts that were attacking Gertrude. Sweet Madeline, a sister whose real name she didn't know. They'd had such plans for the future. She was to visit Madeline in London and see the sights she had heard so much about. Shop in the stores. And talk – yes, above all they were going to talk. Tell everything to each other until there was nothing they didn't know about the other. *Where are you now, my darling sister? And what of my baby . . . No! I cannot bear the agony of leaving her and my Kristof. Oh God!*

The van came to an abrupt halt, skidding on what sounded like pebbles. A beach? A rush of damp salty air, as they opened the doors, confirmed her suspicions. Dragging her from the van caused her further pain, but the impact of it was nothing compared to the extreme terror that gripped her.

'Cut the rope stringing her legs to her wrists, but keep her legs tied together, then stand her up. Take off her blindfold.'

The crashing waves caused spray to dampen her face. It mingled with her tears, icing them as they ran down her face. Through the haze of them she saw François. She hadn't known there was a third person involved. That he, a lifelong friend, believed what she was accused of – and so strongly that he was willing to be part of this – hurt her deeply. His tone told of his disgust and cut the last thread of hope that he would prevent this, as he told her, 'This is where you die, traitor.'

Unable to keep her balance as her legs lost all strength, she toppled over.

'Leave her,' François commanded, then his voice grated with emotion as he added, 'It is fitting that she should die lying down; standing is for heroes.'

A defiance came into her. Staring up at him, she saw him falter as he raised his gun. She shook her head and tried to plead with her eyes. François's expression held nothing but vile hatred.

She didn't register the gun being fired, as a searing, burning sensation took all the space in her head. The world turned into a swirling red mass, before an impenetrable blackness enveloped her. Somewhere in the distance a tiny light broke though. Its beauty beckoned her. Floating towards it brought a peace that settled all around her. The shape of the light changed as she approached. The form of a shadow gradually became clearer. *Papa . . . Papa . . .* A great love encased her, taking away her worldly being and all memories of her time on Earth, and giving her a sense of extreme happiness. A sense of rebirth . . .

23

Alice

ONE MESSAGE BRINGS HOPE, ANOTHER DESPAIR

The letter came enclosed inside one from the MOD. The noise of it plopping through her letter box interrupted Alice's routine of getting ready for work – the humdrum daily toil of admin that she had been reduced to doing since she'd recovered from her injuries. Not that she had given in. She'd taken on new challenges and was in the process of fighting through to full physical fitness, to achieve her dream of going back into action, though so far all requests to do so had been turned down. She knew why. Her mental state wasn't as it should be. The sharpness had gone. A fog of depression hung over her.

Receiving post wasn't an unusual event, but each time something arrived, it raised her hopes. Skipping down the winding staircase, her hand sliding along the highly polished banister, her feet treading the deep, soft carpet, showed up the sharp contrast between her war work and her life now. But living back at home held no comfort for her.

As she neared the bottom step she could see the brown

envelope lying on the silver platter on the hall table – the maid would have put it there. The sight of it stopped her in her tracks, because even from this distance she knew its origin. A dread entered her. Turning the envelope over and over, she went from wishing with all her heart that it didn't contain bad news to a certainty that it did.

The paper knife in her hand shook as she struggled to control the trembling that rippled through her. The grating noise as she opened the envelope frayed her nerves further. Inside it wasn't what she was expecting. It wasn't an official letter. Her name was scrawled in black ink on the envelope inside. Excitement clutched the pit of her stomach at the sight of the crumpled, dirty envelope. The date inside shocked her: 3rd August 1941. Eight months ago!

My darling,

I hope this finds you well and safe. My holiday in Switzerland is to be extended as my broken leg is not looking good. We shall see.

As I cannot travel, my companion will take steps to get this to you, as the post is not reliable. He will also find a way of letting my boss know where I am.

I miss you so much and my heart aches to be with you, but maybe that won't be too long now. Know that I love you, and remember to look up at the stars each night, as that will connect us.

I am yours forever,
Steve xxx

The breath she'd held released itself, but the knot inside her didn't. She couldn't let it unfold. If she did, she would never stop the tide of tears flowing from her. Instead she held the letter to her heart until the urge to undo herself left her.

So Alfonse had taken Steve to Switzerland: *thank God!* And she presumed Alfonse had then delivered this letter to the British agent attached to his unit of the Resistance. That agent must now be home, as he wouldn't have risked posting something to the MOD. But what did it matter? Steve was safe. 'SAFE!' The joy released from shouting this out loud got her standing. With her arms in the air she danced over to the window and opened it, calling out to no one and yet everyone, 'He's safe! He's safe!' Her voice came back at her on the swish of the wind as it bowed the trees in the garden. Flakes of snow danced and floated down to the earth, where they melted. Frost whitened the bare branches, raising the morning light to a picture of loveliness that she hadn't witnessed for a long time, as loveliness hadn't been able to penetrate the dark place she'd been in.

Shivering against the cold, but laughing at her own antics, she closed the window and tucked the letter into her bra, near her heart, and left the house. Her driver waited, his cap covered in snow. *Poor man, if I'd kept him waiting any longer I'd have had to put a carrot in the place where his nose was and two pieces of coal for his eyes!* This ridiculous thought brought another giggle from her. Jenson's look held bewilderment, but she couldn't enlighten him; she would sound so childish, as this lightness inside her made her like a child again and gave her an urge to be very silly. Resisting it, she managed to say, 'Good morning, Jenson. It is a lovely one, don't you think?'

'Mmm, wouldn't say that myself, ma'am.'

'Oh yes, it's a glorious day. Nearly the best ever!' *That will come when Steve comes home, and somehow I am going to find out when that will be.*

Jenson smiled. 'Nice to see you feeling better, ma'am.'

'I am, Jenson. I am.'

Feeling better didn't really describe the emotions bursting for release inside her, but she had no words to explain how she felt.

As the car pulled up outside the War Office, Alice realized she'd travelled through London without seeing any of its wonderful sights. Her head had been with Steve, wondering how he really was and why, after all this time and to her knowledge, he wasn't home. Why was that? Had he deteriorated? Lost his leg even? *Oh God, that could be it!* If he'd lost his leg, he would be of little use. They might even leave him in Switzerland until the war ended. The way things were going, that could be years away, as the whole world was now involved. The Japanese seemed unstoppable, having taken Singapore and invaded Bali, and they now had their sights on the Netherlands. Even the American help wasn't as groundbreaking as everyone had first thought, as they had their own fronts to defend and had suffered heavy losses. At least there was some hope, though, as the news from Libya showed British troops making headway there. But here at home, with rationing gripping everyone harder than ever before, the only relief came from the physical presence of the Americans, or 'Yanks' as everyone was calling them. They gave some hope that their help would reap future rewards. On top of that, the optimism they showed had lifted many a person's spirit.

Alighting from the car and looking over at 10 Downing Street filled her with pride, as it always did. Thank God they had the wonderful Mr Churchill. She did not doubt he would get them through these difficult times. His latest innovation, Operation Outward, held a promise that had given her whole department an excited boost, as they worked through the administration and organization of it and as launch day drew near. The programme would entail attacking Germany with free-flying balloons. These balloons would carry two types of payload: a trailing steel wire that would damage high-voltage power lines by producing short-circuits; and incendiary devices which, it was hoped, would start fires in forests and heathlands. All of those working on the project felt sure that the almost one hundred thousand balloons would cause considerable damage and disruption at hardly any monetary cost and, best of all, no cost in terms of loss of life.

'Jenson, wait here for me. I hope to go to Baker Street. I will let you know.'

Still attached to the SOE, but on loan to the Department of Warfare, Alice gained permission to have a meeting with Captain Bellows. She hadn't spoken to him personally since he'd first interviewed her, with a view to her becoming a Special Operations Executive. There was no need for her to go to Baker Street. On requesting time away from her job to seek an appointment with him, and then telephoning his office, she found that Captain Bellows had appointments at the War Office and would see her whilst he was here.

Her heart thumped as she waited outside the office he had commandeered. His assistant called her in, increasing the drumming in her ears. What she intended was not normal protocol, but nothing could stop her. Besides, he must have an inkling of what she needed to talk about, and he hadn't refused her an audience. This thought gave her hope.

It was hard to read Captain Bellows's expression, which was as nondescript as before. 'Sit down, Alice, it is good to see you. How are you? I am getting good reports of your excellent help here.'

'I am better today than I have been for a long time, which is why I am here. But I think you know that, sir.'

His expression didn't change. 'Enlighten me.'

'I have had word from Ste— Officer Henderson, sir.'

'Yes, I am aware. Every communication comes through me.'

'Please, sir. Please try to get him home.'

'We cannot. Not yet.'

'Why not? And how long have you known where he is?'

'That is not a question you should ask, Officer D'Olivier. You know such information is top secret.' His formal use of her name touched a nerve in her stomach. It showed his anger at her for daring to ask more than she should. She waited, unsure whether she should apologize. Then she felt relief as his voice softened a little. 'I understand you and Officer Henderson have built a relationship that isn't fitting in your position, and this is what is driving you to behave as you are. I know it is difficult for you, but I have crossed a boundary by sending you Officer Henderson's letter. Now, accept that as it is, and carry on as usual. At least you know he is safe.'

'Would I be allowed to go to Switzerland to see him, sir?'

'Certainly not!'

'But why not? I have leave due to me. I can go by train and ship – those waters are safe.'

'Nothing is safe. You seem to have forgotten your training. We are being watched, you are being watched. I don't doubt there are moles everywhere, and that movements are known of each and every one of us. If you go rushing to Officer Henderson, someone may put two and two together and realize who he is. Yes, Switzerland is a neutral country, and we are working with them on a way to get Officer Henderson home without raising suspicion, but for you to go there would put him in jeopardy, as well as our whole mission!'

'Of course – sorry, sir.' *At least I've tricked him into revealing that something is being done to get Steve home. That is enough for me. Now, I can wait.* But his next words took away all her happiness.

'Sit down, Alice.'

This unusual request, and the use of her first name once more, alerted her. 'Is something wrong, sir?'

'Yes. If you hadn't requested to see me, I would have sent for you. In fact I came over to the War Office especially to do so. I have news that I know is not going to be good news for you, but *is* good news for the Special Operations organization and for our country as a whole. We have disposed of the traitor in Paris.'

'No! No, no, no . . . Oh God, no!' She was shattered. *Gertrude – no, not Gertrude.* 'Please, don't tell me . . . they haven't – no!'

'I'm sorry, but yes. And you must try to look on it as a necessary action. A spy has been exterminated, and no matter what the connection to you – and no one outside my office knows of that connection – this has to be a good thing.'

'*It is not good!* That's two of my family – my father and my half-sister – that you have taken, when the real spy goes free. It is Westlin! General Westlin . . . Please listen to me, please . . .' The tears she'd blocked earlier ran down her face, and her mind went into a state where all reason left her.

Without telling it to, her body jumped up. She groped for the door and felt the draught of the corridor as she moved down it. Running took her breath away. Gasping against this restriction, she made it to Westlin's office. Without knocking, she barged in. 'You fucking spy! You murdering traitor! Rat!'

Clawing at him, she took no heed of Westlin commanding her to stop at once or face a charge, but she did see his face pale and a look of horror pass over it as she shouted at him, 'I have proof it is you, you bastard! I have my father's memoirs holding all the evidence he had, but never got to tell. And my father's mistress's account, which she – Elsbeth – could not give at the time, or later. I have it all, you rotten, filthy traitor!'

Strong arms restrained her, lifting her off the cringing Westlin. 'Let me go. It is *him* you should arrest. Him!'

As the security officer manhandled her away, she saw the worried look on the general's face and the beads of sweat running down his blank, pale face. Jerking free, she gathered the spittle in her mouth and spat with all the force she could muster. Though she earned a shove that landed her on her back with a guard's knee on her chest, she had the satisfaction of seeing the spit sliding down Westlin's ashen face.

She sat and waited on the cold, hard bench of the guard-room. Practised at locking her emotions down, she did not give any heed to the consequences she faced; nor could she grieve for Gertrude, or feel for Elsbeth or Juste. Not even her happiness at knowing that Steve was all right, and that work was in progress to get him home, penetrated her. But the longer she stared at the door with her dry, sore eyes, the more she began to see memories from her life in the grooves of the wood's grain. As she relived these memories, any small remaining happiness leaked away and she was left with the misery. She did not want to live any more.

This thought took root. Yes, if she lived she would see Steve, but what did that hold for her now? The war raged on and on, and still she or Steve could be killed. So what did it matter *when* she left this world. There was no 'if' to her death at the moment.

My life is worthless now. In my own way I have given all I can to my country. But the powers that be took even more. They'd taken her family; even her mother was a victim of that. Now a shadow of herself and a drooling mess, she hardly knew who her own daughter was any more. But even if she did, Alice doubted she would care.

And the two people that Captain Bellows and other senior officials had disposed of had been branded as cowards, when they weren't. And now, with her own action in attacking Westlin and accusing him, she herself would be classed as a threat to the team and would more than likely be given a dishonourable discharge. Well, she thought, she would discharge herself – not just from her duty, but from her life.

Undoing her belt, she started to pull it from around her waist. As she did so, the idea came to her to take off her bra, fix it around her neck and then to the belt. She could attach this to the light hanging from the ceiling, by standing on the bench. When all was in place, she would jump. Steve would know why, when he heard about Gertrude's death. *Oh, Gertrude, my sister, my dear, dear sister.*

The door opened and Bellows stood there. She stared at him, her hand still now. If he noticed her belt hanging from her skirt, he didn't remark on it. 'Have you calmed down, Alice?'

She could not answer. No one else had featured in her plan.

'I can cover this up. I don't want it to end as it might. You are a very brave person and have suffered a great deal. Come back to my office, where we can talk. Westlin has been taken for questioning.'

My God! At last . . . With this news Alice's head cleared

and thoughts of ending her life evaporated. What had come over her? She suddenly felt frightened, now that she had an insight into what she was capable of. *Dear God, help me. Don't let me travel the path that my mother has.*

'Sit down, Alice. My assistant is fetching tea. I suggest you have extra sugar in yours, for you have sustained a massive shock. Those who saw your action have been told that you had just heard terrible news and that it involved orders from General Westlin. They understood. They all know that orders are given that cause even our own people to lose their lives – it is how it has to be.'

Sitting down wasn't something she could refuse as her legs gave way. 'You say you have arrested Westlin?'

'Not arrested, no. And as far as all here know, he has been taken home to recover from the attack. But we have asked him to answer some questions. Since you told my superior of your suspicions during your debriefing, we have decided to have him watched. Oh yes, once I heard what you alleged, I wasn't going to take a blasé attitude. Everything we hear of is passed on for investigation. So far there has been nothing to point suspicion at Westlin, but it won't hurt to make him sweat a little, just in case.'

'Thank you. I am deeply sorry for my unprofessional actions, sir.'

'I know. I also know how low it took you. And I understand. I do. I have to do my duty at all times, Alice, and that makes me have to do some very unpleasant things and take actions that are abhorrent to me. Acting on information, I had to give the orders I did. I am deeply sorry for the way that affected you, and will be even more so, if what you say proves to be the truth. Try to understand.'

'I do understand your position, sir. I don't blame you. I

have no proof to give you of my knowledge that Westlin is a traitor other than my father's diaries. And I only have a conviction, based on what I have been told, that my father and half-sister were innocent. I cannot take in what has happened. Why now? How?'

'Gertrude lay low for months, never leaving the house and never putting herself in the line of fire, so to speak. There was one time when she spotted our hit man.'

'She knew she was under suspicion?'

'Yes. A coded message was sent to her by her brother.'

'No, not Juste! Please tell me you are not gunning for Juste.'

'No. His was a natural reaction. We don't look on him as a traitor. He believed his sister, that is all. We do not know where he is. He has disappeared. And the cafe owner has been—'

'Paolo? You have disposed of Paolo . . . ? No!'

'There was no choice. He was still loyal to Gertrude. He passed on the message that she was to be killed. We had to remove him. He could have sent her information that would have been very valuable to Herr Eberhardt.'

'My God! And the others in the group?'

'All still loyal and in contact.'

'Which one killed her?'

'Here, use this.' He handed her a huge white handkerchief – she hadn't realized she needed one. He waited for her to blow her nose. 'I cannot tell you that, Alice. There was more than one, so they themselves don't know which one killed her. They are all attached to another group now – the group that rescued you. They are without an agent at the moment, as we had to lift theirs out. He had been compromised . . .'

'After Gertrude died? Doesn't that tell you something, for Christ's sake? How could Gertrude betray him when she was already dead?' Now she knew she had need of the handker-chief, as a sob caught her voice, bringing a deluge of tears. After a moment she blew her nose again.

'This is all too much for you.'

'No. Please tell me more.'

'Yes, the agent was compromised after Gertrude had died. No one in the war department other than me and my senior knew she had been disposed of, so whoever gave out infor-mation did not realize they no longer had her as a cover.'

'Does he know now?'

'Westlin? Yes, I told him this morning that Gertrude had been shot, and when. His reaction was one of shock. I began to suspect that your accusation of him might have some truth in it then. After all, he knew enough about every operation that went wrong to have been the one to jeopardize it.'

'Oh God!'

'Yes. It was all too late – if only I'd listened to you . . .'

'But you must have listened to me, otherwise why would you bait Westlin – why? Couldn't you have pretended that Gertrude was dead and waited to see if Westlin did anything?'

'You know yourself that wasn't possible, don't you?'

Alice did. It wasn't what she wanted to admit, but with poor Gertrude still alive, how could Captain Bellows be sure that she wasn't the one to compromise the other agent? Alice had to believe that, although he had his suspicions of Westlin, they were – just like hers – almost baseless. Whilst the evidence against Gertrude was damning . . .

Her life took on a new purpose. Now she knew that she had to live. She had to live to prove Gertrude's and her father's innocence beyond any doubt. How she would do that she didn't know. Even her father's writings could not be taken as proof. Bellows had told her that. They would be taken as her father's attempts to exonerate himself, and that was all. Somehow she needed proof, or for Westlin to confess.

'Alice, I want you to take some leave. During it I want you to try and recover. We are getting short of agents, and you will be needed at some point. I still have immense faith in you. To quote a well-known phrase, "Your country needs you".'

'Thank you, sir, I will do my best. In the meantime, can you please get a message to Steve Henderson? You are right, we are in love, and although it is inappropriate we never let it compromise our situation.'

'Well, I wouldn't say that *he* didn't. It wasn't in the plan for him to jump from that plane. He should have returned to base when the mission was aborted. All it has resulted in is his having to be discharged on medical grounds.'

'So he is no longer useful to you. Excuse me for saying so, sir, but sometimes you are all bastards.'

'I know. And, Alice, I understand Henderson. I understand him more than you can know. My only way of helping him not to be disciplined is to keep him where he is, and to continue to say he is unfit for travel. The risk in having him brought home is too great. No one can touch him in Switzerland. I kept him there and sent on the note for you, Alice.'

A blush warmed her cheek at his expression and at the tone of his voice. There was nothing she could say. This was so unexpected. Somehow she stammered, 'Thank you, sir.' What she really wanted to express was her astonishment. After a moment she recovered and anger entered her. If Bellows had feelings for her, how could he have ordered Gertrude's death? But then she understood that he'd *had* to order her death.

She'd received the same training. No one was indispensable. No one . . .

As she left the office Bellows touched her shoulder. It wasn't an inappropriate gesture, given all she'd been through, but when she looked into his eyes she read a confirmation of what she'd guessed. She had to be honest with him. 'I'm sorry, I cannot return your feelings.'

'I know. But know that I will be watching your back for you at all times.'

She nodded. She felt relief as she went through the door and it closed behind her. A longing arose in her as she walked the corridors past averted eyes. She needed to be with Lil. Sensible, loving Lil. And with Mildred and Gillian. Mildred had been happy to come and live amongst people who took things in their stride and knew nothing of her past. She'd even accepted Alice sending the car for her to come and spend time at Alice's home. She hadn't been often, and had spent most of her time with Cook or pottering around the garden, but the fact that she'd been at all was a big stride forward for them both, because up till now they had always been with Gillian and Lil when they were together.

Though not untouched by the war, these three women had something she didn't have: an innocence of the necessary but vile tactics of war. And they could give what she couldn't: uncomplicated and unconditional love to all.

She'd go home and try to contact them. At least she could telephone the nursing home to see if Lil was on duty and ask when her shift ended. Then, if all went to plan, she could collect Lil and take her back to the East End for the evening. Just to be with them, and in their world, was all she desired at the moment . . . Well, not all, but it was the only attainable desire.

*

It would be another three hours until Lil could be free, and that would be too late for today. But Alice learned that it was Lil's afternoon off tomorrow. She would contact Gillian. She had the number of the little corner shop. She'd tell her that she would send a car for Mildred, and would love Mildred to stay over if she would. She hoped with all her heart she would agree.

When she reached home there was a message to say that Mildred would like to come, but not until the morning. That didn't help much, but at least Alice wouldn't have to wait until tomorrow afternoon before seeing anyone.

Feeling restless and disorientated, she donned her waxed coat and wellingtons and walked through her garden into Danson Park. The snow hadn't amounted to much today. Rain had turned what little had been left from the fall of a week ago into slush, and this morning's flurry had made little impact on it. The trees were bare and bleak-looking. They shook with the remains of the snow shower and melted ice, which dripped onto her hood. Some of the drops ran down her face.

The despair she felt made every step heavy-going, but she trudged on, trying to think of anything other than death and destruction and to persuade herself she had more courage than she felt. Agents were badly needed, Bellows had said. And she supposed there were only so many suitable candidates – not in terms of bravery, for the whole country had masses of that as well as many other qualities, but in terms of languages and knowledge of the countries that agents were needed in; these skills were vital, and there were only so many people who possessed them.

Somehow she must lift herself, shelve her grief and personal longings and make herself ready – do whatever it took to get back into the field and be of use to the war effort. Steve would expect that of her, and so would Gertrude.

As she realized this, the park came alive. It was no longer a drab, damp place, but above her the birds quarrelled as they sought to build the best nest for the coming new life. A cluster of snowdrops peeped at her from under a tree, and to her left a carpet of daffodils nodded their hello. On cue, the sun broke through and, as its rays penetrated the branches and dappled a lace-patterned shadow in her path, she noticed everywhere the buds beginning to clothe the trees and bushes. Spring nudged winter for prominence and would win. And she would win, too.

She would ring Bellows and ask him to put her back on the parts of the course she needed to redo to prove herself still capable as an agent, and to consider her back in the fold. Then tomorrow, just for one day, she would allow herself to be Alice, and would laugh and cry with Lil. She needed that.

24

Lil

A WIND OF CHANGE

'Eeh, Gillian, lass, I never thought the day would come when you left to become a Land Girl, but I guess I'm not surprised. Are you sure that is what you want, though?'

'It is. I need to get out of London, Lil, and I'm not made of the stuff that is needed to do much else. Of course I will miss the boys, but I don't feel comfortable going to Ruby's mother-in-law's to see them. I'll keep in touch with them and their dad, though. But since Ruby's gone, nothing is the same.'

'It never can be, love. But going to work in the country? That's a real big change.'

'I know. I'm going to Worcestershire, wherever that is. Cor, luv a duck, it sounds fancy, don't it? Worcestershire . . . ha! 'Ere, I have the address. "Home Farm, Penerston." I know being a Land Girl ain't as good as what you're doing, but—'

'Don't be a daft ha'p'orth – course it is. We're all needed. And you know summat: it feels good to be needed. We women

326

have a lot more to give than men have allowed for in the past, but they're realizing it now all right.'

Gillian's decision to become a Land Girl brought into focus how much she had changed since Lil first knew her. She'd gone from being the young, carefree girl she'd first known to the scarred eighteen-year-old woman in front of her. But at least she was strong enough to take this big step. And then again, they'd all changed – and not all for the better. Life had dealt everyone more than a few blows of late.

Not wanting to dwell on such things, Lil changed the subject. 'Where's Mildred, and what does *she* think about all of this?'

'She doesn't know. I've been afraid to tell her, as it is bound to come as a shock. She's gone to Alice's house up north of London. Alice sends a car for her.'

'Aye, I know she does. But I thought as I was coming . . .'

'I made her go. I don't know why, but when Alice contacted Mildred, I had a feeling there was something wrong. There was an urgency in her message. She said she needed Mildred to go to hers last night, but Mildred didn't feel up to it, so we both thought she ought to go this morning. She'll be back with Alice.'

'I felt there was something not quite right with Alice, too. She rang the hospital and her voice sounded as if she'd been crying, but she just said she'd be all right.'

'There's a lot Alice don't tell us.'

'Aye, and we mustn't ask. By, it'll be good to see her. I ain't seen Alice for a while.' Wanting to change the subject and stop Gillian from speculating about Alice, she said, 'Well, come on then, lass, put the pot on, I could do with a Ruby.'

Gillian laughed. They'd taken to calling a cup of tea 'a Ruby'. It had begun when Lil had mixed up her rhyming slang a while back and had asked for a Ruby Lee. At first the mistake had brought silence, but after a moment they'd all laughed and Gillian had said she could almost hear Ruby splitting her sides. From then on it had stuck, and it felt good to say it. It kept Ruby with them.

Sipping the hot sweet tea, Lil said, 'I have news meself, but I reckon as I'll wait to see Alice and Mildred before saying anything. So, when are you off on your travels then?'

'In two days.'

'As soon as that? Eeh, Gillian, we'll not see each other after this, then.'

'Why? You can visit me and I can visit home.'

'Well, I wasn't going to say until the others were here, but I've joined the Auxiliary Territorial Service and am to be attached to the Queen Alexandra regiment.'

'Blimey, Lil, you kept that quiet! But the Queen Alexandra's nurses, they go where the action is. Oh, Lil, you'll be in the fighting line. No . . .'

'Aye, I will. But, like you, Gillian, I have to do it, lass. I need a change an' all. There's so much that's happened to us, it's hard to live with it all.'

'I know. We never talk of it, Lil, but you don't look on me as a murderer, do you?'

'Naw – never have done and never will. You saved me life, lass. But it were summat to go through, weren't it? The lot of it, and to think my Alfie set it up.'

'We've covered all that, Lil. And we've forgiven Alfie, so you can put a sock in that one right now. No apologies. But I agree, it is a lot to carry around. How do you cope with it?'

'Much the same as you, I reckon. Work hard, try not to give meself time to think, and I shove it to the back of me mind. Though that doesn't mean that I won't talk about it with you, whenever you want to. That's part of our healing: having someone who understands.'

'It is, Lil, it is. I still have nightmares. I don't think I'll ever be able to be with a man. I'm too scared.'

'Aye, it plagues me in the night too, and though I know being with a man can be a really wonderful experience, when you love your man and he is gentle and loving with you, there is this animal side to men that I saw even before all of this, so I'm of the same mind.'

A change came over Gillian at this. For a moment Lil wondered if she'd said something wrong. Gillian lowered her head and, when she did speak, Lil couldn't believe what she said. 'I've heard women go together sometimes – I mean . . . well, live together and love one another, much like men and women do.'

'Naw! They don't, do they? I knew some men were that way inclined, but women? You're not thinking of it, are you?'

'Well . . . Look, we won't see each other for a long time, Lil, but – well, I love you, and we could live together in that way.'

Lil couldn't speak for a moment. Part of her was horrified at what Gillian was proposing, but she knew also that it was because it was strange to her. What she felt wasn't a repulsion, it was just that she'd never considered such a thing, and didn't think she ever would. She wasn't sure what to say next. Gillian saved the moment. 'I – I . . . I don't mean I want to, nor am I asking you. I just think I don't want ever to be with a man, and so this is the way I will go, and I wanted you to know that, if it was possible, then it would be *you* I would choose, and that I love you.'

Recovering, Lil chose her words with care, 'I'm honoured,

lass – it's just that I haven't come across such things and it shocked me. But if it ever occurred to me to do the same, it would be you I chose.' She could feel her face burning, as if she'd sat next to a furnace, and her body felt sticky with the sweat of embarrassment. It was a relief to see the smile on Gillian's face and to hear her words.

'Thanks, Lil. It helps that you are not repulsed by me speaking out in that way. And to know you won't hate me if I do find someone.'

'I could never hate you, lass. Come here.' Holding the trembling Gillian to her, Lil said, 'You're part of me, Gillian. I know no one can take Ruby's place, but I like to think on meself as your big sister. At one time I felt like a mother to you, but that changed after what happened. Anyway, since then I have looked upon you as me sister. And I love you an' all. You're in me heart and that's where you'll stay, no matter what path you choose, love.' Keeping Gillian close to her she thought, *By, I never thought owt like this would happen . . . Nor to know of things such as two women – eeh, I can't imagine it . . . It beggars belief!*

They were still holding one another when a car hooted outside. Letting go, they both ran to the front door. Soon another pair of welcome arms held Lil – those of Alice, who'd beaten Mildred by hopping out of the car much quicker than she could.

Lil could feel the tension in Alice as she hugged her. 'Are you all right, lass?' Alice gave a look that said, 'No, but don't ask', so Lil changed the subject. 'Eeh, lass, you're looking better.'

'I am a lot better, thank you, Lil. And even more so now that I am with you all.' Coming out of the hug, Alice stood aside, leaving Lil to be enveloped in a good old northern welcome from Mildred. 'Eeh, me lass, I've missed thee.' As Mildred gave Lil a big kiss on her cheek, a tear played around Lil's eyes, but she brushed it aside. 'Come on in, the pair of you. I was reet upset to find you weren't here when I got here. Gillian has a Ruby on the go, so we can catch up on all of our news together over a pot.'

Organizing them helped her to compose herself once more. The mood needed lightening, though. By the look of Alice, she had something important to tell, and Lil knew that with her news and Gillian's, there would be plenty of tears ahead and a few shocks for Mildred.

Sitting around the kitchen table chatting about this and that, Alice had taken advantage of a lull in the conversation and was the first to put her future plans to them. 'Well, everyone, I have something to tell you. I'm going to take my service duties up again. I cannot tell you what they are, I know you will understand, but it does mean I am going into training next week and won't be in contact for a long time.'

'Eeh, Alice . . . Eeh, lass, is it dangerous?'

'It could be, Lil. But, you know, last time I went I only had a man – a very dear man – to think about me and to come back to, but now I know I have all of you and a life to come back to; and I know my man is safe. I can't tell you any more than that, my dears, but I know you know what I mean, and you know too why I cannot say any more.'

'Aye, we do, don't we, Mildred?'

'Thou's no need to pick me out, Lil, I know when to hold me tongue.'

They laughed at this indignation from Mildred. She did too, before she said, 'Well, lass, I'm going to miss you. I've loved coming to visit you at your lovely home and doing bits and pieces for you in the garden. It's a good job I'll still have Gillian with me, and Lil to visit me.'

Lil looked down as Mildred said this. 'Sorry, Mildred, but you won't. I'm sorry, love, but I . . . Well, I have joined the ATS, now that I'm fully qualified as a nurse. I'll be working with the QAs and will be going abroad. I don't know where yet, but I know it will be in three weeks and I'll be in training from tomorrow, with no leave. I – I didn't know about Alice's and Gillian's plans when I enlisted.'

'Surely you're not going an' all, Gillian?'

'I am. Oh, love, I'm going to be a Land Girl in Worcestershire!'

Mildred looked from one to the other, her mouth open, her gaze one of fear mixed with shock. 'But . . . Eeh, me lasses, I don't know what to say.'

Taking hold of her, Lil said, 'By, Ma, I'm sorry. None of us knew the others had plans. I don't know what to say. And none of us can get out of it now.'

Mildred stiffened her back for a moment and then relaxed. Lil knew she'd recovered slightly, and the gentle pat on her arm confirmed it as Mildred said, 'It's all reet, lass. I'm proud of you. All of you. And I'll support you and be here for you when you come back. Just make sure you do come back. I don't ever want another of them telegrams . . .'

Her voice caught on a sob as she said this and Lil held her tighter. 'That's not going to happen, Ma. Nothing is going to happen to any of us, I promise you.'

'Aye, it'd be good if you could promise such, but I reckon as Gillian'll be all reet and the change is just what she needs, but with you two I'll be worried every day you're away.'

Alice spoke. 'Look, Mildred, why don't you divide your time between here and my house? You get on well with our cook and the daily, and the gardener loves you and is glad of your help. I could have a bedroom kept ready for you, and my driver would pick you up and bring you back. You could leave some of your things at mine, so you don't have to keep unpacking and packing – what do you think?'

'I'd love that, Alice, ta. It'll be good to keep up with me friends at yours, and me friends round here an' all. Aye, that would suit me to the ground. Ta ever so much.'

'Besides, when you're at Alice's I can ring you and we can have a chat.'

'We can that, Gillian. That'd be grand to hear from at least one of you. But it's going to take some getting used to. I come from being on me own to having you to get meals for and take care of, and these two visiting, and me visiting Alice. And now I'm to go back to being on me own again, worrying about you all. But I guess it's a small part for me to play, compared to what you lasses will be doing. And in your youth an' all – a time when you should be having a good time and going to dances, not risking your lives.'

'We could go to a dance tonight. All of us.' Gillian looked from one to the other of them, her face lit up with excitement. 'There's a dance on at the Palais. And there's a good band playing. I've been to dances of theirs before with Ruby.'

Lil chipped in, before any sadness about Ruby's death threatened the newfound gaiety, 'That'd be grand. Aye and Ruby'll be with us, jiving away in spirit. Let's do it!'

'I'll have to go home for an hour first – I can't go to a dance in this!'

'Not in that jumper you can't, Alice, but there's nothing wrong with your skirt. I have a pretty blouse that would suit you. Cost a packet, it did, and I haven't been anywhere in it yet.'

'But won't you want to wear it, Lil?'

'Naw. I have a frock I haven't worn for ages. That one you made for me, Ma. She's a good seamstress is Ma, learned it in the workhouse and took it up again when she got enough together to get a treadle sewing machine.'

'Aye, I remember: the one I made out of that cloth I bought in Blackburn market. Blue with little daisies on it. By, lass, you looked a picture in it. The style suits you. Go and fetch it. Try it on and come down in it.'

'Let's all have a try-on, eh? Blimey, I ain't felt this bleeding excited for a long time. Come on, Alice, you want to make sure the blouse fits you.'

Not ten minutes had passed before they all stood in front of Mildred for inspection. Lil looked at the others. Alice's height added elegance to her calf-length, straight black skirt, a perfect accompaniment to the lemon chiffon blouse with its many collars, giving a hint of cleavage before they frilled down to her waistline. Little puffed sleeves added a pretty finishing touch. Then there was Gillian, in one of Ruby's loud, red satin frocks. The dress was for an older woman, but Gillian wore it with a charm that made her look as if a little girl had dressed up in her mam's clothes. The dress had a tight skirt and fitted bodice, with ruching from the waist to under the bustline. She looked grown-up and very pretty. Lil's blue dress had a flared skirt. The bodice fitted her shape and had a V neckline. The effect was very feminine. Inside, she felt like a woman again for the first time in ages.

'You all look very nice as you are, but you could do with having something done to your hair. I used to do a bit of hairdressing in me younger days. Go and take off your glad rags and I'll do what I can for you.'

'What about you, Mildred? You're coming aren't you?' Gillian asked.

'Naw, me dancing days are done, lass. Me legs want to be between the sheets at neet, not prancing around.'

At this, Lil looked at Mildred's legs and was shocked to see how swollen they were and the red blotches on them. 'Ma! You never said. Have you seen the doctor?'

'What, and give him a couple of bob that I could buy a nice bit of spam with? Not likely. It's just old age, lass, don't be worrying. I'm reet as ninepins.'

'You may be, but your pins ain't. Eeh, Ma, why didn't you say? You're going to see the doctor tomorrow, whether you like it or not. As it is, it could be treatable – a bit of dropsy, maybe; but you leave it and you'll be in all sorts of problems. Now sit down and put your legs up on the stool. I'll do the girls' hair, and you can put mine up for me when you've rested a while.

The bright lights in the ballroom and the jazzy sound of the music lifted them all as they entered the crowded Palais. Gillian giggled and grabbed Lil and swung her around. Caught up in the beat, Lil felt she could dance her heart out. Alice joined in and all three did their own version of the jitterbug, to the tune of 'Pennsylvania'. A happiness entered Lil and she could see that the others felt it, too. It was as if there was nothing but this joy of abandonment, as they swirled and twisted their bodies, tapping their feet.

'Hey, we can't let you three pretty ladies dance on your own.' Three Yanks stood next to them. Each took the hands of one of the girls and danced off in different directions with them. With the expert guidance of her partner, Lil's feet left her body and took on a mind of their own. When the music finally stopped, sweat ran down her face, but she didn't care. Gasping for breath, she laughed, looking up at him. He had the bluest eyes she'd ever seen. He smiled down at her. His face had a square look to it and his cheeks creased as he smiled, showing chiselled cheekbones. 'Rusty Mandell at your service, ma'am, United States Army, Second Division. I've only been over here for a couple of weeks, and was missing home until tonight. You English folk sure know how to make us guys feel unwelcome at times.'

'Oh? I'm sorry about that. You're not unwelcome – the opposite in fact, for we have been struggling to cope and at times thought we'd go under, so it's good that you're here. We need your help.'

'Glad to give it, ma'am. And your name is?'

'Lil – Lillian Moisley, ATS attached to the Queen Alexandra regiment.'

'You're a soldier?'

'Aye, of sorts I am.' She felt pride as she answered, 'But I ain't a fighting one. I'm a healing one, I hope. The QA is an army of nurses and I have joined the voluntary attachment to them.'

'Oh, I beg your pardon, ma'am . . .'

'Naw, you've not offended me.'

'You sure sound different from other folk I've met in London. Where are you from?'

The conversation flowed easily and, over the course of the evening, Lil's heart began to warm to this man. He looked big and strong and sounded brave when he talked, but underneath she could feel his loneliness at being so far from home. They had a lot in common, as his father was a doctor and Rusty had had plans to enter medical school, until his conscription landed him here, training to be a pilot at Bexhill. As it happened, this wasn't far from where she worked. It was a shame she was only there for two more weeks.

Remembering the others, Lil looked across the room. They were happily engaged in conversation with the other two GIs. Even Gillian was laughing and looked comfortable in the men's company, so Lil's conscience settled. Tonight felt like their last chance to have fun and – a little voice said to her – their last time together for a long time. 'Do you mind if we join me mates? Only we're all going our separate ways after tonight.'

'Really, where ya'all going?'

'You know better than to ask, Soldier.'

His face reddened. 'Sorry, Lil, I can't get used to all this secrecy. I didn't mean . . .'

'I know, but no questions – it puts you under suspicion.'

His hand caught hold of hers as they crossed the room. She didn't remove it. It felt good to hold a manly hand as a friendly gesture and not as one of comfort.

Alice raised her eyebrows as they reached the little group. Lil laughed – it was all she seemed to want to do tonight. After introductions, and looking at Gillian with the fellow who'd taken to her, Lil could hardly believe the conversation she and Gillian had had earlier. It was strange how she hadn't heard of this attraction between women that Gillian spoke of, even though she'd been surrounded by women and gossip in the factory. But then they were not so broad-minded in the north, and such things would be well hidden.

Introducing her friend as Jeff Carter and saying that he was a rodeo rider, Gillian looked the happiest Lil had seen her for a long time. Maybe being with a woman was just something she had considered because she was afraid of men.

*

After the dance was over they walked towards home in silence for a while, but Alice broke it. 'They were nice. It's a pity our blokes haven't given them a better welcome, but the Yanks do seem to have everything we don't. Sid, the one I danced with, told me about their rations, and their meat allowance per day is more than ours for a week! And they all have pockets of money, when our boys can hardly afford to buy a packet of cigarettes.'

'Aye, and not only are they not making the Yanks welcome, but they hate us girls mixing with them. But I don't care. Rusty is one of the nicest blokes I've ever met. A gentleman, who has treated me like I've never been treated afore.'

'Oh . . . Oh, Our Lil is falling heavily—'

'Eeh, don't be daft, Gillian. I just like him, that's all. I gave him Mildred's address, as he wants to hear news of me. There's nowt wrong in that. He's lonely.'

Neither Alice nor Gillian commented. Lil felt a hot flush creep up her face. She'd rather have their banter than this knowing silence, but she forgave them when they came to the front door of Gillian's mam's house. Gillian said, 'Well, this is it.'

A silence fell. It held the sadness of parting. Alice reached out and took Lil's hand. 'Lil, I won't be able to contact you, but know that I will be thinking of you. Please keep safe. You mean a lot to me. You're like a sis – sister. And you, Gillian.' With this Alice pulled them both to her. 'Neither of you will ever know what you have done for me. I have a lot to tell, and I will one day, but not now.'

'Aye, and I feel the same about you lasses. The only good thing about this bloody war is how it brought us together. I hate the thought of not seeing you both for God knows how long.'

'You know, I am separated from the man I love, but every night we look at the stars at the same time, and I know he is doing it too. That one moment brings us together. We three could do the same. My time is ten at night for him. Well, we could do it at a quarter past ten. Wouldn't that be wonderful, and we could send an unspoken message to each other.'

The sound of a sob stopped Alice. Gillian leaned her head on Alice's shoulder, emitting tiny sobs as she tried to suppress her shaking body.

'Awe, lass, don't start – you'll have me blabbering.' But as she said this, Lil felt tears in her eyes and heard a sob from Alice.

They clung together. War had thrown them into each other's lives, but Lil knew in her heart they would be bound together forever . . .

25

Alice

A TRAIN OF DESPAIR, A VISIT OF HOPE

Alice waited. In the distance she could see the smoke from what they called the 'train of despair' billowing into the night air, blocking out the stars. She'd thrown herself into this mission – to help the planned sabotage of the railway line and the rescue of Jews and Roma. This was to be a test for her – a test of her skills in planning, organizing and carrying out a successful assignment, not to mention bonding with a Resistance group once more, now that she had experienced the terrors and heartache of a compromised operation.

Nerves bit into her as she caught Jean's eye. Jean was the leader of the group, and whilst he hadn't been very welcoming to Alice, she had come to respect him and had gained his respect in the process. He nodded. It was an indication that everything was in place. Twenty-five armed men were lying low within yards of her. Each had his own remit. Each waited for the signal.

Thousands of Jews and Roma had been transported along this route from the Dossin Barracks, in Mechelen in Belgium,

340

to Auschwitz concentration camp. The train bearing down on them now held hundreds more. Their intelligence had informed them that the freight cars carrying the prisoners had doors fenced with barbed-wire; this was a new measure and hadn't been present in any of the previous trains.

Stopping the train would be easy, but freeing the prisoners would be more difficult. Luckily a backup team had cutters for the wire and the bolts. Timing was of the essence. Alice hoped she'd worked out everything to the last detail. Night after night she'd come down here to a spot thirty miles from the Dossin Barracks, a woodland area that sloped down to the track. She'd watched the train; timed it; and even, on one occasion, ran towards the line to see how long it would take from her position. She hadn't missed any details. *This mission has to work!*

The ground beneath her shuddered under the impact of the massive convoy of carriages – they were so near now. The time had come. Lifting her arm, she gave the signal. A hand grenade flew past her, its explosion sending debris in all directions. Stones, rubble and clumps of earth landed near her, some hitting her and hurting her arms.

A screeching of brakes and wheels on steel track set her teeth on edge. Sparks splintered the air. German voices cried out, sending shivers of memory through her, but the sound of their own and the Germans' guns firing round after round took away all thoughts, other than those she'd trained her mind to focus on.

'Now!' Her shout sent a stampede of Resistance workers towards the train. Soon carriage doors opened and bewildered faces appeared. 'Run! Run for your lives towards those trees.' The command came over and over again, projecting zombie-like figures into movement. Many fell as they were shot in the back, while others made it to the woods. Alice watched, help-less to do anything more for them, crying as children's bodies did the dance of many bullets, and weeping mothers stood still, waiting for their turn. But many more disappeared into the darkness of the woods, and she held onto this. Aid workers waited for them there. There were plans to move all escapees into hiding. She and her team could do no more than they were doing right then: keeping the Germans at bay and giving the escapees the time they needed.

'The German guards are all dead, Hélène.' This was addressed to Alice. Hélène was her new cover name. It had taken months to get ready for action and gain a new identity. Here, in Belgium, she was passed off as the daughter of a patisserie-shop owner, who had been brought up by her grand-parents in France and had returned to help her father with his shop. The real Hélène Doberson had died as a child; her mother had taken her to France after a divorce from her father, and she'd died of whooping cough. Her father had never been told, and so Alice had turned up one day saying that she was his daughter and had come looking for him. The poor man believed every word, even saying that she looked like his mother, who'd been of German birth and had long blonde hair. This had been a blessing for Alice, as all of his neighbours celebrated her return with him – none of them suspected, but using the poor man had plagued her conscience.

'The mission has been accomplished. We should go. We can do no more.'

'Yes. Jean, we will leave now. I will let HQ know. Well done, everyone.'

'Hush!' Jean gestured to them to be quiet.

A cry came into the silence. Alice ran towards it. A child

whimpered as she neared; across its legs lay the body of a woman. 'Help me to lift her off.'

Her torch lit up the face of a small boy, as she and Jean rolled the woman off him. He looked to be no more than about three years of age. 'Has he been shot?'

Checking him showed that he hadn't been. She was filled with relief. Stretching out her arms, she took the child to her. He did not fight her or show any fear. She stood as she continued to hold him. Jean's voice frightened her. 'What are we to do with him? We cannot take him back with us, and the aid workers and escapees have now left.'

'We can. We pass several safe houses – one of them will take him.'

'No, Hélène, it is too risky.'

'I will take him, if you dare not.'

'Soon the place will be teeming with Germans. They time the train at each station. Besides, how do we know that one of them didn't have time to radio through about the attack? Come, leave the boy.'

'I cannot. You go. I will find the safe house. I have to—'

'For God's sake! How dare you jeopardize this mission, and us, for sentimentality?' Lifting his gun, Jean aimed it at the boy.

'No! You are behaving like a German. This is a child.' Shielding the boy with her arm, she screamed at Jean, 'You kill him and I will kill you!' Her stare held hostility; his held disbelief.

'Come on then. We have to hurry. But I think you are not doing the right thing. We saved upwards of two hundred Jews and Roma – we should have left it at that and disappeared into the night. All the others have done so. Hurry!'

Hurrying didn't prove easy. Stumbling over rutted fields

carrying the boy left her exhausted and falling behind. Stopping to catch her breath made Jean impatient with her once more. She couldn't see his coal-black eyes, but she knew they flared in temper. They were always so hostile, even though he'd come to respect her. 'This is stupid. Here, give him to me,' Jean said.

'No, I don't trust you. You go on – I will make it.'

'You won't, not on your own. It is still around five miles to the nearest safe house. At least let me strap him to your back – it will be easier for you. I promise I won't hurt him.'

Something told her not to, but tiredness and fear that their slow pace would lead to capture had her handing the boy over. Shortly afterwards a muffled shot slung her against a tree. *Oh God, no* . . . 'No, no, no . . . You bastard! You filthy child-killer. I hate you!' Her knees gave way and, as she sank to the ground, her insides crumbled. The child's body dropped down beside her. She pulled him towards her and clung to him. Tears of anger and grief flooded her. Clawing at Jean's feet she brought him to the ground. There they wrestled. 'I'll kill you, I'll kill you . . .' Her hand felt the steel of her knife. Drawing it, she plunged it at him, but he rolled away from her.

'Stop it! It had to be done. The child is nothing – a Jew, or a Rom – nothing . . .'

Hate welled in her. How could Jean have been engaged in rescuing a people he obviously didn't have any respect for? How could he be trusted ever again? 'You have Nazi views! Disgusting prejudices. Why – why did you lead this operation?'

'Not all of what the Nazis preach is bad.'

A sympathizer – Jean had Nazi tendencies. It was her duty to dispose of him. Twisting her arm to avoid his grasp, she plunged her knife towards him once more and this time it sank deep into his chest. Pulling it out in a swift movement, she kicked his body away from her. His moans told her that he would die slowly. Something in her welcomed this. She turned away and ran, scrambling over hedges that tore at her clothes and ripped her skin, but she took no heed of it. In front of her the darkness put up a blank wall, but glancing behind, she saw torches flashing in all directions, searching.

Germans! If they found Jean, would he still be alive? Would he talk? She should have finished him off.

She hurtled forward, her breath catching painfully in her chest. Blinded by hot tears and filled with terror, she stumbled and fell headlong. The ground gave way beneath her. Slithering and sliding, she came to a halt with a bump. She felt damp undergrowth as she got up. There was a stench she could hardly bear. She knew where she was: in a cesspit next to the farm she had walked past day after day, except that this time she had no handkerchief to hold over her nose. Now most of her body had sunk into the fetid mess. Retching brought the bile to her throat. Swallowing the stinging liquid, she thrashed about, trying to grab onto something to help her pull herself out. Her hand caught hold of a branch. She clung to it and pulled herself forward with all her might.

The light of a torch stopped her. It swayed above her, approaching the pit. She froze.

Never did Alice think she would be relieved to be in a cesspit, but she was now as the German walked away cursing the stench and saying nothing would induce him to go further and that he couldn't believe there could be anyone down there.

Hardly daring to breathe, she waited. The lights and the voices of what sounded like half a dozen German soldiers faded. With one more extreme effort, she pulled herself out.

Now she could see the torches again, swishing backwards and forwards as their owners walked with their backs to her across the field in front of her.

The cold damp of the clinging waste-water made her body shiver as she watched and waited, lying low on the ground, the darkness her only shield.

The Germans reached the farm. Shouting and gunshots filled the air, making her fear that some of their unit might have been hiding there and had been discovered. Standing, she tried to see, safe in the knowledge that she couldn't be seen. More gunfire shook her. This wasn't random gunfire, but measured. Shot after shot.

'No, please God, no!' Collapsing in a heap, she gave way to weeping. *How much more? How much more do I have to endure? How much more does the world have to endure? The killing – when will it end?*

When all went silent she lifted her head. A glow had started low in one of the rooms of the farmhouse. After a couple of minutes it took hold and shot flames into the air. Staying down, but still able to see what was happening, Alice watched what seemed like the whole farm burning to the ground. She heard the rumble of trucks and peered to the right of the inferno. A convoy of trucks was heading towards the farm. German soldiers jumped onto the back of them and they sped away, leaving a trail of destruction behind them.

She rose from her crouched position, not knowing where her strength came from, and ran towards the flames. As she neared the farmhouse, she had to stop for a moment as the heat held her at bay. But, as her eyes adjusted, she saw that it was the barns that were on fire and not the house. Approaching to the left of the flames, she managed to reach the house. There was a scream and she turned once more towards the barn. The sound curdled her stomach, as moans of agony came from the same direction. Desperation had her calling out, 'Where are you?' But no one answered. A last cry of death reached her, leaving her shouting out a hate-filled vitriol towards the sky. There could be no God, for no God would stand for this. No God would desert his people in this way. Turning away, she bent over and vomited.

It felt like an intrusion to enter the house. And although she called out, she knew there was no one there, for the eerie silence told her this. She sat at the wooden table in the kitchen with her head in her hands, but lifted her elbows as they started to hurt. Around her was the evidence of a family home: the smells of a kitchen and the warmth of a banked fire in the hearth, on which a kettle belched out steam, lifting its lid up and down. There was still the lingering smell of a casserole from the evening dinner. By all appearances it was as if nothing had happened here. How could those Germans, who were human beings, have carried out such awful acts to the owners, and God knew how many Resistance workers? To force them into a barn and shoot them, and then – not knowing for sure they were all dead – set fire to the barn. As she asked this question she knew the answer. This war had changed everyone, some of them into animals. In many ways she herself was not far behind. How did it happen that she could take a life? That she could kill Jean. *Oh God, when will it end?*

Wiping her tears, she raised her weary body and made herself cross the room and take the kettle from the hob. The weight of it told her it was full. It would be enough to wash in. Something told her that the lady of the house wouldn't have minded her cleaning herself and changing into any clothes that she could find.

As she peeled off her things, her hand rested on her radio pack. Did she have the energy to assemble it? Would it be safe to broadcast? Deciding the answer to both was yes, she set about doing so. She worked out her code, then sent the message: 'Mission successful, but many lives lost. In danger – group diminished – going underground. Will contact when I can.'

She would find out who was left of the group, get them to disband for now and then go to Switzerland and find Steve. She knew where he was, as Bellows had allowed her to send a message to him. It had gone through the MOD to the Red Cross headquarters in Switzerland. Steve was helping to co-ordinate their operations – something she knew he would be good at. Somehow she was going to reach him. She had to. It was the only thing that would keep her sane.

Bellows surprised her. His heart often seemed cold, but in his actions he showed that some warmth had filtered through his steely exterior. A message had come, saying that she was to be air-lifted out, and the aircraft would take her to Switzerland. She still couldn't believe it, as she sat on the floor of the aircraft, waiting. She had to jump from a great height, under cover of darkness, as the aircraft dare not fly low. The Swiss guarded their impartiality very closely, and did not want to be seen to accept British fighter-aircraft on their soil.

She had contact numbers, and would be taken to Officer Steve Henderson at Red Cross headquarters. Once she arrived, she was to prepare Steve for being air-lifted out with her. His case had been looked at, and Bellows had stood up for Steve, telling his superiors that his decision to jump out of the aeroplane into France was because he saw the Germans approaching and wanted to help the stricken Resistance group all he could, with a view to taking the place of the agent on the ground, if she was captured or killed. The explanation had satisfied those who mattered. Steve could come home at last.

The plane door opened with a sucking motion. Staying where she was wasn't an option. She dropped and it took her breath away, and then the wind caught her and a feeling surged through her as if she were a feather, floating down to Earth. She felt a peace she hadn't experienced in a long time. She could swirl around the clouds forever, but a downward pull reminded her to tug on her ripcord and jolted her mind into action: she needed to concentrate on her landing. The pilot had done his best to avoid the mountains and drop her as near the border as he could, flying a little lower than he should. The darkness didn't help, but he had given her a rough idea of where there was a clearing. *Please don't let me land in a tree . . .*

Her body had often shaken with fear, despair and cold, but now the trembles that went through her held an excitement along with anxiety. All that now separated her from Steve was an office door. He knew she was coming. How did he feel? Was he afraid?

Taking a deep breath, she opened the door. He stood looking at her. He had one leg . . . just one leg. Oh God, why hadn't she been told? His face held a question as he leaned on his desk. His eyebrows were raised, as if he wanted to know whether she could still love the broken Steve. She did not have the answer – not in words. He stared at her. His body wobbled on the crutch that he held on to.

'Steve? Oh, Steve.'

Not sure how to approach him, she walked forward instead of charging at him as she wanted to do. Opening her arms, she wrapped them around him. He felt thin. His free arm came round her in a gentle movement. A tear plopped onto her hair. 'Oh Steve, my Steve.' His arm tightened around her. Still he did not speak, but a sob escaped him. 'I'm here, my love, I'm here,' she told him.

He moved her towards a sofa in the corner of the office. The clunk of his crutch behind her tore at her heart, but she didn't stop moving towards the seat. Here they were equals; her Steve could take her in both arms. The love she felt inside, but rarely showed, came to the fore. She wanted to tell him everything – all that had happened, all it had meant to be separated from him. Her whole body gave way. Sobs came out of her from deep inside. It felt as if every part of her wept, as did every part of Steve.

As they clung together and talked, their tears died away. Each helped the other to a better place. A fragile place, but a better one. With everything they'd suffered it would be a long time before they were completely healed – if, indeed, they would be healed at all. There were no miracles available to put things instantly right, but they had each other, and each understood the depth of pain that could be held in a weeping soul. That understanding would be a starting point for them.

'I love you, Alice. Thinking of you has been a double-edged sword for me. In part it has helped me and kept me going, but there has been the worry of not knowing if you were safe and what you were going through. That first note from you was a lifeline, but the news that you were going to Belgium saw me fall into a deep pit of despair.'

'I have seen some horrible things, Steve. They live in my nightmares and disturb me. I am not the girl you knew. But I know I can – we can – heal.'

'We can. Together we can. I am so happy to be coming home. Alice, will you marry me?'

Joy mingled with relief as his words showed her that Steve did not see their future as something to fear, nor did he think she would be repulsed by him in any way. 'Yes, my darling, I will.'

'Come. Let's go to my apartment. I want to make love to you. I want to take every bit of you to me. I'm not sure how we will manage it, but we will.'

'Ha! I'm sure you'll find a way. Here, let me help—'

'No . . . Don't . . .'

She'd gone to help him up. 'I'm sorry,' she said, unsure what to do.

'Oh, darling – yours was a natural reaction, forgive me. But I want you to see me as just as capable as you always did.'

Looking into his tear-stained, puffy face, she knew that no disability would stop her loving him. 'I do, darling, I see only my Steve. As you say, it was a natural reaction.'

After he'd managed to stand, he looked at her as if for the first time. 'You look a mess.'

She laughed at this, knowing it was a 'change-the-subject moment'. She teased him back. 'And so do you! When did you last shave?'

Their laughter was so welcome.

A taxi ride took them to a wooden chalet that Steve called home, and the journey took them about twenty minutes. The bottom half of the chalet was his, while the top half belonged to a young couple. 'They are away at the moment, skiing. Can you imagine that? The world is in turmoil, and the Swiss carry on as normal.'

'Lucky them!'

351

'Yes. Well, darling, here we are.'

The words sounded ordinary, and yet they meant so much. Here they were. The blood and turmoil of war could not touch them, for the peace around them enclosed them now. They were safe for the moment.

Leaning on his crutch, Steve slapped her bottom. 'There's the bathroom. Get in there and get yourself cleaned up for me, wench!'

She loved his humour, and knowing that it was still intact warmed her inside. Giggling a carefree, girlish laugh, she went towards the bathroom. The muscles in her stomach clenched in anticipation.

As the hot water bellowed clouds of steam around them, Steve helped take her clothes off as best he could.

Pulling a chair next to the bath for him, she stepped into the water. He held her hand as she did so. The water burned for a moment. He giggled as she lifted her feet, then leaned forward and put some more cold water in. 'You've gone soft!'

'This is a luxury. Not only have I not had a bath for a while, but when I did, it had to be filled from a kettle, with just enough to cover my—'

'The beautiful heart of you.' His voice caressed her. His fingers entwined in the soft down covering her vagina. They played there for a moment, awakening her fully. 'Sit down, darling, let me wash you.'

Every part of her quivered with the life he had awoken. Leaning over her, he soaped the flannel. With gentle movements he washed her, sometimes rubbing, sometimes holding the sodden flannel and letting the water drip onto her breasts, then watching the droplets run down over her nipples. A frenzy of feelings ran through her, making it hard for her to breathe.

'I think you are all clean now. I can't wait any longer. Let me dry you.'

Standing in front of him, her mouth dry with anticipation, she allowed him to brush her skin with the fluffy towel. Once he stood, she could see how much he wanted her. She stroked him, driving him wild.

'We have to get to the bed. I can't hold out much longer.'

She undressed him, then gently pushed him back from his sitting position on the bed and lowered herself onto him.

The penetration was too much for both of them, as they embraced the feelings that took their bodies. Their cries met each other and they felt the pulsating waves wash over them. As they came down together, they clung to one another.

The blazing world had disappeared behind their own fire, and for one moment they had together found a peace and joy that made their shattered remains whole again.

26

Alice

THE BEGINNING OF THE END

Leaving Steve had been painful, but the war was entering its most important phase and everything they did had to contribute to the big push. That was still only in the planning stage now, but was set for May/June, and all agents who could be spared had been briefed on it and deployed to France.

Waiting until the plane that had dropped her – along with some vital equipment – took off, Alice crouched down, wishing she was going with it, instead of being left here in France once more. This time she was to work in the Normandy area. Juste had contacted HQ. He had a new group ready, but needed help. When she'd first asked to join Juste, her plea had fallen on deaf ears. 'You have emotional ties to him, which might get in the way of duty,' Bellows had said. She'd reminded him of how she'd never baulked at doing her duty, whether that meant killing one of their own or a German. She had then gone on to persuade Bellows to let her join Juste, by pointing out that they were a good team: she had trained him and, with Alfonse bringing some of his men to join them, it

354

had to be Alice who supported them. These men trusted her, knew her and were loyal to her. Eventually Bellows had given in.

Steve had been devastated when she'd told him she was going into the field once more. He had settled well into his War Office job, and worked on implementing the training on new inventions by the boys at The Frythe farmhouse. He had a particular hand in the training of how to operate one-man submarines. Alice wished she and Steve had had that particular marvel when they had to cross the river that night in France in 1941 and had to swim underwater.

Steve had moved into Alice's house in north London as soon as he returned from Switzerland. They had made many adjustments to the house, to make moving around easier for him. They married in a registry office with two strangers as witnesses. Not many people knew about it, not even Lil. But they looked upon the ceremony as giving them the right to be together in the same home, and not as a celebration of their love. That would come when war had ended and they could tell all their friends and family about their relationship and love for one another. They would hold a party to rival all parties, and have a blessing in church, too.

For now Alice had to focus on her job, though she still felt the need to prove to the world that her family were not cowards, but courageous people who did not betray their fellow countrymen. One hope beat inside her: that Alfonse had found intact the tin they had buried containing the last book of her father's memoirs.

'Alice?'

'Juste! Oh, Juste, it is good to see you.' They hugged. She noticed a shadow lurking a little way off in the trees, giving them space for a moment. 'I'm sorry, Juste, so sorr—'

'I have avenged Gertrude's death. François is dead.'

There wasn't anything she could say to this. The man in the shadows stepped forward. 'Alfonse! Oh, this is perfect, the three of us . . .'

Greeting her, Alfonse asked, 'How is Steve?'

Surprised that he knew Steve's name, she told him he was doing well, but had lost his leg. Alfonse expressed his sorrow, but not his surprise.

'Thank you for saving him for me, Alfonse – thank you.'

'I have saved something else. Here!'

The tin felt cold in her hands. 'Is it all right, has it survived?'

'Yes, all intact. Those boxes are well made.'

She wasn't surprised, for the tins were frequently used to hold rations and keep them dry and fresh. She thanked Alfonse and held the tin to her breast. She was so happy to have the diary back. But then she remembered his sacrifice – the killing of his parents in their farmhouse. 'Alfonse, I am so sorry about your parents . . .'

'*Merci*. The pain lives in me without release, but I have had many chances of revenge and I have taken them.'

'I understand. I have been guilty of that myself.'

'Come, we have to go. We cannot linger here. We always have to take great care. We are glad to have you with us, but afraid too, as we believe there is someone connected to you who is the real traitor.'

'There is, Juste, or rather there was. He isn't working in the War Office any longer, for he has disappeared. My boss listened to me and questioned the man – he has not been seen since, and is now a missing person. It is thought he was air-lifted out by the Germans, but no one can be sure. His family say they have had no contact with him, and this is proving to be true, for they are under constant surveillance.'

As they walked across the road and into the field opposite Juste asked, 'Does this mean that your father is in the clear?'

'No, nothing has been concluded. I was told that not even the diary would be proof enough – whatever it might contain – as it would be seen as my father simply trying to justify himself after his death.'

'We will not give up. I will help you. We cannot let it rest. We have to clear Gertrude's name, too. It seems the same man was responsible for passing on the information that she was accused of delivering.'

'You're right, Juste. How we will do it I do not know, but we will find a way. If it takes the rest of our lives, we will find a way.' Changing the subject, she asked, 'Is everything set up for us? Do we have safe houses and a network of helpers?'

'It is. We told British HQ that we could manage and did not need an agent, but communication is difficult without one, and we were told there is new equipment that will help us, but we need to be shown how to use it.'

'I'm glad you contacted HQ. I needed to come back.'

The second field they went through led to a barn where a van waited for them. Its lettering indicated that it was a butcher's delivery van. Alfonse put on a white coat and a striped apron that lay on the front seat. 'I am working as a butcher and deliver to the Germans in the next town every night. But I could not go off my route, so I had to leave the van here. You will have to lie on the floor and I will cover you with these muslins.' The thought of this repulsed her. Though she couldn't see the meat properly, she imagined bits of animal flesh clinging to the muslin. Alfonse laughed at their expressions. 'They are clean muslins. Come on – get down.'

The next hour of the journey bumped and jolted her until her insides felt bruised. But her surprise when Alfonse finally dropped them off made her forget the discomfort, as she asked, 'Is this wise, Juste?'

'No. But for my mother I have taken the chance. She needs to see that you and the diary are safe, for she has worried about you, and the diary is very precious to her. We are based forty kilometres north of here and I visit often, though always at night and I come across the fields.'

Despite the risk, Alice was thrilled to be going to see Elsbeth. She liked her – she was a link to her father, someone who had loved him. She hurried towards the house. 'How is she, Juste? How has she been coping since Gertrude's death?'

They reached the door of the farmhouse, where a strange atmosphere engulfed them. There were no lights on, and the darkness of the place unnerved her. She didn't want to enter. Peering at Juste, she tried to scrutinize his expression. He too looked fearful.

Motioning for her to follow him, he went into the barn attached to the house. 'Come – I do not like this. Mama always leaves a light on.'

'What are you thinking has happened? Oh God, Juste.'

'Stay here. I will have a scout around. I know every nook and cranny of this place. I will be better on my own.'

She nodded. Darkness, cold and fear seeped into her bones. All kinds of awful scenarios went through her mind. Had the locals become afraid of Elsbeth because of her German ancestry? Had the Germans found out about her connections to the Resistance? Had she had an accident and lay helpless inside, or had she died suddenly? Speculation threatened to drive her mad until a noise alerted her.

'It's only me . . .'

Relief at hearing Juste's whisper made her release the breath she'd been holding. 'What is it? What has happened?'

'I do not know. I have been in the house, and everything is in order. Nothing has been disturbed, but there is no sign of Mama. It is a mystery. And I cannot approach the farm workers, for I am supposed still to be in England.'

'Well, at least it isn't looking as if Elsbeth has been taken away or driven out. She must have left willingly. I will go to that cottage down the road where the herdsman lives. I met him before, when I came as Madeline, the university friend of Gertrude. I'll tell him I called in, on the off-chance of stopping for a couple of days, as I have time off work.'

'Yes, that is a good idea. I will wait in the house as it is warmer, though I cannot light a fire or the lamps, for fear that the house is being watched. What if they invite you to stay?'

'I will tell them that I have a key and was told I am welcome any time, and have left clothes and things here. But, of course, that depends on the reason Elsbeth isn't here. If I find out there is something wrong, I will take their hospitality and try to sneak out later, or come to you in the morning . . . Oh, I don't know. Leave it with me. I will do what I can.'

Pulling her jacket around her didn't do anything to shield Alice from the cold. She wasn't able to wear much under her flying suit and, once she'd discarded that, the momentum of getting to safety had kept her warm. Now, with worry seeping through her, the cold took hold of her body and she shivered uncontrollably. As she walked to the cottage down the road her boots squelched in the mud, stirring up unpleasant smells from the dozens of cows that trod this way morning and night on their way to the milking shed. Her stomach churned.

A small light from the cottage ahead guided her. Her knock

on the door echoed as if the place was empty, but through a crack in the shutter a light – no bigger than that from a candle – brightened, as if being brought towards the door where she stood.

The latch clattered in the quiet night, disturbing an owl somewhere above her. It hooted and flapped its wings, making her feel tense and increasing her trepidation. The appearance of a white face shadowed by the flickering light added to her fear, even though she knew it was the herdsman. 'It's me, Madeline. Do you remember me? I visited a few years back. I came to visit Elsbeth again, but nobody is in. Do you know where she is?'

'*Oui*, I remember, there are not many visitors to this part of France. We do not forget those who come. Elsbeth has gone – hounded out. The villagers thought she was spying on them.'

'Was she hurt?'

'No. She has gone to Paris. I am managing the farm. I have a key for the house, Mademoiselle. I know she won't mind you staying. I'll come and light a fire for you. Wait there, I'll fetch some bread and milk for you.'

'No, there is no need. I have a key . . .'

'*Mais oui* – I must. There is nothing in the house.'

Unable to get out of this, she prayed Juste would keep an eye out for her from one of the windows and would see them coming, so that he knew to keep out of sight. Talking loudly as they went into the house, she asked, 'Have you had any contact with Elsbeth since she left?'

'No. I do not know where she is – only where she was heading. She said she would visit Gertrude and stay with her.'

Oh God, did Juste not tell Elsbeth? He said he'd visited

recently, but he didn't answer when I asked him how Elsbeth was coping . . .

'But you, Mademoiselle, how did you get here? Where is your car?'

'A friend dropped me off. He was coming this way, and he is the reason why I came. I am so sorry about Elsbeth. Why, oh why, did the villagers turn on her?'

'A young man was hiding from conscription; he did not want to fight for the Germans. His family needed the money he could earn, but he was arrested. I do not believe Elsbeth had anything to do with it. I heard a rumour they thought it was her, and so I got her out.'

'Thank you.'

'It is nothing. I am loyal to Elsbeth, for she has seen that I and my family are well taken care of over the years. I do not look on her as a German.'

Thankful when the herdsman left, Alice called out to Juste. He'd been waiting in his bedroom. As he shook the cold from him in front of the blazing fire the herdsman had lit, Alice could wait no longer to tackle him. 'Why, Juste? Why have you not told Elsbeth? For God's sake, she has gone to Paris to see Gertrude!'

'I have. Mama knows. I don't know why she told Monsieur Fellena that.'

'Oh. Well, maybe she hasn't accepted it.'

'Yes, she has. It broke her heart, but she did not know how to tell others, in case they asked too many questions and began to suspect there was more to it. I will find Mama. I know she has her favourite places in Paris, and I think she may want to be where Gertrude was last. I just don't know if she realizes how much Paris has changed.'

'Maybe she left a note for you somewhere?'

'That is possible. But for now I am happy that she is safe. We should have something to eat and get to bed. We will have to leave before it is light.'

Huddled up in Gertrude's bed, Alice once more felt the pain of her sister's unjust death. She told herself she would not let herself give way to it. Next to her father's photo there was now one of Gertrude. Lighting a candle near the photos had helped ease some of the pain, as had saying a prayer for them both and trying to imagine them together. 'I will clear your names, I promise,' she'd told the pictures. She opened the last journal and thanked God again for Alfonse having found it. Letting it take her back to a place she did not relish visiting – the time leading up to her father's arrest – she took a deep breath and turned the fragile pages:

Ralph, London, 1915

2nd November 1915: I am extremely worried as I travel home from the terrible debacle of the battle of Loos. Fifty thousand men lost and no victory to report. Even Field Marshal Haig's plan to use gas went wrong, and ended in many casualties and seven deaths amongst our own men. Delays in the arrival of reinforcements didn't help, and blame and suspicion are being bandied about. I have been amongst those questioned about giving information to the Germans, which has frightened me, though no one is even certain that information has been passed on. I am convinced it has, as the Germans always seem one step ahead of us and we have no way of explaining this.

The day before I left to go home they asked me to hand over all of the letters I have received whilst in France. Many were from Elsbeth. This development is giving me grave concern. I cannot wait to visit her, to warn her that she must leave Britain. As a German, she is naturally under suspicion and is being watched.

9th November 1915: I am elated, as at last I can go and see Elsbeth. It has been six months since I saw her last, just before my posting to France. Louise has been very clingy since my return – I fear she knows I have a mistress. Her distress has surprised me, and I have had to offer more comfort and reassurance than I want to. I hate lying, but then Louise has no business questioning me. It is not the place of a wife to do so. Arrangements of the nature we have are unspoken and should remain that way. I am very discreet where Elsbeth is concerned, and that is all Louise should concern herself with. She doesn't want me, or love me. We have long since agreed that I should satisfy my needs elsewhere.

30th November 1915: I have not written for many days as I have been on the run. I will make this last entry and then put this journal into the envelope I have ready. It is addressed to my brother. Please God that Elsbeth will reach him soon. She has all my other journals, and I will instruct Philippe in a separate letter to give her this one. I will also include my last will and testament, which I am of sound mind to make.

I have seen an increased number of military police milling around Dover, where I am now holed up in a small hotel. I have done all I can to disguise myself: shaved off my hair, donned a pair of spectacles, and I will walk with a limping gait when I go out to post this.

Once that is done, I will try to get a passage to France.

I will meet up with Elsbeth and we will somehow make our way down to the south of France where it is safer. But I assume the port is heavily guarded, and don't give much for my chances.

It had been a shock to Elsbeth, as I expected it would be, to know I am under suspicion, but it fitted with some strange happenings that occurred with Captain Westlin, whom I now believe is the real traitor. She is convinced he has something to do with the net of conspiracy that I feel tightening around me. How easily such a net could be woven, as I have given myself an ally in Elsbeth.

It appears that Westlin asked Elsbeth to paint him a specific picture. At first I was mystified as to why this was significant, but she explained that all artists are being watched and some have been arrested. It is suspected, or believed, that spies are getting information to the Germans through their art; a picture can hold many clues and codes.

After Elsbeth finished painting the first picture for Westlin, she heard of two other artists who had worked for him and had then disappeared. She was afraid, especially as he had commissioned her to paint a second painting. Every detail was given specifically to her: place, angle, colour; even objects that weren't in the actual scene were added. I am convinced that this is how Westlin is passing on information to the Germans, whilst at the same time working to uncover anyone thought to be a spy.

When I arrived at Elsbeth's, on my return from the Somme, she took me through to her front room, where her easel stood in the window to enable her to get the best light she could. As we were looking at the commissioned picture, a flash went off outside, just as I pointed out an error that I had spotted concerning the positioning of the

Tower in the scene of London Bridge. Shocked by the sudden flash, I went to look out of the window. Another flash blinded me for a moment. Once the imprint of the blue light faded from my vision, I saw a boy holding a torch and a man whom I immediately knew to be Westlin, as the light from the gas lamp caught him withdrawing from beneath the curtain over his camera. He grabbed the camera and equipment under his arm and ran off.

Running outside, I was just in time to see him round the corner from Elsbeth's road onto another road, which I knew led to Westlin's home. I ran with the greatest of speed and saw him take the steps in front of his house, two at a time. Despite arriving seconds later, I was told by his butler that Westlin had been in bed all day, indisposed with a heavy cold. But what worried me most – especially for my own and Elsbeth's safety – was the presence of Brentworth in Westlin's house.

An expert at developing pictures, Brentworth must have been ready and waiting for Westlin to get back, to start processing the film. Making an excuse, I hurried away, called in on my good friend Monsieur Alberto and begged him, with the aid of a very handsome bribe, to take Elsbeth out of the country.

I hurried back to Elsbeth and we had a swift parting. I had no time to lose. Taking the clothes I had kept at Elsbeth's, I hailed a cab and started on the long criss-cross journey to where I find myself today.

It is with a sorry heart that I close this journal on my life. I feel there is no hope for me now. Many days ago I worked out the damning evidence against me: I keep a German mistress. I have been photographed with her and the picture must contain clues, and in my haste I did not think to destroy it. And my final act of absconding must have sealed the suspicion into a truth. I have been stupid. No one will listen to me, I am sure of that. I have loaded the gun that will execute me – but, I am innocent . . . Innocent.

Alice stared at those last words from her father. Inside she held a pain that clenched the muscles of her heart, but she dared not release it, for fear of losing her strength. Instead she reaffirmed her resolve to make her father's story known and to tell the world that her father was innocent.

Attached to the last page was a letter, which had been opened. It was to Elsbeth. Alice hesitated, but knew Elsbeth had intended her to read it and had left it there so that she would do so:

Elsbeth, my darling,

If you receive this one day, I give you my heart forever. I have lived my happiest moments since we met. Though my dream of us being together does not now look as though it will come true, know that it is what I wanted. Know that you were the only one I loved, and that my continued life with Louise was only a ploy to keep her from a scandal she did not deserve. I hope that one day, if the worst happens, you can use this journal along with your own testament to clear my name, as I fear my capture is imminent and no one will believe me or you, at this moment in time.

Elsbeth, you looked very beautiful and quite rounded, which surprised me, as you have never put weight on before. You told me you had taken to eating more to give you comfort. It suited you, and in my arms you felt wonderful – soft, loving and sort of cushioning. But I

*must not continue to evoke these memories, for they give
me great pain, knowing that I may never have a chance
to see you again. Cherish the love I give you, but don't
mourn me forever. Rather, let me become a beautiful
memory, and find – and give – happiness again.*

I love you, my darling,
Yours,
Ralph x

Alice folded the letter and read the entry underneath it,
which had been written by Elsbeth:

31st January 1916: I could not tell my darling Ralph that
I carried his child. As there was so much danger, I did not
want him distracted by knowing. I hoped never to receive
this journal unless it lay in the hands of my darling Ralph
as he stood in front of me, safely back together with me in
France. But that was not to be. After his last entry he
somehow managed to get this – his last journal – to the
post office. Philippe, in an act that was out of character for
him, was kind enough to bring it to me, as I wasn't at his
house by the time it arrived. I did not feel comfortable
staying with him and his family, and have been staying in
the farmhouse of Monsieur Alberto's parents.

Along with the journal, Philippe brought the terrible
news that ripped my heart into shreds. My darling Ralph
was found guilty of treason and was shot at dawn on 20th
January. His body was disposed of by fire.

Alice drew in a deep breath, swallowing the grief that
threatened to engulf her. She closed her eyes. After a moment
she allowed her mind to work things through.

When her father said he'd had to offer more comfort to Mother than he wanted to, did he mean he'd been forced to sleep with her? *Was that when I was conceived? It must have been, because I was born at the beginning of August 1916! But why – why did Mother want Father to go to her bed, when she'd never wanted him before? Besides, she knew he was having an affair.*

Thinking about it, the letter that Alice had handed over to Westlin was dated around the same time. *My God! Were they having an affair – Mother and Westlin? That must be it, though Westlin did not say so; all he'd said was that he'd been in love with Mother. Maybe Mother was afraid he'd made her pregnant . . . But no, I am not Westlin's daughter – I can't be. I resemble the D'Oliviers too much; and Gertrude, dear Gertrude: she and I were so alike to look at, with the same-coloured eyes and hair. Our height was the same and many of our mannerisms.*

Father hadn't said in his journal that he had slept with her mother, but Alice felt sure that was what he meant – but then he wouldn't write that, would he? Elsbeth was going to read the journal, and he'd want to protect her. Although the way he put it, it was as if he was almost repulsed at having to be with her mother. This realization sent a pang through her heart. Gertrude, as unlucky as she was in life, had been begotten out of love, whereas she had been begotten as a result of her mother's cunning ways.

This thought threatened to overwhelm Alice. Shaking the feeling away, she concentrated on finishing the journal. There were a few more entries by Elsbeth, amongst them details of the two painters whom Westlin had asked to draw landscapes for him and who had since disappeared. Her last diary entry was:

My darling Ralph, I have given birth to our daughter, without you ever knowing that she was conceived. I had hoped to tell you when you came to me, but that never happened.

I have named her Gertrude, meaning 'spear of strength', as that is what our daughter will be. She will know what a good person you were and will love you, as I do. I always believed in you, my darling. Westlin is the traitor, I am sure of it. He conspired to put the blame onto you by commissioning me to paint that picture. I, being your mistress and of German birth, gave him the perfect motive to discredit you, and my paintings pulled the trigger. I am so sorry, my darling.

In a quiet moment after this it struck Alice that there was nothing of Elsbeth's talent as an artist around this farmhouse – not a single picture or any artist's working tools. Nor was there anything in the house to reflect the presence of an artist; it was just a typical French farmhouse.

Staring at the page, Alice started to feel another sadness for Elsbeth. She too had been lost, packed away and reborn as a dutiful wife to Monsieur Alberto.

She looked over at the photo of Gertrude on the dresser. The candlelight flickering in front of it projected life onto it. 'Gertrude, my sister, you truly were a "spear of strength" throughout your life, from the time you were a young girl, keeping strong through all that you endured – bringing yourself back from the brink of degradation and your days as a prostitute, to your time working courageously for us and your country in Herr Eberhardt's residence. Only to suffer the worst injustice: to die the death of a traitor, just as our father did.'

Despite these words breaking her heart, Alice's eyes remained dry as her grief was eclipsed by the sheer hatred that she felt for Westlin and the lives he had terminated or ruined. Her anger reassured her that she would never let Westlin get away with the crimes he had committed. If she couldn't prove his guilt, she would kill him. She had the skills and the passion to enable her to take another's life – war had given her both.

27

Lil

A LETTER – A LOSS

Lil had watched the supplies being loaded onto the train. Amongst them she had seen a couple of mailbags, but hadn't thought there would be a letter for her amongst them.

The wounded had all been transferred to the ambulances that would take them to the hospital ship. The end-carriage of the train held the dead. These were the last to leave, and soon an ambulance would be filled with the bodies. *A last journey for them, but at least, having died on the train, they are going home, unlike millions of other young men, buried in rows and rows of graves in whichever country they fell.* It was funny how she'd come to think of this as a compensation. The horrors she had witnessed had made her cynical.

Turning back towards the carriage that she stood in, she looked at the rows of now-empty bunks. Each one had to be stripped, disinfected and remade. The top bunks were the worst as they were high up; getting the wounded off them had been a job. Her arms burned with the effort it had taken earlier, and her back ached with the strain.

Millie, another volunteer like herself, had helped, and now sat on one of the beds, looking all in.

'Eeh, Millie, lass, you look how I feel. By, lass, getting those wounded soldiers in those ambulances were summat, weren't it?'

'It was. I'm totally done in. Do you reckon it will get easier as we do it more times?'

'It better had be. I dare say we'll develop muscles and will be able to lift them down on our own one-handed!'

'Ha, Lil, does nothing get you down? You're a tonic. Let's have a brew before we start. No one will know – they're all busy doing other things.'

'Good idea, a nice Ruby Lee.'

'You're a funny one. I've never heard some of the sayings you come out with.'

'That's because I made most of them up. Ruby Lee is in honour of me late friend Ruby, who used to make a lovely cuppa, which she called a Rosie Lee.'

'Oh, I've heard that one. That's cockney rhyming slang, ain't it?'

'It is.'

As Millie busied herself with the pot of tea, which she made in the staff kitchen that had once been the guards' carriage, Lil's mind drifted back to Ruby's kitchen for a moment, but she soon jollied herself out of it. Going down that road was too painful.

They were drinking their tea when the Sister came up to them. Neither had seen her approach, but both stood to attention and saluted, after her prompting cough. 'Sorry, ma'am, we just thought to take a break. We'll catch up . . .'

'Sit as you were, Private Moisley and Private Shanly. I don't blame you – a cup of tea is just what we all need at times like this. I have brought your post. The orderly sorted it as soon as it was on board. You all deserve to have it before we get back into the thick of things. Carry on.'

They saluted again, then looked at each other as the Sister retreated. It had taken Lil a while to get used to this ritual. In Crescent Abbey the Sister had been just 'Sister' and the Matron just 'Matron', but in the Army they held officer ranks and had to be respected as such by all, especially by the likes of her and Millie, who were ranked as mere privates.

It surprised her to have any mail. On the last two occasions that post had arrived, which were weeks and weeks apart, there had been nothing for her. Now she held three envelopes, one from each of her loved ones: Gillian, Mildred and, aye, Alice as well.

Getting a letter from Alice was most amazing, as Lil had thought her to be in a place that she couldn't send mail from. But, looking at the envelope, with its crumpled appearance and dirty fingerprints, it had clearly done the rounds several times. This was confirmed when she opened it and saw that it was dated just a few weeks after they'd parted. Alice didn't say anything about where she was or where she was going, but that was understandable. However, what she did say came out of the blue:

Dearest Lil,

I should not be telling you this, but I have to. I am married. It is to be kept a secret for now, but I am so happy that I wanted to share it with you. Our wedding was a registry-office affair, with some strangers to witness it, but when this bloody war is done we will have a real

373

'do', and you and Gillian will be my bridesmaids. Oh, how talking of such things has the heart longing. But it does no good to dwell on them. For now I am very happy and yet extremely sad, as I will have to part from him whom I shall call, for secrecy's sake, Johnny.

I cannot say more, and wasn't going to tell you even, but just had to. I want to say that I am ready for whatever I have to do, and I hope that what you are doing is all you wanted it to be.

Keep safe, my Lil, I love you. See you when we raise the victory flag,

Alice xxx

Oh, Alice, thought Lil. *And I love you, lass. You're like a sister to me. Aye, we're worlds apart, but that don't matter: me and you are kin in all but our standing in life.*

Holding the letter to her, she swallowed hard. Letters from home were always difficult to take, and yet amazing to receive. This one she would cherish, as it would be the last from Alice until the war was over, she was certain of that. *Eeh, I wonder who her fella is?* They all knew Alice had a fella, and somehow the two of them had been brought together, and that's all that mattered.

She shuffled the other two letters and decided to read Mildred's first. With growing joy she read about how Alice had been home on leave and had visited with her young man. But then Mildred started to say things she shouldn't. Would she ever learn?

The poor man is wounded badly, Lil, but is very handsome and a lovely man. He is living in Alice's house, as his parents live a long way away. He will take a desk job

*in the War Office soon, but our poor Alice has to go
away again. Do you reckon she is one of them agents,
Lil? I fear every day for her, and for you. Where are you,
Lil?*

Putting the paper down, Lil could feel an anger rising inside
her: *Ma, Ma, the very thing you fear – by speculating on Alice
as a secret agent – you could make happen by writing such stuff!*

Reading on, she learned how Mrs Rose down the street
had had one of 'them telegrams'. By this Lil knew what
Mildred meant: the poor woman had been told the news that
all mothers dreaded hearing – 'your husband/son/daughter
has been killed on active service'. In this case Lil knew it was
a son: Charlie's elder brother. So it was with sadness, but a
sense of pride too, that she read that young Charlie had
enlisted. Lil could see Charlie in her mind's eye now: a scruffy
young lad standing on a pile of rubble, lost, but trying to
look big. *Well, lad, you're big now and off to fight for your
country. May God keep you safe!*

Lil read on:

*Oh, and I've seen the doctor, Lil, and he said I might
have a bit of a kidney problem; he gave me some horrible
stuff to drink, and I'm to put me legs up for ten minutes
every hour of the day. It don't seem to be working, but I
feel all reet, lass, so don't be worrying about me.*

Oh dear, Ma, that don't sound good, thought Lil. Not worry?
How could she not? That was something she did every day
– and now she had Mildred to worry about, too.

Moving on to Gillian's letter, she opened it with more
anticipation, thinking Gillian would possibly have news of

Rusty. For some reason she'd thought often about the young American she'd met at the dance. Gillian did have news – news that tore at Lil's heart:

> *Dearest Lil,*
>   *I haven't known how to write this letter. I have bleeding sworn at Hitler, I've called on God to kill him, or I will with me bare hands . . . He's taken Rusty. I'm so sorry, Lil. I didn't know whether to write or not, but I could picture you thinking of him now and then, and maybe wondering what had happened, as I think the pair of you were taken with each other . . .*

The note flittered to the floor. Lil's head spun. A sick feeling took her, bubbling up as if it would choke her, although it released itself in a scream: 'No! No, no . . .'

'Lil? Lil, what is it?'

Millie was by her side, looking scared, but with a caring look on her face, too.

How could she tell Millie that she was distraught after hearing that a chap she'd met out of the blue one night had been killed? Why did it hurt so much? Didn't the same thing happen every day of their lives? Didn't they get to know all the lads they nursed, and didn't they dispatch many of them to the morgue? So why did this one affect her so deeply?

The Sister's voice cut into the silence that had fallen. 'Please come to my office, Moisley, and try to hold yourself together as you do.'

'Yes, ma'am.'

Lil bent over and retrieved the letter, then forced her legs to lift her and take her with dignity to the Sister's office, but once there her legs gave way and she slumped onto a chair.

'I gather you have had bad news, Moisley?'

'Yes, ma'am. Sorry, ma'am.' Trying to stand, she found that she couldn't.

'Please remain seated and tell me what has happened.'

'A friend has been killed.' The agony inside her didn't release with this, but tightened even more. She had no tears left in her body. Rusty – a friend, yes, but with hopes of being much more. There, she'd admitted it to herself now. Rusty had woven himself into a cold part of her and warmed it. And a part of her had latched onto that hope, but now whatever she'd dreamed of happening never would. It had ended before it had even begun.

'Take the rest of the day off, Moisley. I am very sorry for your loss. I wish I could give you longer, but I cannot.'

'I just need half an hour, thank you, ma'am, with permission to leave the train and walk along the railway platform for a little while.'

'Very well, I can grant you that. Do you want someone with you?'

'Naw, ma'am. I'll be better on me own.'

'Half an hour it is then. It is now eleven hundred hours.'

Lil's 'Thank you' came from dry, cold lips. These QAs were a wonderfully courageous lot, but military through and through. Everything they said was clipped and like an order – at least it was when speaking to ATS staff. None of them really liked the ATS nurses. There was always an atmosphere.

Once on the platform she found a bench. Ignoring the appreciative whistles of the privates who were still loading supplies onto the train, she sat down.

Her trembling fingers opened the letter again and she read on:

Rusty was on his first assault. Jeff told me about it. He saw the hit. It was direct and it blew the plane up. Rusty wouldn't have suffered, or known that awful moment when the plane spiralled to the ground. I am so sorry, Lil. I know you two had an attraction to each other. Rusty had told Jeff he'd finally plucked up the courage to write you a letter and he would send it to Mildred, but he never had time to do so.

I wish I could give you a hug. I miss you so much, Lil.

Once more Lil stopped reading. The letter rested on her lap. Around her she could hear the noises of the bustling men and the steam belching from a train as it moved away, gathering momentum. A bird sang. It was a sweet chirping that said things were normal for it; it had a nest to build and didn't care what the world below was up to – humans' movements were just a constant annoyance. *Funny I should put all these thoughts into a little bird song, but that's how it is now. Some things carrying on as normal, while others are visiting Hell.*

A deep sigh escaped her as she picked the letter up and finished reading:

Apart from that news, Lil, I am all right. I love it here on the farm. The farmer's daughter, Florrie, is lovely and we are really good friends; well, more than just friends really, you know – I have found my soulmate, Lil.

Alice came to see me, which was nice. She is so happy, but still I think she has a lot of stuff inside her, as if things have closed her down. She said she won't visit for a while now. I miss her too, more than I ever thought I would. She liked Florrie and I think she understood our relationship, though we didn't speak of it.

I went to see Mildred. Her legs are worse – you remember how swollen they were; they are twice that size now and she has a job to walk, but she is very cheerful and having the best life she can in the circumstances.

Well, big sis, take care. Write when you can. Love always,
    Gillian

It was the mention of 'big sis' that hit Lil the hardest, but no release came with the breaking down. It was as if a door was closed and stuck, and she couldn't undo it. It shut the pain away from her heart. She wondered if she would ever get it open again. Poor Rusty – a happy bloke who wished no one any harm, and who had begun to take root in her. One day she'd find out his mam and dad's address and write to them. She'd tell them about how they had met, and how they'd had such a good time, and how he'd spoken of them in loving terms. In the meantime there was work to do . . .

Stuffing the letter into her apron pocket, she thought about the other news in Gillian's letter. *So, Gillian has met someone who makes her happy. Strange to think of it. Aye, and it would be embarrassing to meet this Florrie, though it seems as if it is meant to be.*

But of all the farms Gillian could have gone to, it was funny that it turned out to be the one where Florrie lived. Well, she wished them both well; she just didn't know how she was going to cope with it when she met her.

The carriage that she and Millie worked in was as spotless as it could be, and the train chugged along, following the front line so that, wherever it landed, there would be work to do: wounded to see to, and more horrific sights and happenings to cope with. In the meantime Lil allowed herself a little respite and lay on her bed with her eyes closed.

For the past couple of weeks there had been talk of a big push forward by the Allies. She didn't know whether or not it was propaganda, but she hoped it was true. 'Let's get this war over with,' she said to the bottom of the bunk above her. 'Let's have done with it. All of us are nearly on our knees. We're broken so as we'll never mend. We need an end to it.'

A whistle hailed an inspection. Jumping up and straightening her hair as she ran back to her ward, Lil thanked God she'd had a wash and donned a clean uniform before she lay down, but now prayed that she hadn't creased her uniform too much.

Watching Sister pass each bed gave her the usual feeling of apprehension. Sister always found something to pull them up on. The QA nurse in charge of Lil and Millie walked up and down with Sister, and her glances at them both gave a warning that all Hell would come loose on them, if they let her down.

All went well. But instead of being dismissed, they were told to assemble in the nurses' canteen – one of the best places on the train, which had been fashioned out of what were once the first-class rail carriages. There they found the majority of the staff, all standing to attention, waiting. But the waiting was with an air of trepidation, a tangible feeling that oppressed Lil as soon as she entered. After a few moments she found out why.

Matron – Major Kendle – stood and outlined to them how they were on their way to Normandy. 'This will be a dangerous trip, as many German forces are also making their way there, ready to reinforce troops in the area. The big push has started. The Allied troops have landed. We are about two hundred kilometres away, and it is thought we will come under attack, as the rules of the Geneva Convention may well be broken – as they have been many times before – by the Germans ignoring our Red Cross insignia.

'You are to all put on your battle uniforms and wear them forthwith at all times – even sleep in them – so that you are at the ready, no matter what happens. Our job will be to assist the wounded wherever we can: get them back on the battle-field if possible, or onto ambulances if not. You will be called upon to go above and beyond your duty, but I know you are all extremely capable and you will do us proud. Good luck, everyone.'

A mixture of excitement and sheer terror gripped Lil. This was it then! Oh, they'd been bombed before and had come under fire, but they had been able to outrun the enemy, as their remit had been to get the men out. Now it seemed they were to mend the wounded on the spot and then send them back to fight, or dispatch them home. This would make them a sitting target.

It didn't take long to reach the fringes of the battle, which was hailed by the sound of gunfire and explosions, and planes diving with that awful whining noise that clenched your bowels.

Lil looked at a sea of blood as they passed field after field of dead bodies. Twisted and still, they lay on the red grass, their shapes a tangled carving of brutal humanity. Someone shouted that they'd seen movement in one of the men lying on the ground. Within minutes the train pulled up. Orders were barked out from officers, telling them to search for the wounded. Running in a bent position wasn't easy. Bullets flew within a hair's breadth of Lil's head, explosions blocked her ears and rained shrapnel down on her. She had no time to think. Terror seared through her.

Bodies lay scattered everywhere. Some were hideous, with no faces; others had no limbs, just a trunk and a head; others were headless. A groan alerted her to a live person. Running towards the noise, she dived down beside the soldier, whispering comforting words, only to hear the death-rattle. Touching his hand, she bade him 'Farewell, brave soldier' and rose to run to the next group. Here she found several men alive and called to the stretcher-bearers, 'Over here, quick!' Somehow she and another nurse ferried a dozen wounded back to the train, tripping over arms and legs, squelching in ankle-deep blood puddles as they went.

A hand grenade landed next to Lil just as she reached the steps of the train. Dropping the end of the stretcher that she was carrying, she picked up the grenade and threw it back as hard as she could in a direction where she knew there were only dead personnel. It exploded in mid-air. The blast knocked her off her feet. She landed on top of the poor man she'd dropped. He screamed, and it was a scream that touched every hair on her body and made it stand up. Rolling off him, she tried to say she was sorry, but the blood oozing from his mouth told her he would not hear her. She'd killed him – oh God! She'd killed a man she should have saved!

'Don't take on, lass . . .'

A northern voice. The sound had her trembling. 'He'd not have lived. And you saved many more. Come on, me lass.'

Glancing up, she looked into the face of a stretcher-bearer. Stupidly she asked him, 'Where you from?'

'Top side of Harrogate. Now, come on, lass. Get up and carry on.'

Carry on – however can I carry on . . . ? I've killed one of our own brave soldiers and that will live with me forever.

28

Alice & Lil

THEIR PATHS CROSS

'Hold back. Let the Germans get onto the bridge. Now!' At Alice's command, the sky lit up as if it was daylight. Trucks somersaulted into the flames of the explosion, bodies flew as though they were birds, and bricks scattered, many of them falling within inches of her.

This was a triumphant victory, but not one that she and her Resistance members cheered. An ancient bridge that had stood proudly through the centuries now lay in a heap that they could not see through the cloud of dust. But it was a victory nonetheless, because it would delay the 21st Panzer Division of the German Army in getting to Caen to reinforce other divisions. With a thought of 'Mission accomplished!' Alice felt a pride settle in her.

The euphoria didn't last long, as a moan next to her told her Juste had been hit. 'Oh God, no! Juste, it will be all right. Don't worry.' Not letting her fear for Juste interfere with what she had to do, she shouted orders in every direction.

Soon the river bank was manned with gunmen ready to defend it, against the likelihood of the Germans whom they had not killed regrouping. Once that was done, she could take a minute to see to Juste. 'Alfonse, help! Over here. Juste is hit. See to him – make a stretcher for him. I have to direct the others.'

A shot in their direction had both her and Alfonse ducking low. Alice started firing at the remaining reconnaissance division of the German Army. This was seen as a signal by the rest of the group, as the rat-a-tat of guns firing and hand grenades exploding made for a full-blown battle. They had the upper hand, and picked off the first line of the German defence easily. Once the Germans had their wits about them, though, it became more difficult.

'I'm ready,' Alfonse told her. 'Juste is on the stretcher.'

'Is he badly hurt?'

'It's hard to tell. I can't see him properly. And he is not responding. There is a lot of blood – I felt what seemed like a river of it running from his side as I moved him onto the stretcher.'

'There isn't a moment to lose. We have to get him to that Red Cross train. Fall back to the truck. I'll help to keep the Germans engaged. Get him there, Alfonse, please!'

Reloading as she spoke, Alice renewed her efforts.

A relief greater than any she'd experienced entered her as she heard the German command of: 'Fall back, retreat!' *Thank God!* The German reconnaissance troops were defeated.

On her order, everyone dispersed. It would not be long before the main body of the 21st Panzer Division caught up. Then fresh machine guns and heavy artillery would be used against them, and the sheer numbers of elite German forces would bear down upon them. They wouldn't stand a chance – they had to disperse.

Worrying about Juste, Alice stuck close to the hedgerows and made it to the Red Cross train. The officer she was shown to, the Matron, shook her hand and said, 'I am pleased to meet you. I am guessing what your role is, and that you are an officer. Let no more be said. This way, please. I will show you to your comrade.'

Alice saluted the female major, glad that she had made an assumption and had not questioned her. She followed the Matron through coaches now turned into hospital wards, with bunk beds lining the sides of each carriage. All held the shocking sight of wounded men.

'He's in here, Officer.' But what the Matron said next filled Alice with emotions that she found difficult to cope with. 'Nurse Moisley, one of your patients has a visitor.'

'Lil! Oh, Lil, is it really you?'

'Alice! Oh, Alice, you're safe!'

Lil didn't ask what she was doing here, and Alice didn't expect her to. 'Yes. And with a bit of luck I will be on a plane to England tonight. I am being picked up and taken out of here. My job is done. How is Juste?'

'He is doing fine. The surgeon had no other cases waiting when Juste arrived, and he has been operated on. A bullet has been removed from his side. It missed his vital organs. He has a couple of broken ribs, but he will recover.'

'Good. I couldn't bear to lose him.' As these words left her, she slumped onto the bed behind her.

'Alice! Oh, Alice, are you hurt?'

'No – exhausted.'

'Stay there. We are not expecting any more casualties tonight, for the fighting has moved away from here. We will move with it tomorrow, when we have dispatched today's intake. I'll fetch you a cup of Ruby.'

They both laughed at this – it was refreshing. Up until now Alice had been feeling that she'd never laugh again. 'That will be champion. Is Alfonse – the guy who brought Juste here – all right?'

'Sleeping like a babby. Oh, Alice, it is good to see you. Look, we have a shower room down the corridor. Why don't you take a shower? I'll fetch my dressing gown for you.'

'No, I can't do that, Lil, as much as I would love to. I have a rendezvous near Bénouville Bridge. That is where my pickup point is. Is it far away?'

'I don't know. I will ask one of our dispatch riders to take you. I'll speak to him on me way to making your tea.'

Looking over at the unconscious Juste, Alice thought about their time together: about the assignments that had gone well and those that hadn't. About the loyal men who had fallen, the few who had turned out to be traitors – and about Gertrude. Poor Gertrude: what kind of death did she have? Was it swift, or did they make her suffer? Alice didn't know how François could have been involved, but now he himself was no more. Juste had killed him. It had been an unlawful revenge killing, like her own of Jean. Brushing the thought away, she refused to let it haunt her. Jean had shown Nazi sympathies that could have been dangerous – she would think of that as her reason.

Getting up from her seat, she went over to Juste. 'Hello, my brother – for I will always think of you as that. I will visit when it is all over, and that surely cannot be long. But I have to go. I am tired, and now that your country is forming an army out of all the different Resistance units I will not be needed. Stay safe, my brother, I am proud of you. After this is all over, we will find out the truth and clear the name of our dear ones. We will never give up. I promise.' Bending and kissing his forehead felt strange, for they had never shown any affection between them. 'Lil will look after you. You will like Lil.'

Walking along the corridor away from the sleeping Juste, she found Alfonse chatting to a nurse – well, flirting more like. She had to laugh as she watched them trying to communicate.

'Alfonse says you are very pretty, and would you object to giving him your address at home, so that he can contact you when the war is over?'

When the war is over! They all latched on to that day, but were their hopes in this Allied effort being the one to finish it off too high? *Just get me to that plane and then, apart from the debriefing, that will be that. For me, the war will be over . . . Thank God!*

'Eeh, Millie, what are you up to? Sister is on the prowl, and we haven't got the sluice done yet!'

'Sorry, Lil . . .'

'It was Alfonse's fault.'

'Maybe, Alice. But, Millie, you should have got on with things, to cover for me getting Alice a well-deserved cup of tea. Now hurry, or we'll catch it from Sister if we fall behind. Here, lass, enjoy. Sorry there're no trays or china or silver . . .'

'Oh, I've long left those behind, Lil. Ha, I've been known to drink water out of my boot if I had a thirst!'

'Eeh, I can't imagine it – not you!'

'Yes, me. "Needs must", as they say. Now, Lil, we had better say goodbye. I have to leave once I have drunk this.'

The hug that Lil gave her enclosed Alice in love, tinged with a little fear. 'See you when we raise the victory flag,' they said together, before Lil dashed off.

'Alice . . . ?' Alfonse queried.

'Oh! Yes, Alfonse, it is my real name. Madeline was my cover name. I don't suppose it matters now that you know.'

'I will always think of you as Madeline, and of your bravery. Thank you for what you have done for France.'

'Goodbye, Alfonse. I shall be back when it is all over.'

The motorbike raced to Bénouville Bridge. The bridge, she'd heard, had been a turning point for the invasion, as the 6th Airborne Division had captured it and had effectively thwarted a counter-attack by the Germans.

Within hours Alice was sitting in Captain Bellows's office. It felt strange to be safe. The experience was alien to her. A door slamming somewhere along the corridor made her jump. But what Bellows told her, before he started her debriefing, was news that she did not want to hear, and it affected her more than any fear of loud bangs could. Westlin had committed suicide.

Sitting down, as her legs would not hold her, she looked up at Bellows, shaking her head from side to side. 'No!'

'Yes. His decomposing body was found a few weeks ago in a flat in south London. He left no note, but I think we can assume he was the traitor and that his killing himself was an admission of his guilt.'

'We can assume nothing, sir. I want proof. The bastard! If he was going to take his life, why couldn't he have left an admission and have cleared my father's and Gertrude's names? Why, oh why?' To her horror she realized she was crying. Huge sobs racked her.

'Alice! Alice, you are all in. We will talk some more tomorrow. I will have Steve come and pick you up and take you home. There is little we need to know now. Things are going well. The Allied troops are pushing the Germans back.

There is nothing you can tell us that will either help or hinder that.'

Bellows spoke into his phone. 'Henderson, you may come and get your wife.'

'You know we are married?'

'Yes, I know. I had the devil of a job keeping it quiet, and it went against my principles to do so. You deceived us and, for an agent, that wasn't a good act. But I put my faith in you, and nobody else knows your secret.'

The door opened and Steve stood there. Literally: stood there on two legs. She couldn't speak, for he looked so beautiful and a look of pride glowed from him. 'You have your leg? Oh, Steve, you—'

She didn't finish, for he'd crossed the room and lifted her up. Held in his arms, she felt the last few months of pain, worry and separation drop away. She was back where she should be.

A click alerted them to the door closing. They were alone. Pulling Alice towards him, Steve enclosed her. His lips kissed away her tears as they travelled to her lips. The kiss was gentle and held a promise.

'I have a car outside – let's get home. There is no one there. I have dismissed them all for the day.'

If asked to describe how she felt at this, Alice knew she couldn't have said. Her world joined up at the seams, leaving only small gaps where little pockets of anxiety still nestled – mostly worry for Lil and for Juste. But somehow she would put these out of her mind and would allow her thoughts and her body to surrender to Steve.

The house seemed strange, and she hadn't known it this quiet for a long time. Being within the familiar walls, where love had only come to her in recent years, she felt an immense tiredness pressing down on her.

'A bath for you, my darling, while I make us something to eat.'

'I didn't know you had become so domesticated – you're going soft.' His face dropped as she said this. 'Oh God, Steve, I didn't mean it. It was just me having a bit of banter with you.'

He laughed. 'I know. Now, sit there a moment while I run you a nice bath.'

As he left her, she wished she could cut her tongue out. It was obvious that her words had hit a raw nerve. What had made her say such a thing?

Going after him, she grabbed him from behind. Tiredness drained from her at the feel of him. Making her way around him, she looked up into his face. 'Steve, don't laugh it off. It was insensitive of me. It was a joke, but in poor taste.'

'And we need to have many more such jokes to prise me out of this. I was silly to react as I did. It is me who is insensitive, to have upset you the moment you opened your mouth. Let's start again. Nothing barred – all jokes allowed, no taking things the wrong way or to heart. I'll start with one that isn't a joke: you stink! I want to take you to my bed, but I don't want to come within ten feet of you yet! Let's get you to the bathroom, where I will wash you until I am satisfied you are clean enough!'

'Steve!' Her laughter doubled her over and mingled with his. Memories of visiting him in Switzerland came to her, when, as now, he'd wanted to wash her first. She needed it this time as she'd done then, for the battle that she'd taken part in just a few hours ago still clung to her.

They were back to normal. If 'normal' was what was racing

around inside her. Even the thought of him washing her evoked such intense feelings that she didn't know if she could hold out until declared 'clean for action'.

When she told Steve this, he picked her up and carried her to the bathroom. Plonking her in the empty bath, he turned on the hot and cold taps. The temperature vacillated between the two: one minute the cold tingled, the next she was stomping up and down because her toes were burning, but all the time Steve sponged her down, with sensual movements that threatened to drive her wild.

She bent over, allowing him to wash her hair, relishing the gentle massage of her head. When the moment came to wrap her in a huge towel, he did so slowly, letting his eyes wander over every part of her.

On the bed he finished drying her, and she cried out for him to take her. He took a moment to get his false leg unattached, but then showed an agility she hadn't seen since his injury.

When he entered her she clung to him, knowing herself to be complete once more. Yes, she still had worries and things she had to sort out, but for now she was Mrs Steve Henderson, at home with her husband, and nothing could mar that.

Sometime later she awoke to the delicious smell of dinner cooking. She hadn't even realized she'd fallen asleep. She put on her silk dressing gown, which gave her a feeling of life as she'd always known it. Though she was tainted with horror and seared with guilt, she was loved. She would cling to this last feeling and try to let go of the rest. The whole world had burned – not just her part of it – and all had to recover. Oh, there was a way to go yet before victory could be celebrated, but it looked more than a possibility that it would soon be theirs. The hope was for a new beginning, and carrying old scars into that world wouldn't help. She had to deal with things as best she could.

Over dinner – mustard pork chops with sautéed potatoes and green beans, served with a crisp, dry white wine – she tackled some of the issues she faced. 'Steve, I have read the end of my father's journal. Alfonse found it and brought it to me. The tin it was in had kept it dry and in perfect condition.'

'Oh . . . and?'

'I want to prove the innocence of my father and of Gertrude. I will let you read the journal, but I'm sure you will agree that it does give us something to go on.'

'But with Westlin dead, how will you manage that?'

They chatted this over, but nothing enlightened them as to how to go forward. The important thing to her was that Steve agreed they should still try and prove her father's and Gertrude's innocence.

'I'll start by tackling Mother.'

'But, darling, she's mad! She may not be the most reliable person.'

'I know what she is, Steve. Don't call her mad. But . . . how do you know?'

'I have visited her – I thought you would want me to. We get on very well, but each time I have to remind her who I am.'

'That was very kind of you, though she doesn't deserve it.'

'Darling, you have to live in the now, and the future – it is the only way. No one knows that better than me.'

'I will try speaking to Mother. According to her specialist, the thing about her illness is that her memory loss is more to do with recent events. Apparently patients retain long-term memories, but not memories of what happened last week or even a few minutes ago.'

'Oh, I hadn't realized that. Well, we'll go and visit her tomorrow if you like. I have a few days off to help you settle back in.'

Alice wore court shoes with a little heel, which tapped out a rhythm on the paved drive leading to the home for mentally ill patients that housed her mother. The sound brought back unhappy memories from her childhood – that of her nanny approaching. She gripped Steve's hand.

'Are you all right, darling? Is this visit too soon for you to cope with?'

'It isn't about Mother. Someone else from my past just visited me. One day I will tell you all about it . . .'

'Whenever you are ready, darling.'

They reached the door. Taking a deep breath, she rang the bell and listened to the echo of it as it resounded around the building. A nurse answered the door.

When they walked into her mother's room – a small, plainly furnished, whitewashed space – she saw her mother sitting in a rocking chair next to the low window. Looking through it, Alice could see the drive they had just walked up. Her mother must have been watching them. When Louise turned, her expression held nothing more than it would have done if her daughter had just been out of the room and come back in.

'Hello, Mother.'

'Where is the cup of tea you promised? I have been waiting.'

Alice nearly laughed at this, thinking what a long wait it had been. So, she hadn't been missed. But maybe that was the best way for her mother to look upon it: that Alice had just been fetching a cup of tea. Though she did wonder whether her mother, this woman who had given birth to her, would have cared, had she been well and known the real truth about what Alice's life had been like these past few years. This thought hurt.

Crossing the room, she went to kiss her mother's cheek, but the privilege of doing so was not afforded her, as her mother pulled her head away, striking more pain into Alice. It prompted her to snap out why she was here. 'Well, I may as well get on with it. I want to talk to you about the past, about Daddy and Westlin.'

A gasp from Steve at her frankness made Alice hesitate for a moment, but her mother didn't bat an eyelid. She just said, 'That's all history. What do you want to bring it up for?'

'Because I have met Daddy's mistress and her daughter, my stepsister.'

Her mother's face paled. Steve let out a slow breath, 'Hey, steady on, Alice . . .'

'No. There is no steadying on with this woman. She is brutal and responds to brutal tactics. Well, Mother, it seems you do have feelings about it, although you don't seem surprised. Did you know Elsbeth was pregnant? And me – what about me? Did you beget me out of fear that you were pregnant by Westlin? Oh yes, I know it all. All of it, do you hear me?'

'Alice! Alice, no, please don't do this to your mother, or to yourself. Darling, it isn't right. Please calm down,' Steve begged her.

'No, I will answer her,' Louise replied. 'She has a right to know. Alice, I did think I was pregnant by Stuart Westlin. I loved him. Oh, I loved your father, but not in the same way. Stuart woke me up. Took me to . . . Well, anyway, we had an affair. I didn't worry about it at the time as I knew your father was having a liaison, and we jogged along happily enough. But then I had an infection and . . . well – I had symptoms. My maid said she thought I was pregnant and I became very scared. Ralph would have known; he could have used it to divorce me and cause a scandal. I couldn't take that.'

'And that is why you didn't love me, because you realized I was Daddy's child and not Westlin's?'

Her mother didn't answer for a long time. Alice willed her to say she *did* love her, but that never came. 'I was ill. The strain – everything. Your father's shame, his death, my being ostracized, it was all too much to bear.'

'How much do you think I had to bear: unloved and beaten by you, abused by Nanny?' *Oh God, what am I saying? I never meant to reveal that. What is wrong with me?*

'I – I didn't know . . . Nanny? Oh God, Alice, I didn't know.'

Her mother's shocked face brought the reality of what happened back to Alice. Steve's hand clasped hers, steadying her. Her body didn't resist the gentle pull he gave her. She sat on the chair next to him, thankful for the support. Steve wiped her tears, but didn't counsel her not to speak.

'Yes. Nanny took away my childhood. I – I was so lonely . . . so hurt.'

'I'm sorry. I don't know what to say.'

'You're sorry? What are you sorry for, Mother? What Nanny did, or what you did?'

'Everything.'

This held Alice still. Her mother had said she was sorry. Inside Alice wanted to take the word and strangle her mother with it, but instead she said, 'I forgive you, Mother. I forgive you, but I need something from you.'

'What? What can I give you? I have nothing left. I am not a person, just an empty, unloved shell.'

'You are not unloved. Despite everything, I love you, Mother. And yes, I know you won't remember this conversation, but you do have memories of the past. I almost have proof that Westlin framed Father. That Father was innocent, and it was Westlin who was the traitor.'

Her mother slumped forward onto the tray fixed to her chair, stopping Alice from going any further. 'Mother, what is it? Mother!'

'I'm all right. Oh God, I knew it, but I couldn't prove it. It would have all come out: me being Westlin's mistress, my husband having an affair – everything.'

Feeling a spark of hope, Alice asked, 'What did you know, Mother, tell me?'

'I – I heard . . .' Again her mother slumped forward, but this time it wasn't with the weight of her guilt. Her whole body went into a heap.

'Mother! Mother . . . Oh, Steve . . .'

Steve pulled himself upright and managed to stand faster than she'd ever seen him do since he lost his leg. His hand grasped the bell on her mother's bedside. Reaching Louise's side, Alice held her mother to her, 'Oh, Mother, Mother.'

The grey hair felt soft on her face; the body bony and frail in her arms – and the pain in her heart that these sensations released cut deep.

The nursing staff moved her out of the way. Alice stood looking at the scene and at the doctor testing her mother's vital signs. After a moment he said, 'Your mother is all right, but she seems to have had a minor stroke. These things happen. They sometimes lead to a much bigger stroke, but often they are an isolated incident and may never happen again. They are often a response to shock. You should keep everything around her calm, and make sure she does not worry about anything.'

Standing by the bed where her mother now lay, Alice looked down on what seemed to her like a shrunken tower. Her mother had been that to her – a tower. A tower of hurt, and an impenetrable tower; but now she was the aftermath of a demolition. A destruction wrought by her own daughter. *Why did I do it? Why did I have to confront her? Why now, after all these years? Couldn't I have lived with my knowledge and left her alone?* 'Mother, I am sorry. I didn't mean . . .'

'Sorry? Is there to be no tea then?'

'Yes, there is. I have ordered it for you.' Smiling at the ludicrousness of this, Alice almost thought, *What does everything matter?* Mother had forgotten all that had happened a few minutes ago, and she would never know that her own daughter had attacked her when she could least deal with it.

The old eyes closed, but the hand, patterned with thick veins and still elegant, did not let go of hers. Finding a space on the bed, Alice sat down. She would hold onto this little show of love from her mother and be happy with it. Maybe it was all she deserved.

29

Lil, Alice & Gillian

LONDON,

7TH MAY 1945

VICTORY ANNOUNCED

'Cor, luv a duck, tell me what I 'eard is what I 'eard, Lil.'

Lil couldn't answer Gillian – not in a sane way she couldn't; instead she grasped the hands of this beloved girl and swung her round. 'It's over, it's over!' The joy inside her eclipsed what she'd felt on her discharge, even though that was on medical grounds. It even eclipsed what she'd felt when she turned into this street and came up to the door of what she'd always look on as home – Gillian's mam's house, as she would always think of it.

'Ha, I can't believe it. Bleedin' 'ell! Oh, I wish I was with my Florrie.'

'You should have stayed there, love. I could have seen you another time. We all knew this was imminent. Look, let's turn the radio off and go out, eh? Folk are bound to be in the street celebrating – even the King. That's it! Let's go down to the Mall.'

'Shall we? Oh, I wish Alice was here. The three of us have always said, "See you when they raise the victory flag."'

'Let's call her from the phone box. If she can, I know she'll meet us. We could meet her at the Underground entrance.'

Grabbing their coats, they didn't wait to put them on, but struggled to do so as they walked. The clouds held rain and the wind had a chill to it, but they didn't care, as they were caught up in a flock of folk coming out of their houses.

Cheers echoed around them, hands shook theirs and hasty plans were made about what to do tomorrow: 8th May and the official day of celebration.

'Let's 'ave a street party,' one woman said. And another shouted, 'We could 'ave a bonfire.' To this someone else piped up, 'As long as we don't burn anything that can be salvaged.' 'Well, there's plenty of rubbish we can clear from round here – let's get the boys of the streets 'ereabouts onto it. They'll enjoy that.' 'I reckon as my Charlie will be 'ome soon' . . . And so the chatter went on, ringing in Lil's ears as loudly as all the bells pealing around her, building the excitement that was bubbling up in her till she thought she would have to scream with the sheer joy of it.

'Eeh, Gillian, imagine tomorrow, eh? A street party! It'll be grand.'

The sight of three lads pulling a blackened beam towards them made it all seem real. Here was a remnant of war being prepared to mark the end of the war. But the sight also made Lil feel the sadness of it all. 'Some won't feel like having a good time, I shouldn't wonder, Gillian. Them as have lost so much.'

'I think they will. I think they'll be out in force, just to show them over there that they didn't kill our spirit.'

'Aye, you're reet. And that's a lesson I learned from you

down here. The spirit of the person and the place is summat no one can destroy. Not of you Londoners, they can't. And I'm proud I was down here through it all. Well, most of it.'

'Was it bad over in France, Lil?'

'Aye. I've seen things I'll never get out of me head. But I've also seen courage like I never thought could exist. So the one balances the other, I suppose.'

'Did you never meet anyone? I know it upset you over Rusty going, but – well . . . all them soldiers!'

'I did. I met a man, a French man – he's called Juste. He's a little bit younger than me . . . It's complicated, but he is a sort of relative of Alice, only she doesn't know that I know, so keep that bit to yourself till she sees fit to tell us about it all.'

'A relative of Alice?'

'Aye, I know it sounds incredible, but it's true. Like you've allus said, there's a lot about Alice that she hasn't told us, but it's understandable when you hear it. I can't tell you of it. I reckon as we should wait until she thinks we should know.'

'You've got me wondering now. I wished you hadn't said anything. But anyway, tell me about your man.'

'He isn't *my man* . . . Well, not exactly. Like I said, his name is Juste, spelt J U S T E. He's in the newly formed French Army, but was a Resistance fighter. He's lovely. He was wounded and I nursed him. Something just sort of happened between us – a feeling. Oh, I don't know, it's hard to describe, but I know I can't stop thinking about him and I miss him. I just want to be with him.'

'Blimey, you 'ave got it bad! French, is he? But how can Alice know him? Is that where she's been, in France? But what was she doing . . . ? Oh, Lil, was she a special agent? Them that we heard about, who were so brave in their efforts behind the enemy line?'

'I – I . . . oh, what the hell, it's over now. We can't do any harm talking about it. Yes, she was. She's a very courageous girl. We should be very proud of her.'

'I'm proud of both of you. What you did, Lil, working in that 'ospital train – that was courageous too.'

'Aw, lass, it didn't feel like it; it felt very scary and horrific. But, you know, I'd still be out there and on the train if I hadn't been injured. I'd be going to them concentration camps to help to nurse all of those poor souls that survived their incarceration. Eeh, the things we are hearing, it don't bear thinking about. Despite the fear and the blood and gore, it fulfilled me. I knew I was doing my bit. And you did your bit an' all, lass. You dug for victory!'

'Ha, I bloomin' did, too. Sometimes it felt like I'd reach Australia, I shifted that much muck.'

'Eeh, lass, it's good that it's over with. Let's forget it for one night, eh?'

'Yes, I think we can manage that. Can I link in, or will it 'urt your shoulder?'

'Naw, you'll not hurt me. It's well on the mend. Eeh, I thought me number were up when that bullet hit me. I can't describe the pain and terror of it, but I were in the right place – none better. They soon had me fixed. The worst was having to come home when there was still so much to be done. I felt guilty leaving them all to cope and in danger, but at the same time the happiest I'd been in a long time, at the thought of coming home again.'

'Look, we said we'd forget about it tonight, and that's what we'll do. There's a phone box – let's ring Alice.'

Lil picked up the phone and dialled her number.

'Lil! Oh, I've been willing you to ring. What, Gillian's there? Oh, that's wonderful! Are you all right? I received your letter. Wonderful news about you and Juste. How's your shoulder? I was planning on coming to visit, now that you are home. Mildred's here; she's told me bits, but of course you know that – oh, what wonderful news that was tonight!'

'Eeh, lass, hold your horses. I can't keep up with you.'

'Ha! I'm sorry, I'm just so excited, and now hearing from you is the tops.'

Whatever Alice meant by that, it sounded good. 'We were wondering if you could meet us?'

'What, now? Yes, how marvellous, but oh . . . just a moment.'

'What's she say, Lil?' asked Gillian.

'I'm not sure.' Alice in person was much easier to deal with than Alice on the phone!

'What's that? Are you all right, Lil?'

'Yes, I am Alice. I was talking to Gillian. Can you come?'

'I can. Steve . . . Oh, I haven't told you. Steve's my husband – that's his real name. He has told me to come and see you, and he and I will celebrate tomorrow. Oh, I can't wait to see you. I will be with you soon.'

Lil felt her world complete as they jostled with what seemed like a million and one other folk, walking, running and dancing down the Mall towards Buckingham Palace, all shouting, 'We want the King!' Her own throat felt sore with the chant, and yet even to be doing this and linked in with Gillian and Alice felt like something she could never have imagined.

The rain stopped the carry-on. It pelted down, drenching them. Holding their coats over their heads, they ran for shelter.

Huddled together under the eaves of an empty building, they laughed off their shivers.

'Come back to mine,' said Alice. 'Please, I would love you to. Mildred will be in bed, though. She was going to bed, saying that I was mad to go out and there was time enough to celebrate tomorrow.'

'Ha – she would! Nothing fazes Mildred, or puts her out of her routine.'

'I know. Well, what do you say? We can all have a drink, you can sleep over and then we can drive you back tomorrow. I've such a lot to tell you.'

'Aye, I'm for it. Are you, Gillian?'

'I am.'

'Wait here then. I'll hop over to that telephone box and call my car.'

'You know, Lil,' Gillian said as Alice went to make her phone call, 'now that the war's over, Alice seems a world apart from us.'

'Naw – never think that. Oh, I know we aren't of her station, but she's of ours. She can cross the divide, and she does. We must never become in awe of her, for that would put a rift in our friendship. She wants us to think ourselves the same as her, and I reckon we can. We've all been through the mill together, and we've come out as one.'

'You're right, Lil. It just makes me feel uncomfortable, her sending for her car. And I won't know how to act when we get to her house.'

'Just be yourself. This is Alice you're talking about. Our Alice – she's got no side to her. She's just lived a different life, that's all. And it'll be good to meet her man. Steve, she said he is called.'

*

Not ten minutes later they were sitting in the most beautiful room Lil had ever seen, in front of a log fire that crackled, sending smoke up the chimney. Lil herself felt some of what Gillian had felt – that there was a difference between them and Alice. And with the realization came a shyness. It made her lose her natural way of chatting and caused her to answer Steve's questions with just a yes or a no.

Alice broke the ice. She sat down with her glass of sherry and said, 'Eeh, this'll warm your cockles, it's better than all your Rosie Lees!'

Steve's face was a picture. Gillian let out a pensive giggle, but the mixed-up northern and London accent tickled Lil, so that she burst out laughing. The rest of them joined in, but such was the release that Lil couldn't stop. Her laughter infected the others, till they were all doubled up.

'By, it takes summat to get a night's sleep in this house! What's to do with you all?'

Mildred stood in the doorway with curlers sticking out of her hairnet and a long dressing gown on. Seeing her undid the final knot of tension inside Lil, and she laughed so much her stomach hurt.

'Give over! You're acting like a lot of young 'uns.'

'Eeh, Mildred – Ma. Eeh, come here and give me a hug.'

'You daft ha'p'orth.' This was smothered as Lil pulled Mildred to her. 'By, Ma, it's good to laugh.'

'Aye, and it's good to hear you all. But at this time of night!'

'You've just got the grumps because you've missed out. Well, you needn't – let's pour you a sherry.'

'I'd rather have a drop of port. I'm partial to port.'

This easy exchange amongst the four of them made Lil decide that, no matter where they were, she and Alice could and would always be the same together.

'Well, time to catch up. You first, Lil, tell us all about you and Juste.'

At this from Alice, Steve stood up. 'Time for me to say goodnight, my lovely ladies. Your company on this historical night has been a pleasure, but to sit through your gossiping is something I'm not cut out for.'

It pained Lil to see the difficulty Steve had getting up. But he did it with dignity and something about his struggle reminded her of how they'd all been in the same boat, and nothing had separated the classes then. Oh, there'd been ranks – that had been necessary; but no real class system, not in her line of work. A dying man was a dying man, whether he was a rich one or not. Suddenly she wondered how Steve and Alice would celebrate tomorrow. Theirs would probably be a stilted affair with champagne, and nowhere near as much fun as she, Mildred and Gillian would have in the East End.

'Alice, why don't you and Steve come to our street party tomorrow?' What made her ask she didn't know, but now that she had, she felt glad, because Alice jumped at it.

'Oh, that would be wonderful – a real street party. I've never been to one. Shall we, Steve?'

'I'd love to. Thanks, Lil, that would be a real way to celebrate. Thank you.'

'That's settled then. What shall we bring?'

'Everything and anything you like, Alice. Food, drink, banners if you can get hold of them. And the staff, if they haven't got their own party to go to.'

'Right. Say goodnight to Steve and let's settle down for a women-only chat.' Alice pulled a bell and a man, presumably a servant, came through. He half-bowed to them all and then held the door for Steve as Alice said, 'Goodnight, darling. See you in the morning.' And then to the man, 'That will be all for today. Tell all the staff they can retire now.'

Lil caught a glance from Gillian, but didn't react to it. With the door closed behind Steve, Alice said in a voice that was commanding, 'Now, Lil . . .'

'Juste?'

'Yes. You can't keep us in suspense any longer.'

Telling them all how her friendship with Juste had developed into the two of them falling in love brought him back to Lil, and her heart ached to have him near. He was still engaged in the fighting, and she wanted him safe. 'We plan to marry, once things get back to normal. You know, when he's out of the Army and I'm properly discharged – when I have me papers in me hand. That shouldn't be long now. But Juste . . .'

'What does he look like, Lil?' Gillian asked.

'I have a photo of him here.' They all oohed and aahed over the picture of him, even Alice, as she said she'd never seen Juste look like that, smartly dressed and yet casual, with his shirt bloused over his trousers and his hair tousled. 'He was always in his partisan uniform of grey boilersuit-type dress, and was often dirty and unkempt,' she told them. 'I hadn't realized he was that handsome. He looks like his mother. And speaking of his mother, I – I have something to tell you about Elsbeth . . . Juste's mother.'

Tears flowed down Gillian's cheeks as the story unfolded. As for Lil, she couldn't cry, though the story held such a lot of sadness, but for a long time now she hadn't found it easy to give way to her emotions. She could see the same tightness in Alice. Mildred sniffed more than once, but she was another one who daren't let go.

'Poor Gertrude! And your dad. And, oh, Alice, I don't know what to say . . .'

'Well, I do, Lil. I blame that mother of yours, Alice. She likely could have prevented all of this happening.'

'I have done the same for a long time, Mildred, but in the end I've come to see that many were to blame, except Gertrude. Gertrude did nothing wrong. She remained loyal, even though she fell in love with Herr Eberhardt. But Juste and I are committed to exposing the truth, and one day we will.'

Thinking it looked hopeless, Lil just smiled at Alice. Alice shrugged, but in it there was no hint of her quest being a lost cause; instead a strong determination shone through.

Lil had been dreading the next question that Mildred asked, but she knew it had to come sometime.

'What about you, love, did you find your young man?' Mildred asked Gillian.

Holding her head high, Gillian said, 'No, Mildred. I never want to find one, either. I couldn't bear 'aving one near me – not after the rape. Not in that way. I 'ave some male mates, but that's as far as it goes. But I did find the love of me life, Florrie . . .'

Mildred choked on the sip of port she had taken, spurting sprays of it near and far. Everyone ducked. A silence fell. Lil felt a prickly feeling creep up her neck. Why did Gillian have to be so open about it?

'She's lovely. I really liked her when I met her.' This came from Alice, but it didn't ease the situation.

'Luv a duck, you'd think I'd said I'd fallen for Hitler! It happens. Some men like men and some women like women. Oh, it ain't accepted, but if you three can't do that, then we'll have to part company, because I'm not giving up Florrie for no one.' Gillian's bottom lip quivered as she looked from one to the other.

'We'll learn, Gillian – we will. It's summat as I hadn't heard of, and it don't seem natural, but if that's what you're about, then that's that. I love you like a sister and that will allus stand.'

'Thanks, Lil. I know it is a shock, and I know it has to be kept under the carpet. And I won't embarrass you all. Me and Florrie don't show our affection in public – we can't. But that don't mean we 'ave to give each other up. She don't expect to come to your weddings or anything, but I didn't want to live a lie: not with you three. You're me bleedin' family, ain't you?'

'We are. And I have known relationships like yours at school. I didn't know what they did – well, to be honest, I knew nothing about what a man and woman did together, either. But I learned. I learned in a horrible way what women did together, and it is my own experiences that have repulsed me. But I am not repulsed by your own and Florrie's relationship, and I would love to have you both at my wedding.'

Once more Alice had shocked them, but as she didn't seem to want to say any more, Lil filled the gap, 'And at mine.' Knowing that Alice was already married, she looked over at her, willing her to reveal that she was already married and to prevent the silence from taking root, but it was Mildred who spoke up.

'And, if I were getting married, which I'm not and never will, you could both come to that an' all. Aye, it was a shock to hear, but not to know of. I've seen it all. But you're right to keep it private – folk would hound you.'

'Thanks. And I'm sorry you had a bad experience, Alice. It doesn't 'ave to be like that.'

'I'm sure it doesn't. You look very happy with Florrie and she adores you, I can see that. I'll tell you all what happened one day, but I've drained myself tonight. I just want to say that Steve and I are married. We had to marry in secret, for a number of reasons, but we intend to have a big church wedding soon, and I want you, Lil, and you, Gillian, and Florrie to be my bridesmaids!'

This took the weight off the moment, amidst congratulatory hugs and more tears from Gillian. Lil wondered how she ever thought there could be a rift between Alice and them. Now she knew for sure there never could be.

EPILOGUE
Five Years Later

30

Alice

A JOURNEY OF TRUTH

Alice and Steve stood poised in front of the knocker. Over the fence of the pristine, typically German chalet-style home she could see into the garden. A little girl of around eight years old was being teased by two teenage girls. The sound of laughter, especially that of a child, brought back her longing for her own two little girls, who had been left behind with their nanny. Standing for a moment watching them, Alice reached for Steve's hand.

Two young men were also watching the girls, and beside them and under a tree sat a man in his forties – Herr Eberhardt.

Steve rang the bell on the door, an old-fashioned, black iron bell with a hanging cord, which had to be swung back and forth. The noise it made resounded around the garden. Herr Eberhardt looked up. His face held a question. From what Alice could pick up, he asked one of the girls to go and open the door to them and see what they wanted. The teenage girl, tall and very pretty-looking, gave them a relaxed smile.

'Please ask your father if he will speak with me. I have come from England to see him. It is very important.'

It sounded so simple to say that she had come from England, but that didn't cover all she had done to find this man. Wanted for war crimes, Eberhardt had not moved to one of the usual hideouts, such as South America, but had chosen to live here, on the Bavarian border, in a house nestled in the countryside. The decision had an arrogance about it. His war crimes were not many, for his position hadn't called for him to commit atrocities, being more of an office job. He was not a priority in the hunt for war criminals, but there were proven crimes that could be traced back to his orders – not least that of the murder of Hélène d'Aguste, the maid who had brought Antoine's message to Gertrude. Eberhardt had ordered her torture and hanging.

In the end it had been a journalist who had told Alice where Eberhardt lived. Dawson, an investigative freelance journalist, spent most of his time tracking down lesser war criminals. He had been a war correspondent, and their paths had crossed a few times. He knew of Alice's quest and her belief that Eberhardt could clear Gertrude's name. She didn't ask how he had found Eberhardt, for she had been too elated to care.

Looking now into the piercing but mistrustful grey eyes of Herr Eberhardt put a fear in Alice. She had to handle this carefully, but how? Deciding that telling the truth was the only way, she said, 'We have come to speak to you about Violetta.'

His face lost all its colour. 'Ve vill speak in English. Vhat do you know of her – is she alive? Come in. This vay. This is my study. Ve vill not be disturbed.'

'I am sorry, but Violetta – whose real name was Gertrude – is dead.'

'No! No, no . . .'

There was a knock on the door and a child entered, calling her father's name. Her appearance knocked Alice sideways. The girl looked so like her own eldest daughter. *My God, is she Gertrude's daughter?*

'*Elsbeth, gehen und spielen. Alles ist in Ordnung. Der Vater wird bald sein.*'

As the child left the room obeying her father's command that she should do so, Alice asked, 'Elsbeth?'

'Yes. But tell me who you are, and vhy you are here!'

He listened as Alice told him her relationship to Gertrude, and how Gertrude had been killed.

'But she vas not a traitor – she vas not.' His hands cupped his head. Alice waited.

Steve sat beside her on the chairs that Herr Eberhardt had indicated they should sit on. His face held compassion, as did his voice, as he asked, 'Herr Eberhardt, may I get you a drink: water or . . .'

'Thank you, yes. Over there – vhisky. There are glasses in the cabinet. This is such a shock. I alvays hoped Violetta vould one day valk through the door. Now I know she never vill.'

'Is Elsbeth her daughter?'

'Yes. Violetta – Gertrude – gave her the name. Do you know of it?'

'It is Gertrude's mother's name. She is German, though she lives in France with her son and his wife. Look, there is so much to tell, and to ask. It is a shock to me to know that I have a niece, and yet a wonderful shock, as it means a little of Gertrude lives on.'

'And Elsbeth has a grandmother and an uncle, besides you?'

'And cousins, for we have two girls. And Juste and Lil – that's Elsbeth's uncle and his wife – have twin boys. Mine are four and five years old, and the twins are three.'

'This is all too much to take in. But you came here for a reason other than to tell me my Violetta is dead?'

'Yes, I want to prove that she wasn't a traitor. I want her to receive the posthumous award to which she is entitled, and I want a service to be held in her honour. But I cannot prove she is innocent without you. I have no other way than your testimony.'

'But of course I vill give you a written testimony. I did not know until now that Violetta vorked vith the Resistance. I alvays had my suspicions, but they vere never proved. She never gave me any information. It disturbs me to learn that she vorked against me, used me . . .'

'She loved you. It broke her heart to have to do what she did, and to deceive you. But, just as you and I worked for our countries and what we believed in, so did she. You have to understand that.'

'I do. Though I have to tell you that I did not believe all the idealism of the Nazis. I spouted it, I obeyed orders, but in my heart I believed it wrong.'

Alice wasn't convinced. This was said so many times by war criminals, and by any German they came into contact with. It seemed that none of them had wanted what happened to occur. She believed some of them, but not this man. He had proved his loyalties when he hanged that poor girl. Still, it wasn't her purpose today to take Eberhardt to task over his war record.

'You may have to testify on oath to a tribunal, is that all right? If I can get enough proof, the French authorities will set up a tribunal to clear Gertrude's name.'

Beads of sweat ran down his face. 'This isn't possible. I vould do anything – anything – if I could, but you must know I can't do that. But I am not afraid to speak the truth to you. Any British intelligence ve had came through someone who ve knew at first as Colonel Brown, but I came to know who he really vas. Our intelligence was very good. Ve knew a lot that you British never suspected. Brown's real name vas General Vestlin.'

'My God!' The gasp had Steve moving to her side and asking, 'are you all right, darling?'

'Yes. It's a shock hearing it confirmed after all this time.'

Squeezing her hand to give her comfort, Steve turned to Eberhardt and asked him, 'Herr Eberhardt, are you prepared to let me record you saying what you know? And to give a written statement? I have a tape recorder in my car.'

Eberhardt's hands shook. The whisky in his glass rippled. 'Vill you tell the authorities vhere I am? No matter. It means more to me that I clear my Violetta's – Gertrude's – name. Yes, I vill do as you ask.'

Once Steve had the recorder set up, with a fresh tape on one spool, Eberhardt began.

'Vestlin contacted me soon after the var with Britain started. He said he had vorked with Herr Volf during the 1914–18 conflict and could be of even more use to us now, as he held a higher rank and vas actually vorking in the Var Office. He gave us information that helped us in many battles and thwarted many dissident attacks. He received a fortune – all paid into Swiss bank accounts. Though his contact with us dried up, ve did not know vhy, but assumed he'd been caught.'

Alice felt a bitterness tighten her chest. She had thought that when she finally proved Westlin's guilt she would feel elated, but all she felt now was hatred and yes, despair, because innocent people had died for the crimes Westlin had committed, and because in the end he had still won a victory over her, and she would never see him face justice. 'He took his own life. We were on to him, but we had no solid proof.'

'I see.'

'Is Herr Wolf still alive?' Steve asked.

'He is. Vhy do you ask?'

'It is a long story, involving another of my wife's relatives – her father. He too was wrongly put to death for being a traitor. He was framed by Westlin.'

By the time they had all they needed, Eberhardt had a grey tinge to his skin. His whole body shook, and sweat ran from him. 'Vhat happens now?'

'We will inform the authorities where you are. It will be up to them what they do, but no matter what you did in the past, what you have done today amounts to a great service to justice. Thank you.'

Hearing Steve say this unravelled a little of the knot that had tied Alice's emotions. She looked at Eberhardt, but she did not see a man she could thank. She saw a young girl hanging from a tree.

'Vill you give me some time . . . ?'

'We cannot. We have a journalist with us. He is ready to contact the police the moment we have finished our business with you.'

Eberhardt's throat jerked. For a minute Alice thought he would vomit.

'I have to go to the bathroom. Vill you vait here?'

Alice looked at Steve, who nodded.

They stood there, not speaking. Into the silence came the sound of the children once again. Elsbeth had an infectious giggle and a loud, screechy tone of excitement to her voice as she squealed with joy at whatever the others were doing to her.

A noise Alice had prayed she'd never hear again stopped the child's laughter, and all other sounds and movement. For one moment it seemed as if the whole world had ground to a halt, as the aftermath of the gunshot reverberated around her.

SIX MONTHS LATER

The sun shone on the large group of French and English dignitaries and top military personnel, including General Bellows. It glittered on their medals, as it did on Alice's, Steve's, Lil's and Juste's medals, and very proudly on those worn by the grandmother and grandchild: the two Elsbeths. Elsbeth senior wore the medals of the love of her life, Ralph; Elsbeth junior wore those of her mother, Gertrude.

As the gun salute blasted out, birds took to the air in a squealing frenzy of fear, rising up over Paris and soaring high into the blue sky. Lil's hand found Alice's. Alice could feel it trembling with pride, but, she imagined, with fear too, for she thought the day would never come when the sound did not invoke this emotion in them. But today they stood tall – she and Elsbeth senior the tallest and the proudest, as the two people being honoured were so close to them.

As the beautiful but mournful tones of the 'Last Post' filled the space around them, two hands touched her back; those of Gillian and Florrie, conveying comfort. Alice thought of her mother, who had died suddenly just over a year ago, and wanted to mourn her passing, but at the same time she always held this picture of Louise and Westlin living in eternity together – two people who had done so much damage to others. A little inner voice said, *What does it matter now?* And she knew in that moment she could dispel the bitterness, because what was happening here would blot it out and negate it forever.

Mildred, lovely Mildred, came into her mind. She was now at rest. Oh, how they missed her. She would have been so proud today to have stood in the same group as the man who had done her wrong – Uncle Philippe – and to have looked him in the eye. A smile came to Alice at this thought, and she wondered what Mildred would have said to him. Well, she didn't have to wonder really, as she had a good idea what Mildred would have said, so perhaps it was just as well that everything was as it was.

Steve walked forward towards the bearer of the small casket holding a memento of Gertrude. Taking the folded French flag from the top of it, he marched over to Elsbeth senior and presented it to her. She indicated that it should go to Elsbeth junior, who looked up and smiled as she took it into her outstretched arms. As Alice saw this, she had a fleeting moment when she thought of Eberhardt.

The ending of his life was a tragedy in one way, but in another his act had saved little Elsbeth and his other children from learning all that their father had done. One day they might take the trouble to find out, but at least it wouldn't be in the glare of the public, nor would they have to suffer the agony of his execution day. This way it had been over without them knowing that it was going to happen.

Elsbeth was a happy child. She loved her grandmother, Elsbeth senior, and had settled well with her. All of her cousins loved her too, and Elsbeth spent many weeks with her older siblings, who now lived with an aunt, a sister of their father. Not what you would call a happy ending, for all they had ever known had been torn from them, but then the fingers of war that still clutched at the generations took no heed of people's happiness. Alice wondered if they would ever lose their grip. If anyone would ever really be free again.

Steve turned and marched back to the bearers. Taking the folded British flag, he marched towards Alice. Her tears blurred his progress. She tried to swallow them back. Returning his salute, she took the flag and knew this to be the proudest moment of her life.

As they lowered the tiny symbolic caskets – one for her sister and one for her father – she read her poem, changed a little and with an added verse. Her voice was clear, the words soaring upwards and her heart filling with pride:

> *'I was like a stone covered in moss*
> *For time had stagnated me*
> *The layers had locked in the pain of your loss*
> *And I had to search for the key.*
>
> *As time has given us the courage you showed*
> *The lock is undone and I start anew*
> *So let the world know the debt you are owed*
> *And that I am, and always will be, proud of you.'*

extracts reading groups
competitions books new
discounts extracts extracts
competitions extracts discounts
books new books events
events books extracts reading groups
extracts new titles reading groups
interviews extracts
reading groups events extracts extracts books
books extracts discounts events
new books events events new books extracts
events new interviews new books extracts
discounts extracts discounts books

www.panmacmillan.com

extracts events reading groups
competitions books extracts new